"Loretta Chase at her magical best...shimmers with passion, humor and tenderness." —Mary Jo Putney

"Don't miss it!"
—Stephanie Laurens

Mr. Carsington's sleep was not restful. Mirabel rose and came nearer the bed to study his face. His voice scarcely rose above a murmur, but he was flailing about. She must stop him, or he'd harm himself. So she flung herself across his chest.

He shuddered briefly, then stilled. Mirabel waited, uncertain what to do. Should she let him sleep or wake him? If he slept, he might return to the nightmare.

Everyone said it was a miracle Mr. Carsington had survived until he was found on the battlefield, many hours after the battle. It must have taken unimaginable courage and a will of iron. Not to mention a remarkably strong and resilient body. It was this thought that brought Mirabel back to the present, to where she was, lying across the famously indestructible body. Now she was acutely aware of the hardness and warmth under her. If only . . .

Cautiously, she lifted her head and looked at him . . . and found him looking back at her. His eyes were open. Mirabel swallowed. "Bad dream," she said.

"You had a bad dream?" Mr. Carsington asked.

Miss Wonderful

LORETTA CHASE

B

BERKLEY SENSATION, NEW YORK

This is a work of fiction. Names, characters, places, and incidents either are the product of the author's imagination or are used fictitiously, and any resemblance to actual persons, living or dead, business establishments, events, or locales is entirely coincidental.

MISS WONDERFUL

A Berkley Sensation Book / published by arrangement with the author

PRINTING HISTORY
Berkley Sensation edition / March 2004

Copyright © 2004 by Loretta Chekani.
Cover illustration by One By Two.
Cover design by George Long.
Interior text design by Kristin del Rosario.

ISBN: 0-425-19483-3

BERKLEY SENSATION™
Berkley Sensation Books are published by The Berkley Publishing Group, a division of Penguin Group (USA) Inc., 375 Hudson Street, New York, New York 10014.
BERKLEY SENSATION and the "B" design are trademarks belonging to Penguin Group (USA) Inc.

PRINTED IN THE UNITED STATES OF AMERICA

10 9 8 7 6 5 4 3 2

Prologue

THE Right Honorable Edward Junius Carsington, Earl of Hargate, had five sons, which was three more than he needed. Since Providence—with some help from his wife—had early blessed him with a robust heir and an equally healthy spare, he'd rather the last three infants had been daughters.

This was because his lordship, unlike many of his peers, had a morbid aversion to accumulating debt, and everyone knows that sons, especially a nobleman's sons, are beastly expensive.

The modest schooling aristocratic girls require can be provided well enough at home, while boys must be sent away to public school, then university.

In the course of growing up, properly looked after girls do not get into scrapes their father must pay enormous sums to get them out of. Boys do little else, unless kept in cages, which is impractical.

This, at least, was true of Lord Hargate's boys. Having inherited their parents' good looks, abundant vitality, and strong will, they tumbled into trouble with depressing regularity.

Let us also note that a daughter might be married off quite young at relatively small cost, after which she becomes her husband's problem.

Sons . . . Well, the long and short of it was, their noble father must either buy them places—in government, the church, or the military—or find them wealthy wives.

In the last five years, Lord Hargate's two eldest had done their duty in the matrimonial department. This left the earl free to turn his thoughts to that twenty-nine-year-old Baffle to All Human Understanding, the Honorable Alistair Carsington, his third son.

This was not to say that Alistair was ever far from his father's thoughts. No, indeed, he was present day after day in the form of tradesmen's bills.

"For what he spends on his tailor, bootmaker, hatter, glovemaker, and assorted haberdashers—not to mention the laundresses, wine and spirit merchants, pastry cooks, etc.—I might furnish a naval fleet," his lordship complained to his wife one night as he climbed into bed beside her.

Lady Hargate laid aside the book she'd been reading and gave her full attention to her husband. The countess was dark-haired and statuesque, handsome rather than beautiful, with sparkling black eyes, an intimidating nose, and a strong jaw. Two of her sons had inherited her looks.

The son in question had inherited his father's. They were both tall men built along lean lines, the earl not much thicker about the middle now than he'd been at Alistair's age. They owned the same hawklike profile and the same heavy-lidded eyes, though the earl's were more brown than gold and more deeply lined. Likewise, the father's dark brown hair bore lines of silver. They had the same deep Carsington voice, which emotion—whether positive or negative—roughened into a growl.

Lord Hargate was growling at present.

"You must put a stop to it, Ned," Lady Hargate said.

He turned his gaze full upon her, his eyebrows aloft.

"Yes, I recollect what I told you last year," she said. "I said Alistair fusses overmuch about his appearance because he is self-conscious about being lame. I told you we must be patient. But it is two years and more since he returned from the Continent, and matters do not improve. He is indifferent to everything, it seems, but his clothes."

Lord Hargate frowned. "I never thought I'd see the day we'd be fretting because he *wasn't* in trouble with a woman."

"You must do something, Ned."

"I would, had I the least idea what to do."

"What nonsense!" she said. "If you can manage the royal offspring—not to mention those unruly fellows in the House of Commons—you most certainly can manage your son. You will think of something, I have not the smallest doubt. But I urge you to think of it *soon,* sir."

A week later, in response to Lord Hargate's summons, Alistair Carsington stood by a window in the latter's study, perusing a lengthy document. It contained a list of what his father titled "Episodes of Stupidity," and their cost in pounds, shillings, and pence.

The list of Alistair's indiscretions was short, by some men's standards. The degree of folly and notoriety involved, however, was well above the norm, as he was most unhappily aware.

He did not need the list to remind him: He fell in love quickly, deeply, and disastrously.

For example:

When he was fourteen, it was Clara, the golden-haired, rosy-cheeked daughter of an Eton caretaker. Alistair followed her about like a puppy and spent all his allowance on offerings of sweets and pretty trinkets. One day a jealous rival, a local youth, made provocative remarks. The dispute soon escalated from exchanging insults to exchanging blows. The fight drew a crowd. The ensuing brawl between a group of Alistair's schoolmates and some village boys resulted in two broken noses, six missing teeth, one minor concussion, and considerable property damage. Clara wept over the battered rival and called Alistair a brute. His heart broken, he didn't care that he faced expulsion as well as charges of assault, disturbing the King's peace, inciting a riot, and destruction of property. Lord Hargate was obliged to care, and it cost him a pretty penny.

At age sixteen, it was Verena, whom Alistair met during summer holiday. Because her parents were pious and strict, she read lurid novels in secret and communicated with Alistair in hurried whispers and clandestine letters. One night, as prearranged, he sneaked to her house and threw pebbles at her bedroom window. He'd assumed they would enact some variation of the balcony scene from *Romeo and Juliet*. Verena had other ideas. She threw down a valise, then climbed down a rope of knotted sheets. She would be her parents' prisoner no longer, she said. She would run away with Alistair. Thrilled to rescue a damsel in distress, he didn't worry about money, transportation, lodging, or other such trifles, but instantly agreed. They were caught before they reached the next parish. Her outraged parents wanted him tried for kidnapping and transported to New South Wales. After settling matters, Lord Hargate told his son to find a trollop and stop mooning after gently bred virgins.

At age seventeen, it was Kitty. She was a dressmaker's assistant with enormous blue eyes. From her Alistair learnt, among other things, the finer points of women's fashion. When a jealous, high-born customer's complaints cost Kitty her position, the outraged Alistair published a pamphlet about the injustice. The customer sued for libel, and the dressmaker sought redress for defamation and loss of trade. Lord Hargate did the usual.

At age nineteen it was Gemma, a fashionable milliner. One day, thief-takers stopped their carriage en route to a romantic rural idyll and found in Gemma's boxes some stolen property. She claimed jealous rivals had planted false evidence, and Alistair believed her. His impassioned speech about conspiracies and corrupt officials drew a crowd, which grew disorderly, as crowds often do. The Riot Act was read, and he was taken into custody along with his light-fingered lover. Lord Hargate came to the rescue once more.

At age twenty-one, it was Aimée, a French ballet dancer who transformed Alistair's modest bachelor lodgings into an elegant abode. They gave parties that soon became famous in London's demimonde. Since Aimée's tastes rivaled those of the late Marie Antoinette, and Alistair wouldn't dream of denying her anything, he ended up in a sponging house—last stop before debtors' prison. The earl paid the astronomical debt, found Aimée a position with a touring ballet company, and told Alistair it was time to take up with respectable people and stop making a spectacle of himself.

At age twenty-three, it was Lady Thurlow, Alistair's first and only married paramour. In the *haut ton,* one pursues an adulterous liaison discreetly, to protect the lady's reputation and spare her husband tedious duels and legal actions. But Alistair couldn't hide his feelings, and she had to end the relationship. Unfortunately, a servant stole Alistair's love letters and threatened to publish them. To protect his beloved from scandal and an outraged husband, Alistair, who had no way of raising the enormous ransom demanded, had to ask his father's help.

At twenty-seven came his worst folly. Judith Gilford was the only child of a wealthy, newly knighted widower. She entered Alistair's life early in the new year of 1815. He soon vanquished all rivals, and in February the engagement was announced. By March he was in purgatory.

In public she was lovely to look at and charming to talk to. In private she fell into sulks or threw tantrums when she didn't get exactly what she wanted the instant she wanted it. She expected all attention, always, to focus on her. Her feelings were easily hurt, but she had no regard for anyone else's. She was unkind to family and friends, abusive to servants, and fell into hysterics when anyone tried to soften her temper or language.

And so by March, Alistair was in despair, because a gentleman must not break off an engagement. Since Judith wouldn't, he could only wish he'd be trampled by runaway horses or thrown into the Thames or stabbed to death by footpads. One night, en route to a seamy neighborhood where a violent death was a strong possibility, he stumbled somehow—and he still wasn't sure how—into the comforting arms of a voluptuous courtesan named Helen Waters.

Alistair once again fell madly in love, and once again was indiscreet. Judith found out, made appalling scenes in public, and threatened lawsuits. The scandalmongers loved it. Lord Hargate did not. The next Alistair knew, he was being hustled onto a ship bound for the Continent.

Just in time for Waterloo.

That was the end of the list.

His face hot, Alistair limped away from the window and set the documents on the great desk behind which his father sat watching him.

Affecting a lightness he didn't feel, Alistair said, "Do I receive any credit for not having had an episode since the spring of 1815?"

"You stayed out of trouble only because you were incapacitated for most of that time," Lord Hargate said. "Meanwhile, the tradesmen's bills arrive by the cartload. I cannot decide which is worse. For what you spend on waistcoats you might keep a harem of French whores."

Alistair couldn't deny it. He'd always been particular about his clothes. Perhaps, of late, he devoted more time and thought to his appearance than previously. Perhaps it kept his mind off other things. The fifteenth of June, for instance, the day and night he couldn't remember. Waterloo remained a blur in his mind. He pretended he did remember, as he pretended he didn't notice the difference since he'd come home: the idolatry that made him squirm inwardly, the pity that infuriated him.

He pushed these thoughts away, and frowned at a speck of lint on his coat sleeve. He resisted the urge to brush at it. That would seem a nervous gesture. He was beginning to perspire, but that didn't show. Yet. He prayed his father would finish before his neckcloth wilted.

"I detest talking about money," his father said. "It is vulgar. Unfortunately, the subject can no longer be avoided. If you wish to cheat your younger brothers of what they're entitled to, then so be it."

"My brothers?" Alistair met his father's narrow gaze. "Why should I . . ." He trailed off, because Lord Hargate's mouth was turning up, into the barest hint of a smile.

Oh, that little smile never boded well.

"Let me explain," Lord Hargate said.

"HE gives me until the first of May," Alistair told his friend Lord Gordmor that afternoon. "Have you ever heard anything so diabolical?"

He had arrived while his former comrade-in-arms was dressing. Gordmor had glanced but once at Alistair's face, and sent his manservant away. Once they were private, Alistair described this morning's meeting with his sire.

Unlike the majority of noblemen, the viscount was perfectly capable of dressing himself, and did so while his guest talked.

At present his lordship stood before the glass, tying his neckcloth. Since the process involved not merely tying a proper knot but arranging folds with excruciating exactitude, it usually demanded that one spoil at least half a dozen lengths of starched linen before achieving perfection.

Alistair stood by the dressing room window and watched the passing scene, the arrangement of neckcloths having lost some of its allure since this morning.

"Your father is an enigma to me," Gordmor said.

"He tells me to wed an *heiress*, Gordy. Can you credit it? After the debacle with Judith?"

Gordmor had warned Alistair at the time to be careful: An only child didn't know what it was like to share parents' affection and attention with other siblings, and tended to be overindulged and underdisciplined.

Now Gordy said only, "There must be at least one heiress in England who isn't bracket-faced or ill-natured."

"It makes no difference," Alistair said. "I can't think of marrying until I'm quite elderly and enfeebled: five and forty—no, better, five and fifty. Otherwise, I shall make another catastrophic mistake, and be forced to live with it forever."

"You've merely had bad luck with women," Gordy said.

Alistair shook his head. "No, it is a fatal flaw of character: I fall in love too easily, and always unwisely, and then disaster follows upon disaster. I wonder why my sire doesn't simply choose a rich wife for me. His judgment is sure to be better than mine."

Still, it would rankle, Alistair knew. He would bring his bride nothing. It was hard enough, depending upon his father for funds. To depend upon a wife, to feel beholden to her family . . . The prospect made his skin crawl. He knew other younger sons wed for wealth and no one thought the less of them. It was perfectly acceptable. But he could not quite bring his pride to this point of view. "I wish he had let me stay in the army," he growled.

Gordmor took his eyes off his neckcloth long enough to glance at Alistair. "Perhaps, like some of us, he felt you had used up your quota of battlefield luck. Frankly, I'm glad he blocked that route."

Apparently, Waterloo had tried very hard to kill Alistair. He'd learnt that the foe had shot three horses out from under him, slashed him with sabers, and stuck him with lances. A body of friendly cavalry had ridden over him, a couple of fellows had died on him, and looters had robbed him. Given up for dead, he had lain in the muck among the corpses for hours. He was nearly a corpse when Gordmor found him.

Not that Alistair remembered. He only pretended to. He'd assembled the general picture from others' remarks. He wasn't sure it was all true. Or if it was, it might be greatly exaggerated. He was sure Gordy knew or at least suspected that something had gone awry with Alistair's brain box, but they never spoke of it.

"My father could have let me continue serving King and country," Alistair said. "Then he could not complain of my frittering away my life in idleness."

"But a gentleman is supposed to be idle."

"Not this one," Alistair said. "Not any longer. I must find a way to earn my keep by the first of May."

"Six months," Gordmor murmured. "That should be time enough."

"It had better be. If I haven't found an occupation by then, I must woo and win an heiress. If I fail to do either of these—*he punishes my younger brothers!*"

This had been Lord Hargate's coup de grâce.

The earldom and all its other titles, honors, and privileges, along with most of the family properties, would go to Alistair's oldest brother Benedict when their father died. Great estates were usually entailed this way, to keep them intact over generations. But this only shifted the younger sons' upkeep from father to eldest son. To spare Benedict this burden, his lordship had acquired certain properties, intended to be wedding gifts for his boys.

Today he'd threatened to sell one or both of the younger men's properties and arrange an annuity for Alistair from the proceeds, if Alistair failed to find an occupation—or a well-dowered bride—in the stated time.

"Only your inscrutable father could devise such a scheme," Gordmor said. "I think there is something Oriental about his mind."

"You mean Machiavellian," Alistair said.

"I daresay it is uncomfortable to have so forceful a character for a parent," Gordmor said. "Yet I can't help admiring him. He's a brilliant politician, as all in Parliament know—and tremble, knowing. And even you must admit his strategy is excellent. He struck precisely in your tender spot: those great louts you think of as your baby brothers."

"Tender spots have nothing to do with it," Alistair said. "My brothers annoy me excessively. But I cannot let them be robbed to support me."

"Still, you must admit your father succeeded in unnerving you, which is no small accomplishment. I recall that when the surgeon proposed to saw off your leg, you said, 'What a pity. We had grown so attached.' There was I, blubbering and raving by turns, and you, trampled nearly to pulp, as cool as the Iron Duke himself."

The comparison was absurd. The Duke of Wellington had led his armies time and again to victory. All Alistair had accomplished was to endure long enough to be rescued.

As to his cool demeanor, if he'd taken it all so calmly, why wasn't it plain and clear in his head? Why did the scene remain shrouded, out of his reach?

He turned his back to the window and regarded the man who'd not only saved his life but made sure he kept all his limbs. "You lacked my training, Gordy," he said. "You'd only the one older sister, where I had two older brothers to beat and torment me from the time I could walk."

"My sister finds other ways to torment me," Gordmor said. He shrugged into his coat and gave his reflection a final scrutiny. He was fair-haired, slightly shorter than Alistair's six-plus feet, and a degree burlier in build.

"My tailor does his best with the material at hand," Gordmor said. "Yet spend what I will and do what I will, I always contrive to be a shade less elegant than you."

Alistair's leg was twitching for rest. He left his post at the window and limped to the nearest chair. "It's merely that war wounds are fashionable these days."

"No, it's you. You even limp with address."

"If one must limp, one ought to do it well."

Gordmor only smiled.

"At any rate, I must do you credit," Alistair told his friend. "If not for you, I should be lying very still at this moment."

"Not still," said his lordship. "Decomposing. I believe it is an active process." He moved to a small cabinet and took out a decanter and glasses.

"I thought we were going out," Alistair said.

"Presently." Gordmor poured. "But first I want to talk to you about a canal."

One

Derbyshire, Monday 16 February 1818

MIRABEL Oldridge left the stables and started up the gravel path toward Oldridge Hall. As she was turning into the garden, the footman Joseph burst out of the shrubbery and into the footpath.

Though Miss Oldridge had recently passed her thirty-first birthday, she didn't look it. At the moment—her red-gold hair windblown, her creamy cheeks rosy, and her blue eyes sparkling from exercise—she appeared quite young.

Nonetheless, to all intents and purposes she was the senior member of the family, and it was to Miss Oldridge, not her father, the servants turned when difficulties arose. This perhaps was because her parent so often caused the difficulties.

Joseph's abrupt appearance and breathless state told her there was a difficulty even before he spoke, which he did in a rush and ungrammatically.

"If you please, miss," he said, "there's a gentleman which he came to see Mr. Oldridge. Also which he has an appointment, he says. Which he does, Mr. Benton says, as master's book were open, and Mr. Benton seen it plain as day and in the master's own hand."

If Benton the butler said the diary entry existed, it must, impossible as this seemed.

Mr. Oldridge never made appointments with anybody. His neighbors knew they must arrange social visits with Mirabel if they wished to see her father. Those who came on estate business understood they must deal with Mr. Oldridge's agent Higgins or Mirabel, who supervised the agent.

"Will the gentleman not see Higgins instead?"

"Mr. Benton says it isn't proper, miss, Mr. Higgins being beneath the gentleman's notice. A Mr. Carsington, which his father is the Earl of someplace. Mr. Benton said what it was. A something-gate, only it weren't Billingsgate nor none of them other London ones."

"Carsington?" Mirabel said. "That is the Earl of Hargate's family name." It was an old Derbyshire family, but not one with which she was on visiting terms.

"Yes, that's it, miss. Besides which this is the gentleman what was trampled so heroic at Waterloo, which is why we put him in the drawing room where Mr. Benton says with respect, miss, but it won't do to leave him cooling his heels like he was nobody in particular."

Mirabel glanced down at herself. It had rained off and on all morning. Globs of mud clung to her damp riding dress and, thanks to the walk to and from the stables, thickly caked her boots. Her hair and the hairpins had long since parted ways, and she'd rather not contemplate the state of her bonnet.

She debated what to do. It seemed disrespectful to appear in all her dirt. On the other hand, putting herself right would take ages, and the gentleman—the famous Waterloo hero—had already been kept waiting longer than was courteous.

She picked up her skirts and ran to the house.

• • •

DERBYSHIRE was not where Alistair wanted to be at present. Rural life held no charms for him. He preferred civilization, which meant London.

Oldridge Hall lay far from civilization, in a godforsaken corner of Derbyshire's godforsaken Peak.

Gordmor had aptly, if hoarsely, described the charms of the Peak from his sickbed: "Tourists gawking at picturesque views and the picturesque rustics. Hypochondriacs guzzling mineral waters and splashing in mineral baths. Ghastly roads. No theater, no opera, no clubs. Nothing on earth to do but gape at the view—mountains, valleys, rocks, streams, cows, and sheep—or at rustics, tourists, and invalids."

In mid-February the area lacked even that degree of animation. The landscape was bleak shades of brown and grey, the weather bitterly cold and wet.

But Gordmor's—and thus Alistair's—problem lay here, and could not wait until summer to be solved.

Oldridge Hall was a handsome enough old manor house, greatly enlarged over the years. It was, however, most inconveniently situated at the end of a long stretch of what was humorously called "road" hereabouts: a narrow, rutted track where dust prevailed in dry weather and mud in wet.

Alistair had thought Gordmor exaggerated in describing the condition of the roads. In fact, his lordship had understated the case. Alistair could imagine no area in England more desperately in need of a canal.

Having examined the drawing room's collection of pictures—which included several superlative paintings of Egyptian scenes—and studied the carpet pattern, Alistair walked to the French doors and looked out. The glass doors gave out onto a terrace, which gave way to a profuse arrangement of gardens. Beyond these lay rolling parkland and, farther on, the picturesque hills and dales.

He did not notice any of these landscape features. All he saw was the girl.

She was racing up the terrace stairs, skirts bunched up to her knees, bonnet askew, and a wild mass of hair the color of sunrise dancing about her face.

Even while he was taking in the hair—a whirling fire-ball when a gust of wind caught it—she darted across the terrace. Alistair had an unobstructed view of trim ankles and well-shaped calves before she let the hem drop to cover them.

He opened the door, and she irrupted into the drawing room in a whirl of rain and mud, taking no more heed of her bedraggled state than a dog would.

She smiled.

Her mouth was wide, and so the smile seemed to go on forever, and round and round, encircling him. Her eyes were blue, twilight blue, and for a moment she seemed to be the beginning and end of everything, from the sunrise halo of hair to the dusky blue of her eyes.

For that moment, Alistair didn't know anything else, even his name, until she spoke it.

"Mr. Carsington," she said, and her voice was clear and cool with a trace of a whisper in it.

Hair: sunrise. Eyes: dusk. Voice: night.

"I am Mirabel Oldridge," the night-voice went on.

Mirabel. It meant wonderful. And she was truly—

Alistair caught himself in the nick of time, before his brain disintegrated. *No poetry,* he told himself. *No castles in the air.*

He was here on business and must not forget it.

He could not allow his thoughts to linger, even for an instant, upon any woman . . . no matter how lovely her skin or how warm her smile, like the first warmth of spring after a long, dark winter . . .

No poetry. He must view her as—as a piece of furniture. He must.

If he stumbled into another disaster this time—and disaster was inevitable if a member of the opposite sex was concerned—he would not merely suffer the usual disillusionment, heartbreak, and humiliation.

This time his folly would injure others. His brothers would lose their property, and Gordmor would be, if not utterly ruined, then left in greatly embarrassed circumstances. That was no way to repay the man who'd saved his life, not to mention his leg. Alistair must prove himself worthy of the trust his friend had placed in him.

He must prove as well to Lord Hargate that his third son was not an idle, useless fop of a parasite.

Praying his face told no tales, Alistair casually drew back, bowed, and murmured the usual polite response.

"You wanted my father, I know," the girl said. "He appointed to meet with you today."

"I collect he has been detained elsewhere."

"Exactly," she said. "I have considered engraving that as his epitaph: 'Sylvester Oldridge, Beloved Father, Detained Elsewhere.' Of course, that would truly be the case, would it not, were he in need of an epitaph."

The faint color rising in her cheeks belied the coolness of her voice. It was instinctive to incline toward that hint of a blush, to see if it would grow rosier still.

Rather hastily she moved away and began untying the ribbons of her bonnet.

Alistair came to his senses, straightened, and said composedly, "Since you imply he is not yet in need of it, one may safely assume he is detained only in the usual sense, not the permanent one."

"All too usual," she said. "If you were a moss or a lichen or possessed stamens and pistils or any other uniquely vegetative quality, he would remember the smallest detail about you. But if you were the Archbishop of Canterbury, and the eternal disposition of my father's soul depended upon his meeting you at such and such a time, it would be exactly the same as this."

Alistair was too much occupied with stifling inconvenient feelings to absorb her words. Luckily, her attire finally caught his attention, and this promptly purged his brain of poetic drivel.

The riding dress was of costly fabric and well made, but

in a dowdy style and a shade of green unflattering to her coloring. The bonnet likewise was of superior quality, but frumpy. Alistair was baffled. How could a woman who obviously understood quality have no acquaintance whatsoever with taste or fashion?

The contradiction annoyed him, and this, combined with stifled feelings, perhaps explained why he grew so unreasonably irritated when, instead of untying the bonnet ribbons, she proceeded to tangle them.

"And so I ask you to overlook my father's absence as a quirk or ailment of character," she was saying as she tried to undo the tangle, "and not take offense. *Drat.*" She tugged the ribbons, which only tightened the Gordian knot she'd created.

"May I assist you, Miss Oldridge?" Alistair said.

She retreated a pace. "Thank you, but I do not see why we should both be aggravated by a stubborn bit of ribbon."

He advanced upon her. "I must insist," he said. "You are only making it worse."

She clutched the knotted ribbon with one hand.

"You can't see what you're doing," he said. He nudged her hand.

She brought her hands to her sides and went stiff as a board. Her blue gaze fastened on the knot of his neckcloth.

"I must ask you to tilt your head back," Alistair said.

She did so, and her eyes focused above and somewhere to his right. Her eyelashes were darker than her hair, and long. A wash of pink came and went in her cheeks.

Alistair forced his own gaze lower—past her overwide mouth—to the knot, which was very hard and very small. He had to bend close to look for a likely opening in it.

Instantly he became aware of a scent that wasn't wet wool, but Woman. His heart gave a series of hard thumps.

Resolutely ignoring these disturbances, he managed to get one well-manicured nail into a sliver of an opening. But the ribbon was damp, and the knot gave way not one iota, and he could feel her breath on his face. His pulse picked up speed.

He straightened. "The situation appears hopeless," he said. "I recommend surgery."

Later he would realize he should have recommended she send for her maid, but at the time he was distracted by her lower lip, the corner of which was caught between her teeth.

"Very well, then," she said, still looking at the spot above his head. "Rip it or cut it—whatever is quickest. The thing gives more trouble than it's worth."

Alistair took out his penknife and neatly sliced the ribbon. He longed to tear the bonnet from her head, hack it to shreds, throw it down, and stomp on it, then hurl it into the fire—and by the way, have the milliner pilloried for making it in the first place.

Instead, he withdrew to a safe distance, put away his penknife, and told himself to *calm down*.

Miss Oldridge snatched the bonnet from her head, stared at it for a moment, then carelessly tossed it onto a nearby chair.

"That's better," she said, and beamed up at him once more. "I was beginning to wonder if I must wear the thing for the rest of my life."

The billowing cloud of fiery hair and the smile knocked Alistair's thoughts about as though they were a lot of ninepins in his skull. He firmly put them back to rights.

"I sincerely hope not," he said.

"I do apologize for bothering you with it," she said. "You endured trials enough, I daresay, coming all this way for nothing. Not that I know where you came from."

"Matlock Bath," he said. "Not a great ways by any means. A few miles." At least twenty it had seemed, on filthy roads, under skies spitting icy rain. "There is no harm done. I shall come another day, when it is more convenient." When, he fervently hoped, *she* would be detained elsewhere.

"Unless it is convenient for you to come as a pawpaw tree, it will be another wasted journey," she said. "Even if you should happen to find my father at home, you shan't find him at home, if you take my meaning."

Alistair didn't quite take it, but before he could ask her to explain, a pair of servants entered, bearing trays laden with enough sustenance for a company of Light Dragoons.

"I beg you to partake of some refreshment," she said, "while I withdraw for a moment to make myself presentable. Since you've come all this way, you might as well acquaint me with your errand. Perhaps I can help you."

Alistair was certain it would be fatal to spend any more time alone with her. The smile muddled him horribly.

"Really, Miss Oldridge, it is no great matter," he said. "I can come another day. I plan to stay in the area for some time." As long as was necessary. He'd promised to take care of the problem, and he would not return to London until he'd done so.

"It will be the same no matter what day you come." She started toward the door. "Even if you do run Papa to ground, he won't attend to anything you say." She paused to direct a questioning look at him. "Unless you *are* vegetative?"

"I beg your pardon?"

"Botanical," she said. "I was aware you had been in the army, but that doesn't mean you haven't another occupation in civilian life. Are you botanical?"

"Not in the least," Alistair said.

"Then he won't attend." She continued to the door.

Alistair was beginning to wish he'd let her choke on the bonnet ribbons. He said, "Miss Oldridge, I have a letter from your father, in which he expresses not only a strong interest in my project, but a clear grasp of its implications. I find it difficult to believe that the man who wrote this letter will heed nothing I say."

That stopped her in her tracks. She turned fully toward him, blue eyes wide. "My father has written to you?"

"He replied to my letter *immediately.*"

There was a longish pause before she said, "It is about a project, you said. But not connected to botany."

"A dull matter of business," he said. "A canal."

She paled a little, then her animated face hardened into a polite mask. "Lord Gordmor's canal."

"You have heard about it, then."

"Who has not?"

"Yes, well, there seems to be some misunderstanding about his lordship's plans."

She folded her hands at her waist. "A misunderstanding," she said.

The temperature in the room was rapidly dropping.

"I've come to clear it up," Alistair said. "Lord Gordmor is ill at present—the influenza—but I am a partner in the enterprise and acquainted with every detail. I am sure I can ease your father's apprehensions."

"If you think we are merely *apprehensive,*" she said, "you are laboring under a grievous *mis*apprehension. We—and I believe I speak for the majority of landowners on Longledge Hill—are inalterably opposed to the canal."

"With respect, Miss Oldridge, I believe the proposal has been misrepresented, and I am sure the gentlemen of the Longledge area will, in the interests of fairness, grant me an opportunity to correct and clarify matters. Since your father is by far the largest landowner hereabouts, I wished to speak to him first. His good opinion, I know, will carry great weight with his neighbors."

The corners of her wide mouth turned up a very little, creating a shadow of a smile disagreeably reminiscent of his father's.

"Very well," she said. "We shall search for him. But perhaps you will allow me a few minutes to don something cleaner and drier." She gestured at her riding dress.

Alistair's face heated. He'd become so agitated about smiles and skin and scent that he'd forgotten she was wet and probably chilled. He'd kept her standing about all this time when she must be longing to be free of her damp attire.

He absolutely would *not* think about what getting her

free of it involved . . . the buttons and tapes and corset
strings to be undone . . .

No.

He fixed his mind on canals, coal mines, and steam engines, and apologized for his thoughtlessness.

She coolly dismissed the apology, asked him to make
himself comfortable and take some refreshment, and still
wearing the smile that wasn't one, exited the room.

THE conservatory to which Miss Oldridge—wearing a
different but no more attractive frock—took Alistair rivaled the Prince Regent's at Carlton House. The Regent's,
however, was used primarily for entertaining, and plants
were moved in and out as necessary. Mr. Oldridge's plants
were far more numerous and less mobile.

This was not quite an indoor garden, either. It was more
like a museum or library of plants.

Each specimen was carefully labeled, with extensive
notes and cross-references to others. At intervals, notebooks lay open in the dirt, containing further notes in Latin
in the hand Alistair recognized as Mr. Oldridge's.

Neither the flesh-and-blood hand, however, nor the
gentleman attached to it appeared in the conservatory. The
same held true outside of the house, in the greenhouses and
gardens.

At last one of the gardeners told them Mr. Oldridge had
been absorbed in studying moss life in the higher eleva-
tions. The gardener was fairly certain his master would be
found upon the Heights of Abraham, one of his favorite
spots of late.

Alistair was well aware that the Heights of Abraham
rose in Matlock Bath. Even had he somehow failed to notice the wooded slope with the great mass of rock jutting
up from it directly behind his hotel, he could not help
knowing, because the place abounded in signs and cards
advertising the fact.

He could not believe he'd come all this way on the

damnable road, while the man he sought was back in the village he'd come from, possibly falling off a cliff and breaking his neck at this very moment.

He looked at Miss Oldridge, who was gazing into the distance. He wondered what she was thinking.

He told himself her thoughts were irrelevant. He was here on business. It was her father's views that mattered.

"Your father must be unusually dedicated to his—er— hobby," he said. "Not many people will climb mountains at this time of year. Don't mosses go into hibernation or whatever it is most plants do in winter?"

"I have no idea," she said.

An icy mist was falling, and Alistair's bad leg was taking note of the fact in the form of spasms and shooting pains. She, however, continued walking away from the house, and Alistair limped along beside her.

"You do not share his enthusiasm," he said.

"It is beyond me," she said. "I am so ignorant as to imagine he could find mosses and lichen enough on his own property, instead of tramping all the way over to the Derwent River to look for them. Still, he always contrives to be home in time for his dinner, and I daresay the walking and climbing keep him limber, and at least he isn't— Ah, there he is."

A man of medium height and slender build emerged from an opening in the shrubbery and ambled toward them. He was well protected from the elements in a hat and overcoat of oilcloth, and his battered boots were sturdily made.

As the man drew near, Alistair discerned the family resemblance. Most of Miss Oldridge's features came, he surmised, from the maternal side, but her hair and eyes seemed to be a younger and more vivid version of her father's. Age had dulled rather than greyed his hair and faded his eyes to a paler blue, though his gaze seemed sharp enough.

His countenance offered no sign of recognition, however, when introductions were made.

"Mr. Carsington wrote you a letter, Papa," Miss Oldridge said. "About Lord Gordmor's canal. You made an appointment to meet with Mr. Carsington today."

Mr. Oldridge frowned. "Did I, indeed?" He thought for a moment. "Ah, yes. The canal. That was how Smith made his observations, you know. Fascinating, fascinating. Fossils, too. Most enlightening. Well, sir, you will stay to dinner, I hope."

And away he went, leaving Alistair staring after him.

"He must visit his new specimens," came the cool, whispery voice beside him. "Then he will dress for dinner. In the winter months we dine early. In summer we dine fashionably late. The one place you can be sure to find my father is in the dining room, punctual to the minute. Wherever he may ramble, whatever botanical riddles might fascinate him, he always contrives to be home in good time for dinner. I recommend you accept his invitation. You'll have at least two hours to make your case."

"I should be honored," Alistair said, "but I came unprepared, and have no suitable attire for dinner."

"You are more elegantly dressed than anyone we have dined with in the last decade," Miss Oldridge said. "Not that Papa will notice what you are wearing. And I don't care in the least."

IT was true that Mirabel Oldridge cared little about the minutiae of dress. She rarely took any notice of what others wore and found life simpler when they treated her the same way. She dressed plainly to encourage the many men she dealt with to take her seriously: to *listen* rather than look, and keep their minds on business.

To her great discomfort, however, she had taken excessive and repeated notice of Mr. Carsington, from the crown of his sleek hat to his gleaming boots.

He had not been wearing the hat when she first saw him. As a result she was aware that his hair was a rich brown with golden glints his deep-set eyes seemed to reflect. His face was angular, the profile patrician to the last degree. He was handsome in a brooding sort of way, tall, broad-shouldered, and long-limbed. Even his hands were long. When he had offered to help with the knotted bonnet strings, she had looked at his hands and felt giddy.

Matters did not improve when he'd stood so near to work on the ribbons. She'd caught a whiff of shaving soap or cologne; it was so faint that she couldn't be sure what it was or whether she'd simply imagined it.

But she'd become confused because she was nervous, she told herself, which was perfectly reasonable. She'd been uneasy because she'd been caught unprepared, which was as unpleasant as it was unusual.

One near catastrophe years ago had taught her to keep informed of everything having to do with her father. That way, no one could take advantage of him, or confuse, manipulate, or bully her. That way she would never be at a loss. She would know exactly what to do at all times.

For instance, she read all her father's correspondence and dealt with it. All he ever had to do was read what she'd written and sign his name. In any event, he appeared to read. There was no way to be sure his mind was engaged. He was too busy trying to unlock the secrets of plant reproduction to pay attention to his relatives' letters, or his solicitor's—or any other materials unconnected with botanical pursuits.

Not having opened any letters from Mr. Carsington, Mirabel had no idea what he'd written and couldn't begin to guess how Papa had answered.

If she wished not to be caught unprepared at dinner, she had better fill the gap in her knowledge.

This was why she wasted no time in turning Mr. Carsington over to the servants, who'd see to drying and brushing his "unsuitable" attire and provide whatever else he needed for his toilette.

Yet Mirabel stood for a moment, watching him limp away, only to wish she hadn't, because her heart squeezed, as though it winced for him, which was foolish.

She'd seen and even helped nurse men with worse injuries. She knew men and women who'd suffered as much or more than he had done. She knew of some who'd acted bravely, too, and received not a fraction of the admiration showered upon him. And anyway, she told herself, he was far too elegant and self-assured to need anybody's sympathy.

Mirabel thrust the limp to the back of her mind and hurried to her father's study.

As Joseph had reported, his master's diary lay open to this date, and the appointment was duly noted.

She ransacked the desk but found no trace of Mr. Carsington's letter. Most likely Papa had stuffed it in his pocket and scribbled field notes on it or lost it. The copy of his reply had survived, however, because he'd written it in his memorandum book instead of on a loose sheet of paper.

The letter, dated ten days ago, was as Mr. Carsington described: her father expressed interest, clearly grasped the implications, and seemed most willing to discuss the canal further.

The words made Mirabel's throat hurt.

In the letter she saw the father she'd known once, who took an interest in so many things, so many people. How he'd loved to talk—and listen, too, even to a little girl's prattle. She remembered sitting on the stairs, listening to the voices below, during the frequent dinners and card parties and other social gatherings. How many times had she heard him and her mother in conversation at table, in the library, the sitting room, this study?

But after her mother's death fifteen years ago, he had grown increasingly preoccupied with plant rather than human life. On the rare occasions he did emerge from the realms of botany, it was only for a short time.

Mirabel had missed the most recent occasion. He must have taken notice of the everyday world during the few days she'd spent visiting her former governess in Cromford.

During the visit Mirabel had bought the bonnet with which she'd nearly choked herself this afternoon.

She could not believe she'd let the man unnerve her so completely. It was not as though she'd never encountered his kind before.

During her two London seasons—a lifetime ago, it seemed—she'd met countless men like him: elegant in dress, polished in all the social graces, never at a loss as to what to do or say.

She'd heard the cultivated voices, the drawls and lisps some fashionables affected, the laughter, gossip, and flirtation.

Surely she'd heard voices like his, so low-pitched as to make every commonplace utterance seem of the deepest intimacy, every cliché a delicious secret.

"I have heard and seen them all," she muttered. "He is nothing remarkable, merely another London sophisticate who sees us as provincials and bumpkins. We are all ignorant country folk who don't know what's good for us."

Mr. Carsington would soon discover his error.

Meanwhile, his dinner conversation with Papa should prove vastly entertaining.

Two

WHILE Alistair made no pretense to intellectual brilliance, he was usually capable of putting two and two together, and fairly quickly.

Circumstances this day, however, conspired against him. By Miss Oldridge's abysmal standards he might seem dressed elegantly enough for a country dinner. He knew better.

Thanks to conscientious servants and a good fire, his clothes were brushed and dry. But the clothes were for *afternoon* wear and could not be transformed into acceptable dinner attire by even the most diligent servants.

Furthermore, the staff could not instantly launder and starch his linen. His neckcloth was limp, and creases had formed in the wrong places, which made him wild.

Meanwhile his leg, which hated damp and ought to have lived in Morocco, was punishing him for the ramble in the icy mist by tying itself into throbbing knots.

These annoyances contributed to his failure to realize what any idiot would have divined hours ago.

Miss Oldridge had spoken of stamens and pistils and asked if he was botanical. Alistair had seen the conservatory, the notebooks, the acres of hothouses.

But when he wasn't in a fit over his clothes or being tortured by his leg, he was completely distracted by her. As a result, it wasn't until they met in the drawing room before dinner, and Mr. Oldridge acquainted him with Hedwig's observations on the reproductive organs of mosses, that the truth finally dawned: The man was in the grip of a monomania.

Alistair was familiar with the malady. He had an evangelical sister-in-law and a cousin obsessed with deciphering the Rosetta stone. Since such people rarely, of their own accord, abandoned their chosen place of mental residence, one must take them firmly by the elbow, figuratively speaking, and lead them elsewhere.

Accordingly, at the start of the second course, when his host ceased lecturing to concentrate on carving the goose, Alistair charged into the gap.

"I envy your having so many facts at your command," he said. "I wish you had been able to advise us before we first presented our canal proposal. I do hope you will advise us now."

Mr. Oldridge continued dismantling the fowl, but his mouth pursed and his brows knit.

"We will gladly alter the route, if that is the primary concern," Alistair persisted.

"Can you alter it to another county?" Miss Oldridge asked. "Somersetshire, for instance, where they have already despoiled the countryside with slag heaps?"

Alistair looked across the table at her, which he'd been trying not to do since first clapping eyes on her dinner attire.

Her dress was a cool lavender, when she ought to wear only warm, rich colors. It had a high neck and a lace ruffle to conceal the narrow bit of shoulder and neck the bodice left uncovered. Her glorious hair was stuffed any which way into a clumsy roll at the back of her head. For jewelry she wore a plain silver locket and chain.

Alistair wondered how she could look in her mirror without seeing the obvious: Every article with which she'd chosen to adorn her person was completely, absolutely, and irredeemably *wrong*. She must lack a faculty every other woman in the world possessed. He wondered if hers was a disorder akin to tone deafness, and his irritation with her was what a music lover would feel on hearing an instrument out of tune or a singer off-key.

He wanted to order her back to her room to dress properly, but he couldn't, which was maddening.

This perhaps explained why he answered her in the tone and manner he usually reserved for irritating younger brothers.

He said, "Miss Oldridge, I hope you will permit me to correct a slight misapprehension. Canals do not produce slag heaps. *Collieries* produce slag heaps. At present, only Lord Gordmor is mining coal in your vicinity, and his collieries are nearly fifteen miles from here. The only landscape he is despoiling is his own, because the property is good for nothing else."

"I should think he might graze sheep with less trouble and noise, and do as well," she said.

"You are certainly entitled to entertain any fanciful notions you like," Alistair said. "I should not wish to stifle an active imagination."

Her eyes sparked, but Alistair smoothly addressed his host before she could retort. "We freely admit our motives to be selfish and practical," he said. "The primary aim is a more efficient and cheaper means of transporting coal."

Oldridge, engaged in distributing choice bits of fowl to daughter and guest, merely nodded.

"Lord Gordmor will then be able to bring the coal to more customers," Alistair went on, "and sell it at a lower price. However, he and his customers aren't the only ones who'll profit. The canal will provide you and your neighbors easier access to more goods. Fragile items, traveling smoothly on water rather than bumping along rutted roads, will reach their destinations in one piece. You will have an economical means of conveying manure and agricultural produce to and from the various markets. In short, all in the Longledge environs, from landowner to laborer, will reap its benefits."

"Lord Hargate has not spent much time at his country place of late, even when Parliament is not sitting," Mr. Oldridge said. "Politics can be acutely demanding of the physical and mental faculties and wearing to the spirit. I hope he is well."

"My father is quite well," Alistair said. "I should make clear, however, that he is in no way involved in Lord Gordmor's project."

"I well remember the canal mania of the last century," Oldridge said. "They built the Cromford Canal then, and commenced the Peak Forest. Mr. Carsington, may I press you to try a morsel of curry?"

Alistair was prepared to extol the benefits of Gordmor's canal at length. Still, he was at dinner where, normally, one did not discuss business. He'd introduced the topic only because Miss Oldridge had suggested this would be his best opportunity to make his case.

It was not so hard to set aside business temporarily, however. Alistair was glad of the reminder to savor the food, which was far superior, in both variety and quality of preparation, to what one might reasonably expect so far from civilization.

The cook, clearly, was a treasure. Even the butler and footmen would have passed muster in any great London household, including Hargate House.

What a pity that a woman who otherwise staffed her house so well could not find a lady's maid capable of preventing fashion atrocities.

"How did you come to be interested in canals?" Mr. Oldridge asked him. "Admittedly the engineering feats are fascinating. Yet you do not strike me as a Cambridge man."

"Oxford," Alistair said.

Of the two ancient universities, Cambridge was deemed to offer somewhat greater scope to those of a mathematical or scientific bent.

"Smith was self-taught, I believe," his host said ruminatively. "What do you know of fossils?"

"Apart from the Oxford dons?" Alistair said.

He heard a strangled giggle and looked across the table, but not quickly enough.

Miss Oldridge wore a sober expression in keeping with her sober attire.

Her gaze shifted from her father to Alistair.

"Papa refers to Mr. William Smith's *Strata Identified by Organized Fossils*," she said. "Are you familiar with the work?"

"It sounds far too deep for me," Alistair said, and watched her bite back a smile. She was not immune to feeble puns, then. "I'm no scholar."

"But it concerns mineral deposits," she said. "I should have thought . . ." Her brow wrinkled, much more prettily than her father's did. "It must have been Mr. Smith's geological map you used, then."

"For the canal route?" Alistair said.

"To determine whether it was worthwhile to drill for coal in an area that is all but inaccessible." She tipped her head to one side and studied Alistair as though he were a fossil in dire need of organizing. "England has coal nearly everywhere, but in some places it is difficult and prohibitively expensive either to get to or to transport," she said. "You must have had good reason to believe the coal measures on Lord Gordmor's property were worth so much effort. Or did you simply begin drilling, without considering the practicalities?"

"The Peak is known to be rich in mineral wealth," Alistair said. "Lord Gordmor was bound to find something worth the trouble—lead, limestone, marble, coal."

"Lord Gordmor? But did you not say you were a partner—'acquainted with every detail,' were your words, I think."

"We've been partners since November," he said. "He started the mining operation earlier, not long after returning from the Continent."

The fact was, Gordmor had returned from war to find his finances in alarming disarray. He could not even afford the upkeep of his Northumberland estate. His bailiff had advised him to explore the Derbyshire property, and desperate, Gordy had drilled for coal.

Alistair, however, had no intention of disclosing his friend's personal affairs to an inquisitive young lady—or anyone else for that matter.

"I see." Miss Oldridge lowered her gaze to her plate. "Then you were both with the Duke of Wellington. But you're the one who's famous. Even here, in the wilds of Derbyshire, everyone has heard of you."

Alistair's face grew hot. He didn't know whether she referred to Waterloo or the Episodes of Stupidity. Both matters were for the most part public knowledge, unfortunately. He ought to be indifferent by now to the spectacle of his past rearing its head, it happened so often. But he wasn't indifferent, and he did wish the tales had not traveled quite so far.

"You bear a strong resemblance to Lord Hargate," Mr. Oldridge said. "He has a great many sons, has he not?"

Relieved at the turn of subject, Alistair admitted to having four brothers.

"Some will say that is not a great many," Mr. Oldridge said. "Our unfortunate King has sired fifteen children."

King George III had been for some years completely insane, and thus unfit to handle affairs of state. As a consequence, his eldest son—who, while not insane, would not win any prizes for rational behavior—currently reigned as Prince Regent.

"One might wish our unfortunate monarch had sired fewer children, of better quality," Miss Oldridge said. "Lord and Lady Hargate produced only five boys—yet two are paragons, and one is a famous Waterloo hero. I daresay your younger brothers will prove themselves equally remarkable as they mature."

"You seem to know a great deal about my family, Miss Oldridge," Alistair said.

"As does everyone in Derbyshire," she said. "Yours is one of the county's oldest families. Your father is reputed to be the real power in the House of Lords. Your older brothers have involved themselves in several admirable causes. All the London papers provided extensive accounts of your battlefield exploits, and the local ones devoted oceans of ink to the subject. Even had I somehow contrived to miss your name in print, I could not remain in ignorance. For a time, you were mentioned in every letter I received from friends and family members in London."

Alistair winced inwardly. He'd been involved in barely two days' fighting. He'd been so raw it was a wonder he hadn't shot his own nose off. Why the papers chose to lionize him was a mystery, and an infuriating one at that.

His leg commenced a set of spasms. "That is old news," he said in the chilling drawl that always ended discussion of the subject.

"Not hereabouts," Miss Oldridge said. "I recommend you prepare to endure the admiration of the population."

His frigid tone affected her not a whit. Her cheerful one put him on the alert.

He knew—better than many men, in fact—that a woman's speech could be fraught with hidden meanings bearing no discernible resemblance to the spoken words. He did not always know what a woman *meant,* but he was usually aware that she meant more than she said, and that the "more" was, more often than not, trouble.

He sensed trouble at present, was aware it might at any moment spring out at him from the darkness of her mind, but couldn't perceive what it was.

What he could perceive was her sad excuse for a coiffure coming apart. A cluster of coppery curls had fallen out of the roll and dangled at her neck. Atop her head, curls sprang out singly and in clumps. He watched her push one long tendril out of her face and behind her ear.

It was a gesture a woman might make after she'd undressed and taken down her hair . . . or upon rising from her pillows in the morning . . . or after lovemaking.

She wasn't supposed to do it at the dinner table. She was supposed to arrive there properly coifed and dressed and in perfect order. She wasn't supposed to be tumbling all to pieces, as though she'd been recently ravished.

Alistair told himself to ignore it and brace for trouble. He tried to attend to his meal, but his appetite was gone. He was too aware of her—the fetching gesture, the disorderly curls—and a tension in the air. Even when he looked or turned his mind elsewhere, he couldn't shed his consciousness of her.

Clearly, his host discerned nothing amiss but went on steadily eating, a contented if distant look on his face. It was fortunate he did so much walking and climbing, for the botanist ate enough for any two large men.

Mr. Oldridge talked about experiments with tulips during the remainder of the meal. Finally, Miss Oldridge departed, leaving the men to their port and allowing Alistair to put what was out of sight out of mind.

He fixed his mind on business and commenced making his case for the canal.

While he talked, his host contemplated the chandelier. Still, he must have heard something, because at the end of Alistair's presentation, the botanist said, "Yes, well, I do see your point, but it's complicated, you see."

"Canals are rarely simple matters," Alistair said. "When one is obliged to use other people's land, one must be prepared to accommodate and compensate them, and each party's requirements are bound to be different."

"Yes, yes, but it is very like the tulip experiment," said his host. "Without you apply the *Farina Fecundens,* they will not bear seed. It is explained in Bradley's account, but Miller made similar experiments. You will not find the account in every edition of the *Gardener's Dictionary.* I will lend you one of my copies, and you may read it for yourself."

Following this incomprehensible response, Mr. Oldridge proposed they rejoin Mirabel, who would be awaiting them in the library.

Alistair begged to be excused. It was growing late and he must return to his hotel.

"But you must stay the night," Mr. Oldridge said. "You cannot travel all that way in the dark. The road, I am sorry to say, can be difficult, even in broad day."

Yes, and that is why you need a canal! Alistair wanted to shout.

Since he wanted to, a retreat, clearly, was in order.

At any rate, he needed to think rationally, which meant he must get away. Rational thinking was next to impossible in Miss Oldridge's vicinity.

Matters here were not at all as he and Gordy had supposed. What, precisely, the trouble was, Alistair couldn't say. At present he knew only that both Mr. and Miss Oldridge had an uncanny ability to rattle him, which, as Gordy had remarked, was exceedingly difficult.

Alistair was not high-strung. He might become emotional about women, but his nerves were steady, perhaps to a fault. A jumpier man, he was sure, could not possibly have landed in so many scrapes, because such a man would have hesitated and thought, at least once if not twice.

At present, Alistair's nerves showed alarming signs of fraying.

Even if they'd been their usual rocklike selves, he couldn't stay. He'd worn the same clothes all day—through dinner, no less—which made him a little ill, and no doubt contributed to his prickly mood. To don these same articles of clothing on the morrow was out of the question.

Alistair had borne such privations on the battlefield because he had no choice. Oldridge Hall was not a battlefield—not yet, at any rate.

A short while later, therefore, having also declined his host's offer of a carriage, Alistair set out on horseback, under steadily falling sleet, for Matlock Bath.

MR. Carsington was already on his way before Mirabel learned of his departure.

Her father relayed the news in a state of bewilderment. "He was in a great hurry to go, and it was quite impossible to dissuade him."

Mirabel hurried to the window and looked out. She could see only as far as the light of the library reached, but that was enough to show her the state of things.

"It's sleeting," she said. "I cannot believe you let Lord Hargate's son depart, on horseback, to travel in an ice storm all the way to Matlock."

"Perhaps you are right," he said. "Perhaps I should have summoned some of the largest footmen to subdue him and tie him to . . . something." He looked about as though in search of a suitable something. "But I cannot think how otherwise he was to be prevented."

"Why did you not send for me?"

Her parent frowned. "I cannot say why, but it did not occur to me. I am sorry it did not. The trouble was, he put me in mind of a cactus, and I found myself contemplating the spiny tufts, which might serve a reproductive purpose, though it is generally explained—Why, child, where are you going?"

Mirabel was hurrying out to the hall. "I am going after him, of course. Otherwise, he will break his neck or his horse's leg—or most likely, both—and we shall never hear the end of it. Good God! An earl's son. The Earl of *Hargate*'s son! The famous Waterloo hero, no less—and wounded in the line of duty. Oh, it does not bear thinking of. Really, Papa, you will drive me to distraction one of these days. The man hurls himself to certain death while you are contemplating cactus spines."

"But my dear, it is quite important—"

Mirabel didn't hear him. She was running down the hall.

MOMENTS later, mounted on an unhandsome but surefooted and imperturbable gelding, Mirabel rode out into the night. She caught up with her quarry a short distance past the park gates. The thick sleet had thinned to icy rain, but it could easily thicken and thin again a score of times in the course of the night.

"Mr. Carsington!" she shouted into the downpour. He was only a dark, man-shaped form on a dark, horse-shaped form, but the form was tall enough and sat straight enough, despite the rain pouring from his hat brim down his neck— and anyway who else could it be?

He halted. "Miss Oldridge?" He turned his head her way. It was too dark to see his face. "What are you doing here? Are you mad?"

"You must return to the house at once," she said.

"You must be insane," he said.

"You are no longer in London," she said. "The next house is a mile away. In this weather, it will take you two hours at the very least to reach Matlock Bath—and that is only barring accident."

"It is of vital importance that I return to my hotel," he said. "I beg you to return to your house. They ought not have let you leave. You will catch your death."

"I am but a few minutes from a good blaze," she said. "You are the one who'll catch his death. Then what are we to tell your father?"

"Miss Oldridge, no one tells my father anything," he said.

"Or you, either, I collect."

"Miss Oldridge, while we remain here disputing, the animals grow chilled. I am sure they will be better off moving, yours in the opposite direction of mine. I thank you for your hospitality, and I appreciate your concern for my well-being, but it is quite impossible for me to remain."

"Mr. Carsington, whatever engagements you have for tomorrow—"

"Miss Oldridge, you do not understand: *I have nothing to wear.*"

"You're funning me," she said.

"I never joke about such things," he said.

"Nothing to wear."

"Exactly."

"I see," she said.

She had seen long before now but had failed to come to the logical conclusion. Logic had taken second place to reactions lower on the intellectual plane.

She had observed him closely enough, had been unable to keep from observing.

She had an all too vivid recollection of the way the expensively tailored coat hugged broad shoulders and the powerful torso that tapered to a narrow waist. She had a clear image in her mind's eye of the exquisite embroidery of his silk waistcoat with its one upper button undone . . . and of the snugly fitting breeches outlining muscular thighs . . . and such long legs. Merely recalling sent heat washing through her, though she sat in darkness upon a horse in a cold, driving rain.

She could not help the heat. It was natural enough, she told herself. He was a hero and looked the part: tall, strong, and handsome. Few women could gaze on him unmoved.

All the same, she retained intellect enough to comprehend his irrational determination to travel at night in this filthy weather.

She had not spent two seasons in London without learning something about dandies, and this was a dandy if ever she had met one . . . though she'd never met one quite so imposingly built.

"Well, that's different, then," she said. "Good night, Mr. Carsington."

She turned and rode back to the house.

To her surprise, Mirabel found her father pacing the vestibule when she returned. Usually, he drank his tea in the library while perusing botanical tomes, then proceeded to the conservatory to say good night to the divers vegetable matter therein.

"Oh, dear. You could not persuade him," Papa said as she gave her dripping bonnet and cloak to the footman.

"He has nothing to wear," she said.

Her father blinked at her.

"He is a dandy, Papa," she said. "Deprived of what he deems proper dress, he is like a plant deprived of vital nutrients. He wilts and dies, and one can scarcely imagine the agonies he suffers in the process." She started toward the stairs.

Her father followed her. "I knew something was wrong. It is like the cactus spines."

"Papa, I am wet and somewhat out of sorts, and I should like—"

"But he limps," her father persisted.

"I observed that," Mirabel said. How she wished for a less heartbreakingly gallant manner of limping! It made her feel things she didn't want to and couldn't afford to. And anyway, it was ridiculous at her age, after her experience. . . .

She proceeded up the stairs. "I understand he was quite seriously injured at Waterloo."

Her father trailed after her. "Yes, Benton told me about it. Yet I strongly suspect Mr. Carsington also suffered a head injury without realizing. I have heard of such cases. That would explain, you see."

"Explain what?"

"The cactus spines."

"Papa, I haven't the least idea what you mean."

"No, no, I daresay." She heard his footsteps pause behind her. "Perhaps he will not understand about the tulips, after all. Yes, perhaps you are right. Well, good night, dear."

"Good night, Papa." Mirabel climbed the stairs and went to her room. Though she was tired, she blamed it on overstrained nerves. She had not been prepared. Had she been forewarned of Mr. Carsington's arrival . . . but she hadn't been, had not even imagined this turn of events.

She had made an incorrect assumption about Lord Gordmor that could prove to be disastrous. She'd never dreamt he would be so persistent.

She'd erred, and it was too late to undo the error. All she could do was take a lesson from it. She'd based her calculations on insufficient information. She would not make that mistake twice.

And so, after she had shed her damp clothes and dried off and donned a warm nightgown and robe, she went to her sitting room. There, comfortably ensconced in a soft chair before the fire, she wrote a letter to Lady Sherfield in London. If there was anything about Mr. Carsington Aunt Clothilde didn't know, it wasn't worth knowing.

IT took Alistair the full two hours Miss Oldridge had predicted to traverse the "few miles" from Oldridge Hall to Wilkerson's Hotel, where he was staying.

He arrived soaked to the bone, a condition to which his leg objected in the most strenuous terms, refusing to assist him in any way in climbing the stairs.

But he was used to the leg's tantrums and made it to his bedchamber. There his manservant Crewe expressed his disapproval with a mildly censuring cough and the recommendation of a hot bath.

"It's too late to make the servants haul water up the stairs," Alistair said.

He dropped into a chair near the fire, set his foot on the fender, and started massaging his outraged leg. While doing so, he told his valet about the day's vicissitudes, discreetly excluding his deranged reaction to Miss Oldridge.

"I am sorry, sir, you had a lengthy journey in bad weather to no purpose," Crewe said. "Perhaps I might fetch you a bottle of wine and something to eat?"

"I've been more than amply fed," Alistair said. "Mr.

Oldridge appears to have two great passions: botany and dinner."

"Indeed, sir. The servants here all solemnly swear that he has never once been late to dinner, though he is late or absent in every other circumstance."

"I should have stayed here and listened to servants' gossip," Alistair said, staring into the fire. "As it was, I was ill-prepared for the encounter." The glowing coals brought to mind Miss Oldridge's hair, and the way the candlelight caught it, making it a soft gold at times, a fiery red at others. "His daughter . . ." He hesitated. "She holds amazingly strong opinions for one so young."

"A lady of uncommon character, they say, sir. She would have to be, to manage so large an estate and all her father's business interests."

Alistair looked up from the fire to his servant's face. "Miss Oldridge manages the property?"

"She manages everything. I was told that her bailiff hardly dares draw a breath without her approval. Sir, are you ill? Perhaps I had better fetch that wine. Or a hot posset—indeed, you will not wish to risk a chill at this time, when you have so much to do."

Though he was not ill, Alistair let his valet go to concoct one of his possets.

The master used the time to digest what he'd just heard.

The ill-dressed, inquisitive girl with the fire-colored hair ran one of the largest estates in Derbyshire.

"Well, someone must," he muttered a while later, when he'd finally found a relatively clear perspective on the situation. "*He* doesn't attend to anything else, that's plain enough. As she told me: If it wasn't botanical, he wouldn't attend."

He became aware of Crewe hovering nearby with the hot drink. "I beg your pardon, sir?"

"How old is she?" Alistair demanded. "Not a girl, I'm sure. No girl could possibly—Gad, why didn't I see?" he shook his head and accepted the cup from his valet. "Did the gossips by any chance mention how old Miss Oldridge is?"

"One and thirty," said Crewe.

The sip of posset Alistair had taken went down his windpipe. When he stopped choking and coughing, he laughed. He might as well. It was a fine joke on him.

"One and thirty," he repeated.

"Last month, sir."

"I thought she was a girl," Alistair said. "As anyone would. A slimmish lass, with a mass of coppery hair and great blue eyes and such a smile . . ." He looked down at the drink in his hand, his own smile fading. "God help us. The canal—everything—depends on *her.*"

Three

THE following morning, Mirabel and two servants set out under overcast skies to find Mr. Carsington's body.

They reached Matlock Bath without encountering any corpses, however, and learned from the postmistress that the gentleman had arrived safely the previous night and was staying in Wilkerson's Hotel.

The choice of hotel was surprising. Mirabel had thought he'd be staying up the hill, at the Old Bath Hotel, Matlock Bath's grandest. Instead he'd chosen Wilkerson's, which stood on the South Parade, exposed to all the dirt and noise of coaches coming and going.

When they entered the village, though, the Parade was quiet. By this time the sun had grown bolder, making an occasional dart through the clouds to sparkle on the river and the whitewashed houses pressed against the hillside.

Though the place was as familiar to Mirabel as her own property, she never grew tired of its beauty.

Here the hills rose steeply from the Derwent River, the great limestone crag of the High Tor visible at every turn.

It might have been a castle, with a garden wall along whose sides patches of greenery softened the grey rock.

The spa itself was clean and pretty. Lodging places, shops, and museums clustered along a short stretch of the Museum Parade, and villas peeped out from the greenery on the surrounding hillsides. On the other side of the road, gardens sloped down toward the river. The road followed the river's route, round the mountain rising behind the Heights of Abraham.

It was an easy climb to the Heights, and Mirabel had done it in all seasons. Whenever her cares threatened to overwhelm her, she went there and let her surroundings soothe her.

She had a great deal on her mind this day and experienced more than a little perturbation of spirit. But she hadn't time to let nature calm her.

Instead, having turned over her curricle to the groom and sent her maid Lucy to carry out some errands, Mirabel proceeded to the entrance of Wilkerson's Hotel.

Within, she asked for Mr. Carsington.

Mr. Wilkerson hurried out to her. "I believe he's still abed, Miss Oldridge," he said.

"Still abed?" she repeated. "But it must be noon."

"Just gone half-past eleven, miss," said the innkeeper.

Then she remembered: Members of the *haut ton* rarely rose before noon, usually on account of going to bed about the time dawn was cracking.

Mr. Wilkerson offered to send a servant up to ascertain whether Mr. Carsington was ready to receive visitors.

An image arose in Mirabel's mind of Mr. Carsington pushing tousled gold-streaked brown hair out of his face and blinking sleepily up at . . . someone.

"No, there is no need to disturb him," she said quickly. "I shall be in the village for some hours. I must pay some calls. I can speak to him later in the day."

She noticed her hands were trembling. It must be hunger. She'd been so worried about finding Lord Hargate's son in broken pieces that she'd been able to swallow only a sip of tea and a bite of toast for breakfast. "But first I should like a pot of tea," she added, "and some toast."

She was swiftly conveyed to a private dining room, far from the bustle of the public dining room and tavern. Within minutes the tea and toast appeared.

After she'd emptied plate and teapot, Mirabel's spirits revived. When Mr. Wilkerson came in and asked if she'd like something more—eggs, perhaps, and a few rashers of bacon—she asked for his most detailed local map.

He had any number of such maps, he assured her, as good a selection as one might find in any shop in London, including some handsome hand-tinted ones. He wished the Ordnance Survey map of Derbyshire had been done by now, but it hadn't. "A pity it is, Miss Oldridge," he said. "Very scientifically made, they are, those new maps."

She asked to see what he had, and he brought them to her. Several seemed detailed enough to suit her purposes, and she spread these out on the table, merely to compare. She did not plan a close study until she returned home.

But Mirabel was in certain respects more like her father than she realized. Left to herself—with no interruptions, disturbances, or servants' calls for help— she could become as caught up in working out a riddle as he.

As time passed, she shed by degrees her bonnet and cloak. More than two hours after she'd come, she was still bent over the maps, looking for a way out of her difficulty.

ABOUT this time, Mr. Wilkerson was out in the court-yard, gossiping with a postilion. Consequently, he was unaware that Mr. Carsington had come downstairs and was on his way to the private parlor he'd reserved as his head-quarters. Since Mr. Wilkerson was not there to inform him, and Mr. Carsington did not encounter a servant en route, he had no idea who was in the small dining room nearby.

The door happening to be open, Alistair idly glanced inside as he was passing and discovered directly in his line of vision a small, round, distinctively feminine bottom.

It was draped in green fabric whose fine quality his connoisseur's eye could not fail to discern, even while this same eye was assessing the form beneath and calculating how many layers of cloth came between the dress and skin.

All this was the work of an instant, no more. But she must have heard his footsteps pause. Or perhaps she heard him catch his breath—and snatch his wits back from where they were wandering and remind himself he'd better continue on his way: He could not afford to be distracted by a female, no matter how perfect her derrière.

Whatever the cause, she lifted a head capped with a disheveled mass of coppery hair and turned a deep blue gaze over her shoulder at him . . . and smiled.

It was *she*.

"Miss Oldridge," he said, his voice dropping so low that the two words sounded like "grrrr."

"Mr. Carsington." She straightened and turned fully toward him. "I had not thought you would be up and about at this early hour."

Was she being sarcastic? "It is nearly two o'clock," he said.

Her eyes widened. "Good heavens. Have I been here all this time?"

"I haven't the least idea now long you've been here," he said.

She threw a frowning glance at the map. "Well, I never meant to stay so long. That is, I meant to come back later, when you were awake."

"I am awake."

"Yes, and"—she eyed him up and down—"and looking very neat and elegant."

Alistair wished he could say the same for her. Someone had made a valiant attempt to tame her hair with a braid coiled and pinned on the crown of her head. But of course half the pins were on the floor and the table, and the coil was listing to starboard. His hands itched to get at it and put it right. He clenched them and forced himself to look elsewhere.

Grimly he regarded the expensive dress. This green was even more unbecoming than the shade he'd first seen her wearing. The style—oh, it had no style at all. It was plain and dull and about as flattering as a flour sack.

He turned his gaze to the maps.

"I needed a new one," she said. "We had a very fine map of the area, but my father drowned it in the Derwent River in November."

"I see." He did, all too plainly. "What I don't understand is why you or your father would need one. I was told that yours is one of the older families hereabouts. I should think you'd know the land quite well."

"My own property, yes, but Longledge Hill gets its name from its length, which is considerable," she said. "It actually comprises several hills—far more territory than I or even my father could know intimately." She turned back to the table and pointed to the map. "We have Captain Hughes on one side of us, and Sir Roger Tolbert on the other. Even though we visit frequently, I certainly do not know every stick and stone of their land. I was particularly curious about Lord Gordmor's property, which is actually a good deal less, you see, than fifteen miles away."

"It comes to nearly twice that for carts and packhorses traveling deeply rutted and circuitous roads," Alistair said. "If we could cut a canal in a straight line, it would extend not even ten miles. However, since rocky hills lie along that line, and our route must go round landowners' outbuildings, timber yards, and such—we estimate fifteen miles of canal."

He moved to stand beside her at the table. "Is this why you needed a map? You wished to study our route more carefully? Is it possible you are having second thoughts about your opposition to our plans?"

"No, I'm having second thoughts about Lord Gordmor," she said without looking up.

The fitful sunbeams from the dining room's single window made a fiery froth of the wispy ringlets about her face. The braided coil sagged further toward her ear, which, being small and perfectly shell-shaped, made the imperfect hair arrangement—not to mention every stitch on her persons—all the more aggravating.

"You had perhaps pictured him as one of those rapacious villains of industry who evict humble shepherds and cowherds from their huts and erect immense, smoking factories on what used to be grazing land?" Alistair said.

"No, I had pictured him as being resourceful," she said. "When a solution I devise proves unworkable, I look for another way to solve the problem. But having failed to interest us in his canal, Lord Gordmor has not, as I supposed he would do, exercised his imagination. Instead, he has kept to his original solution. The difference this time is, he's sent in heavy artillery to blast us into submission."

Alistair would have understood immediately what she was saying if his mind had not been otherwise occupied.

The braided coil not only continued to sag but was uncoiling as well. Though he hadn't heard the pins drop, he was sure more were scattered over the map-covered table than a moment ago. Any minute now, her coiffure would tumble completely to pieces. He could barely keep his hands still.

Thus distracted, he said, "Heavy artillery? You cannot think we will bring in our machinery and troops of canal cutters and bully our way through. You are aware, I hope, that we cannot build a canal without an Act of Parliament, and Parliament will not approve a canal proposal the landowners unanimously oppose."

"*You* are the heavy artillery," she said. "In this part of Derbyshire, the Earl of Hargate is at least as important as the Duke of Devonshire. Your family has been here quite as long, and your father is held in exceptionally high esteem. Two of your brothers are paragons, and you are a famous hero. Lord Gordmor chose his partner very wisely, indeed—as well as a convenient time to contract influenza."

Alistair froze, almost literally. After a moment's incredulous outrage, he settled into a cold fury. "Correct me if I have misapprehended, Miss Oldridge," he said with bone-chilling politeness. "You believe Lord Gordmor or I—or perhaps the pair of us—decided to use my family's position and my own notoriety to mow down the opposition? You think that is why I came? To what? Overawe the yokels? Perhaps even touch their hearts with the evidence of my great sacrifice on behalf of King and country?" At the reference to his troublesome leg, a bitter note crept into his voice.

"Lord Gordmor has not a fraction of your impact upon local opinion," she said. "He is not a Derbyshire man. His title is recent, bestowed only in the last half century. And he is not famous." Her chin went up. "I do not see why you take offense. I merely state the simple facts of the case, which should be obvious to everybody—though I suppose no one else will say it to your face."

"You know nothing about Lord Gordmor," Alistair said tightly. "If you did, you would be aware he would never be so dishonorable as to use me or my position to foist a wicked scheme upon anybody."

His leg was twitching angrily. It hated standing too long in one position. He stepped away from the table.

"I said nothing about foisting wicked schemes," she said. "Really, you seem to have a turn for the theatrical, Mr. Carsington." Her brow wrinkled. "Or perhaps they're rhetorical flourishes. 'Overawe the yokels' is apt, but 'rapacious villains' and 'wicked scheme' are off the mark. I do not think your canal is wicked. If a suitor is rejected, it does not follow that he is wicked, merely that he does not suit. Does your leg pain you?"

"Not in the least," he said while a spasm shot through his hip.

She, too, backed away from the table. "I know I'm supposed to take no notice," she said. "But it is never proper to ignore someone's discomfort. You move more stiffly than before. I collect your leg pains you. Perhaps you wish to walk about. Or sit. Or elevate it. I shouldn't keep you here arguing with me, at any rate. I'm sure you have a great many important things to do."

Alistair had many, many important things to do. But she had thrown everything into a tumult, like her hair, and he was not ready to be dismissed. "Miss Oldridge, you know perfectly well that *you* are the most important thing I have to do," he said, and instantly regretted it. Where were his vaunted powers of address? Good grief, where were his *manners?*

He paced to the window and back, and to the window again. His leg treated him to several spasms. It was furious with him.

She watched him, her expression troubled. "The long ride in the cold rain last night cannot have been good for your injury. I did not think of that until now. My great anxiety this morning was finding your broken body in a ditch. I had resigned myself to picking up the pieces. Why am I important?"

Listening to her talk about searching for his broken corpse made Alistair forget what he meant to say. He recalled how she'd left a warm, luxurious house and ridden out in the darkness and freezing rain to bring him back. He could not imagine any other woman—save, perhaps, his mother—doing such a thing. But then, unlike most other women, Miss Oldridge was the responsible member of the family, the one in charge.

The one upon whom his canal depended, he reminded himself.

He should be making the most of this opportunity.

He marshaled his ideas into order. "No one else will speak freely to me," he said. "You said so a moment ago. I need to understand what the objections are to the canal."

"What difference does it make?" she said. "Now you are here, they will melt away like snow under a hot sun."

"But that isn't the way I want to do it!"

She gave him a skeptical look. "Then you shouldn't have come."

Alistair turned away and stared unseeingly out the window while he counted to ten. "Miss Oldridge, I must tell you plainly that you make me want to tear my hair out."

"I wondered what that was," she said.

Alistair turned back sharply. "What *what* was?"

"Heavy weather. It felt as though heavy weather were bearing down upon the room. But it is only you. You have a remarkable force of personality, Mr. Carsington. Why do I make you want to tear your hair out?"

Alistair gazed at her in exasperation. The loosened coil had slid to within a quarter inch of her ear.

He straightened away from the window, marched to the table, swept up a handful of pins, and advanced upon her. "You've lost most of your hairpins," he said.

"Oh, thank you." She put out her hand.

He ignored the outstretched hand, took up the offending braid, coiled it up, set it back where it belonged, and pinned it in place.

She stood rigidly still, her blue gaze fixed on his neckcloth.

Her wild hair was silken soft. His fingers itched to tangle in it.

He quickly finished his work and stood back. "That's better," he said.

For a moment she said nothing. Her gaze went from his face to his hands, then back again. Otherwise, she did not move a muscle, only stood regarding Alistair with the same intensity of expression his cousin applied to Egyptian hieroglyphs.

He said tightly, "It was . . . distracting. Your hair. Coming down."

Her expression did not change.

"One can't . . . think," he added lamely.

But it was no excuse. A gentleman never took such liberties, except with a very near relative or a mistress. He could not believe he'd done it. Yet he did not see how he could help it.

He set his mind—what was left of it—to composing a suitable apology.

She spoke before he could assemble the words.

"So that was what upset you so much," she said. "Well, I should not be surprised. A man who will set out in the dead of night in an ice storm—because he lacks a change of clothes—lives by sartorial standards too lofty for lesser mortals to comprehend." She turned away and began to fold up the maps.

He quickly gathered the shreds of his reason.

"I also have principles, Miss Oldridge," he said, "whether you wish to believe it or not. I should like to persuade the landowners of the merits of Lord Gordmor's canal. I wish to find a way to remove the objectionable elements of the plan, or, if this is impossible, arrive at an acceptable compromise."

"Then go back to London and send someone else to make the case," she said. "You are either sadly deluded or hopelessly idealistic if you think people will deal with you as they deal with ordinary men, even ordinary peers. My neighbors as well as my father left their estate managers to meet with Lord Gordmor's agent. They wouldn't dream of doing so themselves. You my father not only invited to meet with him, but asked to dinner. He even tried to persuade you to stay the night—though Papa is practically a recluse, who would rather talk to plants than people. Sir Roger Tolbert and Captain Hughes, who are more sociable, will call on you and invite you to dine with them. Everyone will ask you to visit and invite you to admire their pets, livestock, and children, especially their daughters."

While she talked, she was trying to roll and fold the maps, and was doing as well as her maid had done with her hair. She wound the rolled ones into cones and spirals and folded the others backwards and sideways and every way but the correct one. By degrees she became lost in a storm of swishing and crackling paper.

Alistair advanced, extracted the maps from her taut grip, and one by one closed them properly. Then he set the lot down on the table, resisting the urge to keep one to swat her with.

She frowned down at the maps. "I had no trouble opening them," she said. "But when it came time to shut them up, they developed a life of their own. I suspect they dislike being closed, and it wants a special knack to coax them."

"No, it wants only simple logic," he said.

"It must be a different form of logic than I ever learned," she said. "But you're an Oxford man, I recall. If only I had gone to university, I, too, should know how to fold a map."

"I wish Oxford had taught me how to get a direct answer to a simple question," he said.

She bestowed upon him a brilliant smile, the one she'd favored him with the previous day, before she'd learnt his errand. Since she'd treated him to only a lesser and chillier variety of smiles since, he was caught unprepared, and his brain reacted as though she'd hit him in the head with a cricket bat.

"You want me to tell you why Lord Gordmor's agent could win no support for his canal," she said. She collected her coat and bonnet.

Alistair collected his wits. "The agent told us no one was willing even to discuss it. Everywhere he went, he was told no and shown the door. Yes, I want you to tell me, Miss Oldridge, since you claim everyone else will be too overawed by my consequence to tell me the truth."

She flung on the cloak. "I most certainly will not tell you," she said. She jammed the bonnet on her head and quickly tied the ribbons. "You have every possible advantage. Everyone will fawn upon you. I do not see your encountering the smallest resistance. The situation is hopeless enough without my giving up to you my single piece of ammunition. Good day, Mr. Carsington."

She snatched up the maps, and out she went, leaving a vexed and baffled Alistair with nothing to do but watch her go, cloak crooked, bonnet lopsided, and perfect backside swaying.

• • • •

IT might have comforted Mr. Carsington to know he was not the only one who was vexed and baffled. Mirabel was disturbed enough to travel another two miles, to Cromford, to seek her former governess's calming presence.

At present they sat in Mrs. Entwhistle's parlor, which was scrupulously neat, attractively decorated, and comfortably upholstered, like its mistress.

The lady, who was ten years older, had married and moved to Cromford shortly after her then-nineteen-year-old charge set out for London and her first season. Mr. Entwhistle had succumbed to a lung fever three years ago. He had provided well enough for his widow, though, to spare her having to return to her old occupation.

"If only I did have a piece of ammunition," Mirabel was telling Mrs. Entwhistle. "But Mr. Carsington will soon discover the main objection. All the Longledge landowners believe the canal will cause too much disruption for too little benefit. Otherwise we should have built our own canal decades ago, when it would have cost far less."

"Men who spend their lives in London cannot conceive of the impact these schemes have on rural communities," Mrs. Entwhistle said. "Even if anyone had explained the problem to Lord Gordmor, he would probably disregard it as provincial prejudice against change and progress."

"I cannot blame him entirely," Mirabel said. "We are at least partly to blame. Had all the landowners made their sentiments clear to his agent, I doubt we should be in this predicament. But none of us took any more notice of him than we have of the others."

The agent's status and power was merely the dim reflection of his employer's, and Lord Gordmor's prestige, as Mirabel had pointed out to Mr. Carsington, was of a dim variety to begin with. To the denizens of Longledge Hill, his representative was merely one in a long line of agents constantly coming and going, trying to promote one speculation or another.

The gentry hereabouts were conservative folk, however. Even at the height of the canal mania, they had considered Mr. Arkwright's Cromford Canal a dubious venture, and the Peak Forest Canal downright risky. So far, events—at least from a financial standpoint—had not proved them wrong. While these canals had greatly improved transportation for the businesses along their routes, neither had yet made substantial profits for the shareholders.

Beyond question the waterways had radically altered both the landscape and the communities through which they passed.

Reaction was even more negative to Lord Gordmor's canal, which would amount to a public highway through Mirabel's and her neighbors' own property.

"You had no way of knowing Lord Gordmor would prove more persistent than the others," Mrs. Entwhistle said.

"It is not the persistence but his choice of representative that disturbs me," Mirabel said. "I *wish* someone had warned me Mr. Carsington was coming. He cannot have written to the other landowners in advance, or everyone would have been talking about it. But I cannot credit his applying only to Papa, the last man in the world to take an interest in a canal—or anything else not possessing roots."

"I suspect Mr. Carsington and Lord Gordmor were not aware of your father's preoccupations," Mrs. Entwhistle said. "They were only aware of his owning the largest property."

"And Papa has done nothing to enlighten them," Mirabel said. "Can you credit his answering Mr. Carsington's letter?"

Mrs. Entwhistle shook her head and agreed it was inexplicable.

"If even my father agreed to meet with Mr. Carsington, you can imagine what the others will do," Mirabel said. "They will wine and dine the famous Waterloo hero, and say yes to everything he proposes, without question. They will accept whatever negligible financial compensation he offers for use of the land, and nod happily to any route he suggests. If anyone proves so bold as to ask for a bridge to get the cows back from the meadows or a curve to take the canal around a plantation instead of straight through it, I shall be much amazed. Meanwhile, we can be sure they will push their daughters and sisters at him, even though he is merely a younger son."

"I imagine he is well-spoken and handsome," Mrs. Entwhistle said as she refilled Mirabel's teacup.

"Exceedingly," Mirabel said grimly. "Tall and broadshouldered, and you would think, since he is so point-perfect in his dress, that he would be stiff, but he is not. He has even accommodated his injury, and contrives to make a limp both manly and graceful and somehow . . . gallant."

"Gallant," Mrs. Entwhistle repeated.

"It is dreadful." Mirabel scowled at her teacup. "He makes me want to cry. In the next moment I want to throw something at him. Besides which, he is impossibly idealistic—or else he is a magnificent actor. I hardly had the heart to tell him no one cares about his noble intentions."

"Dark or fair?" Mrs. Entwhistle asked.

"His hair is thick and brown, but when the light catches it, golden glints appear," Mirabel said. "His eyes are a changeable light brown. They are sleepy-looking," she added. "I could not always be sure he was listening. Or perhaps he was merely bored. Or perhaps my hair offended him so much that he opened his eyes as little as possible."

"Why on earth do you imagine your hair offended him?" Mrs. Entwhistle said. "It is beautiful."

Mirabel shrugged. "Red hair isn't fashionable, especially this odd color, and he must have everything up to the mark. Anyway, my coiffure is never elegant, even at the best of times."

"Because you will not sit still for your maid to do it properly." A lacy cap did not fully conceal Mrs. Entwhistle's own neatly arranged brunette tresses.

"Yes, well, I gave Lucy almost no time this morning, and it came down, as you'd expect."

Mrs. Entwhistle studied Mirabel's hair. "It seems to be in good order now."

"He *fixed* it," Mirabel said. "It is pinned so tight, you would want a pitchfork to dislodge it. I should like to know who taught him to pin up hair. I should have asked—"

"Really, Mirabel."

"—but I was too startled to think of it." *Startled* wasn't the half of what she'd felt. He'd stood so close, she could smell the starch in his neckcloth. And the elusive scent she might have only imagined. But she had not imagined the sudden thumping of her heart and the confusing mix of sensations, of which *surprise* was the mildest.

She had an idea what those sensations were. She was an old maid now, but she'd been young once, and attractive men had vied to stir her interest. They had not all been unsuccessful. It would have been easier for her, perhaps, if one had not succeeded.

But that was long ago, and she'd had a decade to recover. She could remember the wonderful season in London, and William, without pain. That didn't mean she wished to relive the experience. She knew that any attachment must end the same way, and she was not a glutton for punishment.

Not that she was in the least danger at present. Mr. Carsington wanted only one thing from the unfashionable and disheveled Mirabel Oldridge. It wasn't her money and most certainly wasn't her person. He only wanted a piece of information, which he could easily obtain without her help.

Mrs. Entwhistle broke into these meditations. "You said Mr. Carsington was point-perfect in his dress."

"He would put Beau Brummell to shame." Mirabel proceeded to relate the "nothing to wear" conversation in the ice storm.

"That explains a great deal," said Mrs. Entwhistle.

"You know how dandies are," Mirabel said. "Every detail must be precisely so. You would not believe the degree to which my hair upset him. His displeasure set the very air athrob. Finally he told me outright: My hair coming down was *distracting.*"

"Then you are better equipped than you thought," Mrs. Entwhistle said. "You have discovered a weakness in your adversary."

Mirabel stared at her. "What do you mean?"

"I suggest a diversionary movement," said her former governess. "Distract him."

Four

"A dinner party," Alistair repeated expressionlessly.

"Friday. Only three days hence. Deuced short notice, I know." Sir Roger Tolbert spoke between mouthfuls of the heavy meal Wilkerson's cook had provided.

The two men sat in the dining parlor Miss Oldridge had vacated a short time before.

"Nothing so grand as you're used to, daresay," the baronet went on. "Told my lady so. Told her you'd have more pressing engagements. But you know how women are. Get their minds fixed on something."

Alistair nodded sympathetically, while Miss Oldridge's prediction played in his mind: *Sir Roger Tolbert and Captain Hughes . . . will likely call on you and invite you to dine with them.*

At the time, she had upset him, but after she'd gone, Alistair decided the scenario she painted was most unlikely, given the chilly reception with which Gordy's agent had met. Alistair had for this reason written in advance only to

Mr. Oldridge, and citing the agent's experience, asked the gentleman not to mention the visit to anybody.

Once Alistair was here, the news was bound to spread quickly, he knew. But he'd braced himself for a cool reception, if not outright hostility; he was not prepared for a welcoming committee. Even after Miss Oldridge had told him how important he was in the locals' eyes, he'd wanted to believe she'd exaggerated.

He'd expected difficulty and had come prepared to deal with it. He'd seen himself winning over the landowners by dealing fairly with them, listening with an open mind to their objections, and working with them to devise acceptable solutions and compromises. His intentions were good and his heart honest. He was cultivated, tactful, and his manners were faultless—except toward Miss Oldridge. He'd trusted these assets to see him through a difficult battle.

He was not prepared for the entire opposition to surrender the instant he arrived.

Sir Roger had called about half an hour after Miss Oldridge left Wilkerson's, and greeted Alistair like a long-lost son.

The baronet, a man near his father's age, was plump about the middle and bald about the head. At the moment he was laying waste to the spread he'd ordered to sustain him until dinner: mutton, potatoes, a loaf of bread, about a pound each of cheese and butter, and a tankard of ale.

Alistair had a glass of wine. Even if he'd been hungry—unlikely at this hour—he would have lost his appetite as soon as he realized Miss Oldridge had not exaggerated. No one would wait for him to prove his worth or the value of his project. He was Lord Hargate's son, the papers had made a hero of him, and that was enough.

"It is most kind of Lady Tolbert to think of me," Alistair said. "However, as you may have heard, I am here on business."

"Important, daresay."

"Yes, rather." After a pause, while the baronet chewed his mutton, Alistair added, "Lord Gordmor's canal."

Sir Roger's eyebrows went up, but he finished chewing and swallowing calmly enough. "Indeed."

"In fact, I should like to talk to you about it. At a mutually convenient time, that is."

Sir Roger nodded. "Business. Pleasure. Keep separate. Understand."

"Or I could talk to your bailiff, if you prefer," Alistair said.

"Bailiff? Certainly not." The man went on eating.

"But you see, Sir Roger, I should consider it the greatest favor if you—if everyone—would regard me simply as Lord Gordmor's representative. As one in his employ."

The baronet mulled this over while he speared the last of the potatoes onto his plate. "See your point," he said. "Scruples. Do you credit."

"I must make it clear that my father is in no way involved with this project."

"Understand," said Sir Roger. "But my lady won't. All she understands is, your father's Lord Hargate, and you're the famous Waterloo hero. Told her you weren't the lion in the menagerie. Not here to entertain her and the other females." He scowled. "Tears. Buckets of 'em. *Women.*"

Alistair need only recall Judith Gilford's teary temper tantrums to understand how miserable an unhappy woman could make a man. Alistair at least had not been shackled to her and hadn't had to endure it the livelong day and night. A married man must live with it or let himself be driven from his own home.

Making Sir Roger's wife unhappy was not the way to win his respect.

"I had rather be stabbed, slashed, shot at, and trampled by the entire Polish cavalry," Alistair said, "than cause your lady a moment's distress. Please be so good as to tell Lady Tolbert that I shall be honored to wait upon her on Friday."

Friday 20 February

THE dinner party was essentially what Miss Oldridge had predicted.

You'll be . . . invited to admire pets, livestock, and children, especially their daughters.

Sir Roger had talked about Alistair being a lion in the menagerie. As it turned out, it was not Lord Hargate's hero son who was on display but a bevy of maidens, all eager to entertain and entice him.

This was a new experience.

When Alistair had first entered Society, he hadn't worried about anyone's setting marriage traps. He was a younger son, dependent on a father who, while well-to-do, was far from the wealthiest member of the peerage. Lord Hargate, moreover, had four other sons to support.

In other words, Alistair Carsington was no great catch.

His lack of income, however, didn't matter to Judith Gilford. She had enough money for the two of them, with plenty to spare. She might easily have supported a harem, in fact—and it was most unfortunate that the law frowned on polyandry, because it would want at least half a dozen husbands to give Judith all the attention and slavish devotion she craved.

But that was the London social scene, and this was a remote corner of the provinces, where eligible men were about as plentiful as coconut trees.

In eligible young women, on the other hand, the place abounded.

Lady Tolbert's "intimate, quite informal" dinner party comprised more than two dozen guests. Ten of these were misses, all got up in their finest gowns and most flattering coiffures, and all exerting themselves to charm the Earl of Hargate's third son.

Miss Oldridge would have made eleven, but she was hardly a young lady, being on the wrong side of thirty, and she made no effort to charm anybody.

All the other misses wore delicate confections of white

or pastel muslin. These gowns, in defiance of the polar winds rattling the windows, displayed considerable acreage in the way of bosom.

Miss Oldridge wore a grey silk gown designed, apparently, by a strict Presbyterian minister for his grandmother.

She was, determined, it seemed, to drive Alistair insane.

In spite of all his resolutions, she was succeeding.

He'd resolved, since she'd refused to cooperate, to do without her.

He would view her as a piece of furniture standing in his way. He would not bump into or trip over her—figuratively speaking—this night, as he'd done during their previous encounters. This night he would make his way smoothly around her and deal with her neighbors instead. If he won them over, her objections wouldn't matter.

So had he reasoned.

But how was a man to reason, faced with the apparition sitting directly across from him?

No candelabra or other large table decoration obstructed the view. The young ladies clustered nearby were easily entertained. In any event, it was impossible to look away from the horror Miss Oldridge had perpetrated.

The square neckline offered no more than a miserly glimpse of the hollow of her throat. The sleeves ended at her wrists. If not for the high waist underlining her bosom and the slim skirt skimming her hips, a man would hardly know she had any figure at all.

The gown was a shocking waste of exquisite silk and fine workmanship.

Then there was her hair, which was, in a nutshell, unspeakable.

Her maid had driven a rigid—and *crooked*—part through the middle of the glorious red-gold crown of ringlets, flattened it—with a hot iron, it seemed—yanked the lot back, and braided and twisted it into a stiff coil behind. A coronet of braided silver—dented on one side—adorned this outrage.

Only as the meal neared its end did Alistair find a way

to regain a degree of tranquillity. He was mentally re-designing the neckline of the grey gown and cutting the sleeves back to dainty puffs at the shoulders. Much to his annoyance, he had to stop this promising work when Lady Tolbert asked if he had been to Chatsworth.

Alistair focused on his hostess—who, despite having a married daughter Miss Oldridge's age, contrived to appear younger and nearly à la mode—and admitted he had not yet visited the Duke of Devonshire's place, which lay ten miles or so north of Matlock Bath.

"You will wish to visit the Cascade, I am sure," said Lady Tolbert. "A long set of shallow stone stairs runs down a hill. Over these water cascades from reservoirs on the top of the hill above the wood. It is most prettily done, and its effect on the nerves is wonderfully soothing."

Lady Tolbert's nerves, Alistair's valet had informed him, were famous, and the bane of her husband's existence.

Miss Curry, on Alistair's right, said the Cascade sounded ever so romantic, and darted him a demure glance.

"It is most agreeable to contemplate," Lady Tolbert said. "Since you are interested in artificial waterways, Mr. Carsington, you might wish to study it."

Captain Hughes, who sat between Lady Tolbert and Miss Oldridge, observed that the present design dated from the time of Queen Anne.

The naval officer was a dark, dashing fellow in his forties, whom peacetime had marooned on land. Unlike other half-pay captains, he was comfortably settled upon a fair-sized property bordering the Oldridge estate. He might entertain ideas of occupying larger territory, for Alistair thought his manner to Miss Oldridge something more than neighborly.

"I visited the place in my boyhood," the captain said. "It was a hot day, and I, even then, couldn't resist water. I sat down and took off my shoes and stockings to go wading. I'd scarcely begun to splash about when the adults discovered what I was up to and snatched me out. It seems cruel to build such a thing, which little boys can't possibly resist, then forbid them to play there."

"It is good training for adulthood," Alistair said, "when we encounter so much that is irresistible." He let his gaze drift over the range of feminine pulchritude displayed in his vicinity.

His hostess, who was slender and well-preserved, preened a little, and the nearby maidens all blushed.

Except for Miss Oldridge.

Engaged in dissecting a tart, she spoke without looking up from her work. "I understand grown men cannot resist swimming in the canals in full view of canal boat passengers, not to mention the people on shore."

Alistair wasn't at all shocked by Miss Oldridge's referring to naked men in a mixed gathering. He'd already discovered that her speech could be stunningly direct. As well, she was one and thirty, no ingenuous miss like the pretty pea brains surrounding him. Furthermore, country folk tended to be less delicate in their speech than their London counterparts, probably because of all the animals about them, endlessly breeding and birthing.

The Tolberts, certainly, were unpretentious. They served dinner in the traditional way, with all the dishes for each course set out at once. Likewise, male and female guests were not in orderly, even numbers, and sat wherever they liked—though all understood that the places at the head of the table near the hostess were meant for the more important guests.

Some quiet maneuvering had ended in a great many maidens occupying the chairs closest to the guest of honor at the upper half of the table.

Miss Oldridge had not maneuvered. She and Captain Hughes had sat near their hostess at Lady Tolbert's urging.

The captain was regarding Miss Oldridge with amusement. "I take it the fellows were not using bathing machines."

Miss Curry turned scarlet. Miss Earnshaw, beside her,

tittered. But they were ridiculously young, barely out of the schoolroom.

"It is most inconsiderate behavior," said Lady Tolbert. "Only think of the shock to a maiden's sensibilities, should she come upon the men unexpectedly. She might be taken seriously ill as a consequence. I will not dispute that bathing is a healthful exercise—but in the proper time and place. Bathing in a canal." She shook her head. "What next? Roman orgies, I suppose."

"I don't believe I've ever heard of orgiastic swimming in canals," Alistair said.

"A gentleman wrote an angry letter to the *Times* about the swimmers not long ago," said Miss Oldridge. "He said nothing about orgies. But he did mention moral decay."

"The fellows must have been drunk," said the captain.

"Or perhaps it was a very hot day," said Miss Oldridge. "The writer blamed it on the bargemen. He said they were a corrupting influence. I understand they swear shockingly."

"But they would not use bad language on Mr. Carsington's canal," said Miss Earnshaw, throwing a worshipful look Alistair's way. "I am sure he would not permit it."

Before Alistair could invent a response to this fantastically vacuous statement, Miss Oldridge said, "No doubt Mr. Carsington will add that condition to any others the landowners require."

"Since we hope to have many, if not all, of the landowners as canal committee members and shareholders, they will no doubt act vigilantly against the corruption of public morals, Miss Oldridge," he said.

"You will leave the responsibility to them?" she said. She directed a dazzling smile his way, as if he had said something desperately romantic rather than sarcastic. "Well, I know *my* mind is relieved."

Leaving him vexed and dizzy, she turned the smile upon her hostess. "Do you not feel the same, Lady Tolbert?"

"Yes, I suppose," Lady Tolbert said fretfully. "But I had

not thought of so very many strangers coming, and Sir Roger did not mention it."

"I should think we'd be used to strangers, if anyone was," said Captain Hughes.

"But this is not at all like the tourists," said Lady Tolbert. "They at least are respectable persons."

"I am sure the bargemen are respectable in their way," said Miss Oldridge. "And certainly they will seem altogether elegant, after the navigators."

Lady Tolbert put a hand to her throat. "Merciful heaven! Navigators?"

"Miss Oldridge refers to experienced canal diggers," Alistair said. "Skilled laborers." *Not riffraff and vagabonds,* he wanted to add, but didn't. He'd rather not plant any more unpleasant images in Lady Tolbert's head. Miss Oldridge was doing that all too effectively.

"You will not hire local men?" Captain Hughes asked.

"There will be plenty of work for local brickmakers, quarriers, and carpenters," Alistair said. "Still, the contractors must bring in skilled canal diggers—'cutters' they're called."

"No doubt Lord Gordmor will hire only the most respectable contractors," said Miss Oldridge. "In which case, their gangs of workers will not *all* be ruffians. Furthermore, it is possible that the stories of drunken disorder and riots are exaggerated."

"Ruffians?" said Lady Tolbert, turning pale. "Riots?"

"Disorder and riots sometimes occur in places where men are poorly treated and ill-paid," Alistair said quickly. "I can assure you that Lord Gordmor and I will insist upon fair treatment and wages."

"I am confident you will not allow any cutthroats to work for you, either," Miss Oldridge said. "At least not intentionally. Naturally you will demand references for each and every person involved in the canal building, even if the work requires many hundreds."

This was impossible, and she knew it. She might as well expect Captain Hughes to demand references for the men the press gangs forced into naval service. Alistair wanted to point this out, but he doubted Lady Tolbert would find the thought comforting.

Thanks to Miss Oldridge, the lady no doubt envisioned gangs of ruffians roaming at large—raping and pillaging as they went—through the pastoral hamlets and villages and private estates of the Peak.

Unfortunately, the image was not so very farfetched. Only the previous year, right here in Derbyshire, unemployed textile workers had banded together to capture Nottingham Castle. Though troops prevented the threatened mass revolt from materializing, fears of unrest lingered.

"I do hope you will bear in mind, ladies, how many hundreds of miles of canal have been built in this country without incident," Alistair said. "Among them, Derbyshire's Peak Forest and Cromford canals."

"That is an excellent point, Mr. Carsington," said Miss Oldridge. "We should consider another important one: the men will be less inclined to break out in rampages, because the work is less arduous than it was in the old days."

"Indeed, it is," Alistair said. "Much of the backbreaking work is done these days with machinery."

"Quite so," Miss Oldridge said. "Now I think of it, the din of the steam engines and other machines must drown out any swearing, and the smoke will obliterate any disagreeable sights." She beamed at the company.

"Din?" said Lady Tolbert. "Smoke? Sir Roger said nothing about noisy, nasty machines."

Alistair did his best to soothe her while he imagined himself leaping across the table, scooping Miss Oldridge out of her chair, and tossing her out of the nearest window.

Certain inconveniences attended any great building project, he reminded his hostess. While noise and smoke were drawbacks of modern methods, they did greatly shorten the process. Instead of having canal diggers taking up residence for long periods of time—many months, perhaps years—they would come and go in a matter of weeks.

Lady Tolbert listened politely, gave him a sickly smile,

and signaled the other ladies to withdraw from the table. They adjourned to the drawing room, leaving the men to their port.

And while the men drank, Lady Tolbert would spread the contagion to the other wives.

Miss Oldridge had done her work cleverly, the devious creature. Alistair hadn't foreseen the attack, and he'd been unforgivably slow to catch on.

Well, small wonder.

How was he to concentrate on anything when she sat for hours directly in his line of vision, dressed like a fright? How was he to cope with such a spectacle? He couldn't, and so he'd focused on dressing her properly in his mind— or undressing her was more like it, and it would be a public service, really, not to mention economical. That appalling gown might have covered two women.

While he'd been busy mentally disrobing her, the foe had crept up behind him and all but routed him.

He had sat listening to Miss Oldridge poison her hostess's mind while scarcely able to muster his thoughts into order, let alone devise an antidote.

But the women were gone, Alistair consoled himself as the port went round the dining table. He had only to deal with men now. They at least spoke a language one could easily understand. And they played by simpler, if sometimes more brutal rules. All he had to do was play skillfully.

THE men remained in the dining room for nearly an hour, which Mirabel knew was not a good sign. Sir Roger rarely lingered over his port, and if her father was the only one of his guests to drift into the drawing room, it must be because Mr. Carsington had the rest enthralled.

By the time the men finally rejoined the ladies, Papa was long gone. He had wandered out of the drawing room and on to the Tolberts' conservatory.

Until now, the girls had been scattered about the room

in duos and trios, some chatting, some looking at picture books. When Mr. Carsington entered, the chats ended, the books closed, and in a flotilla of pale muslin the maidens sailed, as if carried on a powerful current, toward him.

Mirabel supposed the nautical image arose because she spotted Captain Hughes making his way through the mass of maidens.

He came across the room to the window where Mirabel stood. It was the coldest part of the room, far from the fire. She had retreated there partly because she'd felt agitated and overwarm after dinner and partly because the drafty spot was not inviting to the young ladies. Their innocent joy in the gathering made her feel weary and cross, a sour old spinster.

As she'd hoped, they avoided her chilly corner. Gooseflesh was not attractive, and their current mission was to be as attractive as possible. Eligible gentlemen did not happen into their lives very often, and only Miss Earnshaw had any hopes of a London season in which she'd encounter more. Even that wasn't certain, because Mr. Earnshaw was balking at the expense.

"I'd no idea we had so handsome a fleet hereabouts," the captain said, nodding in the direction from which he'd come. "Or did Lady Tolbert muster them up from forces abroad?"

"I take it you refer to the young ladies," Mirabel said. "She's summoned them from the far corners of the Peak. Now her youngest daughter is wed, she needs someone else's future to arrange."

She did not add her private opinion that the girls, while pretty, were too young and unsophisticated for a man who'd been fêted and petted by London's most fashionable beauties. Too, the girls' gowns must seem sadly outdated and countrified, far beneath his exacting standards.

On the other hand, they were young and fresh, and that was what males liked, all males, of every species.

"Someone should tell her to chart them a different

course," Captain Hughes said. "You're the only vessel in his sights."

Mirabel experienced a spurt of pleasure, which she promptly suppressed. After all, she'd deliberately set out to distract the guest of honor, she reminded herself.

The grey gown was outmoded and graceless to begin with, but in case that wasn't enough, she'd persuaded Lucy to make a few adjustments, transforming it from merely dull and unflattering to hideous. The boring coronet needed only to be stepped on. But the crowning achievement was the coiffure Lucy had so unwillingly executed, declaring afterward that she'd never seen anything so frightful and would never outlive the disgrace.

Mirabel hadn't been prepared, though, for the great number of beautiful young women so prettily garbed. They would make it easy to disregard her.

But Captain Hughes said Mr. Carsington could not ignore her, and the captain was an acutely observant man.

Apparently, she looked horrid enough to distract Mr. Carsington even from the fleet of fresh young beauties.

"I should like to know what game you're playing at," Captain Hughes said, his dark eyes twinkling as he cast a swift glance over her. "Is this rig a part of it? Am I to be treated to an explanation? Or must I continue to play the unwitting accomplice? By gad, when I told my anecdote about the Chatsworth Cascade, I never dreamt you'd use it to launch an attack. You raked the poor fellow from stem to stern. I think his foredeck is still smoking."

"Someone must speak up," Mirabel said. "My neighbors are in danger of forgetting why he is here and what he represents."

The captain looked again toward Mr. Carsington, now surrounded by muslin-garbed vessels. "He might be in the same danger." When he turned back to Mirabel, his expression was more serious. "After the ladies left, he did not once mention the canal," he said.

"Really?" Mirabel looked down at her ugly gown. She had not dared hope her costume would continue to disturb him even while she was out of sight. Mrs. Entwhistle was truly a brilliant strategist.

"I was much amazed," the captain said. "I thought he'd make haste to repair the damage you'd done. Even Lady Tolbert looked at him, for a moment, as though he was the Old Harry himself, and the fellows in hearing range seemed troubled as well. But when he had all the men to himself, Mr. Carsington didn't so much as hint at the subject. Nor did he give anyone else a chance to raise it. Somehow, he had us all talking about ourselves instead."

Mirabel's optimism was swiftly ebbing. "About yourselves," she repeated.

"About our livestock, crops, tenants, and poachers," Captain Hughes explained. "Sir Roger bragged about his greyhounds. The vicar went on about his prize marrows. We yammered and yawed about leaky roofs and wandering pigs and mole catchers. Mr. Carsington must have been bored witless, but he looked as entertained as if we'd been telling bawdy stories."

Mirabel let out a sigh.

"A clever strategy, don't you think?" said the captain.

"Who does not think highly of a good listener?" she said. "Who is not happiest when speaking of himself and his own concerns? By the time you had left the dining room, you were all viewing him as the dearest friend of your bosom, I daresay. And this dear friend happens to be Lord Hargate's son. I can imagine what you were all thinking: What an understanding fellow! Such easy manners! No high and mighty airs about him!"

"I was thinking Mr. Carsington has a great political future ahead of him, if only his father will buy him a seat in Parliament," the captain said.

Like everyone else, Mirabel was fully aware that the House of Commons was not a democratically elected body. The lords of the land controlled the seats, and "winning" one cost about seven or eight thousand pounds.

"I wish Lord Hargate had done so as soon as his son had

recovered enough from his war injuries to stand upon the hustings," Mirabel said.

"Too late for that," said the captain. "We might as well resign ourselves. At least we'll be paid handsomely for use of our property. And we might take consolation in furthering economic progress."

"Really?" Mirabel turned sharply back to him. "Try consoling yourself with this."

She reminded him of the changes that had overtaken pastoral villages from one end of England to the other with the growing network of canals and the industrial areas that grew alongside them. She reminded him that not all factories were as agreeable in appearance or so well-lit as Mr. Arkwright's in Cromford.

She drew a verbal picture of foul-smelling brickyards and their miserable residents, and of the even more desolate world surrounding coal pits. She spoke of winding gears and slag heaps, cranes and coal barges, the hiss and clang of steam engines, the clouds of black smoke and the banshee wail of the whistles. She reminded him they lived at present in an arcadia, one of England's most beautiful places, whose tranquillity they treasured.

She turned toward the window and gestured at the night-blanketed landscape beyond. Growing impassioned as she reminded her neighbor of all they'd invested in their land and the people abiding on it, Mirabel forgot everything else. Consequently, she failed to notice they had company, until a low rumble of a voice jolted her back to the moment.

"Thinking you must be parched with so much talking, Miss Oldridge, I took the liberty of bringing you a cup of tea," Mr. Carsington growled behind her.

Five

MIRABEL turned so abruptly, she nearly knocked the cup and saucer from his hand. But Mr. Carsington moved quickly. His war injuries had definitely not slowed his reflexes.

"Tea's ready?" said Captain Hughes. "Excellent. I feel in need of a stimulant." He fled to his hostess.

Mirabel collected her composure and accepted the tea with steady hands.

"I hope it hasn't cooled too much," Mr. Carsington said. "I've stood here for a time, because I didn't wish to interrupt you."

"You were eavesdropping," she said.

He nodded. "That, too. I was perishing of curiosity. I wanted to know what had roused your passions."

His voice dropped very low, to become more an undercurrent than a sound. Mirabel's pulse rate climbed, along with her temperature.

He studied the floor. "In your agitation, you have shaken loose a great many pins. I cannot decide whether or not it is an improvement." His hooded gaze traveled in the most leisurely manner up the skirt of her gown, lingered briefly at her bodice, then proceeded unhurriedly to the top of her head.

Every inch of the way, Mirabel felt the narrow golden scrutiny—through her heavy silk gown, buckram corset, flannel petticoat, and silk knit drawers—right down to her skin, which it left tingling.

"Is my hair coming down again?" she said composedly. "How vexing. I wish you would show my maid your method with hairpins. I collect you learned that at Oxford, too. Unfortunately, Lucy did not attend university."

"If she had, she might have learnt how to hold her liquor," he said. "Obviously she was drunk when she arranged your hair. But let me correct a misapprehension, Miss Oldridge. I did not learn how to pin up hair at university. I learnt it from a French ballet dancer. She was very expensive. I might have sent you and your maid and all the other ladies in this room to Oxford for what she spent in a twelvemonth."

"You might send us to Paris, but not Oxford," she said. "Perhaps you failed to notice that women are not admitted to our great English universities."

"I've noticed," he said. "It is a great pity."

"I daresay. No ballet dancers to teach you useful skills."

"True." He folded his arms and leant back against the window frame. "Such forms of entertainment are sadly lacking. But I was referring to all members of your sex. I don't see what great harm would result if women were permitted the same sort of education as men."

Mirabel didn't try to hide her disbelief. "I see what you are doing. Having easily made all the gentlemen love you, you suppose you can turn me up sweet as well. You've guessed that I'm a bluestocking, and—"

"I should say 'intellectual,' rather," he said. "You read the desperately difficult-sounding book about the fossils and strata, and no doubt you understood everything your father had to say about mosses and tulips."

"Mr. Carsington, only on rare occasions can I make heads or tails of what my father is saying," she said impatiently. "He has his own unique thought processes, which I do not attempt to follow. I should not advise anyone else to attempt it, either, for that way madness lies. I have my doubts, in fact, as to whether other botanists understand him."

"It would be more useful for me to understand your thought processes than his," he said.

With not-so-steady hands, she set down her neglected tea on a small table nearby. "In order to change my mind?"

"I must do something," he said. "If you speak to the rest of your neighbors as you did to Captain Hughes, I shall be here for months, trying to repair the damage."

"You should have anticipated me and bolstered your cause when you had the opportunity after dinner. You cannot expect me to hold my tongue merely because you are amiable and charming."

His dark eyebrows arched. "You've found my behavior to you amiable and charming?"

"That is not the point," Mirabel said. "The point is, your position and fame don't signify to me, and I won't be seduced by your charm, so I recommend you not take the trouble of exerting it. Also, while I am grateful for your efforts and sacrifice on behalf of your country—"

"Pray let's leave that nonsense out of this," he said stonily.

The frigid tone did not intimidate her. She was accustomed to men using every sort of tactic to make her retreat or yield. She was accustomed to men trying to make her feel insignificant or unsure, and thrusting Keep Out signs in her face. She had learnt to disregard these ploys. She'd had no choice but to learn.

"It isn't nonsense, and I cannot fathom why you would say so," she said. "You fought bravely. You suffered damage, permanent damage. Still, you aren't the only one or the one who suffered most."

He stiffened as though she'd slapped him. But in the

next instant his expression softened into puzzlement, and by degrees the faintest promise of a smile touched the corners of his mouth.

His rigid posture relaxed, too, and he said, "An excellent point, Miss Oldridge."

So, he was not offended. Mirabel's estimation of his character rose a cautious degree. She went on, "It does seem to me that we ought to keep the two matters separate. Gallantry in battle is no assurance of wisdom in other matters."

He regarded her steadily—seriously, she would have thought, but for the smile that yet hovered at his mouth. She wanted to ask what the almost-smile meant. She was tempted, terribly tempted, to touch the place where it lurked. Her heart was beating a little too fast.

She folded her hands at her waist and said, "I wish you to understand that it would make no difference to me if you were the Duke of Wellington. I should still think ill of this canal scheme and do my best to hinder you."

"Have you ever met the Duke of Wellington?" he asked.

"No, but I understand that he, too, is handsome and charming and possesses an immense force of personality. Still, I fancy I could stand up to it."

The amber gaze raked her up and down. "I should like to see that. Perhaps you could."

The slow survey made her knees wobbly. Amusement danced in his eyes, and something inside her danced, too, a darting pleasure and excitement she hadn't felt in a long time: the thrill of flirtation.

But it couldn't be. She was long past flirting age, and dressed like a hag besides.

"All the same," he went on, "I think you would not deny His Grace a fair hearing. Would you not at least tell him what you did and didn't want?"

"Did he tell Napoleon his strategy?" she answered calmly enough, though her mind was neither calm nor clear, and she wasn't sure what she wanted.

"Miss Oldridge, I am not trying to conquer the world," he said. "I only want to build a canal."

She became aware of movement, and glancing past him, noted, with mingled relief and vexation, that the young ladies were casually meandering this way. "Your fleet draws nigh," she said.

He didn't look away from her. "Tell me what's wrong," he said. "Better yet, show me: what you've invested, what you stand to lose. Show me what you were talking about to Captain Hughes."

"You could never understand," she said.

"Suppose I cannot? What will it cost you? A few hours of time?"

Saturday 21 February

CREWE'S cough this morning was low and tragic, telling Alistair that his valet was in the throes of another one of his famous Forebodings.

He'd had one the night before the battle of Waterloo, and blamed the ensuing catastrophe on his master's riding out to battle without him.

Ever since then, Crewe had been convinced he possessed clairvoyant powers.

The tragic cough did not dampen Alistair's mood, which was cheerful, despite his having arisen at the uncivilized hour of nine o'clock. He saw nothing inauspicious about this day. At present, he stood shaving in a pool of sunshine, recalling his after-dinner encounter with Miss Oldridge with the first real pleasure he'd experienced in— Well, he couldn't remember how long it had been.

He remembered the moment of surprised pleasure last night, though, with perfect clarity. He'd gone all stiff and sensitive about his curst fame and his famous dratted injury, and she— But he didn't know how to explain, even to himself, what she'd done. She'd meant it to be a setdown, he supposed, reminding him that he was not the only one who'd fought at Waterloo, not the only one injured, and certainly not the one who'd lost or suffered most.

Even his family, usually brutally direct with one another, tended to skirt the subject of Waterloo when he was about. Only Gordmor, of all his friends, referred easily and comfortably to the lame leg.

Miss Oldridge was the first woman he'd encountered who didn't pretend he wasn't lame and didn't get starry-eyed about his so-called heroics.

She didn't seem to pretend much of anything or to be easily rendered starry-eyed.

Crewe's poignant cough called Alistair back.

"Crewe, do you not see the sun pouring through the window?" Alistair said patiently. "Did you fail to notice that this morning dawned fair, with temperatures well above the freezing mark?"

"I wish I could take heart in the weather, sir," Crewe said. "But after such a dream." He shook his head. "It was so very like the one I dreamt the night before Waterloo."

Alistair paused in his shaving. "Do you mean the one where the footpad cuts my throat and you find me in the alley as the last drops of blood are oozing from my body? Or is it the one where I pitch off the cliff into the sea, and you jump in to save me, but you're too late, and I drown?"

"The cliff, sir," said Crewe. "The sky darkened suddenly, as before a storm, and the remaining light had a peculiar quality. It was as if the sun hung behind a great, green glass. I remember the light in particular as the same I dreamt before that fateful day in June of 1815."

"I'm not riding out to battle," Alistair said. "I'm merely touring Longledge Hill with Miss Oldridge. You may be sure we'll have a servant in attendance. Even in this wilderness, a lady does not go out without protection. Doubtless she'll bring along a large groom of menacing aspect. Should exposure to so much raw nature arouse my passions, he will discourage me from attempting her virtue. Should the scenery produce a similar effect upon her, I reckon I can protect myself."

As he returned to scraping his jaw, he tried to imagine the lady subjecting him to amorous advances. Given her straightforward style, he supposed she'd throw herself at him, literally. He saw her hair tumbling down, and her face upraised to his, and her wide mouth parted . . . and he nicked himself.

Crewe went white. "Sir, I beg you will allow me to assist you." He hurried forward and pressed a towel to the tiny speck of blood near Alistair's ear. "Consider how much weighs upon your mind at present. Is it not the wisest course to allow me to undertake a task requiring one's fullest attention?"

Alistair waved away valet and towel. "If, before Waterloo, the Duke of Wellington could shave himself without fatal results," he said, "I believe I can manage it before ambling along country pathways with a levelheaded—or do I mean hardheaded?—countrywoman."

Crewe subsided into gloomy silence, and Alistair completed his shaving without interruption or injury.

Once the razor was put away and the less hazardous business of dressing commenced, Crewe grew talkative again. Last night, while the master was out, he'd gone to a tavern the local servants frequented, and continued gathering information. He had found out why Lord Gordmor's agent had been turned away, and this news confirmed Alistair's own impression of the situation on Longledge Hill.

About the Oldridges, on the other hand, Crewe had learnt nothing new.

LORD Hargate's heroic son was bored witless.

Mirabel told herself she should have expected it. One hour into the riding tour she was reproaching herself for agreeing to show him her world, especially now, when the landscape was mainly brown, grey, and the drabbest greens.

He could never see it as she did.

Few men could.

Even in Longledge, few truly understood why she'd given more than a decade of her life to this place. Few had any inkling how much she'd given up: the prime of her young womanhood, along with those youthful hopes and dreams. She'd given up as well her one chance at love, because the man she loved was not ready to relinquish his hopes and dreams to make a life with her here.

She had never meant her life to turn out this way.

She'd begun because she had no choice. She'd believed Papa would improve in time, but it never happened. He let all those about him do as they liked. As you'd expect, some took advantage of him. While she was in London, his incompetent—and possibly dishonest—estate manager had made chaos of estate affairs and in a few years nearly destroyed what it had taken generations to build.

At first, Mirabel had taken charge out of necessity. There was no one else to do it. But as time passed, she developed a passion for the land not altogether unlike her father's passion for plants. While he pondered theories of botanical reproduction, she built an arcadia.

She replaced outmoded and inefficient agricultural practices with modern ones, increased farm production, rebuilt the farm village, and began restoring the timber her father had allowed to be nearly decimated.

But to Mr. Carsington, her thriving plantation was only a stand of trees. Her modern cottages were rustic dwellings. Her cultivation methods had something tedious to do with turnips and corn. Her livestock were a lot of boring animals.

Now, as they halted to view the uncultivated slopes of Longledge Hill, Mirabel knew he wouldn't drink in its beauty as she did, or take any more note of it than he'd done any other sight she'd indicated. He'd give it a careless glance, paste a politely indifferent expression on his face, and wait for her to finish talking.

He didn't even remark on how clean and fresh the air was. Why should he? Inhaling the coal smoke–laden air of London for most of his life had killed his sense of smell.

Living there had deadened his other senses as well. He was deaf, dumb, and blind to rural life's beauties and joys.

She'd wasted her time. She'd been a fool to hope he'd understand what she was trying to protect.

A low rumble of a voice cut through the haze of frustration and resentment thickening in her head.

"If your bailiff is incompetent, Miss Oldridge, why do you not find another? Do you keep him out of sentiment? It cannot be for his skill, if he wants so much managing."

Her gaze swiveled sharply to him.

Her astonishment must have shown, because he smiled and added, "Did you think I wasn't attending?"

It was a small, crooked smile, and it made her heart go a little crooked, too, and beat erratically.

As though sensing Mirabel's agitation, her mare Sophy edged away from Mr. Carsington's gelding.

"I thought you had gone to sleep," Mirabel said.

"I was *thinking,*" he said.

"Remarkable," she said. "That never occurred to me."

"I admit it is unusual," he said. "Those who know me will say I'm inclined to act first and think later. But I'm trying to mend my ways."

"I was unaware you had ways in want of mending," she said. "I'd thought all the Carsingtons were paragons."

"The paragons are my two older brothers."

"But you are the famous hero."

His mouth twisted. "I merely contrived not to disgrace myself during the short time in which I fought."

"You are far too modest. You risked your own life several times, to save others."

He gave a short laugh. "That's what men who don't think *do*. We plunge in without considering the consequences. It hardly seems right to call sheer recklessness 'heroic.' However, considering my complete lack of experience; I will take credit for not getting in anybody's way or killing any of my compatriots by accident."

Mirabel wondered why he was so deeply uncomfortable about any mention of his wartime experience. Though he kept his voice light, she'd caught the bitter undertone. She studied his face, but he was on guard now, and his strongly sculpted features told her nothing.

"You're impulsive, you mean," she said. "That is the fault you are trying to mend."

"If only that were the sum total of my faults," he said. "I fear I'm not one of the Carsington paragons, and not likely to become one."

"I hope you do not," she said. "You are trouble enough as it is, even in your desperately flawed state."

He was a greater trouble than Mirabel was prepared for.

This day's journey was futile. He'd never see what she'd achieved or have any inkling of what she'd sacrificed to achieve it. He wouldn't understand why she'd bothered. She didn't know how to explain about her bailiff, why she supervised him so closely. She was not about to delve into ancient history or explain an anxiety even she wasn't sure was completely rational. Those were private matters, and he was a stranger, a London-bred stranger.

He was incapable of seeing the value of a place like Longledge Hill, and so could never comprehend the harm his canal would do.

But this wasn't the worst of her troubles.

While he'd looked and seen nothing, Mirabel had caught a glimpse of the man behind the flawlessly groomed exterior.

The glimpse made her want to know more.

She knew this was a bad sign, and ordered herself not to probe further.

"Have you seen enough of Longledge Hill?" she said. "We can turn back any time you like."

"I doubt I've seen enough," he said.

"Very well." Mirabel gave Sophy leave to walk on. The gelding and his rider promptly followed suit, and her groom Jock trailed behind at a discreet distance.

• • •

ALISTAIR meanwhile was regretting his recent impulse. He was beginning to wish he hadn't challenged Miss Oldridge to take him on this tour. She was muddling him horribly, and this time it wasn't completely the fault of her clothes, though they were maddening enough.

Her slate blue riding dress was five years out of date, her round cork hat was losing its trimming—which didn't match the dress—and her green boots clashed with everything.

The ridiculous rig was all the more vexing because she was a skilled and elegant horsewoman. Though he knew any number of women who rode well, he greatly doubted any of them—except perhaps his mother—would attempt this ancient packhorse trail, which was growing narrower, steeper, more rutted and obstacle-fraught by the minute. Miss Oldridge, on a high-strung mare named Sophy, rode with fluid ease.

Alistair's own mount was a powerful gelding of far less volatile temperament.

Normally, he would have preferred an animal not quite so tame. At present, however, he had strong reason to doubt his judgment.

It was true he was impulsive and reckless—but only with his own life and limb. He was never so cavalier with others' lives, including those of dumb animals.

The other night, when he'd ridden back to the hotel in the icy rain, was a glaring exception. He hadn't yet forgiven himself for the chance he'd taken with Mr. Wilkerson's horse. If she'd been a fraction less sturdy and surefooted, she could have been seriously injured. Alistair had rather not contemplate the suffering the animal might have endured or the only way to end it.

With this folly in mind, he'd taken Miss Oldridge's advice and borrowed for the tour one of her horses, because they were more accustomed to the local terrain.

"It is not much farther now," she called back to him as they entered a wooded part of the hill. "We come to an outlook a short way ahead. We can pause there for a while, then begin the journey back."

"We're not going to the top?"

She halted, and he did likewise, careful to keep a distance from her skittish mare.

"We're nearing the end of the old packhorse trail," she said. "Farther up, the way becomes too steep and rocky for the horses to manage safely."

"You've never been up there, then?"

"On foot," she said.

"We can dismount," Alistair said. "Your groom can look after the horses."

She glanced at his bad leg.

He set his jaw and waited.

"The ground will be slippery after so much rain," she said.

His mind flashed an image: shadowy figures scrambling for footing on ground slippery with blood.

He wasn't sure whether it was real or his mind playing tricks. Either way, he couldn't speak of it. One did not speak of such things, especially to women.

"You've made the climb wearing layers of skirts and petticoats," he said. "My leg will not hinder me a fraction as much."

"That does not mean you ought to punish it," she said. "Pray recollect, you are unfamiliar with the terrain, you are not a countryman—"

"No, I'm a soft, decadent Londoner, is that it?"

"I'm not blind," she said. "I can see you are not soft. Except perhaps for your vanity. Yours is amazingly sensitive, I note."

"I've been trampled by cavalry and survived," he said. "I believe I can climb a hill and live."

"Mr. Carsington, even Captain Hughes, who can still climb a mast and run along those whatever they are—yards, I believe he calls them—even he would think twice before undertaking the upper slope at this time of year."

"If I were as old as Captain Hughes, I should keep away altogether."

"It is a pity you are not old enough to have some sense," she said.

"If an elderly gentleman like the captain can manage the hill in summer, I reckon I can manage it on a balmy spring day."

"Elderly?" She stared at him for a moment, then said, as patiently as to a child, "It is *February*. And while the day did begin mildly enough, the wind has picked up." She looked up. "Also, it looks like rain."

Alistair looked up as well. The scattered clouds had grown and spread, but they were pale and unthreatening, with large patches of blue between. "Not for hours," he said. "I shall be snug in my hotel long before the weather turns. Tell me the truth, Miss Oldridge. If you were on your own this day, would you stop halfway, or continue?"

"I've lived here my whole life," she said. "I played here as a child. Obviously my case is altogether different from yours. Common sense should tell you to heed those with greater experience." She let out a huff of impatience. "I do not understand why a gentleman of your intelligence would allow his pride and vanity to dictate to his common sense—but I can see it is no use arguing."

She hardly raised her voice, but her tone was sharp, and her mare, growing uneasy, started backing off the path.

Alistair wished she had chosen a less temperamental mount for this journey. Sophy had a look in her eye he didn't like. If she bolted—

"I beg you to attend to your mare," he said, his calm voice belying the alarm twisting his gut.

But before he finished speaking, she had the horse quieted and guided her on. She made it all seem as effortless as if she were promenading along Hyde Park's Rotten Row, rather than a narrow trail through a steeply angled landscape of rock and timber.

Still, the terrain wanted his full attention. To avoid distracting her again, Alistair held his tongue until they reached the outlook.

There, to his relief, she dismounted and let the groom take charge of her horse. Alistair did likewise.

The site was not the narrow ledge he'd pictured but a broad, rough terrace in the hillside. A handful of boulders adorned a thin carpet of brown, unidentifiable vegetation. One forlorn shrub grew out of a crack near the outer edge.

From this vantage point he looked out over the moors while his guide explained the difference between black and white lands. The black referred to the blackish-brown heath covering the ground, making it look like a landscape in Hell. The white lands had more green vegetation—some parts had even been limed and reclaimed—though at this time of year it was hard to tell the difference.

"You must know this isn't nature's work," he said. "The moorlands were once forests. Then the great monasteries went into the wool business. No new trees grew to replace those cut down, because the sheep ate everything: the saplings, then the grasses that took the place of the trees, and eventually, all the grass. The sweet soil washed away and left your picturesque moorland, where only matgrass and heath can grow."

"You think it's ugly," she said, turning away from him toward the bleak landscape beyond and below.

Surprised by the despairing note in her voice, Alistair moved nearer.

Since her round riding hat was small, with only the narrowest brim, he had no trouble seeing her face. The profile view revealed red-gold curls dancing wildly in the wind—and a creamy countenance the air and exercise had tinged pink. No tear trickled from the too-blue eye and along the straight nose, and the soft, pink lips didn't tremble.

Her chin jutted out a bit, but that seemed to be her usual way, looking defiant or stubborn or in general uninterested in trying to please anybody.

All the same, she struck him at this moment as young, far younger than her years . . . and lost.

Alistair told himself his romantic imagination was at work and overdoing it. She was one and thirty years old and had for a decade managed a large estate and handled all her father's affairs. Even Alistair could see she'd done this successfully. The estate, clearly, was thriving.

Furthermore, according to Crewe, her neighbors generally agreed that she had a good head for business. Alistair understood how great a compliment this was and how very clever, strong-willed, and confident she must be to have earned it. Men usually resented women encroaching on their turf and would go out of their way to create difficulties for them.

In Longledge, however, most of the men—of both high and low degree—respected Miss Oldridge's judgment and admired what she had done with her father's property. She even had the power to sway opinions, as he'd discovered last night when he'd eavesdropped on her impassioned speech to Captain Hughes. The words had moved Alistair then, and troubled him yet.

Still, capable and strong-willed though she was, Alistair couldn't shake off the feeling that she was lost, or vulnerable, or needful of something. He didn't know what it was, but he sensed he'd somehow hurt or disappointed her, and this at least he must try to remedy.

He must do so, not because she was a damsel in distress, he told himself, but because he needed her on his side. She had influence with the landowners. His motives were purely businesslike and practical.

"To prepare for this mission," he said, "I perused, among other volumes, Mr. John Farey's *General View of the Agriculture and Minerals of Derbyshire*. Mr. Farey calls the moorlands 'disgusting' and the plants growing here 'noxious and useless.' While I will admit it is not the prettiest sight I have ever seen, I shouldn't call it ugly or disgusting. *Dramatic* would be my word."

She looked at him full on, the great blue eyes wary. "You are humoring me."

"Miss Oldridge, the labor of humoring you far exceeds

the bounds of my patience," he said. "When I am with you, I can barely remember my manners."

She smiled then, and his heart warmed as though it basked in summer sunshine. His brain, unfortunately, warmed as well, and commenced melting. He doubted he'd ever encountered a weapon more deadly than that smile.

"Your manners are otherwise very beautiful," she said. "Several parties last night remarked that you belonged in the diplomatic corps."

"How much more agreeable it would be for you," he said, "were I spending this day with the Tsar in St. Petersburg."

"I was thinking of someplace warmer," she said.

"Hades?"

She laughed, and the light sound had the same whispery quality as her speaking voice. "I was thinking of Calcutta or Bombay."

"Of course. There I might die of any number of contagions, if the heatstroke didn't kill me first."

"I don't wish you dead," she said. "I wish you well and thriving—elsewhere."

"You could nudge me over the ledge," he said, "if your groom happened to look away for a moment. It would confirm my valet's Foreboding, and my father's prediction of my coming to no good end. And everyone would be happy."

Her smile faded. "Why would your father predict such a thing? You cannot be so desperately flawed as all that."

"My sire finds me expensive and troublesome to keep," he said. "I am, actually."

She studied him for a moment, her blue gaze traveling the full length from the crown of his sleek hat to the toes of his top boots. "I can believe you are expensive."

Alistair told himself she could discern no fault with his attire. No one ever could. All the same, he felt himself flushing under her scrutiny, which vexed him.

He became aware of dirt on his well-buffed boots, and thought the hem of his overcoat wasn't quite straight. He was not sure his coats ever hung precisely as they should, because of his leg. The curst leg spoilt everything. He was sure it had become shorter than the right one, no matter what his tailor claimed. He wished he'd worn a riding coat, so the disparity would be less evident.

He found her looking at him questioningly. "It isn't only my clothes," he said.

"No, certainly not," she said. "There are the expensive ballet dancers."

"Yes, that sort of thing. And the lawsuits. And the sponging houses. And— Oh, the list is immensely long."

"Lawsuits," she repeated. "Sponging houses. Well, well. You grow more complicated by the moment."

"But I am mending my ways," Alistair said. "The canal is completely respectable."

"Yet your valet has forebodings, you said."

"Not about the canal. About me. Crewe often has them. He believes his dreams predict the future."

Alistair told her about the cliff dream, and the odd light, and how Crewe had had the same dream before Waterloo.

When he was done, she said, "If you do happen to fall, you may well break your neck. Drowning, on the other hand, would be difficult. The largest body of water nearby is the Briar Brook, which isn't deep enough."

"Then it should be safe enough for me to continue up the hillside with you," he said.

"You mean *dangerous* enough. If it were safe, you would be as bored with the prospect as you have been with everything else."

"You thought I was bored?" It was his turn to smile. "Well, then, perhaps you're not as clever as I'd supposed."

Six

MR. Carsington's golden eyes danced, and the smile—the complete article, not a crooked bit of one—was devastating.

Mirabel quickly looked away and started up the path while mentally flagellating herself.

She should not have let the conversation become personal.

She had thought him possessed of the unshakable aristocratic self-assurance she'd encountered so often in London and found as unfathomable as her father did the mating habits of lichen. But Mr. Carsington had a chink in his armor. He wasn't as sure of himself as it seemed.

This wasn't the only way she'd mistaken him. His discomfort with mention of his wartime heroics wasn't the usual becoming modesty, false or otherwise. He was truly uneasy, and she found herself wondering what troubled him so much about it, and wishing he'd tell her so that she could set him right.

She'd found out, too, that for all his vanity about his appearance, he was far from happy with himself.

She hadn't reached this conclusion because he spoke of reforming. After all, men—especially rakes and other ne'er-do-wells—commonly pacified women by promising to reform. Even Papa did it, about twice a year, with most sincere intentions—which he'd forget the instant the next botanical riddle happened along.

No, it wasn't the talk of mending his ways. It was the troubled expression in Mr. Carsington's eyes and the change in his tone when he spoke of his father. That note in his voice struck a painful chord within her. She recognized the frustration: the sense of failure no matter what one did, the awareness of a vast, unbridgeable gap.

"I can walk and talk at the same time," came Mr. Carsington's deep rumble from behind her.

He was very close behind her, she discovered as she glanced back. "I'm *thinking*," she said.

"But women are much more complicated beings than men," he said. "I believe you can even hold more than one thought in your mind at once. Surely you must be able to think and walk and talk simultaneously."

"I was wondering if you practice the bored look in the mirror," she said. "You are so very good at it. I feared you would fall asleep and tumble from your horse. Since you've already read Mr. Farey's book, what I've had to say about Longledge Hill must seem tedious repetition."

"It wasn't what you had to say about farming," he said. "I'd already read enough about Derbyshire agriculture to make me want to hang myself. It's *you* I find interesting."

Mirabel's heart twisted about again. "I'm a farmer," she said. "It isn't in the least exciting."

"Why don't you leave managing the estate to Higgins?" he said. "Why don't you let him do what he was hired for, while you go to London and enjoy yourself? If the social whirl proves too frivolous, you might find scores of other intellectual ladies to talk to and attend lectures with."

She remembered, rather wistfully, the joys of London.

Aunt Clothilde never gave up urging her to visit. One day, perhaps, Mirabel would. But not yet, not now, certainly, when everything she loved was threatened.

"You are so kind," she said. "I wish you as far as Calcutta. You only wish me as far as London."

"You've evaded the question twice and thus doubled my curiosity. Have you a lover here?"

A lover? *She?* Was he serious?

Mirabel stopped short. He trod on her heel, and her foot slipped. Then she was toppling backward, flailing for balance. He caught hold of her waist and righted her. It was done in an instant. But he didn't let go.

She heard his quick intake of breath and looked up to meet his strangely intent golden gaze. Her own breath came quicker, and her heart skittered against her rib cage.

His hands were big and warm, his grip firm, and she thought he must sense the commotion within her. She ought to pull away, but she didn't want to. She only wanted to look up into his eyes, trying to read them and daring to hope she wasn't the only one in a commotion.

He bent a hairsbreadth closer. "What a little waist you have," he said in a soft, puzzled voice. "I should never have guessed."

She was not little, but he was so much larger. Her head came only to his immaculately shaven chin. She stood near enough to feel his breath on her face, near enough to detect the elusive scent she still had no name for. She saw the faint network of scars on the underside of his jaw and wanted to put her hand up and lay it against his cheek. She didn't know why or what it would achieve, only that she wanted to.

It took nearly all her willpower *not* to do it, to gather her composure and say, so very casually, "If you are done measuring me, Mr. Carsington, I believe I can contrive to walk on unaided."

He took his time straightening and was slow and deliberate releasing her. Even after he'd fully let go, she could feel the pressure and warmth of his hands. She knew a boundary had been crossed, and if she did not take very great care, she would soon have no boundaries left.

"You gave me a fright," he said. "I had a vision of you tumbling down the rocky hillside. My heart still pounds."

Mirabel's did, too, with everything but fear. "Perhaps if you would not follow so closely, we should be less likely to stumble into each other," she said while hoping she would not be tempted to do so accidentally on purpose.

"A good point," he agreed. "I should have paid more attention to where I was walking as well. But I was caught up in admiring the view, you see."

To the right, the left, and straight ahead the view consisted of trees, limestone rocks, scraggy bushes, and dirt. A smattering of evergreens provided the only bright color in the dreary landscape.

"The scenery here is hardly worth the climb, I should say," she said.

"Not from my perspective," he said.

Heat washed through her. She understood his meaning. She had not spent two seasons in London without learning how to detect innuendo. She pretended not to understand, though she could not pretend it dismayed her. It had been a very long time since an attractive man had made improper remarks about her person. She'd forgotten how agreeable it was.

A small, insistent voice in the back of her head made warning noises, and she remembered how agreeable he'd made himself to all the men last night.

"For the present, you would be wiser to watch the path," she said.

"I shall try to be wise, Miss Oldridge."

Mirabel walked on.

"About your lover," he began after a moment.

She did not mind flirtation and a bit of impropriety. She had never been missish. But she could not let herself fall victim to his charm. And she most certainly would not explain private matters to him. "I cannot believe you think

I've undertaken all that I have, merely to be near a man," she said quellingly.

"What a pity. I was picturing clandestine meetings, perhaps on that ledge overlooking the romantic moors."

"You are certainly entitled to entertain any fanciful notions you like," she said, repeating his patronizing retort of a few days earlier. "I should not wish to stifle an active imagination."

He laughed. "Touché, Miss Oldridge."

As the path rounded a sharp curve, Mirabel felt the air change. She looked up. The clouds were thickening. She paused. This time he was prepared, and they didn't collide.

He came up beside her and stood nearer than was strictly proper. He was breathing hard—winded, apparently.

He could not be accustomed to such climbs, and his leg must be hurting as well. "I think the weather may change more quickly than you estimated," she said. "Perhaps we'd better turn back."

He eyed the forbidding hillside. "Let's go a bit farther. Where's the Briar Brook?"

"Not far," she said. "But there's hardly any path at all up ahead, and the climb is much steeper."

"So it appears," he said. "It's been ages since I scrambled up a rocky hillside. I should like to see if I can still do it."

Mirabel would have argued, but the longing look he directed at the rocky terrain ahead stopped her tongue.

He wasn't quite whole, and she was sure it vexed him more than he let on. The appearance of easy grace must want hard work to maintain. Yet no matter how hard he worked, he'd never move as smoothly and effortlessly as he'd done before Waterloo.

She wished he wouldn't let it vex him. No one with working eyesight could possibly perceive him as defective or weak. But even she had enough delicacy not to broach so personal a topic—not that he'd heed her if she did.

Instead, she agreed to continue, and he managed so well

and was so pleased with himself that she led him farther than she'd meant to.

He told her he should have realized one didn't need an even gait to get over and around rocks. "Think of crabs," he said. Exaggerating his limp, he started moving sideways, hurrying up the hill ahead of her.

Mirabel laughed, throwing her head back. That was when she felt the first raindrops.

She called out to him.

He paid no attention but raced up among the rocks, almost as quick as a crab. A moment later, the sky turned black, and the drops swelled into a deluge.

And in the next moment, she saw him slip, and fall, and tumble down into the rocky stream. There he remained, terribly still, when she reached him.

THE world went black, briefly. When Alistair came to, he wasn't sure whether it was day or night or where he was.

A low-hanging sky the color of coal smoke spewed cold, lashing rain. He closed his eyes and tried not to think, but his mind hurried along anyway.

How bad was it? How many holes had the enemy made in him? How swiftly would his strength ebb away?

How soon, he wondered, would the life leak out of him, and was that better than being rescued and somehow patched up so that, mutilated and incapacitated, he could die a long, slow death over years instead of hours?

Artillery blasted nearby, and the air filled with smoke. He heard men scream in agony. Rifle fire. More smoke. Horses thundering toward him.

They crashed over him, bringing oblivion. But not for long. He soon woke again, to stench and smoke and the cries of the dying, man and beast.

He woke as well to the pain, which created a world of its own, making the grim scene about him seem a degree less immediate.

The pain loomed large, dimming everything else. At first it was one steady throb like his heartbeat. Then other variations came and went, driving aches and spasms through him, these lesser torments darting in and out from under the great, steady drumbeat.

All the world narrowed to only him and to the one human sensation in all its shades and variations. Pain, he discovered, was a fugue, and a kaleidoscope, and it hardly mattered what you called it, since it was the only thing.

"Mr. Carsington."

Night music in the fugue.

That was wrong.

Alistair opened his eyes. Blue, blue eyes looked into his. A halo of fiery fluff above the eyes. Upon the fluff perched the aged hat with its tattered trim. Above and beyond the hat was the black sky, disgorging forty days and forty nights of rain.

"You are conscious," the night voice said. "Can you speak? Can you tell me where it hurts?"

"Nowhere," he said. _Everywhere._ His leg was on fire. Had he been shot? But no, that was years ago. This was now. The girl. The redhead. Ah, yes, he remembered: silken soft hair the color of sunrise . . . twilight eyes . . . the sweet, slender waist under his hands. When was that? Why had he let her go?

"I know you are hurt," she said. "Tell me where. I dare not move you until I know. But I must move you. You cannot lie in the Briar Brook all day. Please do be sensible. Where does it hurt?"

"Nowhere," he said. "Not in the least. Perfectly well." He tried to lift his head, but pain shot down from his hip to his ankle. He caught his breath. It was only his plaguy leg, he told himself. Nothing to panic about.

"Catch my breath," he gasped. "Up in a moment." He managed to lift his head and wrap one arm around a rock. He rested his head on the rock as though it were a pillow. Rain beat on his bare head. Where was his hat? He must find his hat. In a minute, he'd get up and look for it.

"Jock!" she called. "Jock!"

Who was Jock? Not her lover. She'd said she hadn't one. He shouldn't have asked. He'd done other things he shouldn't. He remembered watching her hips sway and his all but announcing his approval of her handsome derrière. Because they'd been alone. No groom of menacing aspect. *Jock. The groom.*

"Horses," he said. "He can't leave the horses."

The smoky haze settled in again. Around him, the animals' screams mingled with the men's. He smelled blood. Men's or horses? He was going to be sick and disgrace himself.

"Get up, you fool," he mumbled. "Help your comrades."

The night voice, shaky now, called Alistair out of the haze. "Don't try to speak, Mr. Carsington. Let's save our strength, shall we? Jock won't hear me in all this, at any rate."

She was right. In this storm, who would hear their shouts for help?

The icy stream rushed around and over him, banging his legs against the rocks.

"I must check for broken bones," she said. "If you're in one piece, we should be able to get you out of the brook without too much difficulty."

One piece, yes. He saw the stack of bloody limbs. He didn't want his leg thrown into that ghastly heap.

"Flesh wound," he mumbled. "No call to get excited."

"Save your strength," she said. "I'll make it quick."

Firm, confident hands moved over his neck and shoulders. He closed his eyes, and the dark world swam back into his mind.

He heard the din of artillery, which couldn't quite drown out the groans and screams. The pain made him shake, and he was growing numb with cold. He thought about Kitty and Gemma and Aimée and Helen, about warm beds and soft hands. He would die here and never feel a woman's hands on him again.

A moment later Alistair came back to the pounding rain

and the woman leaning over him, whose expert hands traveled down his limbs, gently pressing, probing.

He found his wits and his voice. "Are you a doctor, too, Miss Oldridge?"

"I've had more practice with animals," she said. "Still, I should be able to recognize a broken bone if I encounter one."

When she reached his left ankle, the jolt of pain made him sit up sharply.

"There's the trouble," she said. "It could be a great deal worse. You were rather cruelly knocked about when you fell. I'm fairly certain you've sprained your ankle, and you've undoubtedly wrenched some muscles. But nothing seems to be broken."

Banged about. Bruised. Muscles wrenched here and there. That was all. Why the devil did it hurt so much? And what was wrong with his brain?

"Knew it was nothing," he gasped. "Sprained ankle."

"I should hardly call it *nothing,*" she said sharply. "You have all the old hurts from battle, and you are wet and chilled to the bone." While she spoke, she was helping him to his feet.

Even with her help, the process was awkward and maddeningly slow. Also excruciating, thanks to the damaged ankle competing with his mangled upper leg.

Not only did every movement hurt, but his muscles were no longer fully under his command and kept going into spasms. The pain and shakiness, the crashing stream, the slippery stones, the blinding rain, and his sodden clothes combined to make him feel like the cripple he'd worked so hard not to become.

Alistair made himself work now, though his body wanted to give up, and a part of his mind wished he'd broken his neck so he wouldn't have to fight anymore.

But that was a tiny despised part of himself he usually kept locked away. Self-pity disgusted him. He'd seen what others endured and knew how trivial by comparison his own difficulties were.

He told himself to be grateful he had a strong-minded countrywoman to lean on, who did not burst into tears or fly into a panic, but stayed as cool and steady as any comrade-in-arms.

With her, he waded—lurched, rather—to a section of the bank where a gravel bed allowed for a reasonably secure footing, and climbed out.

Henceforth the going became a degree easier. The ground was slippery, and they traveled steeply downhill rather than up, but they steadied each other. Eventually they reached the outlook, where a worried Jock was preparing to set out after them.

MIRABEL had had a good deal of practice in appearing to have everything under control. Where business was concerned, one must preserve an unruffled demeanor, even if a late freeze decimated the orchards, or a prolonged spell of wet weather rotted half the winter's hay supply, or the sheep began dying of a mystery ailment.

As Captain Hughes would say, she was captain of the ship, and the well-being of vessel and crew depended on her. Any symptoms of confusion, hesitation, doubt, or alarm she displayed would swiftly infect others, undermining morale and endangering both crew and vessel.

She'd taken over her father's affairs because he'd abandoned command, leaving the estate drifting toward the rocks and endangering the livelihoods of all the people who depended upon it.

After more than a decade of shouldering her father's responsibilities, it was second nature to take firm command of a situation, even if within, Mirabel felt hopelessly confused or frightened witless.

From the time Mr. Carsington tumbled into the Briar Brook, she was as near hysteria as she'd ever been in her life. When she'd scrambled down to the water, her heart was thundering in her ears. The sheeting rain blurred her vision, and she couldn't be sure if his chest was going up and down or not. Her hands shook so much she couldn't tell whether he had a pulse.

Fortunately, he opened his eyes, and after a moment seemed to recognize her, and she calmed enough to think, though not as clearly as she'd like.

On the way back to Oldridge Hall, her mind continued to clear. Consequently, by the time a brace of servants had eased Mr. Carsington from his horse and loaded him onto a ladder, she knew something more was wrong with him than a sprained ankle.

He would protest being carried, then begin mumbling again, apparently oblivious to his immediate surroundings. Inside the house, he repeated this set of behaviors while the servants carried him down the hall and up the stairs to the yellow guest suite.

It would have been easier to put him in one of the ground-floor rooms, but a ground-floor room would be easier for a man with an injured ankle to escape from. Mirabel was certain he'd try to escape. After all, he hadn't brought a change of clothes. If an ice storm couldn't deter him, she doubted very much that a sprained ankle would.

She had to make him to stay put, at least until Dr. Woodfrey had examined him.

She saw Mr. Carsington transferred from the litter to a chair, supervised the process of peeling off his sodden outer garments, and got his injured foot propped up. After sending the footman Thomas for the tool she needed, she signaled Joseph to remain nearby. She thought it best to prepare her guest for the destruction of his costly boots.

She told him hot water was on the way, and he'd soon be able to wash. "But I'm afraid we must cut off your boot."

He took the news calmly, merely staring at the floor. Water dripped from his hair, which fell into his face.

"It's wet," he said. "Who'd have thought a man could spill so much—" He dragged his wet hair back and peered closer. "Oh. Water. My boots. Crewe will be in fits."

His head came up suddenly, and his feverish golden gaze met hers. "I have to take off my clothes." He yanked at his sodden neckcloth.

Mirabel stopped his hand. "The cloth is soaked and difficult to manage. You're shivering. Let me help."

He frowned, then let go of the linen and lifted his chin.

Mirabel bent and started working at the knot, keeping her hands steady through sheer will. "Papa doesn't have a valet," she said, "or I'd send him to you." She got the knot loosened enough to draw the ends of the cloth through. Once the boots were off, she could let the servants finish undressing him and help him bathe.

"The Duke of Wellington doesn't keep a manservant, either," Mr. Carsington said. "His Grace does for himself. I could do without. But Crewe's looked after me forever. He goes with me everywhere. Here. There." He let out a shuddering sigh, and his gaze became distant. "I'll get up in a moment. Have to help. Can't lie here. Gad, what a waste. What will they put on the gravestone?"

He subsided into the odd murmuring again. Mirabel didn't want to think about what caused it. She was certain sprained ankles didn't set off delirium.

She remembered her mother's feverish babbling in those last days—and hastily put it out of her mind. She told herself to concentrate on getting this man clean and warm as quickly as possible.

"Mr. Carsington, we must cut off your boots," she said, keeping her voice steady. "They're ruined anyway."

He nodded, and she started to unwind the neckcloth.

Thomas entered with the knife she'd asked for. Mr. Carsington looked up at the servant and stiffened. "No cutting," he said. "It's only a flesh wound."

Mirabel let go of the neckcloth and lightly touched his forehead. His skin was hot.

"Your boots are wet through," she said gently. "Your ankle is tender and probably swollen. Pulling off the boot might worsen the injury."

He blinked up at her, and his gaze seemed to clear. "Yes. The boots. Of course. I'll do it."

"You're chilled," she said. "Your hands are unsteady. Please be sensible and let Joseph do it."

Mr. Carsington looked at his own long hands, which he couldn't keep quite still. "Not Joseph." He looked up at her. "You. Cool, steady hands. We have to keep our heads, don't we? Slice 'em both up good and proper, Miss Oldridge. The boots, I mean. And pay no mind if I sob while you do it. These boots were so very dear." He grinned at her like a mischievous boy. "I made that vile pun just for you. It made you smile, too. You've a soft spot for puns, I know."

He did make Mirabel smile in spite of her alarm. She took the knife from Thomas, knelt by the patient's chair, and began the operation.

ONCE the boots were off, the servants proceeded with their usual smooth efficiency. In a very short time, Mr. Carsington was clean, warm, and dry. He let them put him to bed with his foot propped up on pillows and an oilcloth bag of ice tucked about his ankle. He seemed comfortable enough when Mirabel came in later and found him dozing.

He slept for a time, then grew restless and mumbled the way he'd done when she'd examined him in the brook. She tried to quiet him, but he only grew more agitated.

"I can't lie here," he said, struggling up onto the pillows. The front of his nightshirt opened to a wide V, exposing a portion of his chest and the curling, dark gold hair lightly covering it. The hair was damp, as was the edge of the shirt opening. A muscle throbbed in his neck. "Where are my clothes?"

Mirabel reminded him that his clothes were wet, and the servants were taking care of them.

"Oh," he said, and fell back upon the pillows.

She rose and drew the bedclothes over him. "You're

worn out," she said. "You've sprained your ankle, and I think you've taken a chill. Please rest."

"Gad, I'm so muddled," he said. "Did I fall on my head?" He closed his eyes, and she commenced pacing the room, wishing the doctor would hurry.

Not half an hour later, Mr. Carsington was flinging off the bedclothes and—apparently oblivious to the fact that he was baring his long, muscled legs to her view—shouting for his manservant.

Joseph, who was in attendance, hurried to him, but the patient thrust him aside and leapt from the bed, only to let out a ferocious oath and grab the back of Mirabel's vacated chair for balance.

"It's supposed to walk!" he raged. "This leg is supposed to walk! What the devil is wrong with it?"

"Sir!" came a firm masculine voice from the doorway. "Compose yourself."

Mr. Carsington stilled, his gaze riveted on the figure in the doorway.

Captain Hughes strode into the room. "What is the meaning of this uproar, sir?"

Mr. Carsington sank into the chair and shook his head, as though trying to clear it.

"Mr. Carsington is not quite himself," Mirabel said calmly while her heart pounded and her insides worked themselves into knots. "He's sprained his ankle and . . ."

She took a steadying breath. "I don't know whether he has sustained a concussion or taken a chill, but he is unwell."

"I heard about the accident," the captain said. "I was on my way from Matlock when I met up with the lad you sent for Dr. Woodfrey. The doctor will be a while, I'm afraid. He's up to his elbows in emergencies."

"I never take ill," Mr. Carsington said. He sat sideways, his right arm draped over the back of the chair. "Never. All the same. That great, reeking heap. You wouldn't have left it there, either. I've a strong stomach, but it was sickening. And they were in such an infernal hurry. You know what they're like." He addressed the last sentence to Captain Hughes, who couldn't have had any more idea what he meant than Mirabel did.

But the captain nodded and said, "I daresay I do."

"Or maybe not," said Mr. Carsington. "I seem to be talking gibberish. I fell on my head, didn't I? Yes, of course. Exactly what I needed about now: brain damage."

Seven

CALM *down,* Alistair told himself. *Be a man, damn you.*

At the moment, if he was a man, it was no one he recognized. He wasn't certain he could move without vomiting. He wasn't sure what had happened, whether the butchering was done or not. He told himself to think about something else, anything else.

Crewe. His premonition. Ridiculous. This was war. The odds of being wounded, maimed, killed, were high. Better than fifty-fifty. Still, Alistair hadn't been fully prepared for the extent of the carnage. Acres of corpses, so many of his friends about him. The dead and dying who fell into the muck, never to rise again.

He became aware of a woman's voice nearby. And a man's. Not Gordy's. Whose? He wished he could unscrew his head from his neck, take it apart, and fix it.

"Not feeling quite the thing, I daresay?" the male voice said.

"There's an understatement," Alistair said.

"You said you were unwell," the voice said. "Something sickened you. Do you recollect? A reeking heap, you said."

Had he spoken aloud? They were mere thoughts, unworthy ones. And anyway, it was a dream. It couldn't be true. He scarcely knew what fear was. He would never behave so disgracefully, become sick over a bit of unpleasantness, like a girl. His father would be ashamed if he found out. But he wouldn't. It wasn't true, couldn't be.

"Did I?" Alistair said. "How odd. I don't recall." He took a shallow breath. "Are they done with the leg yet?"

Was it gone, tossed onto the heap with the other limbs?

"Do you know where you are, sir?" came the voice again in the clearly recognizable accents of authority. A man used to command. An officer, of course.

"Do you know where you are, sir?" the voice repeated. "Do you know me?"

Alistair opened his eyes. The world about him spun at first, then gradually slowed and settled down. He realized he was in a room, not a surgeon's tent. The man standing before him was familiar.

"Captain Hughes," he said, keeping his voice steady while he tried to untangle nightmare from reality.

"You had a fall," the captain said. "You sprained your ankle, and by the sounds of it, got your brain knocked about your skull. Happened to me once. Rigging fell on me, knocked me bung upwards. But it's nothing to worry about. Your brain box will sort itself out in time."

Alistair rubbed his forehead. It ached, but the pain was nothing to the pounding misery of the left side of his body. "A fall. Yes, of course. Hit my head, no doubt. Temporarily unhinged. That explains."

Then he remembered leaping from bed, half-naked . . . a pale, startled face nearby . . . blue eyes, wide with alarm.

He looked about the room and found her standing by the fire, her hands folded at her waist.

Oh, delightful. He'd been carrying on like a lunatic in front of *her.* "Miss Oldridge," he said.

"You know me," she said.

"For the moment, yes. It seems I've made a thorough spectacle of myself."

"It was nothing so very dreadful," she said. "You did not at any time make any less sense than Papa does. Nonetheless, we should all feel easier in our minds if you would return to bed."

At that minute Alistair recalled that he was still half-naked, clad only in a shirt that didn't belong to him. The fabric was coarser than what he was accustomed to. Looking on the bright side, however, it was large enough to conceal the ugly network of scars on his thigh.

He waved off the captain's offer of assistance and started toward the bed, which was only a few paces away.

Miss Oldridge walked to a window and looked out, tactfully allowing him to complete the clumsy transfer of his mangled body to the bed.

The room was quiet but for the rain beating against the windows. The sound was soothing. The bedclothes emitted a faint lavender scent. Everything surrounding him was immaculate, well-ordered, and peaceful.

He could not believe he'd confused this place with a world belonging to nightmares.

"You look in better trim already," Captain Hughes said. "Not the wild-eyed fellow I found when I burst in so unceremoniously." He turned his attention to the figure by the window. "I hope you will forgive my lapse of manners, Miss Oldridge. I was downstairs in the hall, waiting to learn if you'd any orders for me, when I got wind of the disturbance on the upper decks."

"You've nothing to apologize for," she said. "For all you knew, my father might have set a room on fire again."

Alistair was brooding about brain damage, having discovered no other way of accounting for his outrageous behavior. Her words tore him out of his self-absorption and brought him bolt upright in bed, setting the entire left side of his damaged body athrob. He ignored the pain.

"Again?" he said. "Is Mr. Oldridge in the habit of setting rooms ablaze?"

"It was only the once, some nine or ten years ago," Miss Oldridge said. "While looking at a letter from my Aunt Clothilde he had a sudden insight about Egyptian date palms. They plague him from time to time, for reasons no one else but he and perhaps three other botanical persons in the world understand. As best he recollected afterward, this was such a time. He jumped up from the writing desk, upsetting a candle, which he was too excited to notice."

She came away from the window. "Luckily, a servant did notice soon after Papa hurried out. The only damage was some charring of the writing desk, a partly singed rug, and a lingering smell of smoke."

"I feel much better," Alistair said. "At least I did not burn down the house."

She approached the bed and studied him critically. "Your color is healthier than it was a short while ago. Not so feverish. All the same, we ought to put more ice on your ankle. Would you like some for your head as well?"

Alistair had almost forgotten his aching head. The violent throbbing along his left leg had claimed center stage. "Indeed, I would," he said. "You are most kind to think of it. For my part, I shall attempt to await the doctor quietly, if not rationally."

She smiled, and the room seemed to grow brighter, though rain continued beating at the darkened windows. "I'm vastly relieved to hear it," she said.

DR. Woodfrey did not arrive until very late in the day. He was young—barely thirty—small, wiry, and energetic, and accustomed to traveling in every kind of weather. Still, there was only one of him, and the storm's suddenness and violence had caused numerous mishaps in addition to making the roads all but impassable.

In spite of this, Dr. Woodfrey was his usual brisk, lively self when he reached Oldridge Hall. After briefly conferring with Mirabel and Captain Hughes, he went straight up to Mr. Carsington. Mirabel and the captain retired to the library to await the medical verdict.

The doctor joined them about half an hour later and was commencing his diagnosis when Mr. Oldridge hurried in, his countenance troubled. Arriving home in good time for dinner, he had seen Dr. Woodfrey's carriage and was greatly alarmed, believing Mirabel had been taken ill.

Concealing her amazement at his (a) noticing so unbotanical an object as a carriage, (b) recognizing whose it was, and (c) worrying about her, Mirabel explained about Mr. Carsington's fall and strange behavior thereafter.

"Good heavens!" said Mr. Oldridge. "His head is not broken, I hope. The ground can be deceiving in certain places, especially near the old mines. I have tumbled more than once. Luckily, we Oldridges have strong skulls."

"His head is not broken," Dr. Woodfrey assured him.

"Is it fever, then?" Mirabel said. "Is that what makes him delirious?"

"He is not feverish at present," the doctor said. "He was fully rational the entire time I was with him."

Nonetheless, he went on to say, the patient might have sustained a concussion, albeit a mild one. By all accounts, he had lost consciousness for no more than a minute or two—perhaps merely seconds—and did not display symptoms associated with severe brain injury: he was not sleepy and dull-witted or vomiting or taking fits. Still, he must be watched carefully for the next eight and forty hours.

Dr. Woodfrey was concerned as well that a cold or affection of the lungs might manifest themselves during this interval. These concerns, combined with the sprained ankle, argued strongly against the gentleman's expressed wish to return immediately to his hotel.

Having rendered this verdict, the doctor took Mirabel aside to give her specific instructions.

"It is of sovereign importance that our patient remain where he is," Dr. Woodfrey told her. "In addition to his brain and ankle, which need rest in order to heal properly, he displays symptoms of a fatigue of the nerves. This may prove even more worrisome. Acute fatigue has been known to set off hallucinations and other irrational behavior, which would explain what you took to be delirium."

Mirabel could not believe Mr. Carsington suffered from any sort of fatigue or nervous condition.

True, he had mastered the fashionable appearance of boredom and lassitude, but he was far from feeble. On the contrary, he was dangerously compelling.

She recalled his hands on her waist, and her physical awareness of his strength, and her heated, nearly demented reaction. She could not remember when the mere proximity of a man had disturbed her so profoundly. Even William, whom she'd loved so fiercely, had not made her feel so much with so little effort.

William, too, had been abundantly masculine, forceful, and dashing. But he had not made her feel, palpably, every change of mood as she did in Mr. Carsington's vicinity: the displeasure that set the very air athrob—and more troubling, the easy charm, as palpable as a caress, she found nigh impossible to withstand.

She recalled the pun about his expensive boots—"so very dear"—and the lighthearted boy's grin, and said, "He is the last man on earth I should have thought weary and worn out."

"I agree he looks healthy enough," said Dr. Woodfrey. "But today's shock has disrupted a delicate balance. The best medicine is rest. I shall leave it to you how to accomplish this. You are a resourceful young woman."

He gave a few simple instructions about diet and treatment, regretfully declined her invitation to dinner, and departed to attend the next patient, leaving Mirabel to devise a means of managing a man even the Earl of Hargate found troublesome.

"WOODFREY is wrong." Alistair made this pronouncement in the imperious accents his father employed to stifle all argument. It wasn't easy to appear magisterial while sitting in bed, wearing only a nightshirt, and propped up with pillows, but he was not about to be bullied by an elfin doctor and a disheveled young woman.

The latter was regarding him with an anxious expression that made him uneasy.

"I am not sure you are in a condition to judge with any accuracy what is best for you," Miss Oldridge said.

"I can judge better than he," Alistair said. "Woodfrey doesn't know me. I have inherited my paternal grandmother's constitution. She is four score and two, goes out at least three nights a week, and is a terror at whist. She is in full possession of her wits and in complete command of everyone else, for time has only honed the deadly fine edge of her tongue. She would never allow herself to be confined to bed for a mere sprained ankle and a bump on the head."

Miss Oldridge did not immediately respond. She nodded at the footman, and he took away Alistair's dinner tray.

Since she had kept him company while he ate, she must have seen that his appetite was in fine order. He'd left not a crumb behind.

When the servant was gone, she walked from the fire to the window at the opposite end of the room. It wasn't her first such journey. Even while inhaling his dinner, Alistair had watched the rhythmic sway of her hips as she came and went. Now the food was gone, he could give her his undivided attention.

She wore a wine-colored sarcenet dress trimmed in blue. The style was too severe and the colors weren't quite right for her complexion, but it was the least unflattering dress she'd worn so far.

Her inept maid had made an attempt to dress her hair in the antique Roman style fashionable several years ago. As one would expect, the two knots at the back of her head were coming unknotted.

Reflected light from the candles and fire glimmered along a trail of hairpins to and from the chimneypiece. He found the sight arousing, heaven help him.

On the positive side, if mere hairpins could arouse him, he could not be anywhere near death's door.

"If your ankle is not allowed to rest, it will not heal properly," she said when she returned to the fire. "It will become weak and susceptible to repeated sprains."

"Your miniature doctor exaggerates the danger," Alistair said. "Medical men always make dire predictions. That way, if one dies, it isn't their fault, and if one recovers, it's due to their brilliance."

"Everyone knows what happens with sprains," she said. "At least in the country we do. You would be foolish to take such a risk. You especially cannot afford a weak ankle. It will undo all you've accomplished in recovering use of your leg."

The speech was as simple and blunt as a club to the head, and equally effective.

His leg was fussy and uncooperative at the best of a times. Given a weak ankle, it might refuse to perform at all.

Alistair had the usual quantity of masculine pride. On the other hand, he was not a dumb brute. He refused to behave like an idiot merely to appease his pride.

"It grieves me to say this, but you have made an excellent point," he said. "We must on no account upset the famous leg. There is no predicting what it will do."

Her taut expression eased. She approached, took the chair by the bed, and folded her hands in her lap. "It is understandable, your being upset," she said. "Anyone who's endured a long period of immobility, as you have done, must cherish his freedom of movement. Even a day or two of being confined to bed must seem a great deal to you."

"Oh, I shouldn't mind that so much," he said. "By dint of long study, I've mastered the art of lounging about or sleeping away the day instead of doing something noble or at least useful. No, no, it isn't that. The trouble is, I'm sick to death of pandering to this capricious limb."

She glanced at the peak in the bedclothes under which

his injured foot reposed upon a pillow, then looked quizzically at him. "Pandering?"

"Let me tell you about this leg, Miss Oldridge," he said. "This used to be a modest, well-behaved leg, quietly going about its business, troubling nobody. But ever since it was hurt, it has become tyrannical."

Her expression eased another degree, and amusement glinted in her eyes, like faint, distant stars in a midsummer night's sky.

Encouraged, he went on, "This limb is selfish, surly, and ungrateful. When English medical expertise declared the case hopeless, we took the leg to a Turkish healer. He plied it with exotic unguents and cleaned and dressed it several times a day. By this means he staved off the fatal and malodorous infection it should have suffered otherwise. Was the leg grateful? Did it go back to work like a proper leg? No, it did not."

Lips twitching, she made a sympathetic murmur.

"This limb, madam," he said, "demanded months of boring exercises before it would condescend to perform the simplest movements. Even now, after nearly three years of devoted care and maintenance, it will fly into a fit over damp weather. And this, may I remind you, is an *English* leg, not one of your delicate foreign varieties."

Her mouth quivered, and laughter danced in her eyes.

Something quivered and danced within him, and his mind filled with the wrong thoughts—of touching his lips to the tiny laugh line at the corner of her eye, of bringing his mouth to her quivering one.

He kept talking. "In any case, it won't go anywhere willingly at present. How on earth did I imagine I should be able to hop up from bed and trot along to the hotel?"

She said, not too steadily, "You did fall on your head. On a r-rock." She stifled a giggle.

Alistair had always found giggling girls tedious. He told himself to be bored with her, too, but it was impossible. Her choked laughter made his heart so light, it seemed to float within him, and his mind was light and floating, too—not good, and he thought, *Oh, no, I shall soon like her, and that won't do because we know where it must lead. Stop charming her, you numskull.*

He couldn't stop.

He sighed theatrically. "Since a graceful exit is out of the question, I must accept my fate with humble resignation. I shall lie here looking wan and brave. Now and again, perhaps you would be so good, Miss Oldridge, as to stop by to admire my quiet fortitude." He settled back upon the pillows and donned a heroic expression.

She laughed then, out loud, her eyes crinkling into narrow blue slits.

The cool, whispery sound wafted inside him and stirred again the place already disturbed with the erotic allure of hairpins and the untoward delight he took in a poorly suppressed giggle.

But before Alistair could say or do anything fatally stupid, Mr. Oldridge entered, carrying a large volume.

"Mr. Carsington is not to read, Papa," the daughter said. "Dr. Woodfrey said he is not to exert his mental faculties."

"I know," her father said. "He is not to be overstimulated. That is why I have brought *Prodromus Systematis Naturalis Regni Vegetabilis.* I sent my sister a copy some time ago, and she has written her thanks more than once. Clothilde says it is a most restful book. Whenever she finds herself in a state of agitation or unhealthy excitement, she reads it. Infallibly, after a page or two, she tells me, she subsides into a pleasantly drowsy state." He beamed at Alistair. "I shall read to you—but if you find it too sensational, we shall try something else."

MR. Oldridge had a soothing voice, and of the Latin words he uttered, Alistair understood about one in ten. Having some dim idea that he'd be quizzed later, he struggled to follow.

He didn't remember falling asleep. He simply went

from one place to another in the night, from a warm, clean bedroom to a battlefield.

The smell made him sick, and his foot slipped on the slick ground. He lost his hold of Gordy and slid downward toward the muck, the hideous muck that wasn't simply mud, but blood and other things human. Parts. Bits and pieces.

It had nearly swallowed him, that unspeakable mire.

Don't think about it, he told himself as Gordy dragged him up again.

But the horror was everywhere. There was no escaping it, all the long way to the tent. Then he spied the thing, the ghastly thing, worse than any sight in a shambles. No butcher dealt in parts like these.

He looked away, but not before he saw the arm, muddied and bloodied linen stuck to it, a bit of ruffle at the lifeless wrist.

The scene dissolved into haze. He became aware of voices. He couldn't understand it all, but he grasped enough.

"No," he said. "They're *wrong.* It's only a flesh wound. I refuse."

There was more murmuring, headshaking, voices growing sharp and impatient. They hadn't time to dig out bits of bone and metal and wood, the surgeons said. They couldn't be sure of getting it all. What they were sure of was infection, gangrene. The leg must come off or he'd die, slowly and horribly.

All Alistair could think of was the heap he'd seen, and someone tossing his leg onto it. After all those hours of hanging on, fighting fear and despair . . . was this what he'd been saved for? An impatient surgeon wielding a saw? Had he endured all those long hours only to be mutilated?

"They don't know," he gasped. "They know only one way. We must go away from here."

"Yes, yes, but please wake up."

He felt a hand on his shoulder. He brought his hand up,

and covered it. "Yes, steady," he said. "You need only steady me, and I'll do perfectly well."

"Of course you will. Only do wake up."

It was a woman's voice, an Englishwoman who spoke in the accents of his own class. The night voice.

Alistair opened his eyes. The world about him was so quiet, he could hear the faint crackle of the fire. The room was lit as before, and he had no trouble recognizing the woman leaning over him.

"That's better," she said. "Do you know me?"

"Of course." He smiled up at her. He'd been dreaming, that was all.

Relief was too small a word for what he felt. He'd been crawling through Hell for half eternity, it seemed, and come out on the other side. He didn't know where he was now. Not Heaven, he was sure, and glad of it, for he wasn't quite ready to give up the things of this earth—like the sight and scent of a pretty woman bending so near that he might easily reach up and bring his hand to the back of her neck, and draw her down. . . .

But this would be wrong, he remembered, and not only wrong but stupid beyond permission.

He suppressed a groan and squeezed the hand upon his shoulder. He had only to turn his head to kiss it . . . but he mustn't because that, too, was wrong, though he couldn't remember why.

"I must have fallen asleep," he said. "Bad dream."

"What is your name?" she said.

He gazed blankly at her.

"What is your name?" she repeated.

He gave an uneasy laugh. "Don't you know me, Miss Oldridge? Am I so changed?" He hadn't changed. He was the same man as before. Only a little deformed.

"I am supposed to ask you at intervals what your name is," she said, so crisp and businesslike. "I am to ask other simple questions as well. To determine whether your brain has been injured."

Her brisk tone swept away his anxiety and made him

want to tug her down and kiss her until she had not a sensible thought left in her head. But he mustn't because . . . Ah, yes. She was a gently bred maiden, and there were certain lines a gentleman didn't cross. Having sorted out that matter, his mind produced another rational thought: She shouldn't be here, so late at night, alone with him.

Reluctantly, he released the soft hand, pushed himself up on the pillows, and looked about the dimly lit room.

"Where is your father?" he said.

"I sent him to bed an hour ago. I couldn't sleep, and he is not the most reliable person to keep watch over a sickbed."

"I'm not sick," Alistair said. "I have a sprained ankle and possibly a concussion, that is all. It cannot be a severe concussion, as I have no trouble recollecting the fact that my name is Alistair Carsington, that Weston makes my coats, Hoby my boots—By the way, the pair you hacked to pieces came from Hoby only a fortnight ago. And Locke makes my hats. My waistcoats—"

"That will do," she said. "I am not greatly interested in the numerous parties involved in assembling you. I daresay it's as complicated as fitting out a ship, and of the same crucial importance to you as proper nautical accoutrements are to Captain Hughes. But it does not matter to me in the least."

"Does it not?" he said. "Perhaps my brain is more grievously injured than we thought, for I distinctly recollect your mentioning, more than once, my being elegantly turned out."

She straightened and took a step back from the bed. "It was an observation," she said curtly. "Nothing more."

What Alistair observed was that she must have pinned up her own hair, because it not only made no pretense at style but was falling in her face. A tangled clump of light copper curls dangled at her shoulder.

As to her clothes, either she'd slept in them or had thrown them on with more than her usual careless haste. Her frock was the one she'd worn earlier, but she was not wearing a corset. He could tell by the way the garment hung, especially by the way it outlined her bosom.

He *wished* she'd put on the corset. He wished he could be sure all her buttons were buttoned and all her tapes tied. But he knew she must be half undone, and he could not stop his mind from undoing the rest. He told himself not to think about her underthings and the naked body underneath, but he was a man, and it was too late. Minus the corset's artificial upthrust, the true shape and size of her breasts was easy to picture. He couldn't help estimating how few layers of underthings the wrinkled dress concealed: a chemise, perhaps, and very likely, nothing else.

He remembered how small her waist was and the sweet curve of her bottom and the bewitching sway of her hips.

He bore all this manfully.

But then he recalled the way her hand, soft and warm, fit under his, and a longing seized him, so fierce and wrenching that for a moment he couldn't breathe.

"You had better go back to bed," he said, his voice harsh. "You ought not have come here, especially in the middle of the night. It is shockingly improper."

"Indeed, it is," she said. "You have dropped hints leading me to suspect you are a rake—"

"A *rake?*" Alistair came up from the pillows, and the movement outraged his leg and ankle, both of which went into spasms. He winced, and hastily smoothed the bedclothes to make her think their rumpled state was what caused him pain. "I'm nothing of the kind," he muttered.

"But you spoke so casually to me of your expensive ballet dancer."

"One ballet dancer doesn't make a man a rake. If I were . . ." He trailed off. If he were a rake, he'd think nothing of coaxing her into bed with him. She had no idea what it cost a fellow to behave like a gentleman in these circumstances. He wished his father could see him now.

No, on second thought, it was better his lordship remained one hundred fifty miles away.

His oblivious seductress, meanwhile, was looking elsewhere, her brow creased. "Now I remember," she said. "My Aunt Clothilde writes me all the London gossip, and I am sure you figured in at least one of her epistles—before the battle in which you behaved so gallantly, I mean. Aunt tells me all the scandal about everybody, but it is hard to keep track of the names of people one's never met. Yet I'm certain yours came up. Now what was it?"

She settled into the chair beside the bed and appeared to cudgel her brains.

Alistair sighed. "Pray don't tax your memory," he said. "The scandals attached to my name are numerous."

Her gaze returned to his face, and she tipped her head to one side to study him.

He was not used to women, to anyone, studying him so openly. He was not used, he realized, to anyone's taking the trouble. No one else looked deeper, past the elegant appearance and charm. He wondered uneasily if anything of value existed beneath the polished surface.

"Do all the scandals involve women?" she said.

"Yes, of course. However—"

"Exactly how many scandals? Or are they too numerous to count in your present delicate state? Recollect you are not to tax your brain."

He recalled his father's list. "Seven—no, eight, technically."

"Technically." Her expression was unreadable.

"One scandal involved two women. But it was my last," he added. "And it was nearly three years ago."

"Then you are a reformed rake."

"To reform, I must first be a rake, which I never was. Not that it matters," he added irritably. "The difference between me and a libertine will seem a mere technicality to you. You will believe I am splitting hairs very fine, indeed. Not that you ought to be thinking about such subjects, or that I had any business speaking of my mistresses to a lady. I cannot imagine what possessed me to mention the ballet dancer. I must have been addled. Perhaps it is this infernally clean country air. I think it makes me giddy."

"Good heavens, I did not intend to make you so agitated," she said.

"I am not agitated," he lied. He was horny and frustrated. He was the next thing to naked, confined to bed, with a half-dressed woman within arm's reach—all this while the rest of the household was sound asleep. He would defy a saint to remain serene in such circumstances.

"Dr. Woodfrey believes you suffer from a fatigue of the nerves," she said.

"Nerves?" Alistair repeated indignantly. "I have no nerves to speak of. Ask anybody. I am the least excitable person you will ever meet." After a pause, he added, "I admit I find you somewhat provoking. But I think you do it on purpose—oh, not altogether. I suppose you can't help that." He made an impatient gesture indicating her hair and attire. "It is an affliction, like tone deafness." He waved her off. "Now please go away."

She smiled.

Oh, no.

The smile curled about his heart and squeezed it and threatened to strangle the remnants of his reason. "You're amused," he said accusingly. She didn't recognize the danger. She was in no way on guard. He would have to guard them both—and really, it was too much to ask, after such a day and night.

"I find *you* amusing," she said. "You are the most amusing man I have met in a very long time."

A soft bed . . . a warm woman, laughing in his arms. His pulse was racing.

His gaze swept the room and fell upon the botany book her father had left behind.

The soporific book.

"Well, if you can't tear yourself away, Miss Oldridge," he said, "perhaps you would be so good as to read to me."

Eight

CAPTAIN Hughes arrived at Mrs. Entwhistle's domicile late Sunday morning.

When the maid ushered him into the cozy parlor, the lady of the house evidenced no great delight at seeing him.

She appeared less pleased when he told her his errand.

"You cannot be proposing that I appear, uninvited, *on the Sabbath,* with my baggage, upon Mirabel's doorstep," the former governess said in tones that had seldom failed to quell rambunctious pupils.

The intimidating tone did not match the lady's appearance. She was not tall and gaunt and dressed in severe black, but a plump, attractive woman of middle height and middle age, prettily garbed in a ruffled white morning dress and lacy cap.

The neatly appointed parlor felt very small to the captain. True, he was accustomed to the crowded quarters of a ship. He was also accustomed, however, to being master of the vessel, having the windward side of the quarterdeck entirely to himself, should he choose to walk about and cogitate, and the freedom to climb aloft to the crow's nest if he wished, should he feel the need to clear his head.

Feeling overlarge and clumsy in Mrs. Entwhistle's neat parlor, he stood stiffly by the chimneypiece, whence he dared not move lest he knock something over. Since the look in her intelligent brown eyes did nothing to put him at ease, he was not his usual coolly commanding self.

"Dash it, Flo—I mean, Mrs. Entwhistle, you know it won't occur to her to invite you," he said. "She sent for Carsington's manservant last night because it was the practical thing to do. But she isn't accustomed to consider proprieties. The neighbors'll consider 'em, though. You know that as well as I do. All the Peak knows her father isn't a proper chaperon."

"You said Mr. Carsington is incapacitated."

"He has a sprained ankle and a bump on the head," said Captain Hughes. "If you think this would incapacitate an otherwise healthy young aristocrat, you're naive beyond permission. I trust I needn't explain to you what such fellows' morals are like."

"His morals don't signify," said Mrs. Entwhistle. "But perhaps you are implying that Mirabel is so weak-willed—or perhaps love-starved—as to forget her own? Pray sit down. You ought not make a lady crane her neck to look at you."

He sought the chair farthest from hers and perched uneasily on its edge. "You think I'm officious," he said. "A meddler."

"I am not certain what to think," she said. "Perhaps you are jealous."

For a moment he stared at her in plain disbelief. Then he let out a roar of laughter.

She did not so much as crack a smile.

"D'ye think so, truly?" he said. "Well, whether it's so or not, that don't change the facts, madam. The fact is, people gossip, and they like nothing better than cutting up others' reputations. Fond as most of the neighborhood is of Miss Oldridge, and understanding of her situation, they're too human to resist scandal. You know we've precious little scandal in Longledge, which means the smallest particle goes a long way."

"It is absurd to imagine Mirabel would commit an indiscretion," the lady said coldly.

The captain's patience deserted him. "I hope you won't be so fatuous as to tell me she's past it," he said. "A spinster Miss Oldridge may be, but she's far from a dried-up one. Besides which—not to mince matters—she's still young enough to breed. Which means she's by no means too old to be seduced—or suspected of it. That's good enough for the tongue waggers."

The lady glared at him.

Over the course of a not exactly smooth-sailing naval career, Captain Hughes had been glared at by admirals and boards of inquiry. While Mrs. Entwhistle's cross look got under his skin more than those of thick-headed naval authorities and politicians had ever done, he was a crusty old salt who could bear it for as long as she chose to inflict it.

"I shall write a letter, tactfully hinting at proprieties," the lady said at last. "If Mirabel chooses to invite me, I shall go. I cannot possibly invite myself."

"What nonsense!" said the captain. *"I'm* inviting you."

"Oldridge Hall isn't your house, though you seem to run tame in it," she said.

"What a stickler you've come to be!" he said. "Was that Entwhistle's influence? You used to be so jolly. So was Miss Oldridge, when you were there. You were exactly what the girl needed. I always said so. It was clear enough to me, being away so much. I could see the difference when I came home, the first time, after Mrs. Oldridge died."

Mrs. Entwhistle leapt up from her chair, ruffles fluttering. "I wish I saw a difference in you!" she cried. "You are as great a booby as ever. Mirabel is one and thirty years old. A handsome young man has practically fallen into her lap—and you fret about protecting her virtue. What about her *happiness?"*

For a moment the captain was so astonished, he forgot his manners. Belatedly, he rose, too. "I say, Flora—I mean, Mrs. Entwhistle—are you matchmaking?"

She lifted her dimpled chin. "I prefer to think of it as letting Nature take her course."

"In my experience, Nature ain't at all reliable," the captain said. "If she was, ships wouldn't need sails or rudders, would they?"

THE captain was right to fret about gossip, for Miss Oldridge had enemies.

Some twenty miles away, in the valley at the other end of Longledge Hill, Caleb Finch was busy this Sunday encouraging the villagers to imagine the worst about her.

He had come from Northumberland a few days earlier ostensibly because he suspected mismanagement of his master Lord Gordmor's coal mines. Caleb certainly was well qualified to judge, being a master of chicanery, connivery, double-dealing, and double-crossing. However, his real reason for returning was to make trouble for Miss Oldridge.

He had attended church partly to impress the locals with his piety and partly because it offered an opportunity to make mischief among the greatest number of people with the smallest amount of effort. His sober black suit hanging from his tall, lanky frame, his sparse, greying hair slicked back, he was clean and proper on the outside and convinced he was equally so on the inside.

By some mental sleight of hand, his lies, frauds, and subterfuges always had a moral rationale. Since Caleb was no intellectual giant, the rationale usually boiled down to a simple proposition. For instance: *This fellow has something I don't have, which can't be right, and so if I get it from him—it don't matter how—I've righted matters.*

Eleven years ago, Miss Oldridge had committed the hateful crime of making him stop righting matters for himself with her father's wealth. She had dismissed him with-

out a reference, saying he was incompetent. After that, no
one for miles around Longledge would employ him. He'd
had to seek work elsewhere.

A wiser man would have counted his blessings. She
might have had him charged with a long list of property
crimes. She might have let him figure out how to account
to a magistrate for improperly kept books and the mysterious disappearance of large quantities of livestock, produce, timber, and numerous other articles. Instead, she had
given him the benefit of the doubt.

But Caleb wasn't grateful. He didn't take the opportunity to turn over a new leaf. It was easier to nurse the
grudge for ten years and more and jump at any opportunity
to make unpleasantness for her.

For instance, he was delighted with his master's plans
for a canal, because it would go through the Oldridge property and be a constant misery to Miss Oldridge.

And so, after church, when he heard of Mr. Carsington's accident, Caleb was not slow to cast Miss Oldridge in
the worst possible light. He donned a pious look and said
he *hoped* it was an accident. When asked what he meant,
Caleb was only too happy to explain. He meant, he said,
that some people might ask what was they doing up that
high on the hill on a day like that? The London gentleman
probably didn't know no better. But what was the lady
thinking, taking him all the way up there? And where was
her groom all this time? Why weren't he with 'em?

Within minutes, these and similar remarks had traveled
through the congregation, where they met with incredulity
and dismissals for the most part, e.g., "Where does that
man get his ideas?" Or, "I do believe every word of par-
son's sermon went in one a them big ears of his and
straight out the other."

But here and there were like-minded individuals who
loved nothing better than tearing others down, especially
others prettier or wealthier or better-natured than they.
These persons were happy to imagine the worst.

They took up Caleb's version of What Really Happened, and embroidered on it, and passed it on to every other small-minded individual they knew.

By Sunday afternoon, it had traveled the full length of Longledge Hill to the parish in which Miss Oldridge resided.

CAPTAIN Hughes delivered Mrs. Entwhistle early in the afternoon.

By this time, Crewe, who'd arrived at daybreak, had put away the belongings deemed necessary for a few days' stay.

According to Captain Hughes, who paid the patient a brief visit, these essentials were "sufficient to equip a seventy-four and every man-jack upon it."

Yet he admitted to the ladies that the valet had everything stowed neatly enough, and Mr. Carsington appeared more at ease than before.

Certainly when Mirabel entered the room sometime later, her houseguest appeared more elegant. Nothing the captain had said prepared her, though, for the full effect of Mr. Carsington's appearance.

Her houseguest lounged in a cushioned armchair before the fire. He wore a fine silk dressing gown over a shirt of feather-light lawn, complete with elaborately arranged neckcloth. A pair of wide trousers hung loosely over the long legs. Upon his feet—his naked feet—were Turkish slippers.

She told herself it was wise not to attempt stockings. While his ankle was not badly swollen, it must be tender. She told herself to note how the injured foot was wrapped and propped up exactly as the doctor had ordered.

But she couldn't focus. Though her guest was more fully dressed than when she'd last seen him—last night, when she should *not* have been here—he was a great deal more exposed.

Under the bedclothes, those long legs had been mere shapes. Now they stretched out shamelessly before her.

The soft cloth of his trousers clung to their contours, reminding her of the rock-hard muscle she'd felt when she'd examined him for injuries. Then she'd been too anxious, too busy suppressing panic to feel anything else. Now . . .

She looked away, scanning the room as though making sure all was in order.

It wasn't, not in any order she recognized. The very atmosphere had changed.

Starched white linen and dark wool and leather . . . masculine toiletries crowding the dressing table . . . a shaving box . . . the scents of palm soap and boot polish . . . and him.

The room was *male,* and he dominated it.

She felt his gaze upon her and gathered her composure. "You seem more comfortable, Mr. Carsington," she said. "I am glad of it."

"I told you I was an expert at lounging about," he said.

He was far beyond expert. He made his very surroundings seem languid, sultry, and . . . sinful.

Which was absurd. Her imagination was running away with her. Mirabel told herself to be sensible and directed her attention to the tray her servant carried. Dr. Woodfrey had ordered light meals, several times a day, and she had accompanied the latest one.

She watched Crewe relieve her servant of the tray and set the dishes out upon the small table.

When all was arranged to his satisfaction, the valet drew up a chair for her. She sat, wishing she felt as much in command of herself as her guest seemed to be.

Crewe discreetly withdrew to a far corner of the large room.

"You look like an Eastern potentate," she told Mr. Carsington.

"I am not partial to these trousers," he said. "They are rather faddish, and I can't recollect what possessed me to buy them. But Crewe would not let me wear breeches or pantaloons because they are made to fit snugly. He feared my ankle would be jostled when I put them on."

She remembered, too vividly, the long, muscled legs thrust out from under bedclothes. Her mouth went dry. She folded her hands tightly in her lap. "Crewe is most sensible," she said.

"Regrettably, I am not allowed stockings, either, for the same reason, and I am sure it isn't proper for you to see my bare ankles, Miss Oldridge."

She'd seen a great deal too much for her peace of mind: the way his shirt had fallen open during his momentary delirium, and the hard, muscled chest glinting gold.

She said lightly, "What a fuss everyone makes about proprieties. But put your mind at rest. My former governess has arrived to protect my reputation, and so you needn't fear that the sight of a bit of your bare skin will corrupt my morals."

"I envy your mastery of your feelings," he said softly. "I doubt I could gaze unmoved at *your* naked ankles."

Heat spilled outward from somewhere in the center of herself and washed over every inch of her skin.

A cough came from the other end of the room. Mr. Carsington looked impatiently at his valet. "What is it now, Crewe?"

"I merely wished to observe, sir, that the cook went to great trouble to tempt your appetite, and certain delicacies do not improve with the passage of time."

By the time her guest's attention reverted to her, Mirabel had her mind back in working order. He was teasing, she told herself. For Society beaux, such gallantries were a habit. Flirtation and innuendo were merely a part of conversation. They even whispered naughty remarks in the ears of elderly ladies.

It was absurd to imagine that a pair of thirty-one-year-old ankles, bare or otherwise, could stir any strong emotion in him.

"Will you not join me?" he said. "Your cook seems to have provided enough for a regiment."

"She's accustomed to Papa's appetite, which is prodigious," Mirabel said. "Still, this is not an excessive meal for a man of your size, and I am not at all hungry. But perhaps you would prefer to dine in private."

She had better leave. She had come only to look in on him. She would gain nothing by lingering. She had softened toward him too much already. If she did not have a care, she would become infatuated—absurd at her age, and dangerous to more than her virtue.

She rose.

"I vastly prefer your company," he said.

Mirabel sat down again.

TO Alistair's annoyance, as soon as he'd finished eating, Miss Oldridge once more rose to depart.

"Mrs. Entwhistle will wonder what's become of me," she said. "I told her I would look in on you briefly."

"To admire my quiet fortitude?" he said.

"Yes, and to make sure you didn't feel abandoned," she said. "I hope you don't think that is the case. You would be overrun with visitors had Dr. Woodfrey not forbidden it. But he says you are not to tax yourself in any way."

"All I have done is sit here and eat and talk," Alistair said.

"That isn't all," she said. "You have exerted yourself to be witty and charming. It is pleasant for me but not good for you."

"I was not exerting myself," he said. "Wit and charm come naturally to me."

"Then perhaps it isn't good for *me*," she said, and quickly added, "While I sit here being charmed and amused, a dozen important tasks are left undone."

He slumped in his chair. "I am crushed. There is something in your life more important than I. Well, then, I must bear it and find some trivial tasks I shall pretend are more important than you. Crewe, bring me pen and paper. I shall write some letters."

"Certainly not," she said. "You are not to tax your brain."

"I must let Lord Gordmor know I am temporarily laid up. He will be expecting to hear from me, anyway."

"I sent an express letter to him this morning," she said. "And another to your parents."

"To my parents?" Alistair started up from the chair, and his leg and ankle brutally reminded him to stay put. He sank back down, gripping the chair arms. "Who told you to write to my parents?"

"My conscience," she said. "Your friends and family are bound to hear of your accident before long. I did not want them to be troubled with the usual garbled and exaggerated version of events. You will not believe the rumors flying already."

Alistair had enough experience with rumors to know that they generally defied all laws of reason and oftentimes far outstripped his wildest imaginings.

Now, too late, he saw the fatal errors he'd made. He'd paid too much attention to her. He'd singled her out at the Tolberts' party. He'd gone riding with her, accompanied only by a groom. He'd spent the better part of the night with her, unchaperoned, in his *bedroom*. It wasn't hard to guess what people would think.

"It is believed in some quarters that I deliberately lured you to a dangerous spot and attempted to cause a fatal accident," she said.

Once again Alistair experienced the sensation of being struck from behind with a large club. "You *what?*"

"Pushed you into the brook," she said.

"But that's absurd. Why would you try to kill me?"

"The canal."

For a moment, Alistair didn't know what she was talking about. In the next, he was cursing himself.

He'd forgotten that to her he was an invader, a despoiler, the minion of a villainous viscount.

He'd forgotten, in fact, to *think*—except with his reproductive organs.

He'd been celibate too long, that was the trouble. He'd

avoided women until his leg was healed and working, more or less. Since then . . .

Well, he wasn't sure what had held him back. He'd been numb or not fully awake in some way. But wasn't it typical that after nearly three years of apathy toward the fair sex, he should choose now, of all times, to wake up from the coma or whatever it had been?

Wasn't it typical that he should choose her—an unmarried lady—when the world abounded in merry widows and straying matrons and out-and-out harlots?

Instead of concentrating on business, he'd wallowed in fantasies that every gentlemanly principle forbade his acting upon.

Perhaps his brain really was damaged.

All this went rapidly through the remnants of what used to be his mind while he mustered a faint smile and said, "Murder. Over a canal. The folk hereabouts must be desperate indeed for excitement."

He looked toward his valet. "Crewe, have you heard anything of this?"

The manservant's gaze darted from one to the other.

"Don't mind me," Miss Oldridge said. "You've heard about it belowstairs, naturally."

"The matter was mentioned, miss, in my presence," he said. "The staff were as one in their indignation. They said you would never behave in so dastardly a manner."

"Certainly not," Alistair said with a dismissive wave of his hand. "Who in his right mind could believe Miss Oldridge capable of devious behavior?"

Crewe gave one of his expressive little coughs.

"What is it, Crewe?" Alistair said. "Have you something to add?"

"Ahem. No, sir."

"I believe, were Crewe less discreet, he would tell you my staff are certain I would never do anything I might be hanged for," Miss Oldridge said. "This is true. I have always believed that anyone who must violate the law to achieve his purposes must lack either intelligence or imagination, probably both."

"Those are words to make a man's blood run cold," Alistair said. In fact, what he saw in her blue eyes made him uneasy. "I begin to suspect, Miss Oldridge, that the world would be a safer place were you lacking in both articles."

"I hope I am not lacking," she said. "I should never stand a chance against you otherwise. While my conscience is clear on the score of your accident, I admit it was fortuitous. But I detect heavy weather bearing down upon me, which means I've upset you—and I did promise Dr. Woodfrey that we would keep you calm and rested."

She gave him a quick smile, and Alistair, numskull that he was, felt cheated. He wanted more: the dancing light in her eyes, the whispery laughter.

And when he watched her depart, red-gold curls springing loose from their pins, hem dragging to one side, and hips swaying, he was not thinking about ways to succeed with the canal, upon which so much depended, but about the speediest means of luring her back.

He forgot altogether to wonder exactly what she meant by "fortuitous."

MIRABEL decided she'd better not visit the patient again until the following day, when she'd had time to recover her common sense—and she must not forget to take Mrs. Entwhistle with her.

Mr. Carsington was not left solitary, however.

Her father went upstairs after dinner and stayed with their guest for a good while. When he returned to the library, he informed Mirabel and Mrs. Entwhistle that Mr. Carsington had fallen asleep while being enlightened regarding the differences between Linnaeus's and Jussieu's systems of botanical classification.

"He was vastly interested to learn that the one is founded on the sexes of plants, while the other takes into account the natural affinities," Papa informed them. "Mr.

Carsington made a witty remark regarding natural affinities, which I cannot recollect at the moment. He also drew an analogy . . ." Papa trailed off, his brows knitting. "I meant to mention the date palms. He has a cousin, a lady of unusual linguistic talents, who is trying to decipher the Rosetta stone, and this put me in mind of the Egyptian date palms. But he made me laugh, and I forgot, and then we spoke of something else, and by degrees, he fell asleep. Yet I do not think it is sufficiently restful. I do not like to tell Dr. Woodfrey his business, but I am surprised he did not prescribe a dose of laudanum."

"I believe laudanum is not advised in cases of suspected concussion," said Mrs. Entwhistle.

"It was only recently that Brown brought Jussieu into favor in England," said Papa. "We were sadly isolated in our thinking. One must go abroad, you see, and seek other opinions. Captain Hughes, for instance."

"What about Captain Hughes?" Mirabel said. "I cannot follow you at all, Papa."

He gazed not at Mirabel but through her, with the faraway look she knew all too well. "The juices extracted from the seed pod of the poppy possess remarkable curative powers," he said. "These properties have been remarked upon time and again, going back to Hippocrates himself. The Egyptians knew it as well, I am certain. Once they succeed in unlocking those secrets—and they are bound to, one of these days—what a vast store of knowledge will be opened up! I should like to meet his cousin."

Mirabel looked blankly at Mrs. Entwhistle, who responded with a similarly uncomprehending expression.

Mirabel regarded her father. With a shake of his head, he came out of his musings. He walked to a bookshelf and plucked out a large volume.

"Papa?"

"Yes, my dear?"

"Papa, you mentioned Captain Hughes a moment ago," Mirabel said.

"Yes." Her father started toward the door.

"Did you mention him to any particular purpose?"

"Oh, yes. Concussions. Perhaps he, too, thinks this does not fully explain. He would know better than I."

Mirabel's parent departed, leaving those behind mystified, as usual.

THE letters from Oldridge Hall, written by Miss Oldridge and signed by her father, reached their London destinations after midnight.

The arrival of express letters at odd hours was a common enough occurrence in Lord Hargate's household. Though not a member of the ministry, he was active behind the scenes and sent and received nearly as many urgent messages as did Lord Liverpool, First Lord of the Treasury.

Consequently, the letter aroused no panic at Hargate House. Having passed the usual quiet Sunday, the earl and his lady were at home, in the latter's boudoir. They were enjoying a lively dispute about their eldest offspring's domestic affairs when the servant brought them the letter.

Upon seeing where it had come from, Lord Hargate merely raised his eyebrows and passed the missive to his wife to read, which she did, aloud.

When she had done, his lordship shrugged and refilled his wine goblet. "Only a sprained ankle. Confined to Oldridge Hall. It might have been worse."

"I rather think," said her ladyship, "it could not be better."

THE missive from Oldridge Hall awakened far more consternation in Lord Gordmor's breast, thanks to his sister.

Lady Wallantree had elected to spend a dull Sunday evening with her convalescing brother who, even when ill, was less tedious company than her husband. She was about to order her carriage brought round for the return home when the servant entered the parlor with the letter.

Express letters being very expensive, they were not frequently used outside military or political circles and seldom carried glad tidings. As a result, in less exalted households than those of prime ministers and Earls of Hargate, they tended to stir excitement, if not alarm.

Lady Wallantree had no intention of dying of curiosity. By now her family was asleep. Only a few servants would be sitting up waiting for her. She saw no reason to inconvenience herself for the sake of mere servants.

She no more valued her brother's privacy than she did her servants' or family's comfort. After giving him two seconds to read the letter, she snatched it from him.

He sank back onto his chaise longue with a sigh and wondered why, of the two people in the world for whom the influenza held no terrors, one must be one hundred fifty miles away in Derbyshire and the other must be his sister.

"Perhaps you will be so good as to acquaint me with its contents when it is convenient, Henrietta," Lord Gordmor said.

She read it aloud to him.

He was still trying to digest the news and decide how he felt about it, when she said, "I am very glad Carsington is not seriously injured, but I could wish for your sake he had ended in any other house but Oldridge Hall. Though Oldridge has signed it, the letter is in a woman's hand."

"I wouldn't know, scarcely having a glimpse before it was torn—"

"I have a strong suspicion the woman is Oldridge's daughter," his sister continued. "The one who jilted William Poynton and led him to make such a fool of himself." She pursed her lips and considered. "But that was before your time. You were still at school. She must be past thirty now, and those kinds of looks fade quickly. Not that she was a great beauty twelve years ago. She would never have taken at all—that apricot-colored hair and such singular manners, my dear. But who could overlook the fortune? That was why half the peerage threw their sons at her. Yes, Douglas, I know you will say your friend's taste is impeccable, and he is incorruptible as well, like the rest of the family. But keep in mind that, even if Oldridge remarries—"

"Henrietta, what are you saying?" Lord Gordmor broke in crossly. "A few simple points, if you please, in a logical order. Recollect I have been ill, and my head is not strong."

She gave him back the letter. "In plain terms, then: As soon as you are strong enough to travel, you must go to Derbyshire. I do not wish to alarm you, and I hope I am wrong, but I strongly suspect that both your friend Mr. Carsington and your canal are in very great danger."

Nine

MIRABEL woke at two o'clock in the morning—the same time she'd awoken yesterday—and couldn't get back to sleep. She lit a candle, flung on a dressing gown and slippers, and paced her bedroom for a while. This accomplished nothing.

At last she took up the candle, left her bedroom, and padded along to the guest wing.

The door to Mr. Carsington's chamber was left ajar in case Crewe needed to summon help quickly. In a chair by the door a footman slumped, snoring steadily.

Mirabel crept past him into the bedroom, where a single candle burned.

Crewe rose as she entered. She set her candle on the mantel of the fireplace. The valet approached her.

"He's all right, miss," he murmured.

"You're not," she said in the same low tones.

Though the light was dim and wavering, she easily discerned the worry and weariness etched in the loyal servant's countenance. She wondered how many nights, after Waterloo, he had kept watch over his master.

"I'm sure you've been worried to death about him," she said. "I'll wager you haven't had a moment's rest since getting word of the accident."

Crewe denied feeling any fatigue or undue worry.

"You will be of little help to Mr. Carsington if you get no sleep this night," she said. "An hour or two's rest will do you good. I'll keep watch in the meantime."

The valet protested. Mirabel's very sensible arguments—about his needing rest to be of full use to his master, and his being within easy call should any difficulties arise—fell on deaf ears. But when she gave her word of honor not to kill his master in his sleep, Crewe looked very shocked, stammered an apology—he never meant to imply any such thing and never dreamt it, for a minute—and meekly took himself into the adjoining room.

He left the connecting door open.

Mirabel settled into the chair by the bed and studied Crewe's master.

During her discussion with his manservant, Mr. Carsington had got himself turned about. He now lay partly on his stomach, and the shape of the bedclothes outlining his body told her his injured foot had slipped from its pillow. She debated whether to waken the footman to help her turn the patient onto his back again. Before she could decide, she found herself recalling her father's remarks about laudanum, Egyptians, and Captain Hughes.

What had led Papa to that sequence of thoughts?

He said Mr. Carsington's sleep was not restful.

Mirabel rose and came nearer to the bed to study his face. It seemed peaceful enough, and strangely youthful, with his tousled hair falling over his brow. She could see the boy he must have been. He snored softly, rather like a lion purring, but it was uneven.

She linked her hands behind her back because she was dreadfully tempted to smooth his hair back from his face, as though he were that young boy, as though the gesture would be enough to soothe him.

The soft snoring stopped, and he shuddered.

Mirabel's hands would not remain sensibly behind her back. She reached out and lightly brushed his hair back. She stroked his cheek.

He stirred and began to mumble. At first it was only incomprehensible strings of sounds. Then came a hoarse whisper: "Zorah. We must find her."

More muttering. By degrees, Mirabel began to distinguish phrases here and there. Something about being sick. Something about butchers.

He began to toss and turn. "Get away . . . no . . . can't look at it . . . vultures . . . I knew him . . . No, don't talk. Never say. Didn't see. Make a joke. Ha. Ha. Attached to it. Getting on so well together. Gordy, find her. Flesh wound. Zorah. She said. Get me away. *Don't let them.*"

His voice scarcely rose above a murmur, but he was flailing about. She must stop him, or he'd tumble out of bed or otherwise harm himself.

She touched his shoulder. "Mr. Carsington," she said gently, "please wake up."

He jerked away and kicked at the bedclothes. "Can't breathe. Get them off. Sick. Sick. God help us." He threw himself toward the edge of the bed.

Mirabel flung herself across his chest.

He shuddered briefly, then stilled.

Mirabel waited, uncertain what to do. Had she truly calmed him, turned his sleeping mind elsewhere, or was it only a pause? Should she let him sleep or wake him? If he slept, he might return to the nightmare.

She listened to his breathing. Not slow. Not like peaceful sleep. She remembered what her father had said, how sure he'd been that Mr. Carsington had suffered a head injury at Waterloo. She recalled what she'd read of his actions in battle, and of what he'd endured afterward. He'd been believed dead and might have died in fact, if his friend Lord Gordmor hadn't scoured the battlefield for him, through the night, among acres of corpses. Was this what the famous hero dreamt of?

He didn't want to talk about the battle or hear about it. Perhaps in his place, she would feel the same. He could not wish to be reminded of what must have been the most horrendous experience of his life.

Everyone said it was a miracle he'd survived until he was found, many hours after the battle. It must have taken unimaginable courage and a will of iron. Not to mention a remarkably strong and resilient body.

It was this thought that brought her back to the present, to where she was, lying across the famously indestructible body.

His chest rose and fell under her, but now she became aware of more than its unsteady rise and fall.

He'd pushed away the bedclothes. His nightshirt had fallen open. She hadn't thought about his state of undress. She'd simply acted to quiet him. Now she was conscious of the faint friction of her nightgown against his shirt, of the place where the flannel of her gown brushed his bare skin, of the edge of the shirt opening touching her cheek. Her breasts were crushed against his chest, and she was acutely aware now of the hardness and warmth under her, of the hurried, irregular rise and fall, a countertempo to the quickened, unsteady beat of her heart.

She felt again, as though it were happening now, his hands circling her waist and saw once more the intent golden gaze, the lurking smile.

If only . . .

She took a deep breath, and let it out, and told herself to get up. Cautiously, she lifted her head and looked at him . . . and found him looking back at her.

His eyes were open and dark but for the faint gleam of reflected candlelight.

Mirabel swallowed. "Bad dream," she said.

"You had a bad dream?" His voice was a sleepy rumble. He smiled lazily, and his hands slid up to her hips.

His hands were so very warm, and as they stole up farther, her mind slowed.

She wanted to stop thinking entirely and let those long hands slide over her. She wanted to touch her lips to that sleepy smile. . . .

Seduction, a voice called to her from far, far away.

It was the faint voice of her rapidly disappearing intellect. She didn't want to call it back, but she'd had years of practice in overcoming such inclinations, in doing what had to be done, like it or not.

Swallowing a sigh, she wriggled away from the insidious hands, slid off the bed, and stood back out of reach. As though she were in any real danger. As though he would, if wide awake instead of half asleep and thinking of someone else—by name of Zorah, perhaps—reach for her.

"*You* had a bad dream," she said.

"And you were comforting me," he said.

She clenched her hands. "I tried to keep you from throwing yourself on the floor. You were thrashing about. I should have called for help, but it was quickest to—to—"

"Jump on me." His mouth quivered.

Mirabel's face burned, and she reacted instinctively, attacking from an unexpected quarter, as she'd learnt to do when cornered and made to defend herself. "Who is Zorah?"

His amusement vanished, and the atmosphere instantly thickened.

She knew she wasn't to upset him, but she was too angry with circumstance, with fate, to behave sensibly. "You spoke her name more than once," she persisted. "You wanted to find her. I take it she's important."

He raised himself up on the pillows. Though he did so without wincing, Mirabel knew it hurt. She could tell by the way his features hardened. She cursed her bad temper and self-pity and wayward tongue.

"Never mind," she said. "It is none of my business. I panicked. And behaved stupidly. I should have let Crewe stay. He would have known what to do."

Mr. Carsington looked about the dimly lit room. "Where is he?"

"I sent him to bed," Mirabel said. "He looked so tired and worried."

"Do you never sleep, Miss Oldridge?"

"No, I always prowl about the house in the dead of night, looking for unsuspecting gentlemen to leap upon." She realized her dressing gown was falling open. Not that there was anything to see. Her sensible flannel nightgown left everything to the imagination.

Nonetheless, she drew the dressing gown closed and began tying the ribbons. "Not that we ever had any unsuspecting gentlemen here before," she went on into the pulsing silence. "But if we had, I should have leapt upon them, too. So you are not to think there is anything out of the way about my behavior."

"You are tying those ribbons into knots," he said.

She looked down at her too-busy fingers. "Yes, well, I could be calmer, I daresay."

"I'm sorry I gave you a fright," he said.

"Fright," she repeated, still gazing at her hands as though she didn't know what they were. "Yes." She felt a wild urge to laugh and another to sob and another to fly from the room. She sat down heavily in the chair by the bed and buried her face in her hands. "Give me a moment," she mumbled. To her dismay, tears welled. What was wrong with her? She never cried. Was she hysterical?

"You have enough to worry about without worrying about me," he said. "It's a wonder you don't collapse from the weight of your responsibilities. I am sorry to add to it."

"Oh, you are nothing." She waved a hand to dismiss the notion but did not trust herself enough to lift her head.

"Don't be ridiculous. I am the Earl of Hargate's son, and a famous dratted hero besides, and now you are saddled with my care. If I should accidentally do myself a fatal injury, you will be blamed for not taking proper care of me—or even for hastening my demise, perhaps. Small wonder you can't sleep. I shouldn't care to be in your shoes—er—slippers, for the world."

Mirabel looked up then and found him regarding her with a troubled expression.

"Not that I have any idea what it's like," he added. "I've never had to be responsible for anybody. Nothing—nobody—has ever depended on me. It makes one feel rather pointless. Well, not altogether. Certain people rely upon me to set an example in the way of neckcloth arrangements."

She smiled in spite of herself. "Oh, more than that, I'll warrant," she said. "Your waistcoats are paragons, beautiful without being showy. You have the knack for not overdoing, which is exceedingly rare among dandies. Beau Brummell was one of the few who possessed it. So great a gift is also a great responsibility."

"Yes, well, there you have it. My great responsibility is to look beautiful."

And he carried it out to perfection, Mirabel thought. Even now, with his hair tousled and night shirt rumpled, he seemed a work of art to her. It took enormous will to keep her eyes from straying lower than his bared neck, to the crooked V of the shirt opening.

She told herself not to think about it, either: the hard muscle of his upper torso, and how soft and fragile she'd felt . . . how she'd longed to touch him . . . how she'd relished the feel of his long hands curling over her hips, sliding upward. . . .

She turned away and stared hard in the direction of the fire, which had dwindled to glowing embers.

"You asked about Zorah." His voice had dropped so low it seemed to vibrate inside her.

"It doesn't matter," Mirabel said. "It's none of my business. She's one of the seven or eight, I suppose."

"No, a camp follower," he said, frowning. "She was at Waterloo. When they found me. I . . ." He paused. "I couldn't remember."

•　•　•

ALISTAIR had never said it aloud before, in plain words, and almost wished he hadn't now. But it was very late, and the household was asleep, and he seemed to be still half-dreaming.

He'd come out of a nightmare to a warm armful of woman. He'd come to consciousness inhaling her scent while her hair tickled his cheek.

In the next moment he was being swept this way and that in emotional crosscurrents.

She was, he'd recollected, the wrong woman—the one he mustn't have—and he wondered if this was some hellish trial he must endure to pay for his youthful misdeeds.

And then, watching her struggle not to weep—with exhaustion, no doubt—he'd remembered he was a trial to her, one more burden in an already overburdened life.

He could not pretend, not to her.

"I don't—didn't—remember," he repeated. "It's driven me wild. It was not even three years ago. A battle, perhaps the most famous since Trafalgar—I was there—and I can't—couldn't—remember."

"Good heavens," she said, "that is the last thing on earth I would have . . ." She frowned. "Amnesia. So that is what Papa—" She broke off and looked up at him. "You were very much knocked about. It is perfectly understandable. And then, yesterday, when you fell into the Briar Brook—"

"On my head," he said wryly.

"It must have jarred the memories loose."

"It's still only bits and pieces," he said. "The battle itself remains hazy—an infernal din amid clouds of smoke. Perhaps that's how it was. Every so often the smoke clears, and I have a moment of clarity. But not the important moments, the times when . . ." He hesitated. "The heroic feats you read about. I still can't remember those. Only the aftermath, when the din has stopped and the smoke has cleared and the quiet seems unearthly. I come to, and it's dark. I'm pinned down. And there's a smell, indescribably vile."

Alistair paused and shut his eyes. She didn't need to hear about this. What was the matter with him?

He'd said far too much and was on the brink of revealing more: about the dream that had felt so real, true, familiar. Those endless hours spent trapped under a corpse, in the muck, suffocating in that stench.

"So many hurt," she said softly. "So many dead. Two soldiers died on top of you. There were wounded and dead everywhere. I've sat by deathbeds, but I cannot imagine what a battlefield must be like."

A charnel house. A hellish mire. He'd thought they would never find him, that they'd already given up on him. He didn't know how long he'd lain there. It seemed like years passed while he was sinking into the ooze, rotting to death by slow degrees.

"Don't try to imagine it," he said.

She met his gaze. "To us at home, war is made out to be grand and glorious. But I don't see how it could be anything but filthy and horrible beyond imagining." He heard her breath catch as she added, "And heartbreaking."

Someone dear to her must have died there, he thought. That would help explain why she buried herself in this out-of-the-way place.

"You lost a loved one?" he said. "At Waterloo?"

"A loved one?" She shook her head. "It is the end of so many young lives that makes me sick at heart."

He decided not to probe further. "Lives lost, yes—that's the hard price," he said. "But there's honor in fighting and dying that way. It is a great chance for a man to do something truly worthwhile. And a battle is glorious, in a way. Especially such a battle, against a monster like Napoleon. It is the nearest one can come to being like the knights in legend, slaying dragons and ogres and evil magicians."

As soon as he said it, he regretted it. He sounded like a boy prating of fairy tales.

Miss Oldridge was looking at him, her expression impossible to read.

He'd revealed far too much. He searched for some

witty, ironic remark, but before his sluggish brain could respond, she spoke.

"You are so complicated," she said. "No sooner do I believe I've sorted you out than you do or say something to overthrow my neat theories."

"You have theories about me?" he said lightly, snatching at the chance to redirect the conversation. "Can it be, Miss Oldridge, that there is time in your busy, responsible life for thoughts of me?"

"I make the time," she said, "much as the Duke of Wellington made time to think about Napoleon."

It was a douse of cold water, and Alistair told himself he needed it and ought to be grateful to her for stopping him before he opened his heart to her.

He was her enemy, because of Gordy's canal. She did not forget it. He should not, either.

He should remember what he'd come here for.

He should never forget that not only his best friend's but his brothers' future depended on it, and it was his last chance to redeem himself in his father's eyes.

"I haven't come to conquer the Peak and make its inhabitants my subjects," he said. "I am not your enemy. Furthermore, I must tell you that on any number of grounds I must take issue with your comparing me to Bonaparte. Have you any idea what the man wore to his coronation? A toga!"

She smiled and shook her head. "It would be so much easier if you were more monsterlike. I wish you could contrive to be more disagreeable, or boring, at least."

He wanted to ask how unmonsterlike, how undisagreeable she found him. He wanted to know how he could make it harder for her to hate him. But he'd already said too much, felt too much. He'd already gone farther than was sensible in the circumstances, the curst circumstances.

If only . . .

No. None of those worthless *if onlys*.

"Given a choice, I'd rather be thought loathsome," he said. "I can think of few worse fates than being deemed boring. An incorrectly starched neckcloth, perhaps. Hessians worn with breeches. Waistcoat buttons left undone with a plain shirt." He shuddered theatrically.

She laughed softly and rose. "How can I hate a man who does not take himself seriously?"

She did not hate him.

His heart gave a thump of relief, but he played his part. With a shocked look he said, "Miss Oldridge, I assure you I could not be more serious, especially about the matter of wearing one's upper waistcoat buttons undone with a plain shirt—or wearing them fully buttoned with a frilled one."

. . . unless she was the one who did the unbuttoning, he could have added. Then he wouldn't care what kind of shirt he wore.

He remembered the hurried thudding of her heart against his chest, and his own heart banging against his ribs.

He remembered the sweet curve of her hips under his hands.

He remembered the warm fragrance of her skin.

No, he must forget these things. Otherwise, he would make more mistakes, do something irreparably stupid.

Remember Gordy instead, he told himself. *Remember the man who refused to believe, as everyone else did, that you were dead, the man who, near dead himself with fatigue, searched the filthy, reeking battlefield for you.*

He told himself to remember his younger brothers, who would be robbed to support their feckless brother.

He told himself to remember their sire, whose third son had disappointed him time and time again.

He came out of these unhappy reflections to find his tormentor anxiously searching his countenance. He wondered how long he'd been silent, fighting with himself.

She rose and said, "I have kept you up talking too long. If you are ill tomorrow, it will be my fault, and Crewe will never trust me again. I solemnly promised not to do you any harm."

"You did me no harm," Alistair said. "The opposite,

rather. I'm grateful to be rescued from that dream." He could not resist adding, "Thank you for jumping on me."

"Pray don't mention it," she said, heading for the door. "The pleasure was mine, Mr. Carsington."

ONLY a few ill-natured persons believed Mirabel would go so far as to push Lord Hargate's son into the Briar Brook. This did not mean the rest were not exchanging other theories, very like the sort of damaging gossip Captain Hughes had predicted.

The vicar's wife, Mrs. Dunnet, who was partial to Mirabel, paid a call on Monday. In the drawing room, over tea and cakes, she tactfully made Mirabel and Mrs. Entwhistle aware of the local mood, as ascertained from conversations heard after church the previous day and in the course of this morning's calls.

"I am sure Mr. Dunnet has preached more than once about idle rumors and bearing false witness," the vicar's wife said. "The trouble is, most of his listeners assume his words apply to everyone else but them."

"I daresay most of the talk reflects discontent and vexation rather than true malice," said Mrs. Entwhistle. "And we mustn't forget Caleb Finch's friends. They've never forgiven Mirabel for dismissing him."

At the mention of her former bailiff, Mirabel got up from her chair and walked to the French doors. The day was overcast. That was like Caleb Finch, she thought. She had not seen him in years, yet he hung over her world and darkened it.

She had only herself to blame.

She should have brought charges against him; she knew that now. But at the time she'd been scarcely twenty years old, unsure of her evidence, unsure of herself, and sadly naive about business.

As well, William had arrived in the midst of it, and she'd been trying to make him understand why the wedding must be put off, why she couldn't go away with him, not then, while the estate was falling to pieces.

"My dear."

Mirabel turned at the sound of her governess's voice and mustered a smile. "How I should like to forget Caleb Finch. Is he back again?"

How she wished she'd had the courage years ago to bring him before the law. He might have been transported—along with some of the friends who'd connived with him to take advantage of her father.

"He is not in Longledge," said Mrs. Entwhistle.

"He could hardly wish to show his face here," said Mrs. Dunnet. "I have not heard him mentioned this age. Even his friends don't speak openly of him."

"Caleb Finch's allies are a minor irritation," Mrs. Entwhistle said. "My great concern is the respectable people of Longledge. If we do not soon quiet them, your reputation will be in tatters."

Mirabel wished she didn't need to worry about her reputation and the effect of rumors on it. But she couldn't afford any smirch on her character. She would lose all the influence she had worked so hard to win. No one would pay any attention to her objections to the canal.

"I am not at all sure how one goes about stopping such talk," she said. "Denial only makes matters worse."

"One needs to understand the causes," said Mrs. Entwhistle. "I believe we may blame envy."

"Envy?" Mirabel returned to her chair. Mrs. Entwhistle had a remarkable grasp of human nature.

"You have a celebrated person under your roof," that lady explained. "But at present, your neighbors are forbidden to visit him. Everyone, naturally, wants to be made an exception to the rule. They see that Captain Hughes is an exception, as am I, and do not understand why they should not be as well."

"I will not turn you out, or turn Captain Hughes away, merely so as to offend nobody," Mirabel said. "They will only find something else to be vexed about."

"You need not turn anybody out," said Mrs. Entwhistle. "It is simple enough to quiet such talk."

Mrs. Dunnet laughed. "It cannot be so simple as all that, or else I am very stupid. Nothing I said availed."

"It is only that people long for excitement," Mrs. Entwhistle said. "They wish to learn whether mysterious new injuries appear daily, or whether Mr. Carsington evidences symptoms of poisoning—or whether he is even alive." The widow's dark eyes twinkled. "The devil makes talk for idle tongues, and why not? It is February, this is a small community, and people have no other entertainment. If I were you, I should entertain them, Mirabel."

"I hope you are not proposing I poison my guest in order to keep my neighbors amused," Mirabel said.

"I propose that you rearrange your schedule for today," her former governess said. "Put business aside and spend the time visiting your neighbors instead. Be sure to give them every possible detail about your exalted guest. Also—and this is most important, Mirabel—you must beseech their advice regarding his care."

The vicar's wife turned an admiring gaze upon the plump, beruffled widow. "How astute you are," Mrs. Dunnet said. "That will be worth a hundred sermons, though you must never tell Mr. Dunnet I said so."

MIRABEL'S Aunt Clothilde had sent Mrs. Entwhistle to Oldridge Hall fifteen years ago. She was intended to be more of a companion than a teacher for the motherless girl, since by that time Mirabel's education was essentially complete. The governess had found a household devastated and demoralized by the death of its beloved mistress. In short order she rebuilt morale and, as Captain Hughes put it, "Got 'em all shipshape again."

In doing so, she had given Mirabel the kind of education her mother might have done, one that extended far beyond the schoolroom. Mirabel had profitably employed this knowledge a few years later, when she had to give up

her romantic dreams and return home from London to prevent another shipwreck.

This was why Mirabel didn't question Mrs. Entwhistle's counsel but promptly followed it.

As a result, Mirabel spent all of Monday, well into the
evening, listening to various ladies' tender expressions
of pity for Mr. Carsington's sufferings. She accepted
with a straight face and humble gratitude their medical
receipts guaranteed to cure everything from chapped lips
to deafness.

She listened to advice about forestalling lung fever and
stoically bore their reminiscences of the great influenza
outbreak of '03, which had killed her mother. She waited
while they wrote notes to the patient and promised to deliver them to him as soon as Dr. Woodfrey deemed his
brain strong enough for reading. She went home at last in
a carriage loaded with jellies, conserves, syrups, and
enough Balm of Gilead Oil to cover Prussia.

She arrived shortly after dinner and found Mrs. Ent-
whistle in the library conversing with Captain Hughes.
Papa, she was informed, had gone upstairs to keep Mr.
Carsington company.

"I had fully intended to have my tea upstairs with the
patient," Mrs. Entwhistle said. "But when Captain Hughes
told us during dinner that Mr. Carsington seemed to be in
low spirits today, your father insisted on visiting him. He
said he knew exactly the thing to alleviate the trouble."

Mirabel recalled her father's confused idea that laudanum was somehow the answer to Mr. Carsington's mysterious problems.

She did not know for sure that laudanum would do him
any harm. On the other hand, she couldn't be sure it would
do him any good, and she most certainly had no idea
whether her father had any inkling of proper dosage.

Mirabel ran out of the library and up the stairs.

Ten

HEART pounding, Mirabel burst into the room, ran to the bed—and stopped short.

Mr. Carsington was not in the bed, drugged unconscious or otherwise.

She looked about her and found three pairs of eyes regarding her with varying degrees of perplexity.

Crewe had paused in the act of trimming a candle.

Papa was rising from his chair.

Mr. Carsington lifted his head from the hand it had been leaning on and, after a moment, smiled a small, secretive smile.

The back of her neck tingled.

"Oh," she said. "I thought you were sleeping."

His smile widened. Mirabel abruptly recalled what she'd done in the early hours of morning—and her sarcastic remark about leaping upon gentlemen in their sleep.

Her face grew very hot.

"Never mind," she said. She started to turn away.

"Please don't go, Miss Oldridge," Mr. Carsington said.

"Your father and I were talking about Egyptian date palms. I should like to hear your views."

Perhaps his smile hadn't meant what she thought it did. Perhaps it had been a smile of relief at her interrupting a deadly boring botanical lecture.

Her father gestured at the chair he'd vacated, and Mirabel took it. She could not run away, no matter how embarrassed she was.

While botany was less likely to prove fatal than an opiate overdose, it was not without its dangers. From date palms, Papa might proceed to Sumatran camphor trees, in which case Mr. Carsington was sure to throw himself out of the window.

"We were speaking of young men sowing wild oats," her parent said, "and I remarked that this may well be a law of nature. In ancient Egypt, I was telling Mr. Carsington, only female date palms were cultivated. Wild males were brought from the desert to fertilize them."

"I could not understand why the Egyptians should go to so much bother," Mr. Carsington said. "Why not use cultivated males as well as females? But you are better versed than I in agriculture. What is your opinion?"

"I can think of three reasons," she said. "Tradition, superstition, or—and this, I fear, is not always the rule in agricultural practices—the wild males had been proven to produce fruit either in greater quantity or of superior quality."

"The Babylonians suspended male clusters from wild dates over the females," Papa said. "Many nations of Asia and Africa used this combination."

"Then it would appear to be a widespread practice," Mirabel said. "Yet I don't see what it has to do with the human species sowing wild oats. To my knowledge, date palms do not possess intellectual powers, let alone principles. They cannot decide how to act. They are governed entirely by natural laws."

"But the young are governed more by nature—by natural feelings, in other words—than by intellect and moral principle," her father said. "For example, would either of you claim to be the same person you were, say, a decade or so ago? At that time, as I recollect, Mirabel, you were in London, breaking hearts left and right—"

"I was *what?*" Mirabel stared at her father. He could not have said what she thought he did.

"Were you really?" said Mr. Carsington. "Well, that is interesting. You grow more complicated by the minute, Miss Oldridge."

ALISTAIR wished he had a way of capturing the moment, for the look Miss Oldridge gave her father was priceless. If the botanist had suddenly sprouted palm fronds and date clusters, she could not have appeared more dumbfounded.

She quickly composed herself, however, and directed a level gaze at Alistair. "This is absurd," she said.

"You never told me you'd been to London," he said.

"It was ages ago," she said. "You weren't even born yet."

He laughed. "No doubt my father wished I hadn't been. Some ten or so years ago I incited a riot near Kensington Gate."

"A riot?" she said. "You started a riot?"

"Did you not read of it? The tale was in all the papers."

"I don't remember," she said.

"You had too much on your mind, I daresay. All those hearts you had to break."

Alistair thought she was well on her way to breaking his.

This day had dragged on so slowly, grey and dismal. He hadn't realized how low his spirits had sunk until now. He'd hardly noticed his state of mind, it was so familiar, this melancholy.

Then she'd burst into the room and he'd thought his heart, in pure joy, would burst from his chest.

Numskull heart. She would break it, and forget about it

as quickly and easily as she'd forgotten all the others. It would serve him right. He should guard it better, lock it away and keep his mind on business. Should, should, should. But he couldn't summon the will to resist her, to stifle the happiness he felt when she came into the room.

He watched her summon her wits, saw her baffled blue gaze clear, and waited for her answer.

She leaned toward him and whispered, "I beg you will not place too much credence in what Papa says about my time in London. I cannot think where he comes by the notion that I am a femme fatale. Perhaps he has confused me with my Aunt Clothilde. She was a famous beauty. She is still, actually. Men are always falling in love with her."

Alistair leaned toward her. "Perhaps it runs in the family," he whispered back.

She gave him a quick, uncomprehending look, then coloring, drew back. "Oh," she said. "You are flirting with me."

If only it were so simple and innocent. But it was not. The game he played at present was more dangerous than mere flirtation. He knew this, but he couldn't—or wouldn't—help himself.

"Do you mind?" he said.

"No." Her brow wrinkled. "Doubtless you find it more amusing than date palms. But I am out of practice, and—" She broke off and looked about the room. "Where is Papa? Where is Crewe?"

Alistair gave the room a quick survey. Their chaperons were nowhere in sight. "They seem to have abandoned us," he said softly. "I wish you would take advantage."

"Of what?"

"Me," he said. "I am helpless, confined to this chair. I am not to put any weight on my left foot. I am completely at your mercy. Break my heart. Please. Get it over with."

"You are delirious," she said. "Papa was talking about camphor trees, wasn't he? I must tell Mrs. Entwhistle not to let—"

"Very well. If you will make me leave my chair . . ." Alistair started to get up.

She sprang up from her chair, thrust her hand against his chest, and pushed him back down.

He looked up at her. Her hand stayed on his chest. She didn't move, didn't speak, only watched him, her gaze scanning his face.

Finally, she lifted her hand. He waited for the slap he so richly deserved.

She laid the palm of her hand against his cheek.

It was nothing, really, the merest touch, but it was everything, too, to him, and he might as well have been struck by lightning, for it blasted to pieces what remained of his judgment and all those noble principles regarding the lines a gentleman may and may not cross.

He turned his head and pressed his lips against the soft flesh of her hand, and heard her quick intake of breath.

His own breathing grew hurried. He'd done nothing but miss her and indulge in hopeless fantasies since she'd left this room in the dark hours of morning.

He couldn't banish the memory of her scent and the supple curves of her body.

Now he drank in that scent while tracing the soft curves of her palm with his lips. Her hand trembled, but she didn't draw it away, and when he kissed her wrist, he found her pulse beating as frantically as his heart did.

Her fingers curled into a fist against his cheek. He kissed her knuckles.

She pulled her hand away.

He looked up.

Her countenance was wiped clean of expression.

From behind him came a small, disapproving cough.

Alistair suppressed the oath rising to his lips, turned toward his valet, and said, "Oh there you are, Crewe. I wondered where you'd got to."

"I beg your pardon, sir," the valet said. "Thinking Mr. Oldridge had remained, I assumed my presence was not required, and stepped into the next room to attend to a few tasks."

"I collect it was the date palms," said Miss Oldridge coolly. "They have driven me to distant parts of the house often enough. When that subject comes up, the wisest course is flight. I applaud your good sense, Crewe."

She turned an unreadable gaze upon Alistair. "Perhaps I had better warn you about the camphor tree of Sumatra. Papa has recently read an *Asiatic Journal* article devoted to the topic."

"I am not sure I know what a camphor tree is," Alistair said.

"I strongly recommend that you do not ask him to enlighten you," she said.

"I certainly shan't ask Mr. Oldridge to read the article to me," Alistair said. "Your father has a soothing voice, and botanical prose is terrifically boring. I'll only fall asleep without learning a thing. Look at what he brought this time. Can you wonder at my preferring to discuss date palms with him?"

Miss Oldridge glanced at the table, where a copy of De Candolle's *Elementary Principles of Botany* lay.

"In any case, I like conversing with your father," Alistair said quite truthfully. Despite what he'd learned about Oldridge as well as what Alistair observed and what he'd surmised, he couldn't dislike the gentleman.

"No one converses with my father," the daughter said. "Not as normal human beings understand conversation. It is all detours and tangents and non sequiturs."

"You have too many responsibilities pressing upon you," Alistair said. "You haven't time to follow the meanderings of his mind, let alone sort them out. I, however, am completely at leisure at present. I can listen and puzzle over the connections between one idea and the next. It is fascinating."

Her expression sharpened, and her blue gaze fixed upon him with an intensity he could only wish were amorous.

But he knew better. He had said something wrong. He

didn't know what it was, but he had no doubt he was about to suffer the consequences.

"Fascinating," she said quietly. "Of course you would say so. You are such a good listener. You let him ramble on about botany the way you let the other gentlemen hold forth about their hounds and poachers and mole catchers."

Something was springing out at Alistair from the darkness of her mind, but he could not yet make out what it was.

"Mole catchers?" he said lightly while he braced himself to be torn to pieces.

"I listened all day to ladies' remedies for ailments ranging from warts to consumption," she said. "It was tedious and annoying. But the exercise resulted in my neighbors thinking more kindly of me."

Alistair caught on. "Miss Oldridge, it is not—"

"When you first came here, you told me why you'd contacted Papa first," she said. "Since he's the largest landowner hereabouts, you assumed his opinion of the canal would carry great weight with his neighbors. I thought that by now you would have realized my father takes no notice of practical concerns, such as the prospect of coal barges or passenger boats filled with drunken aristocrats cruising through his meadows."

"Miss Oldridge—"

"You are wasting your time cultivating my father," she said. "In the first place, he dotes upon you already. In the second, he hasn't the remotest interest in your canal." She lifted her chin. "In your place I should stick to seducing his daughter, since she, as anyone can tell you, is your most dangerous—and determined—opposition."

"Miss—"

But she, knowing a good exit line when she'd uttered one, swept out of the room before he could utter another syllable.

He listened to her footsteps fade.

From another corner of the room came a pitying cough.

• • •

LATE the following afternoon, Mirabel was in her father's study, answering his correspondence.

She had found the perfect way of keeping Mr. Carsington at the very back of her mind, instead of occupying every cubic inch of that organ: property law. She was locked in a desperate battle with the legal jargon of a letter from her father's solicitor when she became aware of a series of faint thumps from the hall.

She assumed a servant had dropped something. If the problem was serious, she'd soon learn of it.

She returned to the solicitor's letter.

"I must speak to you," a voice rumbled from near at hand—and nearly catapulted her from her chair.

But composure was reflexive. Mirabel kept her seat, dropping only the pen with which she'd been making notes. *Replevins*, *mesnes*, *distreins*, and writs of *cessavit*, however, all flew out of her head.

Mr. Carsington stood in the doorway, leaning on a cane. He was fully dressed. His linen was immaculately white and crisply starched. His sleek brown coat hugged his broad shoulders as though it were a second—and costly—skin. She was not sufficiently versed in men's fashion to identify his inexpressibles as pantaloons, breeches, or trousers. All she knew was that they fit snugly, outlining the long, muscular legs she'd seen in their natural state.

That recollection brought a host of others, and a rush of longing swept in with them, and in that moment she saw the truth, so stark there was no disregarding it.

She'd crossed a boundary.

She was infatuated.

She'd done it without realizing, and now that she understood, it was too late. She had no way back to safety.

She must simply endure it, and hide it, pretending she felt nothing, that, for instance, the room had not grown too small, suddenly, and too warm.

"This is most unwise," she told him. "Your ankle is not strong enough for traipsing about the house."

"Today Dr. Woodfrey told me I might take some mild exercise, as long as I used a cane, and put as little weight upon my foot as possible," he said, advancing into the room, which seemed to shrink further. "My leg has given me a good deal of practice with the method."

Cautiously she stood. She braced her hands on the desk. "I strongly doubt that Dr. Woodfrey's idea of 'mild exercise' is a hike from the guest wing, down a long staircase, and several hundred feet to the coldest part of the house," she said.

"I don't care what his idea is," Mr. Carsington said. His voice dropped to a throbbing undercurrent. "I must speak to you. About yesterday. You accused me of seducing you."

"You need not announce it to the household." Mirabel hastily skirted the desk, and him, and closed the door. She stood in front of the door, in case she needed to make a speedy exit . . . before she added a blatant outrage to her rapidly mounting heap of indiscretions, something she couldn't cover up with sarcasm or by taking the offensive, as she'd done previously.

He remained where he was, but a pace or two away.

"You announced it in front of my valet," he said.

"I forgot he was there," she said. "Crewe is discreet to the point of invisibility."

"His master is not," said Mr. Carsington. "I am indiscreet, and very stupid at times, but I am not duplicitous. I do not go about seducing women in order to further business aims."

"I see," she said. "You do it merely for amusement."

He regarded her with half-closed eyes, yet she detected the glitter in them. "I am not the one who left London strewn with broken hearts," he said.

Was he mocking her? "I told you that was nonsense," she said tightly.

"You made a start at breaking mine," he said.

"I *what?*" She could not believe her ears. "Are you delirious?"

"You accused me of seducing you," he said. "You seem to have forgotten who made the first move."

It had been she, and she couldn't pretend otherwise. Heat washed over her, not all of it from shame.

She remembered the feel of his mouth against her hand, and the way the world had gone away. She experienced again the spill of sensations she had no name for, and the sense of toppling off balance. She did not know how to come right, and wasn't sure she wanted to.

She looked up and saw his mouth curve a very little. It seemed like a taunt, daring her to contradict him. She didn't want to. All she wanted to do was lay her fingers over his mouth and feel those sensations again. She didn't want to talk or listen or think. She didn't want to be sensible. She was always sensible and thinking ahead. She was one and thirty years old. Why could she not be a fool this once?

"Well, if you must split hairs so fine," she said unsteadily.

"I certainly must," he said. "Furthermore, I am not cultivating your father. He has been kind and amiable to me, and altogether impossible to dislike, even for *your* sake. If anyone is being won over, it is I. This is why—"

He broke off with a gasp as she grabbed his lapels. "Miss Oldridge."

She looked up at him.

He looked down at her hands. "You're *wrinkling* my coat," he said in horrified tones.

Mirabel smiled, though her heart banged as loudly as a cannon volley.

His gaze went from her hands to her mouth, and the horrified look faded. His eyes darkened.

Her breath came and went too fast, and her knees wanted to buckle. She tipped her head back.

He bent toward her—then drew back. "No. There is too much at stake. I cannot be—"

Mirabel tugged on the lapels, pulling him to her, and kissed him, full on the lips.

It was like kissing a block of wood.

Her spirits, a moment ago so agitated, plunged into a black abyss.

She started to draw away.

"Oh, don't look like that," he said. "I am only—It isn't that I don't want . . . Oh, what's the use?"

He let go of the cane, and it toppled to the floor.

He caught her face in his hands and gazed at her for a long moment. She brought her hands up to cover his. They were warm, and his touch was gentle, as though she were fragile. She wasn't, and for a moment, nothing at all made sense, and butterflies fluttered in the pit of her stomach.

Then he lowered his mouth to hers, and with the first gentle pressure of his lips, the world changed.

Mirabel had been kissed before, and passionately, too, and she'd responded passionately because she'd been in love.

But this was different, as different as another universe, and she didn't care about passion or love, only that it was sweet and made her limbs weak.

He wrapped his arms about her, and drew her closer, and deepened the kiss. The intimacy of it, the first taste of him, made her shiver. It shut down her mind as well, and left her in a haze of feeling. She was aware of the tickle of his neckcloth and the faint mingled fragrances of starch and soap and something else, something far headier: the scent of his skin. She wanted to bury her face in his neck. She wanted to feel his skin against hers, everywhere.

She pressed herself closer, tucking into the hard length of his body. His arms tightened about her, so strong, and she, who'd spent years relying only on her own strength, ached with the sweetness of it. To be held so, to want and be wanted—it hurt, and the hurt showed her how carefully, safely numb she'd been all these long years.

She didn't want to be safe now. Their kiss grew fiercer, much more wicked, and hazy pleasure thickened into intoxication. She dragged her hands through his hair and broke the kiss to press her mouth to the corner of his, the place where he hid his smiles. She drank in the scent of him, male and clean yet dark, too, and faintly dangerous, like the hint of danger in his bedchamber, the languor that seemed to hang in the air, the sultry atmosphere, hinting at sin.

He turned his head and teased as she did, his mouth caressing her cheek, her jaw, her neck. Some sound escaped her, foreign. A sigh, a moan. She felt his hands slide downward to cup her bottom. She gasped at the intimacy, those long hands, touching her *there*—and then he was lifting her up, as smoothly and easily as if she were made of air. A moment later he'd deposited her, breathless, on the desk.

He leaned in and kissed her, and she forgot she was shocked, forgot everything but him. Instinctively, she opened her legs so that he could get closer, and when he did, she wrapped her arms about his neck. He made a sound, something between a groan and a growl, and broke the kiss. For a moment he rested his forehead against hers.

He drew a long, shaky breath, then lifted his head. He tangled his fingers in her hair and drew her head back and looked at her. He was breathing hard, and his eyes were very dark.

"Now would be a good time to tell me to stop," he growled.

"Oh," Mirabel said. It was hard to get out the one syllable, and it sounded thick and muffled, not her voice at all. "Yes. Thank you. I didn't know. When." *Didn't know. Didn't care.*

"I thought not." He dragged his fingers through her hair and smiled rather sadly, then let go and took a step back. "It is fortunate for you that I am mending my ways. And may I say that it is uphill work."

She wished he'd picked another time to mend his ways.

He cleared his throat. "You took a great chance, leaving it to me to call a halt to the proceedings. Another few minutes, and I should have had all your buttons and strings undone—at which point I should be beyond caring about the consequences."

"Oh," Mirabel said, and then, as his words sank in. *"Oh." Another few minutes. What would it have been like?*

"I should like to know what use it is to have a chaperon when she is never about when she is needed," he said irritably. "If the lady were doing her job, this sort of thing would not happen."

"It isn't as though I do this sort of thing all the time," Mirabel said.

"That is obvious," he said.

She slid down from the desk. "I'm sorry if my lack of skill annoys you. I should be much better at this if I had practice, but as you can imagine, the opportunities are rare." She sighed. "Nonexistent, actually."

"That isn't the issue! The issue is your ignorance about protecting your virtue. Someone should have taught you ages ago—"

"I was taught," she said. "But it *was* ages ago, and I barely remember, and anyway, I am not sure what the point is of protecting it anymore."

"The point?" he said. "The *point?*"

"It does not seem very important," she said. It seemed completely wrong at the moment, in fact. Perverse.

"It doesn't need a point." He raked his fingers through his hair, adding to the wonderful disorder she'd made. "It is a moral principle. Part of the higher order of things. A matter of honor."

"Honor is so important to men," she said. "Can you not look after it yourself, if it is so important? You should have fought me off the way you fought the French. You should not leave it all to me. I do not have seven or eight love affairs' worth of experience in these things. It is most unjust to expect a woman of little experience to resist an attractive man of extensive experience."

"It is unjust," he said between his teeth, "but that is the way it *is*. I cannot believe I am trying to explain the facts of life to a woman of one and thirty. Men are *animals*, Miss Oldridge. It is most unwise to leave such things to us. This is a perfect example. I had resolved, most firmly, to remain deaf, dumb, and blind to your attractions."

"My attract—"

"I am here on crucial business," he went on. "The most important of my life. You can have no inkling how much depends upon it. Yet every encounter with you serves only to drive it farther and farther from my mind. This must not continue. I cannot become entangled with you, no matter how much I want to."

"No matter how much you—"

"When you are about, I forget why I am here and how much depends upon me," he said. "The longer I am under this roof, the more addled I become. I cannot believe I went to the length of hunting you down this day. But yes, I can, as I can believe what followed. If I remain any longer, I shall turn into a dithering imbecile—and your reputation will be in shreds."

If he remained? Mirabel's lust-drugged mind abruptly cleared. "You cannot be thinking of leaving," she said. "I am sure Dr. Woodfrey did not give permission for that."

It was then she noticed the discarded cane lying on the floor. "Oh, I had forgotten your ankle," she said. "You are not supposed to put any weight on it." She was sure he wasn't supposed to be picking up a woman who weighed rather more than air. If his ankle did not heal properly, it would be her fault. "I should have considered—"

He picked up the cane. "Pray do not add me to your responsibilities," he said. "You have more than enough. I have far too few. I reckon I can meet the challenge of being responsible for myself, if nothing else." He limped to the desk and collected a handful of hairpins. "Here, let me do something useful. It will reduce the whispering in the servants' hall if you do not emerge from this room looking as though your houseguest had ravished you."

AWARE he must leave before his limited willpower gave way, Alistair made quick work of Miss Oldridge's hair. Then, ignoring her protests, he hastened to his chamber and ordered Crewe to start packing.

Crewe didn't argue. He only gave a sad little cough and donned a stoic expression. This was his way of saying, "You are wrong, tragically wrong."

Alistair ignored it.

He could not ignore Captain Hughes, however, who marched in a short time later without so much as a by-your-leave, and briskly announced that Mr. Carsington would stay at his house.

Alistair thanked him and politely declined.

"I must urge you to reconsider," said the captain. "If you return to Wilkerson's, Miss Oldridge will worry herself sick."

"There is nothing to worry about," Alistair said. "I only need to rest, which I can do as well in my hotel as here." He doubted he would rest at all until he was far away from Mirabel Oldridge. If not for the canal, he would head straight back to London this instant.

"She's worried about Crewe," Hughes said. "He sits up with you most of the night, she says, then attends you all day. At the hotel, he'll have no help. There aren't enough servants, and they are always busy. He'll have to supervise Wilkerson's cook closely as well, because she can't be relied upon to prepare correctly the light dishes Dr. Woodfrey has prescribed. In short, Miss Oldridge asks you to consider your valet if you won't consider yourself."

Alistair looked at Crewe, who went on with the packing, pretending to be deaf.

"Miss Oldridge blames herself for upsetting you," the captain went on.

"She did not upset me," Alistair said. "I am entirely to blame."

Hughes rolled his eyes. "I cannot believe these dramatics—about a canal, no less! I couldn't believe my ears when Miss Oldridge declared she'd go with Mrs. Entwhistle to Cromford, so that you'd remain here."

"That's ridiculous," Alistair said. "I have no wish to drive the lady from her own home."

"I should hope not. She'll spend the whole time fretting about everything here, and what is or isn't being done in her absence, and what might go wrong, and a hundred other anxieties. Not to mention that Mrs. Entwhistle will be obliged to pack again and travel, when she's scarcely arrived."

"Miss Oldridge oughtn't have so much to worry about!" Alistair snapped. "I like Mr. Oldridge, but it is wrong for him to leave everything to her. If he must indulge his botanical passions, he should hire a proper steward to look after estate business. It is unreasonable to expect her to be both mistress of the house and lord of the manor. Have you seen her desk? Great heaps of letters in that beastly law hand—and judging by the expression on her face when I entered, it was about as plain to her as Chinese is to me."

Alistair wished he could forget what he'd seen during the moment he'd stood unnoticed in the study doorway, watching her. She was dragging one hand through her hair, covering the legal correspondence with hairpins. In the other she had a pen whose ink she'd spattered on her sleeve.

But it was her face that troubled him most. She looked so weary and despairing. He wanted to scoop her up in his arms and carry her away—on his white charger, no doubt.

"She's clever and capable," he said tightly, "but it is too much for one person. Even my father, who reads every confounded tradesman's bill and can tell me to the farthing how much I have outspent each quarter's allowance—even he leaves the better part of managing his properties to his agents. He has a secretary as well. Miss Oldridge does it all herself and receives no thanks or even acknowledgment. It is a wonder she hasn't had every feminine feeling ground out of her by now. That only her wardrobe and hair suffer is a testament to what I consider a miraculous resilience."

"You don't know the half of it," said Captain Hughes. "Maybe there's no reason for you to know. But I can tell you that you don't improve matters by running away to Wilkerson's."

Eleven

ALISTAIR might have withstood the other arguments, though they sent his conscience into spasms.

What demolished his resistance was the *You don't know the half of it,* and the captain's tone, hinting at revelations to come.

Alistair wished he could pretend his motive was practical: The more he knew about Miss Oldridge, the better equipped he would be to either win her support for the canal or weaken her influence over others.

But that was a monstrous lie. The truth was, he wanted to know more about her in the same way he wanted more of her on every other count—because he was thoroughly, fatally, besotted.

His case being fatal, he yielded to the captain and moved next door.

Though not built on the grand scale of Oldridge Hall, Bramblehurst was not the country cottage one might envision as the residence of a half-pay captain. It was not, furthermore, a typically untidy bachelor abode. The place was scrubbed and polished to within an inch of its life. Captain Hughes obviously believed naval discipline applied as well on land as at sea.

He adhered as strictly to Dr. Woodfrey's rules as if they came direct from the Admiralty.

He rigorously enforced the "no visitors" and "no mental exertion" rules, and made certain Alistair had the proper amount of exercise. He shared his guest's restricted diet, much as he would have shared his officers' privations during extended periods between ports. He was a congenial and thoughtful host, who neither intruded too much upon his guest's solitude nor left Alistair too much on his own.

Nonetheless, the nightmares worsened, night by night, revealing more of what had previously remained hidden in a dark corner of Alistair's mind. Now he wasn't sure which was worse: the gaping hole in his memory and the nagging anxiety that something was irreparably wrong there, or the moments of painfully vivid recollection that revealed a man he hardly recognized, one who was antithesis of all he'd supposed himself to be.

He didn't know how much to believe. Were these true memories, as they seemed? Or were they distortions, as dreams so often were?

He kept these worries to himself, however, as he'd kept the missing piece of memory secret—with one exception—along with the uncertainty it produced about the health and wholeness of his mind.

Every morning at breakfast, when the captain asked if he'd slept well, Alistair claimed he'd slept like a top.

But on Friday when he gave the usual answer, Hughes shook his head. "I wonder how you can sleep so soundly with such dismal results," he said. "Your eyes are sunk halfway into your skull, and it appears someone has blacked both your eyes. You're not lying awake fretting about your canal, I hope."

"Certainly not," Alistair said. "That accomplishes nothing."

"You shouldn't weary your mind with trying to guess

what Miss Oldridge will do, either," said the captain. "You'll imagine she'll act according to rational rules of engagement, when in fact she'll do nothing of the kind."

"Ah, well, women's and men's minds are different," Alistair said.

"The most desperate engagement I ever undertook at sea was child's play compared to the smallest dispute with a woman," the captain said. "They invent their own weapons, their own rules—and change 'em when the whim takes 'em. You'd think that a fellow who's seen the world a dozen times over—a fellow a very few years short of the half-century mark—" Black eyebrows knit and an angry glitter in his eye, he plunged his fork into a slab of bacon. "You'd think that an old sailor would have learnt their ways by now, or at least learnt to steer clear."

"But if we steered clear, life would lose so much of its sweetness—and more than a little of its excitement," Alistair said. As he looked back on the years since Waterloo, the womanless years, the time seemed dreary beyond describing. How had he lived through it? He was amazed he hadn't hanged himself.

They ate in silence for a time.

Then the captain muttered, "But *he* must take some of the blame. Stuffy, preachy little pig's rump. What possessed her to marry him, I'll never know. She said he was settled. *Settled.*"

Alistair's jaw dropped. Hastily, he reassembled his composure. "Miss Oldridge has been married?" The union had been annulled, of course, else she wouldn't be "Miss Oldridge."

She might not be a virgin, then, after all, which meant the rules had changed.

As soon as he thought it, he was furious with himself. He could not believe he'd grown so deranged as to look for loopholes that would permit him to bed her.

He found the captain regarding him gravely. "Not Miss O," he said. "I was speaking—grumbling—about the other lady. Mrs. E. Talking to myself. We old bachelors do that sometimes." He went on eating.

"I see," Alistair said. "The other lady." The captain's woman troubles were located in the person of Mrs. Entwhistle, not Miss Oldridge . . . who had never been married.

Of course she hadn't been. Hadn't she told him she was inexperienced? She was untouched. And she had not been saving herself for *him*.

"Miss Oldridge likes 'em lively," Captain Hughes said after a moment. "Or at least she did. The fellow she was to be shackled to was a man of spirit. I was sure he'd carry all before him. Not the sort to take no for an answer. When she broke it off, he followed her here and insisted on staying until she got matters sorted out."

In response to Alistair's questioning look, the captain explained. Following his wife's death, Mr. Oldridge had neglected his affairs sadly, and his estate began a swift descent downhill. Matters had reached a crisis shortly after Miss Oldridge became engaged in London. She broke it off and returned home. This was eleven years ago.

"Mr. Oldridge's affairs were in a wretched tangle," the captain went on. "Anyone could see it would take years to sort out. I believe one or two matters are still in dispute, in the lawyers' hands."

That would explain, Alistair thought, why she supervised her bailiff so closely.

"But how was William Poynton to wait years in Derbyshire?" Captain Hughes said.

"Poynton?" Alistair said. "William Poynton, the artist?"

The captain nodded. "He was only starting out then. He'd been commissioned to paint a mural in some Venetian nobleman's palazzo. A great opportunity. He couldn't tell the *signore* to wait two or three or five years. Today he could. Not then."

Poynton was a highly regarded artist who traveled extensively abroad. Alistair remembered the marvelous Egyptian scenes hanging in the drawing room of Oldridge Hall. Poynton's work, of course.

"She had to save the estate, and he had to make his name," the captain said. "Mrs. E claims he should have waited. After a year or two, she says, the girl would have been less fearful about leaving the place in charge of a new bailiff. That's absurd, and so I've told her. Poynton could no more turn down the commission or bid his patron wait than I could decline a ship or tell the Admiralty Board it wasn't convenient at the moment. When you're at the bottom, and your superiors offer a step up the ladder, you don't make conditions."

"But to give a woman up for the sake of professional advancement?" Alistair said. "He couldn't have truly loved her."

The captain shook his head. "Poynton was mad in love with her. It was the talk of London. He came here *after* she'd broken off with him. All the world knew of it. But he cared nothing for what a pitiful spectacle he must appear to his sophisticated friends."

"He's an artist," Alistair said. "They go in for such theatrical gestures. They are masters at grand passions. I don't call that love. If he had truly loved her, he would have found a way."

THOUGH he'd turned the breakfast conversation to topics other than Mr. Carsington's unhealthy appearance, and was much encouraged by his reaction to the Poynton matter, Captain Hughes was not at all sanguine about his guest's health. Instead of steadily improving, he seemed to be growing steadily worse.

His confidence in Dr. Woodfrey shaken, the captain sought out Mrs. Entwhistle. While he enjoyed arguing with her and often contradicted her "insights" regarding human nature, Captain Hughes had nearly as high a regard for her intelligence as for her physical attributes.

A short time after breakfast, he met up with her in the park of Oldridge Hall. As he'd hoped, she was taking her usual brisk morning walk along the same woodland path she'd favored during her governess days.

In the old days she dressed simply in dull shades of grey and brown, as her position required. These days she was more colorful. This morning she wore a red pelisse. The matching bonnet was a fetching concoction of feathers and ruffles.

Captain Hughes paid her compliments, which she accepted with indifference, never slackening her pace. She grew more interested, however, when he told her how his guest reacted to the Poynton story. She agreed that Mr. Carsington's affections seemed to be engaged.

The affair could not progress, however, if the man's health was failing, and this Captain Hughes explained, was his primary concern at present.

"I can't believe he looks so ill because he's languishing for Miss Oldridge," he said. "If you tell me this is the case, I'll be ill myself."

"Yesterday Mirabel received a letter from her aunt in London," said Mrs. Entwhistle. "It included a detailed account, which she read to me, of Mr. Carsington's love affairs. Given this report, I believe it is safe to say that languishing is not in his style. His style runs rather to dramatic scenes, impassioned speeches, and riots. These activities require a degree of physical effort incompatible with pining away or languishing."

"Riots?" said the captain. "Over *women?*"

Mrs. Entwhistle's frivolous bonnet bobbed up and down.

"Well, that's more like it then," the captain said. "A man of action, exactly as I supposed him."

"Regrettably, your perceptions are not as acute as some people believe," Mrs. Entwhistle said. "Mr. Oldridge is convinced that you alone understand what is wrong with Mr. Carsington."

The captain looked at her incredulously. "I?"

Another bob of the bonnet. "Something to do with

Egyptians, poppies, and . . ." She thought for a moment, biting her lip in a way that made Captain Hughes impatient.

"Egyptians?" he said. "Poppies? What the dev—How is a fellow to make heads or tails of that?"

"Mr. Oldridge wondered at Dr. Woodfrey's not prescribing laudanum," she said. "If I understand correctly, Mr. Oldridge does not believe a concussion is the trouble. He seems sure that you know what the ailment is. He has mentioned this more than once."

"I only know Carsington don't sleep and won't admit it," Captain Hughes said. "I thought he was worrying about his canal, or about Miss Oldridge blasting holes in his . . ."

He trailed off, because something was teasing in a far corner of his mind. It was like a dot of white sail on the horizon just far enough away to elude identification. He waited, but it never drew nearer.

"There's no help for it," he said at last. "I'll have to talk to Mr. Oldridge myself. It'll end in a headache, but it's in a good cause, I reckon."

MIRABEL, meanwhile, was also hearing about Mr. Carsington. While Captain Hughes was hunting down her father for enlightenment, she was receiving enlightenment from a group of ordinary women concerned about their and their husbands' livelihoods.

Her mother had started the informal meetings many years earlier. The women gathered once a month to discuss worthy community projects and how best to carry them out. The meeting also provided an opportunity to air grievances before the one local member best circumstanced to address them: the lady of Oldridge Hall.

At one such meeting, eleven years ago, she'd gleaned the first clues about Caleb Finch.

The current topic was Mr. Carsington.

By now everyone knew why Lord Hargate's third son

had come to this part of Derbyshire. Not everyone was as thrilled as the gentry families with unmarried daughters.

The miller Jacob Ridler, like millers everywhere a canal had ever been proposed, was vehemently opposed, according to his wife. But he wasn't the only one. Even those who'd seemingly benefit objected: the lime burners to the north, who needed coal for their kilns, for instance; purveyors of the various minerals, who had to transport heavy loads; and farmers looking to sell their produce and manure beyond the local market.

"The water is a great worry, miss," Mary Ann Ingsole, a farmer's wife, said while they prepared clothes for a needy family. "If the canal drains away Jacob Ridler's water, he can't run the mill. Then where do we grind our corn?"

"My Tom says they'll send all our mutton, beef, and corn on barges down to London and leave us to live on potatoes," another woman said grimly.

"Jacob says they have to build a reservoir," said Mrs. Ridler. "But where, miss? Where's a big enough parcel of land that don't have a farm or quarry or livestock on it?"

"They don't build reservoirs proper," said another. "They burst, and somebody's killed."

These were merely a few of the objections. Mirabel listened to them all. When the women had finished unburdening themselves, she said, "I've made no secret of my opposition. But I'm only one woman, and it's the men who'll decide this."

Mr. Carsington must hold a public meeting to form a canal committee and draft a petition to Parliament, she explained. This would offer the best opportunity for those opposed to speak up.

"But they won't," Mary Ann Ingsole said. "Even Hiram, who as you know never fears to speak his mind, don't like to come out against Lord Hargate's son."

"Same with all of them," said the woman beside her. "They grumble at home and amongst themselves, but they'd as soon be pilloried as say anything against him in public."

"Jacob said he'd feel like a traitor. Everyone knows how Mr. Carsington got hurt. It was plain soldiers he risked his life for, like our own menfolk."

"Besides which, Lord Hargate and the older sons have done so much good hereabouts."

"If it was anyone else but him, the men'd loosen their tongues, to be sure, miss."

Mirabel had realized the local gentry would prefer to avoid conflict with a member of Lord Hargate's family, consoling themselves with their material gains from the canal. She had not imagined, though, that prosperous tradesmen and farmers would behave like medieval serfs.

If no one would speak up, she could not mount a successful opposition. Her counterpetition to Parliament would be dismissed out of hand.

She left the meeting and climbed into the gig, her spirits at low ebb.

Canal projects had been killed before, and she knew how it had been done. She had money enough to mount a battle that would tie up the parliamentary committee until Judgment Day with lawyers, witnesses, and petitions.

But she couldn't do it alone. She was a woman, and couldn't vote. Parliament would take no notice of her objections. They certainly wouldn't believe she spoke for others if not one of these others would make the slightest murmur against the canal.

It was her own fault, she told herself, for not devising a better counterattack. If she'd devoted less attention to Mr. Carsington's manly beauty and more to the canal, if she'd occupied her mind with business instead of finding pretexts to throw herself into his arms, she might have weakened his position by now.

Instead, he was advancing at a prodigious rate, without doing a single thing. From Sir Roger on down, everyone simply surrendered to the famous Waterloo hero.

And how could she blame them, when she, too, had surrendered—not her opposition to the canal, but everything else: her intellect and morals, her common sense and pride.

Not to mention she'd put herself in precisely the situation she'd been so determined to avoid.

Once again, as she'd done eleven years ago with Mr. Poynton, she was going to make herself completely wretched because of a man.

Why couldn't she, just once, become smitten with a man whose plans and ambitions were not in irreconcilable conflict with hers?

She released a sigh and tried to let her surroundings quiet her mind.

It was early afternoon, and cold, though not bitterly so. Masses of grey clouds shifted restlessly overhead.

She drove along one of the deep, twisting country lanes Mr. Carsington so abhorred. In spring, the roadside would be thick with wildflowers, and the trees would form a graceful green archway over the road. At present, the lane was a study in drab greens and dull browns, lonely and melancholy to some eyes, perhaps.

It was not so to hers.

She could hear the wind make the evergreens seem to whisper among themselves, and she could watch it catch up handfuls of last autumn's fallen leaves and scatter them, as a fairy queen's attendants might strew flower petals along their lady's path.

The steady clip-clop of her horse's hooves, the sigh of the wind, the nearby chirp of an optimistic bird, the chatter of a squirrel—all these simple country sights and sounds about her gradually soothed her troubled heart.

As the unnatural gloom dissipated, Mirabel's natural buoyancy returned. Few cases were truly hopeless, she told herself. They only appeared so to people lacking courage and imagination. She was not one of those people.

She should not feel stupid because she hadn't yet discovered a way to defeat Mr. Carsington.

Aunt Clothilde was one of London's most fashionable hostesses. Married to Lord Sherfield, an active politician, she dealt with politicians daily. Yet even she had admitted Mr. Carsington was a challenge.

For a man, Lady Sherfield had written, he was amazingly intelligent. He was chivalrous as well. Even his affairs—the "seven or eight" he'd referred to, which Aunt Clothilde had described in juicy detail—only testified to his noble qualities. He did not use and discard women, as rakes did. He was loyal to a fault, even with harlots and thieves. He was gallant and honorable. . . .

Then Mirabel saw it, the glimmer of hope.

Hadn't he said, time and again, that he wanted to understand the objections, so that he could address them? It had upset him when she'd told him that people were too overawed by his family and his fame to contradict him.

He had restrained himself with her, he said, because he wanted to behave honorably.

How would he feel, then, if she told him what the women had said today? How would he feel upon learning that simple, hardworking people were too mindful of his heroism and sacrifice and his family's long list of good deeds, to express their true feelings?

If she could make him understand how very great and unfair his advantage was, perhaps he'd return to London and let someone else take his place here. Even with Lord Gordmor, the ordinary people would stand a better chance. Respect for his title would not stop them from speaking out on behalf of their families and their livelihoods.

Surely Mr. Carsington's honor would oblige him to leave the field to a less godlike individual.

And when he was gone?

She mustn't think about that.

Luckily, she had only a short way to go, and her resolve hadn't time to melt away under the memory of boyish grins and pathetic puns and feverish kisses.

She still had her priorities in order a short while later, when she drove up to Captain Hughes's door.

But before she could climb down from the gig, his butler came out and told her, with effusive apologies, that they weren't receiving visitors. The master had gone out and left strict orders: Mr. Carsington was not to be disturbed under any circumstances.

"Nancarrow, this is absurd," Mirabel said. "You know that Mr. Carsington was staying at Oldridge Hall recently. I'm sure Dr. Woodfrey never forbade *my* visiting."

The butler's face turned bright red. "I'm sorry, miss," he said. "Orders is orders. I'm obliged particular not to make exceptions, as it sets a bad example, and bound to lead to mutiny."

Nancarrow was the captain's former boatswain, and fanatically devoted.

"Very well," Mirabel said, though it wasn't well at all. "Perhaps you would be so good as to provide me with pen, ink, and paper, that I might write Mr. Carsington a note."

"No letters, miss," said Nancarrow. "Too taxing for the gentleman's brain."

"It is only a few lines," Mirabel began, then thought better of it. Unlike her own butler, Nancarrow was unaccustomed to thinking for himself, and could not, as Benton did, distinguish the proper circumstances for making exceptions to general rules. If she pressed the matter, she would only vex herself and make him miserable.

She drove away.

But not, as Nancarrow assumed, home.

ALISTAIR returned from his daily perambulation of the captain's neatly manicured park about the time the gig made a detour, invisible to Nancarrow, onto a back lane.

Unaware of the recent dispute at the front of the house, Alistair was startled when a shower of pebbles struck his bedroom window, which was on the first floor at the back of the house.

Advancing to the window, he beheld Miss Oldridge standing in a flower bed below. His spirits instantly broke free of the gloomy mire into which they'd been steadily sinking since breakfast.

He opened the window. "Miss—"

"Shhhh!" She pointed to one side. Alistair looked. A tall, ancient-looking ladder stood against the building. While he watched in blank disbelief, she shifted the decrepit ladder until it rested next to his bedroom window.

"Miss Oldridge," he began.

She gave him an admonishing look and put her finger to her lips. Then she began climbing up.

Alistair wondered if he was dreaming. Since this was far pleasanter than his usual dreams, he was content to enjoy it for as long as it lasted.

In very short order, the top of her ugly grey bonnet was level with the window ledge. An instant later, she was looking up at him, as though it were an everyday sort of thing for her to be perched on a rickety ladder a full story above ground level.

Dizzy, Alistair gazed into her twilight blue eyes and debated whether it was safe to sweep her off the ladder and into his arms.

"Mr. Carsington," she said.

"Miss Oldridge."

She beamed up at him. "I have come to beg a boon."

The smile reduced his brain to jelly. "Anything," he said.

"I thought you would wish to be apprised . . ." Her brow creased. She leant back, her smile fading.

Alistair grabbed the ladder. "Don't do that! Are you insane?"

"You're very ill," she said. "No wonder Nancarrow was so obstinate. I should have realized." She started to climb down.

"I am not ill," he said.

She paused. "You look dreadful. I am sure you should not be standing at an open window."

"Miss Oldridge, if you do not tell me what this is about, I shall climb down after you," he said. "Without my overcoat *or* my hat."

She came back up. "You'll do nothing of the kind," she

said. "I only came about business. I had not considered how much it would tax your mind."

"What business? You said you wanted a boon."

"In a manner of speaking." She stared at the rung she was holding. "But I did not think it through. I had not taken into account your great debt to Lord Gordmor. To have to choose between fair play and loyalty—" She shook her head. "It is too much to burden you with when you are ill."

"I am not ill," he said.

She looked up at him. "Something is wrong."

"Yes, something is wrong," he said. "Something is terribly wrong. You. Me. This." A sweep of his hand took in the space between them. "What is between us."

She looked down toward the ground—a dreadfully long way down, it seemed to him. Her gloved hands curved more tightly about the rung she held onto. "I wish you had not said that," she said.

"I didn't mean to. But you—" He broke off, because she was ascending, quickly, and then she was shifting onto the ledge.

"Good God!" Heart pounding, he grabbed her and hauled her inside.

He wanted to shake her, but she broke free and stepped back out of reach.

"You could have been killed," he growled.

"Only if you dropped me." Her voice was shaky. "You shouldn't have grabbed me. I knew what I was doing."

"Did you?"

"I'm a countrywoman." She straightened her bonnet. "Not like your London ladies."

"No, not at all," he said. "You are not like anybody. You are—you are—"

Her blue gaze lifted to his, and memories flooded him: every look, every touch . . . the whispery sound of her voice, the infinite variety of her smiles . . . the sweet yielding of her body. He, with his renowned tact and powers of address—he, who'd always used words so effortlessly, couldn't string a thought together, let alone find words to express what he felt.

He made a helpless gesture and said stupidly, inadequately, "You are turning everything upside down and inside out."

She flung herself at him, wrapping her arms about his waist and smashing her ugly bonnet against his chest simultaneously.

He caught his breath, closed his arms tightly about her, and crushed her to him.

"You shouldn't have come," he growled into the top of her bonnet. "But I'm so glad you did."

"I should have stayed away, but I couldn't," she said, her voice muffled against his coat. "I jumped at the first excuse."

"I've missed you so much," he said.

"Good. I've been perfectly wretched about you." She drew back enough to look up into his face. "Ever since you left, I've been wishing we'd finished what we started. I've wished you hadn't stopped. I've wished you had undone all my buttons and strings and didn't care about the consequences."

"You don't know what you're saying," he said. He did, and wished he didn't. He was not made of iron.

"I'm telling you the truth," she said. "Why should I pretend? I'm always making excuses, telling myself as well as you tales to protect . . ." Her voice wavered. "I don't know what I'm protecting. My vanity. My pride."

"Your honor," he said.

"Must I protect it?" she said. "Shall I leave now? Why didn't you chase me away before I spoke?" She pulled away, her lower lip trembling. "Wretched man."

"My dear . . ." Oh, he was lost. He wished she'd simply stick a dagger in his heart and be done with it.

"Your dear," she said. "Your dear." She gave a short laugh and wiped her eyes. "Oh, don't look so—so—Don't look that way. I shan't weep. I despise women who use tears to get what they want. I was merely overcome for a moment. With exasperation."

"I should give anything," he said, "to have it otherwise."

There was a long, taut pause. Then she said, "You wish I were not a gently bred maiden, is that it? If I were not an unwed lady, what then?" She pulled off her gloves and dropped them on the floor. Then she began to untie her bonnet ribbons. "What then?" she repeated. "What if I were not quite a lady, after all?"

Alistair stared at the gloves and at her naked hands, swiftly undoing the ribbons. "You cannot be . . ." He trailed off while his mind struggled with an incredible possibility.

She pulled off the bonnet and tossed it onto a chair.

"No," he said.

She began unbuttoning her pelisse. "I am one and thirty years old," she said. "I should like to gather my rosebuds before the petals shrivel up and fall off."

Twelve

THE expression on his magnificently patrician countenance was priceless. If she hadn't been so nervous,
Mirabel would have laughed. But she was quaking in her
boots, and if she paused, even to laugh, she would lose her
courage.

"This joke is not amusing," he said.

"I've never been more serious in my life," she said.

He'd said he missed her. He'd said he had feelings for
her. Perhaps those feelings simply added up to lust, but that
was all right. What she felt was lust, too.

It had been so long since she'd felt desire, so very long
since a man had returned her feelings. She had held back
with William and preserved her virtue for honor's sake.
She'd let the man she loved go, for duty's sake. She would
not let honor and duty rule this time, not completely.

She and Mr. Carsington were alone, and this time they
were not under her father's roof or at the hotel. No one had
seen her enter his bedroom, and no one need see her leave
it. Such an opportunity would never come again.

She didn't want to die a maiden. She had to know what it was like to experience and express passion. She must experience, once, what it was to be made love to by the man one longed for.

He started toward her. She backed away. "You must do up those buttons," he said so very sternly, "or I shall do them up for you." He advanced.

She retreated.

The room was a fraction of the size of his bedchamber at Oldridge Hall. Its furnishings, combined with his belongings, created a course of obstacles and left him little space to maneuver round them. She knew he daren't chance overturning a chair or table or toppling any of the breakables, which seemed to be everywhere. The noise would bring the staff running.

He limped cautiously after her, and she retreated, while her unsteady fingers moved down the front of the pelisse.

"Miss Oldridge, this is a very dangerous game," he said. "Someone might hear us."

"Then lower your voice," she said.

She leapt up onto the bed, and standing a hairsbreadth out of his reach, quickly shrugged out of the pelisse. She threw it at him, and it caught him in the face. He held it there for a moment, then crushed it against his chest.

"You must not," he said hoarsely. "It is wicked to do this to me. It holds . . ." He swallowed. "It holds your warmth, your scent."

Her heart thumped frantically.

"This is most unwise," he said. "And unfair."

"You leave me no choice," she said. "You and your dratted honor."

"You must not do this," he said. "You must *not.*"

"We'll never have another chance," she said.

WE'LL *never have another chance.*

Alistair tried to tell himself it didn't matter. He could no more dishonor her here than under her father's roof.

She was struggling with the fastenings of her dress.

They were at the back. He might have undone them so easily.

He clenched his hands and stood motionless.

Without help, she couldn't get the dress off. He must *not* help her.

"I've spent my life doing my duty," she went on while trying to twist her dress about in order to get to the buttons and strings. "I don't regret it. Not altogether. But I know I'll regret you."

"My dear—"

"Don't say that!"

"You *are* dear. If you were not—But we cannot—We must talk. I beg you to stop disrobing. It's impossible to talk rationally while you're doing that."

"I'm always so rational," she said. "Always doing the right thing. Why may I not, once, do the wrong thing?"

"Yes, you may, another time. But not *now*."

"You said you missed me, you were wretched without me," she said. "When you go back to London, you'll have other ladies to make you forget me. I shan't have anyone like you. I don't want to wish I'd taken a chance. I don't want to regret. Now is all I have. Do you not see? Time is running out for me."

She gave up fumbling with the dress fastenings and grabbed the bedpost instead. She lifted her right foot, unfastened her half boot, and after a short struggle and a few stumbles, pulled it off.

He could not let her continue. He started toward the bed.

"Don't think of it," she said. "I am very nervous and liable to scream."

Alistair took a step back. She was nervous already. Very likely her courage would soon fail her altogether—before his resolve failed him, he prayed. Before he forgot what honor was. He must pretend. He was good at that. He must pretend he felt nothing.

He moved away, brushed her ugly bonnet from the

chair, sat down, and folded his arms. "Very well," he said. "Take off all your clothes. Writhe in the bed naked, if you wish. It is nothing I haven't seen before and won't again. As you say, there have been and will be other women in my life. *Many* other women. If I grow very bored, perhaps I shall take another turn about the garden."

He watched the other boot sail past him. Luckily it was soft, and the carpet was thick. It landed with a faint thud.

Her garters went next.

Alistair stared at his boots.

Something soft and slithery landed on his head. He snatched it off, opening his eyes. It was a stocking, still holding the shape of her leg. He swallowed a groan.

Another stocking landed at his feet. He stared at it, dragging his fingers through his hair.

He heard a faint *whoosh,* and a pair of silk knit drawers swirled onto his knee and slid to the floor.

He told himself to pretend it was something else, but he couldn't. In his mind's eye he saw feathery, pale copper curls in the most secret, most feminine of places. Slowly he looked up toward the bed.

Her fiery hair was tumbling about her shoulders, and her dress was twisted sideways. She had her skirts hiked up to her thighs while she worked at untying her petticoat. He had already seen her ankles and calves, the first time he'd seen her. He knew they were shapely. But he hadn't seen nearly so much of them, and he hadn't seen those sweetly curving limbs bare.

She had a beauty mark near the crook of her left knee.

"Miss Oldridge," he said thickly. "Mirabel."

"I have never had to do this from the inside out before," she said. "It is no small challenge." She tugged the petticoat down and stepped out of it. She stood for a moment, her skirts bunched in her hands, and looked at him.

"Your legs are very beautiful," he said. *Please cover them up,* he should have added. He didn't. Not that it would have made a whit of difference.

She glanced down at her legs. "Yes, they are good, I

think. But no one ever sees them. The rest of me is good as well. And it is all *going to waste!*"

Then at last he saw the trouble.

She lived in this out-of-the-way place with a father who was mainly absent, in spirit if not in body. She worked day after day, and no one took much notice of what she did. There was no one to applaud her accomplishments, let alone to admire or flirt with her. There was no one to tell her how pretty she was, no one to appreciate her wit, her intelligence, her caring and affectionate heart.

Why should she care how she dressed, or whether her hair was tidy or not, when she was, to all intents and purposes, invisible?

"I see you," he said. He got up and crossed to the bed. She stepped back, out of reach.

"You are beautiful," he said. "I would give anything in the world to have you. But I cannot, because I am not in a position to marry you."

"Of course we cannot marry," she said. "It is very likely you will build your horrid canal and destroy everything I hold dear, and I shall hate you for it. If you fail, it will be my doing, and you'll hate me for it. At this moment, we are in charity with each other, but it cannot last. If we do not make love now, we never will. You will have other opportunities with other women, I know. But I am not likely to meet another man for whom I have feelings as strong as those I have for you."

She spoke quietly and composedly, but the color came and went in her cheeks. She stood stiffly, her skirts still bunched in her tightly clenched hands.

No tears glistened in her eyes, and her lips didn't tremble, but her chin jutted out, brave or defiant or merely obstinate, he couldn't tell.

All Alistair knew was that he wanted what she wanted, and he felt like a beast, making her beg. He would feel like a beast afterward, too, no matter what he did.

He would do what she wanted and what he wanted, and work out the moral difficulties later.

After all, he told himself, he wasn't a schoolboy. He knew ways to make love without ruining her.

He and Judith Gilford had taken full advantage of the rare, brief occasions they'd been alone together. He'd had time enough to relieve his affianced bride of her virginity. She, certainly, hadn't tried to protect it.

Yet he'd controlled himself.

He might be stupid, but he was not without scruples.

He told himself this as he pulled off his coat.

He tossed the coat aside, unbuttoned his waistcoat, swiftly removed it, and threw it on top of the coat. He untied and unwound his neckcloth and flung it aside. It landed on top of her drawers.

Alistair heard her suck in her breath.

His own breathing was shallow. He told himself to calm down and keep a level head. He pulled off his boots.

Then he looked at the woman standing on the bed, letting his gaze travel slowly from her bare toes upward, over the graceful turn of her ankles, the sweet curve of her calves, the teasing dot at the crook of her knee . . . and up the gentle swell of her thighs.

He climbed onto the bed and on hands and knees crept toward her, across the counterpane marked with her boot prints.

She didn't move a muscle, only stood holding her skirts as before. Nearing, he saw the tiny beauty mark was a misshapen heart, upside down. He kissed it. Her leg trembled.

He hooked his arm round her knees and brought her down.

He heard the soft, choked cry of surprise and the light thud as she landed among the pillows. Then he was crawling over her, and she was clutching fistfuls of his shirt and pulling him down to her.

He meant to be gentle and careful, but it was nearly impossible. He was like a man who'd wandered the desert for days, weeks, years. She was the oasis, fresh and clean and sweet. Every other woman he'd ever known seemed merely a mirage. Only she was real.

Her scent was everywhere, dizzying. He'd held her pelisse to his face, inhaling her helplessly, and the scent brought back everything he'd tried to forget: the first taste of her, as fresh as morning, and the artless ardor of her kiss . . . the warmth of her body on top of his, her heart thumping against his chest, her hair tickling his chin.

Now she was here, in his arms.

We'll never have another chance.

He deepened the kiss, and the sweetness darkened. A lover's dusk settled in, with darkness to come. All the world gone . . . only they two, alone.

His hands moved to her back, and he undid the fastenings he'd vowed not to touch: first the dress's buttons and tapes, then the corset strings. Then he was pushing the lot—bodice, corset, chemise—down to her hips . . .

. . . and then he forgot how to breathe.

He'd pictured in his mind the shape of her breasts, but he could never have imagined how perfect they were, firm and velvety smooth, tipped with delicate pink buds. He had not quite envisioned the flawless curve of her stomach and the enticing dip of her navel. He had not imagined he would stop suddenly, and look at her, and realize she was everything in the world he'd ever wanted.

"Mirabel," he said softly. Wonderful. Miraculous. He drew his hand, so lightly, over her breast.

She rose to his touch, the delicate bud tightening and darkening. "Oh," she said. It was the softest of sighs, the gentlest exhalation, yet it told him everything—of the pleasure she took, the trust she gave, the wanting she felt, undisguised.

He slid his hands over the silken curve of her belly. She moved under his hand, her uninhibited response urging him on, and his touch grew less delicate, more possessive. He stroked over the velvety skin, the perfect curves, and she moved with every stroke, giving completely, trustingly, without fear or shame. The more he tasted and touched, the more she gave, and the more he wanted.

His mind was a haze of wanting, and she was everything he'd ever wanted.

He kissed her deeply, as though he must get to the heart of her, and she caught her fingers in his hair and answered with the same urgency. The taste of her was so clean and sweet, innocent but not shy. It was like drinking the nectar of the wildflowers blooming defiantly in the most forbidding moorland.

"Mirabel." A murmur against her eager, welcoming mouth.

"Yes, yes, yes," she whispered.

Yes yes yes.

He pushed dress and corset and chemise over her hips and down, scarcely heeding what he did, only wanting them out of the way. He shed his own remaining garments in the same mindless way, caring for nothing but to taste her mouth again, and her skin, and to learn every inch of her body with his hands, his mouth.

Perhaps he was aware, in some distant corner of his mind, of where he was and who she was and what he'd intended, of what was right and what was wrong. But the awareness slid farther and farther away while her hands moved over him, too, as she learnt from him to be bold, as she discovered how to stir his hunger for her.

Right and wrong receded and faded while desire blazed ever fiercer and wilder. Her tongue tangled with his, her fingers dug into his shoulders, and their bodies tangled, too, as he rolled with her onto their sides. All the while they demanded more of each other, and the clinging kiss deepened, into a heated mimicry of coitus.

He was still aware, in some faraway place, of what he'd intended and what honor demanded. But she clung to him, and he'd rather die than let go of her, so warm, and silken soft, and passionate.

He dragged her up tight against him, and heard her soft gasp.

"It's all right," he whispered.

It wasn't. She was an innocent, else his arousal would not have shocked her.

Stop, he told himself. *Stop now.*

But she didn't recoil. She wasn't afraid, though his swollen *membrum virile* throbbed against her belly.

"Oh, my goodness," she said, her voice a choked whisper. She moved her hips against his. Then, *"Oh."*

He had no thoughts left, only a hot haze of consciousness. "I want you," he growled. "So very much."

"Yes," she said. "Yes, please."

Yes, please.

He slid his hand between her legs.

She made a soft, startled sound, then relaxed and yielded, trusting him.

He slipped his fingers through the feather-soft curls and gently caressed her. Again she stiffened, and again, in the next moment, she surrendered to the intimate touch, moving against his hand, seeking more. Her soft hands moved more possessively over his shoulders, his arms, sending rivers of heat coursing down to the pit of his belly, making a hot darkness of his mind.

His caresses grew less gentle, and her hands tightened on his arms. "Oh, yes, please. Oh, yes. Dear God I—" and then she was shuddering to a climax, then another, and another.

He felt her pulsing pleasure ricochet through him, felt it course through his veins and reverberate in muscle and sinew. She was slick under his hand, and he was half mad with joy and need. She writhed against him. "Oh, please. Please." She caught her fingers in his hair and dragged his mouth to hers, and it was sin he tasted this time, hot and sweet carnal sin. He needed to drain every drop, to be inside her, to feel that madly pulsing pleasure from within.

Still half lost in the tumultuous kiss, he drew her leg up over his hip. He stroked more deeply with his fingers, readying her, though she was silky moist already, and his fingers trembled with need. She wanted him. He wanted her, more than anything in the world.

He poised himself to enter.

She slid her hand down his belly, and he groaned against her mouth. She was murmuring. He couldn't understand. His mind was thick and dark and hot.

Then he felt her hand close over his rod. The thick, black world went blinding white, her touch a lightning strike, blasting through him. It jolted through muscle and pumped through vein . . . and he exploded, spilling himself onto her belly.

HE took Mirabel with him when he rolled off her and she, mere putty in those long, knowing hands, went easily. A delirious happiness filled her being, while pure physical pleasure cascaded over her skin and through her veins and made her tremble.

He drew her close and tucked her up against him, her backside pressing against his groin. She nestled there comfortably and thought hazily that this was where she belonged, must have always belonged. He was big and warm and wonderfully solid. She reached back and stroked the taut, muscular thigh pressed to hers. She felt him wince, and consciousness stumbled back, and she realized she'd run her hand over the wounded thigh. What she felt against her palm was a tangle of smooth, raised scar tissue.

"I'm sorry," she whispered. "Does it pain you?"

He made an odd sound, a laugh or a groan or something in between. "No, sweet, not at all. Another kind of suffering."

He pressed his mouth to her neck, and she shivered.

"Like that," he said.

Pleasure. It pleased him when she touched him. She knew that. She'd felt his pleasure, an echo of her own, with every caress. It was as though he were an echo of her and she of him. It was as though they'd always known each other, been part of each other, but some interruption had come, separating them for a time.

She could not speak of it yet. What had happened to her

was too magical. What she'd felt was beyond any words she possessed. To have him touch her so intimately, to give herself up completely—it was so wonderful it hurt. If only she'd realized what would happen when she touched him so brazenly, she wouldn't have done it. She'd wanted him inside her.

But no, it was better this way, for both of them. No consequences.

She swallowed the lump forming in her throat.

"It's that tyrannical leg," she said. "Always wanting attention. Let me look at it."

"It isn't pretty," he said. "But what do you care? You see the beauty in the black moorlands, where others see ugliness and bleakness. And anyway, you're a country-woman. You've no doubt watched cattle, sheep, and pigs give birth. You must have a wonderfully strong stomach."

"Women are not so squeamish as men," she said.

"Squeamish?" He laughed.

She turned in his arms, paused to kiss his neck and shoulder, then regarded the damaged limb.

The injury was more extensive than she'd imagined. Not one, but a large tangle of scars spread from his hip nearly to his knee.

"It must have been a fearful wound," she said. "Wounds, I mean. It is amazing you were able to keep the leg and live."

She felt him stiffen.

"Shall I change the subject?" she asked.

It was a while before he answered, his voice very low, "The surgeons said they must take it off. I wouldn't let them. I was . . ." A long pause. "I'm not sure I was rational at the time. But Gordy was, and he seconded me."

"You must have lost a great deal of blood," she said. "That would make it hard to think clearly."

He buried his face in her hair.

"And your having lost so much blood would make it very risky to amputate," she went on. "I hadn't thought of that. I suppose the surgeons did not know what else to do.

Neither would I, come to that. I don't know how you found the Turkish healer, but he—or she—seems to have saved your life. You were fortunate your friend was there. Lord Gordmor."

She owed this magical interlude to her enemy, then. She'd soared to the stars and back because of him. The man aiming to destroy her world had saved this man's life.

She would not think about it.

She stroked over his chest, over the silky hair. "There's more gold," she murmured.

"There's what?"

"More gold in the hair on your chest than on your head." She looked up and met an unreadable amber gaze. "I have paid very close attention to these little details," she added.

She'd been memorizing him, so that later . . .

She put that thought aside, too. She wanted to concentrate on *now.* It would be over all too soon.

Now she was warm and content and safe, and still at one with him. Soon . . .

Soon. Oh, Lord, how long had she been here?

Pleasure and warmth began to dissolve as reality slithered back in, the snake in the garden.

She looked up at him. "I must go," she said.

His arms tightened about her.

"I must leave now," she said. "I cannot stay all afternoon . . . though I wish I could."

His gaze darkened. "We need to talk first," he said.

"We can talk another time," she said.

"About us," he said.

"There isn't—won't be—any 'us.'"

"I think we must talk about marriage," he said.

Her heart skipped and fluttered, exultant and fearful at once. Mad and sane at the same time.

She drew in a long, steadying breath and let it out, and rested her head upon his chest. "I'm a countrywoman, as you pointed out," she said. "I know how animals are impregnated. You did not impregnate me."

He gave a short laugh. "It was not for want of trying. But you—Gad, with you I have all the control of a horny schoolboy."

She lifted her hand and laid the palm against his cheek. "I regret nothing," she said. "You must not, either. You are not responsible for my virtue. You did not trick or deceive me. I knew what I was doing."

"It doesn't matter," he said. "I knew what I was doing, too—or thought I did. I never meant for it to go so far."

"I did," she said.

"That makes no difference," he said.

"Don't tell me it's a question of honor."

"Not simply honor," he said. "Honor and affection. I care for you."

It came then, all unbidden, the memory: William, storming through her ravaged plantation, pulling her into his arms. *I love you, Mirabel. Don't ruin two lives. Don't make me go away without you.*

She'd held firm then, though she was so deeply in love, because too much was at stake.

This was mere infatuation, she told herself. Yielding to it would render everything she'd done pointless. She would have sacrificed William's love for nothing. All these years of working to save the place she loved, the place her mother had loved—all for nothing.

She tried to wriggle free. The powerful arms did not give way one iota. "Mr. Carsington," she said.

"Alistair," he said.

"Mr. Carsington," she said firmly. "Pray use your head. Marriage is out of the question. In a very short time we shall be at odds, and you may be certain I shall fight you, mercilessly, with every weapon at my disposal. This—this interlude, as agreeable as it has been . . ." She trailed off, honesty getting the better of her. "Not agreeable. It was . . . perfect. And I care for you, too, but I do not see how any woman could help it. I cannot allow these feelings or our . . . intimacy to influence me."

He kissed her forehead.

She wanted to cry.

"I refuse to believe the situation cannot be resolved more happily," he said. "We have not even had a proper discussion about it."

"There is only one feasible route for your friend's canal," she said. "Believe me, I've searched for alternatives. There aren't any."

"The route can be shaped in various ways," he said.

"The result will be the same," she said. "You will make a public highway through my peaceful, backward world, and it will change beyond recognition and beyond recall. I cannot let that happen. To an outsider, Longledge is like a hundred other rustic places. But to me it is unique and precious."

"My dear, I understand that."

The gentleness of his voice nearly undid her. Tears itched at the corners of her eyes. Her throat ached.

She set her fist against his chest and pushed. This time he let her go.

She started to get up. He sighed and said, "Wait."

He got up, crossed the room to the washstand, and filled the basin.

For a moment she watched his long, powerful body move, so graceful in spite of the limp. Then she looked away.

He brought her the basin and a towel.

She hurriedly washed herself while he, still magnificently, unself-consciously naked, slowly went about gathering her clothes.

He came to the bed and sat down, his arms filled with her garments. He did not give them to her but sat staring at them.

She dug out her chemise and drawers and wriggled into them. She found her stockings, sat down beside him and, with shaking fingers, drew them on.

When she was sure she could trust herself to speak again, she said, "I understand you, too. I know you are loyal and high-minded—"

"It was not very high-minded to debauch you," he growled. He set her clothes down next to her, got up, grabbed his breeches, and pulled them on.

"I asked—no, *demanded*—to be debauched," she said.

"Don't be absurd."

He plucked her garters from the heap of clothes, started to give them to her, then snatched them back. He knelt and tied them. When he was done, he kissed the beauty mark near her knee.

The kiss made a shambles of her resolve. It took all her willpower to maintain a pretense of objectivity.

"It isn't your fault," she said. "I did everything I could think of to seduce you. It was wrong of me. I should not have taken advantage of a sick man, but I am not an over-scrupulous woman." She stood. "I would be much obliged if you would help me with my stays and frock."

He stared at her for the longest time, his dark amber gaze so searching. Then he did as she asked.

He laced up her corset with disconcerting efficiency.

She wondered how many women—in addition to the seven or eight she knew of—he'd dressed and undressed. She felt a pang, surprisingly painful, of some emotion she hoped was not jealousy.

In another few moments, he'd helped her into her dress and fastened it. Her hair took more time, because the pins were everywhere. Still, to her it seemed to take no time at all.

But she had no excuse now to delay her departure, and so she started toward the window.

He caught her arm and drew her back.

"Mirabel, there are other matters to consider besides the canal," he said. "If there is the least blemish on your reputation because of me—"

"You worry too much," she said, though worry niggled at her, too. Her effectiveness in the community depended on her neighbors' respect for her, which would vanish if any hint of today's adventure got out. Yet she went on coolly, "This isn't London's beau monde, ruled by a small court of capricious matrons. My neighbors are not such high sticklers. I should have to commit a hanging offense before they would cut me. Actually, being suspected of a dalliance with you may increase my social credit and make me appear more interesting and dashing."

His countenance hardened. He did not release her arm, only stood looking at her, his eyes dark.

"That will happen only if they do suspect," she said. "Which is most unlikely—unless you make me late getting home."

"But if they do, I will hear of it," he said. "And I will do what is right."

She had no doubt he would try. He had probably been born wearing shining armor. And it was typical of fate's perversity to send Sir Galahad into her life only to lay waste, like any evil dragon, to everything she held dear.

She mustered a cheerful smile. "If my neighbors suspect I've been naughty, they'll entertain themselves with watching to discover if I am increasing," she said. "When it finally becomes clear that Lord Hargate's war hero son did not get a bastard on me, they will turn to a new sensation. Sorley's pig will eat Mrs. Ridler's nasturtiums. One of the vicar's prize marrows will disappear mysteriously the night before the fair. Mrs. Earnshaw's housekeeper will see a ghost in the stillroom."

She reached up with her free hand and stroked his jaw. "I must go now."

He released her and turned away.

Mirabel hurried to the window and climbed out.

She didn't let herself look back.

She'd have the rest of her life for looking back.

Thirteen

THOUGH it was futile to attempt to keep secrets from one's manservant, Alistair tried. He dressed quickly, found a brush, and whisked at the footprints on the counterpane.

He heard Crewe come in, sighed, and went on brushing.

The valet approached, sponge in hand. "If you will permit me, sir," he said. "A damp sponge may better serve the purpose."

Alistair moved away.

Crewe rubbed at the spots. "You have inserted your waistcoat buttons through the wrong buttonholes," he informed his master, "and a hairpin is caught in the right sleeve of your coat."

"Damn me to Hell," Alistair muttered. He rebuttoned the waistcoat and removed the hairpin. There would be more among the bedclothes and pillows, but he must trust Crewe to remove all such evidence before the maids could spot it.

Maids. Had anyone else come upstairs?

"Crewe, the other servants . . ."

"No one else has come near this part of the house for the last hour or more," his faithful valet said. "Upon ascertaining that you would prefer not to be disturbed, I decided to seek domestic advice from Captain Hughes's staff. They were so good as to vouchsafe to me their favorite receipts for preparing scouring balls, and their opinions as to whether it was preferable to use soap or spirit of wine to clean gold lace and embroidery."

Crewe had kept the other servants away, in other words.

If only the man had shown less tact and burst in upon his master before the master could embark upon an act of stupidity far surpassing anything he had done previously.

But it was not Crewe's job to do Alistair's thinking for him. The master proving bereft of morals, the servant had acted to shield the lady from discovery and disgrace.

"You are a paragon, Crewe, do you know that?" Alistair said. "You are the wisest and most faithful of servants."

"It is no hardship to serve a good master, and they are rarer than many people think," said Crewe. Having removed the last vestiges of Miss Oldridge's footprints, he commenced remaking the bed. "They seem, however, not so rare a species in this corner of Derbyshire. Captain Hughes's staff are devoted to him and cannot sing his praises loud enough. As to the inhabitants of Oldridge Hall, I have personal experience of their kindness and generosity."

The bed now rid of all traces of recent events, Crewe turned his attention to the carpet. He collected three hairpins, a broken button, a minute piece of lace, and some odd bits of thread.

While the servant scoured the room for other compromising evidence, his master made a decision.

Two hours later, while Captain Hughes was in a hothouse, trying to wrench Mr. Oldridge's attention from a dingy green something-or-other, Mr. Carsington and his manservant were riding back to Matlock Bath.

• • •

BY the time she reached home, Mirabel had begun to understand why maidens were strictly cautioned to protect their virtue and save their virginity for the wedding night.

She'd seen animals breed and thought she had an idea of what happened between men and women. But she'd left something out of the equation.

Animals didn't make love. It was purely physical.

Somehow, in her addled, ignorant mind, she'd assumed it would be that way: physical, pleasurable, and a relief of some kind—a release of pent-up feeling.

She hadn't guessed how sweet it could be or how the sweetness, as much as the passion, would intensify all she'd felt before.

She hadn't an inkling of how much it would hurt to say no when he spoke of marriage, and to make him—and herself—face the hard facts and the vast gulf dividing them.

She hadn't realized how painful and difficult it would be to drive away.

Now she realized she'd made a terrible mistake.

But it was done and couldn't be undone.

She would have what she'd wanted—or what she'd thought she'd wanted: an experience, a memory.

In time, she'd learn to dwell on the memory with pleasure, she told herself. She would remember that a man— She smiled ruefully. No, not merely a man. A handsome knight had ridden into her life, and for a time, he'd made her feel like the fair damsel in a romantic tale. For part of an afternoon, she'd had a happy ending.

That's more than you had yesterday, she told herself.

And so, resolved to be cheerful, she went home. Not feeling quite ready to face Mrs. Entwhistle, Mirabel went to her study.

This was a mistake, because she no sooner sat at the desk than she remembered the first, feverish embrace . . . the strong hands lifting her onto the desk—

She pushed away the recollection.

"Later," she muttered. "Later you can mope."

She forced her mind to the event that had precipitated today's fatal error: the women of Longledge and their husbands—the tradesmen and farmers who wouldn't speak up.

She got up from the desk and walked to the window and looked out on the fading afternoon. This window didn't offer much of a view, but even this slice—a glimpse of the trees that had so narrowly escaped Caleb Finch's saws—was balm to her wounded spirit.

As regrets softened and faded a degree, she turned over in her mind her original plan.

It had not been well thought out, true. While Mr. Carsington would not want to take unfair advantage, he also couldn't shirk his responsibility to the man who'd saved his life. How could he face Lord Gordmor and say, "I'm sorry, but I had to come back because no one would fight with me. Except for one love-starved spinster, they will all do anything I say. You'd better go instead, because they'll give you a proper fight."

Now that she played the scene out in her mind, she saw how ridiculous it sounded. Lord Gordmor wouldn't think his friend was disloyal; he'd think Mr. Carsington was insane.

He would think . . .

"Insane," she said softly. "Ailing. Getting worse. Insomnia. A fatigue of the nerves. The doctor said so."

And quickly, before her conscience could gather strength enough to stop her, she sat down and started writing the letters.

It did not take long, and when she was done, she went in search of her father, to get his signature.

According to Benton, Mr. Oldridge was unlikely to have gone far this day. A new specimen from foreign parts had been delivered this morning, and he was exceedingly worried about it.

She found her parent in a hothouse, frowning over a droopy piece of unidentifiable plant life. Captain Hughes was with him, apparently attempting the impossible: an intelligible conversation.

She greeted the captain, and after apologizing for the interruption said, "Papa, I need you to sign these two letters."

"Yes, my dear. In a moment."

Where her parent was concerned, "in a moment" could easily mean "not in this lifetime" and, possibly, "not for all eternity."

"I'm afraid it cannot wait, Papa," Mirabel said. "We have not a minute to lose. These messages must go out express."

Her father turned away from the plant to her and blinked. "Good heavens. What has happened?"

"You need not make yourself anxious," she said. "I have the matter in hand. Only sign them, please. It is improper for me to do so."

Since he was constantly making notes about his collection of vegetable matter, pen and ink were nearby. He did not, however, merely run an absent eye over the letters as usual and scribble his name. This time he read.

When he had done reading, he did not immediately take up his pen. Instead, he looked at her, much in the way he'd been scrutinizing his enfeebled new plant.

Mirabel assured herself that no one, and most especially not Sylvester Oldridge, could possibly deduce from looking at her face that, a few hours ago, she had lain naked in the arms of the Earl of Hargate's third son. Nor could Papa ascertain from her features the disgracefully wanton means by which she'd managed the feat.

"I do not think——" he began.

He did not complete the thought, because at that moment, Captain Hughes's footman Dobbs hurried into the hothouse, red-faced and panting.

"Beggin' pardon, sir—sirs—miss—but Mr. Nancarrow tole me to cut along smartly to the captain, as it won't wait and——"

"Then get on with it," the captain cut in. "What's amiss?"

"It's Mr. Carsington, sir. He's run away."

"Ah, well," said Papa. He moved away and signed the letters.

Mirabel could only stare at the servant.

"Have your wits gone begging?" the captain said to Dobbs. "The man's too sick to run away. More likely he walked too far and got lost, or collapsed from fatigue."

"Don't look like it, sir. He went with Mr. Crewe, and they took their horses."

"And no one made a move to stop them? Is Nancarrow incapacitated? Why didn't he send for me the instant he knew of it?"

"He did, sir. He only just found out hisself. Had the news from the stables. At first we thought it was one of the stablemen's jokes. But when I went up to Mr. Carsington's room, all his things was packed up, and the window was open."

"The *window?* Don't tell me the man climbed down on knotted sheets."

"No, sir. Mr. Vince took out the ladder this morning to check the rainwater heads, and he must've forgot it, because there it was, sir, right alongside Mr. Carsington's window."

THE second express letter from Oldridge Hall was delivered before cockcrow on Saturday, and awakened Lord Gordmor from a dead sleep.

With trembling hands, he tore the letter open. When he finished reading it, he swore violently.

He got up. Returning to sleep was out of the question. He paced his bedroom for a time, then summoned his manservant and told him to start packing.

It was well before the valet's normal time of rising. He blinked several times to assure himself this was his master, wide awake at this unspeakable hour, and proposing to travel.

But he only said, "Yes, my lord. Where to, my lord?"

"The ends of the earth, God help me," said his lordship. "Derbyshire."

SINCE Lord Gordmor expected to make a longish stay in the wilds of the East Midlands, his servants would need several hours to complete the packing.

Shortly before noon on Saturday, therefore, the viscount called on his sister.

She was still abed when he arrived, and listlessly sipping her chocolate. She grew more animated, however, when he told her about the letter.

She had a great deal to say, most of it to the tune of "I told you so."

"You did not tell me Car would become so ill," Gordmor snapped, after the tragic chorus had gone on, in his opinion, more than long enough.

"I knew he was not the man for the task," she said. "You won't admit it, and no one will speak of it openly, but all the world whispers that he hasn't been right since Waterloo. He spends more time with his tailor than anyone else—not to mention that he's scarcely looked at a woman since he came back. I always said it was a pernicious melancholia at the very least, but who listens to me?"

"A per-*what?* I don't recall your ever—"

"Now he is many miles away from all his friends," she went on, "surrounded by people who bear you—and by association, him—a great deal of ill will." She adjusted her frilly nightcap. "Very well, if you will look at me in that disagreeable way, I shall say not another word on the subject. But I am glad you are going at last, and only hope it is not too late."

• • •

LORD Gordmor called next upon Lord and Lady Hargate. He found only her ladyship at home. Having risen and breakfasted long since, she met him in the drawing room.

"Oh, you've come about Alistair," she said after they'd exchanged the usual courtesies. "We had an express this morning. Poor Mr. Oldridge is greatly concerned. But he has only a daughter and no experience of sons. I am sure his fears are exaggerated."

If the Hargates were unconcerned, the letter to the parents must have been far less candid than the one to the friend and partner.

"I trust that is the case, your ladyship," Gordmor said. "Nonetheless, I cannot be easy until I see for myself. I mean to set out for Derbyshire this day."

Her sleek eyebrows went up. "Are you sure you are well enough?"

Lord Gordmor assured her he was fully recovered from the influenza.

She studied him for what seemed a very long time before she said, "You are pale, but that may be the consequence of spending so many weeks indoors. I daresay you know your own constitution best. You are concerned, naturally, about the canal business."

"I had planned to deal with the Derbyshire side of matters myself," he said. "Then I fell ill and had no way of knowing how long I should be incapacitated."

"Time is of the essence, I understand," she said. "If Parliament does not pass your canal act before they rise for the summer, you might have to wait as long as another year to begin your work. We cannot be certain whether Parliament will sit again in the autumn."

"At any rate, we should prefer to begin digging in the good weather," he said.

The truth was, the work *must* begin this summer, sooner if possible.

Every delay would make the project more expensive. At

some point, it would become prohibitively so. More than one canal had languished, partly built, for lack of funds.

Meanwhile, Gordmor's mines would languish as well. While Peak coal was not renowned for its quality or quantity, it was adequate to fuel the steam engines used in local industries, devices which could only increase in number in the coming years.

His coal need not travel far, certainly not all the way to London. He only needed to transport it quickly and cheaply to customers ten or twenty miles away.

Once he could sell easily to larger markets, his bailiff had told him, it would be economically feasible to invest more in the mines and get more out of them. Moreover, once he had cheap transport, other minerals would justify the costs of getting them out of the ground. His Derbyshire property would eventually bring in a handsome income, rather than the meager funds it now provided.

He did not express his anxieties or his ambitions to the countess. He preferred not to dwell on them in his thoughts, either. This day, however, while he preserved his usual unflappable demeanor, they raced through his mind.

"Alistair did explain the scheme to me in great detail before he left," the countess said. "I was pleased to see him so enthusiastic. I had begun to fear he would never recover his spirits."

"He only wanted a challenge," Gordmor said. "Something to rouse his fighting spirit again."

She regarded him consideringly. "All the same, you are uneasy letting him fight alone."

"I confess I am, your ladyship. But then, as you are aware, a great deal is at stake, for both of us."

MORE than Alistair Carsington's fighting spirit was roused at present.

His conscience had become a Fury as fierce as any in Greek myth, and that was only a fraction of the turmoil in his heart.

He spent the rest of Friday poring over all the maps Wilkerson had, and making notes.

On Saturday, he rode out to Gordy's mines to see the lay of the land for himself.

On Sunday, he walked the short distance from his hotel to the village of Matlock. There he attended services at its ancient church and prayed for divine guidance, as his brain wasn't offering any.

He left the church feeling no more enlightened than he had after studying the maps or the mines and their environs.

He stayed after the regular parishioners had left, and walked about the churchyard, reading inscriptions.

Alistair knew none of the Oldridge family would be buried here. They had their own ancient church in Long-ledge. Their relatives would be interred there or in a mau-soleum on the estate.

He hadn't come to look for anybody's ancestors, how-ever. He simply had no reason to hurry back to his hotel. He could not conduct any business on this day. Without business, he had little to distract him from the viper's nest of problems that had developed out of what was supposed to have been a simple matter of a waterway.

He had dreaded the coming of Sunday with its dearth of distractions. He would have too much time to think, and since he couldn't think to any useful purpose, he'd rather have something to do.

Still, the familiar rituals in the unfamiliar church, among strangers, quieted his inner turmoil somewhat. The hilly churchyard, with its weathered and crooked stones, brought a measure of tranquillity as well.

The day was cool but not cold, the sky cloudy but not darkly so. Here and there a tree seemed to have taken heart that spring was coming and cautiously hinted at budding.

He slowly limped among the stones, pausing now and then to read those that were legible. Among the newer graves he found that of a Waterloo man.

Alistair laid his hand upon the simple headstone and stood there for a time.

That calmed him, too.

He didn't ask himself why Waterloo had slaughtered this man and spared him. He knew there was no answer, no rhyme or reason to these matters. He knew he hadn't been spared to any particular purpose. Nonetheless, unlike this poor fellow, Alistair was alive; it was up to him to give purpose to the life he'd been granted.

Thus spiritually fortified, he returned to his hotel and, in defiance of Dr. Woodfrey, read the newspapers Crewe had obtained the previous day and wrote half a dozen letters.

2 March

ON Monday morning, shortly before ten o'clock, Mirabel drove her curricle into Matlock Bath. She paid a visit to the postmistress and another to the proprietress of the newsroom and circulating library. Since these ladies could circulate news faster than the post or press, it was the quickest way to let all the world know her errand and, she hoped, keep gossip about her destination to a minimum.

Thence she proceeded to Wilkerson's Hotel, where she requested an inn servant unload her carriage. When the servant had carried the contents into the building, she asked for Crewe.

The valet appeared within a few minutes, his expression professionally clear of any signs of curiosity or anxiety.

"I need not ask how your master does," she said. "I know you take excellent care of him and make sure he adheres to Dr. Woodfrey's regimen."

"Well, as to that, miss—"

"I know you do the best you can, in difficult circumstances," she said. "I have only come to deliver to him some items we'd forgotten." She indicated the baskets the inn servant had set down nearby.

Though Crewe said nothing, he could not altogether conceal his bafflement when he glanced at the baskets.

Mirabel was well aware that Captain Hughes had sent

Mr. Carsington's belongings on to the hotel early on Saturday. This was what his ex-guest had requested in the note he'd left before escaping . . . via the ladder Mirabel had forgotten to move back to its original position.

"Some days ago, the ladies of Longledge Hill were so generous as to vouchsafe to me a number of remedies for Mr. Carsington," she explained to Crewe. She took out a list from her reticule. "You will find several conserves and cordials, an essence for relief of headache, a vegetable syrup for something or other—but there is a note attached to the jar, and you may find out for yourself. Let me see what else. Acid elixir of vitriol—excellent for flatulencies, I am told. Asafetida pills—which serve as well for hysteric complaints as for asthma, though in different dosages. Edinburgh yellow balsam. Daffy's elixir. Several jellies. Receipts for cooling drinks, wheys, possets, and wormwood ale."

Crewe's eyes widened. "Indeed, miss. Most . . . generous of the ladies."

"When Mr. Carsington returns to London, he might set up as an apothecary," she said.

"I thank you for the suggestion, Miss Oldridge," came a growl from behind her.

Mirabel whipped about.

The famous Waterloo hero stood but a few feet behind her, leaning on a cane, his beaver hat in his other hand.

He had, as usual, not a hair out of place. His collar points touched the firm line of his jaw. His neckcloth was its usual crisp perfection. The green tailcoat fit smoothly over the wide shoulders and chest and tapered to his lean waist. The trousers . . .

Her mind flooded with images: those long, muscular legs tangled with hers, the powerful arms pulling her close, the so-skillful hands moving over her skin, touching her in the most intimate places . . . the touch of his lips on the back of her neck . . . the murmured endearments.

She directed her gaze to his face, and aware she was flushed from head to toe, lifted her chin.

He regarded the baskets, then her.

"Flatulencies?" he said, eyebrows aloft. "Hysteric complaints?"

"The former is sometimes a consequence of immobility," Mirabel said. "The latter appears to be the way some of the ladies have interpreted Dr. Woodfrey's diagnosis of a fatigue of the nerves."

"My nerves are not fatigued," he said. "I am quite well."

He wasn't. His golden eyes were sunk in dark hollows.

"Your eyes," she began. Automatically her hand started to rise, to touch his cheek, but she drew it back and clutched her reticule with both hands.

"It's nothing to do with illness," he said. "I wish you would not—" He broke off and glanced about.

Crewe was making himself invisible as usual. However, the inn servant who'd carried in the baskets lingered in the hall. A maid had appeared as well and was dusting industriously nearby.

Mr. Carsington grew formal, asking after Mr. Oldridge and Mrs. Entwhistle.

Informed that they were well, he said, "I must not keep you, Miss Oldridge. I know you have many important claims upon your time. I will walk out with you, if I may. I contemplate a visit to the petrifying wells. Everyone tells me these natural wonders are not to be missed."

Mirabel assented with matching formality.

Once they were outside, strolling on the Parade and out of curious servants' earshot, he said in a low voice, "I wish you would put your mind at ease. I'm not in the least unwell. I only look haggard because of not getting a proper night's sleep. I keep fighting the confounded battle, night after night. Ah, yes, and there is a woman who plagues me as well."

Mirabel did not want to be the one who kept him awake. Yet she couldn't help but be glad that he thought of her. And she couldn't help wishing she might be there when the nightmares plagued him. She could hold him and . . . No, she couldn't. And anyway, before long he would be gone and out of her reach. Either his parents or Lord Gordmor would come soon and take matters out of his hands. And hers.

Once he was gone, she would become herself again. Eventually.

"You might try the baths," she said. "You will have them all to yourself, and the proprietors will give you every attention."

He sighed. "Very well, I shall try the famous baths. I have decided, at any rate, to become acquainted with all the tradesmen, museum keepers, and guides. Along with all the gossip, I might pick up an idea or insight that will help me solve the canal problem."

Mirabel had already tried. She'd looked at the problem from every possible angle and discovered no acceptable compromises, let alone alternatives. The canal must travel along relatively level ground. Between Lord Gordmor's mines and the Cromford Canal, the only stretch of such ground lay exactly where Lord Gordmor wished to build his waterway.

She had hoped to find he'd made a grave miscalculation, but he hadn't.

If there had been any other way . . .

There wasn't. She had searched and searched. Her only hope of defeating the canal scheme was to get rid of Mr. Carsington.

It would be better for everyone if he were gone. Better for her heart, certainly.

She had not expected to see him this day. She'd come early on purpose to forestall that possibility—or so she'd persuaded herself.

Liar, liar. She was still pretending, making excuses. Had she not come herself instead of sending servants with the boxes? Obviously she'd been hoping to hear his voice or catch one last glimpse of him.

And she'd made everything worse. A word, a glimpse, wouldn't suffice. She wondered what would. Nothing within the realm of possibility, certainly. The longer she remained near him, the harder she made it for herself.

She must turn away, go on about her business, her pretend business.

She looked up into the strongly chiseled countenance, into the burning gold of his eyes.

"I have not been to the petrifying wells in a long time," she said. "I wonder if my glove is still being incrustated."

Fourteen

LONG before he came, Alistair had been aware of the resort's various natural phenomena. The famous waters from Matlock Bath's mineral springs, for instance, offered other excitement besides baths.

The water was known for depositing a calcareous encrustation upon objects over which it flowed. At the petrifying wells, the results were displayed for the edification of visitors.

Miss Oldridge's glove had either long since been removed or had, over time, resolved into an anonymous lump of calcified matter. Still, other marvels remained. The keeper of the place was delighted to show Lord Hargate's famous son a petrified broom, a wig, and a bird's nest. Miss Oldridge persuaded Alistair to sacrifice his gloves, which, she whispered, would be of immense interest to tourists in the months and years to come.

"Duke Nicholas of Russia paid Matlock Bath a visit two years ago, in February, no less," she told Alistair after they left the place and started back toward Wilkerson's. "Being

Russian, he probably thought the weather balmy. The year before, we had Archdukes John and Louis of Austria. They are mere foreigners, however. Your visit the well keeper will boast of till his dying day, and your gloves will be pointed out to visitors with hushed reverence. When word gets out that a petrifying well in Matlock Bath is in possession of your gloves—not merely one, but the pair—tourists will flock to the place to view these holy relics."

Alistair looked down at her. She was smiling, and mischief twinkled in her far-too-blue eyes, and he longed to draw her into his arms and kiss her witless.

"Those were exquisitely made gloves," he said with feigned sorrow. "I shall never be able to replace them, and Crewe will never forgive me. But if the sacrifice improves trade, I must not repine."

"You may be sure that any business you patronize will make the most of it," she said. "Foreign noblemen are as common as flies these days, but such a heroic personage as Lord Hargate's son—"

"I'm not heroic," he said, careful to keep his voice light. "It's utter nonsense."

She stopped and turned to him. "It isn't nonsense. How can you think it is?"

They stood upon the South Parade, close by Wilkerson's and in full view and hearing of a number of interested passersby. Alistair knew he should return to the hotel and let her go on her way, but he wasn't ready to let her go. Not yet. She of all people needed to understand.

He remembered what she'd said about his wounded leg: that the odds had been against him either way. She'd shown him that he'd had as good a reason to say no to the surgeons as he had to say yes. He only wished he'd said no because he'd weighed the odds, not because he was terrified. He'd never forgive himself for that fear.

That, at least, was his own secret.

His alleged heroism was public, a difficulty he encountered almost daily. It was a thorn in his side, digging deeper and deeper as time passed. Perhaps if one person in the world—the one who meant the most to him—knew the truth, he could bear it better. He wished he could tell her all, but he couldn't. Still, he could tell her a part.

He looked about, but there was no place in the picturesque resort where they might be private without stirring gossip.

He was not entirely surprised when she, evidently guessing what he wanted, came to his rescue.

"Have you seen the view of Matlock Bath from farther up the hill?" she said. She nodded toward the road next to Wilkerson's, which led to the Heights of Abraham. "There is an excellent outlook but a short way up."

She started that way, and he went with her.

When they were out of the spa's earshot, she said, "I don't know why you must fight the battle of Waterloo night after night. I wish I knew of a posset or syrup to help you sleep peacefully. My father thinks the remedy is laudanum. Perhaps you might consult an apothecary about a small dose. Perhaps if the battle didn't haunt your dreams, you would not be so tetchy about the subject."

The battle wasn't all that haunted him, but he mustn't speak of the rest: how he longed for her, how he missed the sound of her voice, her scent, her touch.

"I am tetchy about being made out to be hero," he said. "I've borne it for a long time because I couldn't remember what happened that day. I had to take others' word for it. Now that I do remember, I can't bear your having the wrong idea of me. I value your good opinion—oh, and your affection, though I should not speak of that—I value these too much to have them under false pretenses."

She stared at him, blue eyes wide with disbelief. "What are you saying? False pretenses? There were eyewitnesses to your many acts of bravery."

"Others did as much and more," he said. "My actions were nothing extraordinary. There were men who'd been with Wellington for years, who acted with surpassing courage and gallantry. If you knew their stories, you would understand how demented it seems to me to be singled out as the hero."

She walked on, saying nothing. Alistair ached to tell her all. The full truth. What had happened at the surgeon's tent. Perhaps in time he would. Perhaps in time, if she would give him time, he would find the courage.

One step at a time down from the hero's pedestal.

He limped on with her in silence, glancing from time to time at her profile, wondering if she was reassessing him, and if her affection would survive the process. She was frowning. Oh, why had he not held his tongue?

"Last week, I had a letter from my Aunt Clothilde," she said. "It described in detail your tumultuous love affairs. Aunt never expurgates on my account, you see. She wrote about the riot at Kensington Gate, the pamphlets, the sponging house, the lawsuits, and the rest. Then I better understood why the Earl of Hargate said you were expensive and troublesome to keep."

Alistair felt the old weight descending upon him, the sense of pointlessness and weariness he hadn't felt in weeks. His past was like an albatross round his neck. It would cost him her affection, canal or no canal.

"I suppose this is the price one pays for having a forceful and exciting character," she went on. "You attract the press. The newspapers made you famous, not solely because of your deeds—though you are entitled to be proud of them—but because you made a grand story."

He heard the lilt in her voice and dared another glance at her face. A hint of a smile played at the corners of her soft lips, and humor danced in her blue eyes.

He remembered her bursting through the doors of the drawing room that first day, eyes sparkling, face lit . . . and the sunny smile wrapping about him and warming him . . . and all the shades and variations of that smile he'd seen since.

He remembered how the sight of her had lightened his heart, as the smallest change in her expression did now.

"A grand story?" he repeated.

"There was the scandal in London, the broken engagement, and the courtesan," she said. "Then the outraged father, sending you abroad. *As a diplomatic aide*. Lord Hargate never meant for you to be fighting, did he?"

"Certainly not. My sire deems me undisciplined and rebellious and altogether unfit for military service."

"But you were not the sort of man to sit tamely in Brussels while the others went to war," she went on. "Few know how you managed it. Those who do know won't say. Most of us know only that you somehow wangled a place for yourself and ended up in the thick of the fighting."

"At such times, the commanders are glad to have every man they can get," Alistair said. "I had friends from school who put in a good word for me, and I was persistent—attached myself like a barnacle. It was easier to let me in than to get rid of me."

"However it was done, you proved your mettle in battle," she said. "At risk of your own life, time and again, you rescued injured men of every rank. You fought bravely. You endured, even after you'd fallen. Then there was the dramatic tale of Lord Gordmor hunting through the darkness for you among the dead and dying, and the miracle of your recovery from grievous injuries. You see? It is a grand story, Mr. Carsington."

Alistair did see the full picture at last. He stopped and, leaning on his walking stick, stared at the ground while his mind played out the scenes in his head, like the scenes of a play. At the finale, he saw his family descend en masse and bear away the prodigal son to England.

And he laughed—from embarrassment or relief or perhaps simply because of the ridiculousness of his life.

Then he raised his head—a moment too late to discern the worried glance she cast him—and gazed at her, and said, "It is as you said that time when you came to Wilkerson's. You are the only one who would say such things to my face. Even my best friend . . ." He trailed off, grinning. "Poor Gordy. But why should he enlighten me as to the true nature of my fame when even my brothers—who are never in the least shy about setting me down—held their tongues?"

"They should have told you," she said. "But perhaps they didn't realize how deeply the matter distressed you."

Alistair shrugged. "My family never talks about it, at least not in my presence." After a moment, he added, "And I've done everything possible to discourage them and everyone else from discussing it."

He straightened, and it was then, for the first time since they'd set out, he noticed his surroundings.

What he saw robbed him of speech.

Immense rock formations thrust out from the hillside. Massive, stony obelisks lay strewn about, like ninepins. Upon them grew the lichens and mosses that so fascinated Mr. Oldridge. Trees and shrubs wedged in the spaces between rocks, and a sampling of braver and hardier wild plants hinted at the profusion that must appear in warmer seasons. Alistair heard water dripping from somewhere in the mountain, the same water that trickled through the petrifying wells.

The trees and rocks shut out everything else. He and she might have been on some fairy-tale island. He turned slowly round, gazing in wonder like a child.

"This site is called the Romantic Rocks," came her cool voice from a distance. "In the height of the season, it is overrun with tourists."

He looked at her.

She sat on one of the obelisk-like stones, her hands folded. Her dull grey bonnet and cloak blended into her surroundings, drawing all the attention to her glowing countenance and the fiery curls framing it.

"You love this place," he said.

"Not simply this spot," she said. "I am a part of the Peak, and it is part of me. My mother told me she fell in love with this part of Derbyshire when she fell in love with my father. Some of my earliest memories are of walking with her up to the Heights of Abraham. We often came to these rocks. We visited the caverns, too. We went to the baths and the petrifying wells. We took a boat across the river to the Lovers' Walks. We even made trips to Chatsworth and the other great houses. We never grew tired of the sights." Her voice softened with nostalgia. "Sometimes on our expeditions, we would sketch and paint. Sometimes my father came along. In those days, he was fascinated with botany, but in a more rational way. Mama made him wonderfully detailed paintings of plants and flowers."

Alistair walked to her and sat down beside her, thinking no more of his expensively tailored coat and the effect of moss and lichen upon it than she did of her unfashionable cloak.

"Your father loved her very much," he said.

She nodded. Her eyes glistened.

"If she was at all like you, I can understand your father's shutting himself off from the world for all these years," he said. "It is only a few days since last I saw you, yet to me it has seemed a dark and wearisome eternity."

She stood abruptly. "You are not to make love to me," she said in clipped tones. "I should not have taken you here. I should have stopped at the first picturesque viewpoint, as I meant—or thought I meant. I seem to persist in doing the exact opposite of what I ought to do."

Alistair rose as well, though more stiffly, for the rock was chilly and his leg had not forgiven him for the visit to the cold, damp petrifying well. "Love makes people behave strangely," he said.

"I am not in love with you," she said. "It is an infatuation. I have heard of such derangements happening to elderly spinsters."

"You are neither elderly nor deranged," he said. "Perhaps you are merely infatuated with me, but I am over head and ears in love with you, Mirabel."

She turned away. "I advise you to conquer the passion," she said in a voice as cold and brittle as ice, "because absolutely nothing will come of it."

Whatever Alistair might have expected, it wasn't this.

All the glow had gone out of her in an instant, and all the warmth and trust and affection.

He stood, chilled and uncomprehending, staring after her as she hurried away.

IN case her frigid leave-taking failed to discourage him from following, Mirabel made a quick detour and hurried down a well-concealed bypath.

She would not cry. She could not cry. In a few minutes, she would be back upon the South Parade, and people must not see her with red eyes and nose. If they did, the news would be all over Matlock in an hour, and traveling over the surrounding hills and dales in two.

She would have plenty of time to cry later, she told herself.

Alistair Carsington would soon be gone.

Still, at least this would be a clean break. If she had broken off cleanly with William Poynton in London eleven years ago, he would have stayed away. He would not have followed her here, and tried to change her mind, and made her more miserable than she was already—though he never meant to—and she would not have added to his unhappiness.

That was what came of trying to break off with someone kindly and gently: You only made it drag on longer and made everyone involved more wretched.

No, this way was better, Mirabel told herself. It would have been far better had she turned cold and cruel before Mr. Carsington declared his feelings. But she had been weak, wanting another minute with him before they separated forever, then another minute and another.

Still, she would have hurt him no matter when she did it, and perhaps it was only fair he wound her, too.

I am over head and ears in love with you, Mirabel.

Who would have thought those words—the sweetest any woman could wish to hear—could hurt so very much?

Still, she knew they would both heal. In time.

Meanwhile, something far more important than her heart was at stake.

She had no choice. She must get rid of him.

IT took Alistair only a minute or so to absorb the blow and set out after her, but it was a minute too long.

Though he went as fast as his leg would let him, he caught no glimpse of the grey bonnet.

Not until he came out of the walkway into the main road at Wilkerson's did he see her. It was the back of her, however, upon the curricle, with a smallish groom perched behind. The vehicle was fast disappearing from view.

He hurried into the hotel to order a horse and narrowly missed colliding with a servant hurrying out at the same moment.

"There you are, sir," said the servant. "There is a—"

"I want a horse," Alistair cut in. "Pray make haste."

"Yes, sir, but—"

"A horse, with a saddle upon it, quickly," Alistair snapped. "If it is not too terribly inconvenient."

The servant scurried out.

"And where were you thinking of going in such a lather, Car, if a fellow may be so impertinent as to ask?"

Alistair turned toward the familiar voice.

Lord Gordmor stood in the doorway leading to the private rooms. He wore a mud-spattered overcoat, and his boots looked as though they'd been dragged through a swamp and chewed on by crocodiles.

Alistair quickly collected himself. He was growing used to shocks. "You look like the devil," he told his friend. "I should ask what brings you here, but I am in rather a hurry. Why don't you have a bath or something? We'll talk when I get back."

"Ah, no, dear heart. I think we must talk now."

"Later," said Alistair. "There is something I must take care of first."

"Car, I have come a hundred fifty miles by post chaise,"

said his lordship. "A drunken idiot driving a phaeton four-in-hand ran us into a ditch late on Saturday, ten miles from anywhere in every direction. We spent most of the following day trying to find a soul willing to break the Sabbath to repair our vehicle. I have had not a wink of sleep since Oldridge's express came—which, by the way, it seems his daughter wrote. It broke my repose hours before any cock thought of crowing on Saturday."

Alistair had started to turn away, planning to run to the stables and saddle a horse himself if necessary. Gordy's last sentence brought him back sharply.

The only express messages Miss Oldridge had mentioned to him had gone out more than a week earlier.

"An express?" he said. "From Oldridge Hall? On Saturday *last?* Only three days ago?"

"You have calculated the number of days correctly," Gordy said. "I rejoice to find your brain damage has not affected the simple arithmetic functions."

"Brain damage." It took Alistair no time at all to put two and two together. "I see," he said calmly, though his voice dropped a full octave. "What other interesting news was Miss Oldridge so good as to communicate?"

THE two men adjourned to Alistair's private parlor. There Gordy handed him the latest urgent missive from Oldridge Hall.

Alistair read it while his lordship ate a much-belated breakfast.

Though Mr. Oldridge had signed the letter, the loopy swirls covering both sides of the paper were no more his than was the prose style. Alistair was certain both writing and contents were solely Miss Oldridge's.

Judging by the penmanship alone, one would guess her nature to be fanciful and her brain to be as feathery light and undisciplined as her hair.

The penmanship was sadly deceptive. Miss Oldridge's nature was candid to a shocking degree, down-to-earth, practical . . . and fiercely passionate. The brain under that fiery cloud of wild, silken hair was as soft and fuzzy as the average rapier.

She translated Dr. Woodfrey's "fatigue of the nerves" as "nervous collapse." The bump on the head became a brain injury. Citing Alistair's sunken, shadowed eyes, she hinted at his sinking into a decline. She compared his sleeplessness to Lady Macbeth's sleepwalking and Hamlet's restlessness—implying, in short, that Alistair was declining into insanity. Adding insult to injury, she made good use of his implying Dr. Woodfrey was an incompetent country quack. She recommended Mr. Carsington be examined in London by "medical practitioners better versed in diseases of the mind."

She modestly declared herself no expert in these cases. Perhaps she was mistaken. Indeed, she hoped she was, for Lord Gordmor's sake. Naturally, he knew best, but she would hesitate to leave her business affairs in the hands of a man who was not right in the head.

Long after Alistair had read it, twice—first in outraged disbelief and then with a grudging admiration—he continued to gaze at the series of whirls and swirls with which she'd covered the pages. Had he been alone, he would have traced those loops and twirls with his finger.

He had enough self-command not to do that, but not enough to remember to return the letter to Gordy. Instead, Alistair folded it up and tucked it inside his waistcoat next to his heart.

By the time he realized what he'd done, it was too late. He found Gordy regarding him quizzically over the rim of his ale tankard.

"Doubtless Oldridge—or his daughter—exaggerates the case," said his lordship. "Still, you must have a competent London physician look at you. The fall into the mountain stream cannot have done you any good, and—not to put too fine a point on it—we both know your brain box was not in perfect order after Waterloo."

"I had a fever then," Alistair said tightly. "I was delirious. The two conditions often go together."

"But when the fever passed, you didn't remember the
battle," his friend said. "You didn't know how you'd hurt
your leg. You didn't remember fighting. You wouldn't
have believed me if I hadn't brought in all those fellows to
talk about what you did."

"You knew," Alistair said.

"Of course I knew," Gordy said. "I've known you
since we were children. I know when something's wrong.
Hasn't it occurred to you that the recent bump on the head
might have further damaged a place already fragile?"

"I had amnesia," Alistair said. Gordy looked dubious.

"Amnesia," Alistair repeated. He almost added *you
idiot,* but he recalled it was Miss Oldridge who'd first put
a name to the ailment, so he was as much an idiot as
Gordy—and everyone else who'd noticed and failed to
mention it—for not grasping the obvious.

"Amnesia," Gordy said.

"Yes. The recent bump on the head *restored my memory.*"

"But you look ill, Car. Almost as bad as you did when
Zorah and I carried you out of the surgeon's tent."

"That's because of the insomnia," Alistair said.

"I see. Amnesia and insomnia. Anything else?"

"I'm not insane," Alistair said.

"I did not say you were. Nonetheless—"

"Mental disease wouldn't have occurred to you if Miss
Oldridge's letter didn't suggest it," Alistair said impatiently. "She's manipulating you, don't you see? She's trying to get rid of me."

Gordy's pale eyebrows climbed upward. "Really? This
is novel. More often than not, one is obliged to peel the
women off you. Even Judith Gilford would have taken you
back—especially after Waterloo—if only you had gone
back to her and groveled a little."

"I used her abominably," Alistair muttered. "I am
ashamed to think of it."

"Car, we both know she was impossible."

"That is no excuse for betraying her with another woman—and worse, humiliating her by doing so publicly," Alistair said. "Small wonder Miss Oldridge doesn't trust me to represent her interests fairly."

Lord Gordmor set down his tankard. "I beg your pardon. I am not sure I heard aright. *Her* interests?"

"Everyone's interests," Alistair said. "She speaks for the others on Longledge Hill, because they are too overawed by my father and my so-called heroics to speak for themselves."

After a short, stunned silence, his lordship spoke: "In other words, Miss Oldridge is the only one who has raised any objections to the canal. Our only opposition is a woman. Who cannot vote. Who controls not a single seat in the House of Commons."

"She isn't the only opposition," Alistair said. "She is the only one who dares to voice her objections."

"My dear fellow, it is not our job to encourage the timid to speak up," Gordmor said patiently. "It is our job to build a canal. At present, our only opposition is a woman—which is the same as no opposition at all. We must strike while the iron is hot."

"We aren't ready to strike," Alistair said. "For two weeks I've been shut away. That old hen Woodfrey forbade me to see anyone or even read a letter. I haven't so much as begun discussing the canal with the landowners."

"You don't need to *discuss* it."

"Gordy, these people are not the enemy. We need to come to an agreement, not mow them down."

Lord Gordmor rose. "You are my dearest friend in all the world, Car, but I cannot let your conscience or brain injury or whatever it is ruin a great opportunity. Too much is at stake. If you were more composed in your mind, you would realize it. I wish I could wait for you to become composed, but I cannot. I am going out now to place a notice in the papers for the canal committee meeting."

"Now?" Alistair said, aghast. "For when?"

"A week from Wednesday. The local announcement

will appear in Wednesday's Derby *Mercury*. That will prevent anyone's complaining of insufficient notice—though all of Derbyshire knows of our plans by now. I can only pray Wednesday is not too late."

Fifteen

MIRABEL'S mother was not buried in the Longledge churchyard but in the family's mausoleum.

Built early in the previous century, the circular, Palladian-style structure stood on a rise at some distance from the house, past the bridge spanning a man-made river created at about the same time.

Two hours after leaving Matlock Bath, Mirabel stood there, drinking in the view whose beauty never failed to bring her a degree of peace, no matter how bleak or impossible her life might seem at the time.

"Oh, Mama, what on earth am I to do?" she said.

No answer was forthcoming. Mirabel had not spoken aloud expecting one. She'd spoken only because there was no one alive to whom she could fully open her heart.

She continued walking from one pillar to the next while telling her mother—and any other entombed ancestors who cared to listen—all about the last few weeks.

The March wind blew strong this day, and its whistles and moans as it swept round and through the edifice easily drowned out her voice as well as the hoofbeats upon the bridge below.

At one point, she caught a faint whinny, but the wind blew it away, and she assumed it was Sophy, who was in one of her moods. Today the mare had taken a dislike to the bridge and could barely be got across it. Once across, she refused to go anywhere but downhill and would not take her mistress up toward the mausoleum.

Every now and again, Sophy developed one of these inexplicable aversions. In no humor for a war of wills with an animal many times her size and weight, Mirabel simply gave in. She tethered the mare near the bridge and walked the rest of the way.

At the moment, she stood on the other side of the building, gazing at the place where Lord Gordmor's canal would cut through the landscape. Consequently, she didn't see the tall figure dismount, tether his horse near Sophy, and begin limping determinedly up the hill.

Mirabel was still staring in frustration at the invisible canal when she heard the footsteps upon the stone floor. She turned that way, and felt her heart leap, most painfully.

She lifted her chin and donned her haughtiest, coldest expression. "Mr. Carsington," she said curtly.

"You wicked, wicked girl," he said.

His gold eyes sparked, and his color was up. The air thickened and crackled as though a storm brewed nearby.

She knew he was the storm and what she felt was the force of his anger. It was as palpable as the charm that made even practiced courtesans fall helplessly in love with him. She wanted to back away, out of range of that compelling force, but pride wouldn't let her retreat.

She lifted her chin a degree higher. "It is nothing to me what you think of me," she said. "You are nothing to me at all."

"You are the worst of liars." He advanced.

She was an instant too slow to react, and he caught her and pulled her into his arms. She twisted and ducked her head. If he kissed her, she would go to pieces.

He didn't kiss her. He only crushed her to him and held her while he rumbled into her bonnet, "Woodfrey's a quack, is he? I walk in my sleep and talk to myself, do I? I ought to be examined by practitioners familiar with *diseases of the mind,* ought I? And you would not put your business affairs in the hands of a man who was *not right in the head.* Oh, no, indeed. But then, you will not put your affairs in anyone's hands. Your body is another matter, I believe."

Mirabel could have fought until he let her go. He was too chivalrous not to let go if she struggled. But she didn't want to be let go.

He'd been stealing her heart, bit by bit, since the day she'd met him. Soon she'd have no part left to call her own. She knew that this time the heartache would be worse, much worse than what she'd endured when she'd given up William. Yet she'd bear it in order to have this moment.

"I'm sorry," she said, her voice muffled against his coat.

Mr. Carsington had no difficulty hearing the apology, apparently, for he detached her from his coat and stepped back a pace to hold her at arm's length and look at her. "The letter to Gordmor was monstrous underhand, Mirabel. If I didn't know you better, it would make me think you had seduced me on purpose to *make* me insane."

"Oh, no," she said. "What I told you then was the truth, I vow."

"You said you had strong feelings for me."

"Yes, and what good do they do anybody?" she cried. "They won't make that troublesome canal of yours vanish, will they? And *there* is where it will go." She nodded in the direction of the canal route through the landscape. "You will spoil Mama's view—and all her work as well as mine—and every time I come here I will see it and it will h-hurt me."

Her eyes filled, and her throat tightened.

"Your mother's work," he repeated after a moment. Mirabel nodded. The intensity of her grief took her by surprise, and she couldn't yet trust herself to speak. She had not cried in front of anyone since her mother died. Tears should be private. And anyway, they made men cross or uneasy or confused or, more usually, all three at once.

He let go of her and moved away. He stood for a time looking where she'd indicated. Then he came back and took her hand.

"The landscape design is hers, I take it?" he said.

He had given Mirabel the moment she needed to regain her composure.

"My mother was an artist," she said, her voice steady now. "In other circumstances, if she'd been a man, she might have become another Capability Brown."

SHE didn't need to say more.

Alistair had understood from the moment she spoke of the canal's spoiling her mother's view. But once begun, Mirabel continued smoothly enough. Talking seemed to calm her.

She told the story, both hers and that of the land. In her mind, evidently, these were one and the same thing.

She told him how the estate had evolved over the years, and how the greatest change occurred nearly a century ago, when the mausoleum was built and the grounds redesigned. It was an attempt at the naturalistic style of which Lancelot "Capability" Brown had been the master.

The result, however, had never been entirely satisfactory, and over time, various elements had been let to deteriorate either because they were undesirable or had proved impractical.

It was Alicia Oldridge who had begun transforming the place, over the course of the nearly twenty years she had been married. She had died without completing her plans. Mirabel knew every detail, however. Her mother had shared her ideas and enthusiasm from the time her daughter was old enough to comprehend them.

"She made this view," the daughter was saying now.

"There used to be a summerhouse halfway down the hill, above the bridge. She had it moved and tucked away among those trees, so that you come across it unexpectedly when you follow the winding path along the river."

She pointed to another place, where she had made changes according to her mother's plans. She described so vividly what had been there before that Alistair could see clearly, in his mind's eye, both the extent of the transformation and its artistry and subtlety.

When she had taken him fully round the colonnade encircling the mausoleum and given him the history of the corresponding views, she fell silent.

Something in the quiet, and in her stance, made him wonder if she was regretting the revelations.

He studied her profile. Then he bent his head slightly, trying discreetly for a better look.

She did not seem aware of him. Though her gaze was fixed upon a distant spot, he doubted she saw that, either. Her eyes held the faraway expression he'd observed more than once in her father's. She looked at the distant place exactly as Mr. Oldridge had gazed at the chandelier on the evening when Alistair first tried to enlist him on the side of the canal.

Then, slowly, the corner of her mouth began to turn up a very, very little.

Alistair directed his own gaze straight ahead. "I should give anything," he said, "to know what is going through that busy mind of yours."

"I was trying to think of ways to get rid of you, but my brain won't cooperate," she said. "Or my heart. Or whatever it is. I try to think, but then I see you . . . naked."

His head swiveled so sharply it was a wonder it didn't fly clean off his neck. "You *what?*"

"You," she said. "Naked."

For a time, he had done very well, not thinking of her naked. This day he had only held her in his arms, and not for so very long, either. Not nearly long enough.

He had not kissed her or attempted to remove so much

as a glove, though he would give anything to taste her mouth again, to feel her hands on him. She had only to touch his face and the world changed, came right.

Yet somehow he'd resisted desire, and so he'd flattered himself that he was maturing after all. This time he would not be so unspeakably stupid as before.

But she no sooner said the fatal words than he saw her standing upon the bed with her skirts hiked up to her thighs, revealing . . . oh, no, the tiny, lopsided, upside down heart at the crook of her knee . . . and then she was down upon the bed . . . the perfect breasts tipped with sweet, pink buds . . . the feather-soft curls between her pretty legs.

He remembered the scent and taste of her skin. He remembered the trust, the tenderness, the passion.

He squared his shoulders and set his jaw. "When we are wed, you may see me naked all you like," he said. "Until then, it would be best not to refer to the subject."

"We are not going to be wed," she said.

"Yes, we are, though it may take some time." He turned her toward him, careful to keep his hands only lightly upon her shoulders. "You must not take off your clothes in front of any other man, Mirabel."

"Certainly not," she said. "It isn't the sort of thing I make a practice of. It is only you—"

"That is precisely what I am saying," he said. "Only *me*. That is the point—one of the points—of being married."

"It did not seem to be a very important point for Lady Thurlow," she said.

Curse her aunt! The Thurlow affair was not public knowledge. How had she found out? And what was she thinking, to communicate such knowledge to an innocent?

"You may not cast my youthful indiscretions in my face," he said. "My father performs that service admirably. Furthermore, I am mending my ways. If I were not, I should take advantage of this moment. We're alone. No one is watching."

They were alone. No one was watching. And he didn't

want to reform. He wanted to be worse than he'd ever been before. He wanted to snatch any opportunity offered, to do whatever was necessary to have her, and honor be damned.

The distance between them was so great, and so very small. The very air between them vibrated.

He closed the space in a single stride, pulled her into his arms, and kissed her.

And she kissed him back, surrendering instantly, her soft mouth yielding to the first light pressure of his. Her hands came up, cupping his face, holding him—as though she needed to, as though he wasn't already bound to her.

He undid the bonnet ribbons, and tossed the ugly thing aside, and dragged his fingers through the unruly copper-tinted curls. She knocked his hat off, and laughed against his mouth, and the husky, wicked sound echoed inside him. She was innocent in so many ways, yet she tasted and sounded like sin and made him drunk with longing.

He undid the fastenings of her hideous cloak and slid his hands over her bosom, down over the delicious little waist, down over the voluptuous curve of her hips and perfect derrière.

She moved under his hands, unself-consciously enjoying and seeking more, and driving him wild with frustration. Too many garments, too many obstacles. He reclaimed her mouth, kissing her deeply, ferociously, while he eased her back against a pillar.

He pushed the cloak off her shoulders. While it slid to the stone floor, he was undoing the fastenings of her bodice, then dragging it down. He broke the kiss to bury his face in her neck and drink in her scent. He trailed kisses along her shoulder and down to the edge of her chemise, to the smooth swell of her breasts, straining at the confining corset.

She held him there, her hands stroking through his hair. She kissed the top of his head, an unexpected tenderness in the midst of mindless passion. A wild rush of feeling tore through him, as though some inner dam had burst. He could not get enough of her, could not get close enough.

He dragged up her skirts and petticoats—too much in the way—and his hand slid up her inner thigh to the opening of her silk drawers. She pushed against his hand. "Oh, please." Her voice was a soft moan laced with laughter. "Oh, no. Oh, please, yes."

He sank to his knees and kissed her in that soft, most feminine of secret places, and heard her suck in her breath and let it out on a sigh. "Oh," she whispered. "Oh, that is *wicked.*"

Laughter, still, the faintest trace. And he laughed, too, inwardly, with a wicked joy, while he made love to her with his lips, his tongue, while he held her beautiful, trembling legs and felt her body convulse, wave after wave of shuddering pleasure. Pleasure raced through him, too, in waves of liquid heat. It flooded his brain, submerging the last bits of reason and principle, and roared through his blood to swirl dangerously in the pit of his belly.

He kissed the inside of her knee, where the funny, upside down heart was. Then, when she was still weak and helpless, trembling in the aftermath of euphoria, he rose, to make her his, because he must. He was hot and mad with need, his swollen rod straining toward her.

But as he reached for the first trouser button, a gust of wind shrieked and whistled through the colonnade, so sharp and sudden that it startled him to consciousness.

The wind screamed like an angry ghost, and he remembered where they were: her mother's burial place.

A chill colder than the March wind went through him. He let her dress fall, and brought his hands to her shoulders, and leaning forward, rested his forehead against hers, and waited for his breath to come back and his thundering heart to slow.

When he could speak he said thickly, "My reform is not progressing as well as I thought. I was sure I could resist doing something scandalous with you against one of these columns."

"I hoped you would not resist," she said. "But I had no idea there was anything so scandalous as *that.*"

He lifted his head and met her dazed blue gaze.

"You like to flirt with danger, I see," he said.

"No, not at all," she said. "I am always so careful and sensible. But you make me so . . ." She looked away. "Happy. The word is inadequate. My heart lightens when you are by, and I feel like a girl again."

His heart ached. All he wanted was to make her happy, and all he seemed to do was cause her trouble. His demented lust: Twice he'd come a heartbeat away from deflowering her. His curst, crucial canal scheme: The great obstacle between them was his only hope for the economic independence that would let him offer for her honorably and proudly.

He mustered a smile. "You mean I make you foolish."

She laughed. "Yes, that, too. And you are foolish to come here. You should have taken the bad-tasting medicine I administered before and let it cure you."

"When you told me to conquer my passion, you mean."

"I was trying to make it easier for us both," she said. Belatedly she noticed her state of undress. She tugged at her bodice. "Oh, look what you've done. I wish my maid were half as quick as you. I cannot believe you have had only seven or eight romantic episodes. It is hard to believe you've done anything else your whole life but dress and undress women, you are so expert at it."

At the moment, he wasn't sure he possessed any other talent. But he said nothing, only turned her about and did up the fastenings. He found her cloak and bonnet. He draped the ugly cloak over her shoulders. He did not attempt to retrieve the many lost hairpins but arranged her hair as best he could with the few remaining and stuffed the lot into the hideous bonnet.

As soon as he was done, he wanted to take everything off again. "When we are wed," he said, "the first thing I'll do is burn every last stitch of the abomination you call a wardrobe."

"We are not going to be wed," she said. "I have a weakness for you. I am deeply infatuated. This may cause me to forget, temporarily, what modest behavior is supposed to be, but I cannot forget why you are here."

"I don't expect you to forget it," he said. "I only ask you to try not to underestimate me. I know a solution exists."

She shut her eyes and let out a weary sigh, then opened them again and said, "Do you think I haven't tried to find one? I know Longledge far better than you, and I have searched and searched and turned the matter this way and that. If I thought a solution was possible, do you think I would have written that letter to Lord Gordmor?"

He recalled, then, why he'd come—or part of the reason, the rational part. He had to tell her. He couldn't let her learn it first from the newspaper on Wednesday. "Mirabel, I wish you hadn't written to him," he began. "I wish you'd trusted me. Now you've left us no time at all."

He hesitated. He'd come to warn her, but he'd forgotten about Gordy, what he owed him. It would seem like disloyalty. Yet Alistair had to warn her: It would be dishonorable, and the worst sort of betrayal, not to.

"No doubt your friend will make haste to hold his canal committee meeting," she said, the previously sultry voice now brisk and businesslike. "If he is wise, he will send the notice express this day to the papers, to make sure it arrives in time for this Wednesday's Derby *Mercury.*"

She already knew. Of course she would. Everyone said she had a good head for business. She understood how such matters were managed. She must know that parliamentary orders required the canal committee meeting announcement to appear in both the London *Gazette* and the local paper. Was that what she had been studying the other day? Was that what all those legal papers were about? Had she already begun planning how to throw legal obstacles in their way?

He told himself he must resist the temptation to interrogate her. Where she was concerned, Gordy must do his own spying. And she must do her own spying on Gordy.

How in blazes was a man to work out all the niceties of loyalties in such a case as this?

"He does not wish to lose a minute of time," Alistair hedged. "All the same, you must trust me to see the matter dealt with fairly."

"If you want the matter dealt with fairly, you must go back to London," she said. "I had expected you would be on your way by now."

"Yes, I know you had counted on my departing—or being taken back, rather, in a strait-waistcoat, no doubt."

"You are under a great strain, though you won't admit it," she said. "You cannot look after my interests and Lord Gordmor's at the same time. They are mutually exclusive. It is no wonder you dream incessantly of war, when you are fighting with yourself."

She moved closer and took both his hands in hers. "I have looked after my own and my father's affairs for more than ten years. This is not the first crisis I have confronted. I am not helpless or stupid."

"I know that," he said. "Still, it doesn't mean the man who loves you may not try to help you."

"I fear it does," she said. "I cannot fight properly when you are by. You make me deranged."

"It is not a fraction of what you do to me," he said, tangling his fingers with hers.

Gently she drew her hands away and folded them at her waist. "If you truly wish to give me a fighting chance, you must keep away from me. I can accomplish nothing productive while you are near. London would be best."

"I refuse to run away, merely because the situation is difficult," he said.

She huffed an impatient sigh. "If Lord Gordmor is truly the friend one supposes him to be, he will consider your well-being and insist upon your leaving. If he is so selfish as to keep you—or you persist in this hopeless—"

"For God's sake, Mirabel," he broke in. "You know my history. I *always* get into disastrous situations. Never once in my life have I had to get myself out of one. I am nine and twenty. And I am quite done with letting others fight my battles, while I go on my way feeling stupid and use-less—until I stumble into the next difficulty."

She studied his face briefly, walked away, and came back again. "I did not mean to treat you like a child," she said. "You are not in the least childish. You should not feel stupid or useless. I don't know why you do. We are all of us stumbling. Life is puzzling and difficult."

"I mean to puzzle it out," he said, "and find a solution for us."

She smiled then, a sunburst of a smile. "You will make me believe you, against all reason. Very well. Stay or leave, as you choose, of course."

"I am most certainly not leaving," he said.

She nodded. "As you wish." She stepped back a pace: Her chin went up, and her tone became coolly polite. "At present, you are Lord Gordmor's representative. Kindly be so good as to convey a message to his lordship. You may tell him I speak on behalf of my father, who does not con-sent to his lordship's putting a canal through this property. Tell him Mr. Oldridge is inalterably opposed to a canal in the Longledge environs and will fight him with every means at his disposal, both here and, if necessary, in Lon-don before Parliament. It would be well to warn his lord-ship, furthermore, that the Oldridge resources are by no means small. Will you do this for me, sir?"

The abrupt change, the cold, determined tone, took Al-istair aback. But only for a moment. He was growing used to being clubbed from behind, and recovered his poise with the speed and agility that practice so often brings.

"Certainly, Miss Oldridge." He bowed. "Will there be anything else?"

"Not at present," she said. "If I think of anything, I will send for you." She gave him a dismissive wave, which was hardly the good-bye he wanted.

But he'd already had more of her than he had any right to. He allowed himself one quick, longing glance at the column against which he'd introduced her to a pleasure far beyond her innocent imaginings.

Then he told himself that he'd more or less insisted on her treating him like an intelligent business representative, and that as Gordy's representative he'd never expected or wanted special treatment. Moreover, he had already received a great deal more of the romantic variety than he ought.

If he wanted tender good-byes, he'd better earn the right, with marriage. He could not wed until he had the means to support her. This would not happen until he and Gordmor made a success of the mines, which depended on the canal.

In short, this would-be knight in shining armor had several dragons to slay before he could sweep the fair damsel up onto his charger and gallop away.

And so he bade her a polite good day and started away. He'd gone but a few steps when he abruptly turned back, clasped her arms, and gave her one quick, ferocious kiss.

Then, leaving her to totter back against the column, he limped down the hill.

He did not look back, but he smiled.

WHEN Alistair returned to Wilkerson's, he found Lord Gordmor in the private dining parlor, keeping company with another tankard of ale.

Alistair ordered one for himself. After it had come and the servant departed, he delivered Miss Oldridge's message.

Gordmor took the news calmly enough. "It is no worse than we expected," he said. "Better, actually. When you set out from London, we supposed all the landowners were against us. Instead, our foe turns out to be only one of them." He drank. "All the same, I must insist upon your returning to Town."

"That is out of the question," Alistair said.

"Your loyalties are divided," his friend said. "I know you well enough to know where it must lead. You will try to accommodate opposing interests, which will only drive you mad. You look ill enough as it is. Your parents will wonder why I snatched you from the brink of death in Belgium only to let you be driven mad in Derbyshire. Furthermore, you are supposed to be the London representative. This was how we originally agreed to divide the work, if you recall."

"My life is always complicated," Alistair said. "It is time I learnt to manage it."

"I should like to know what you propose to do this time," Gordy said. "You have fallen in love with a woman who is determined to destroy us. Or am I mistaken? Perhaps you raced after Miss Oldridge in order to enlighten her regarding the relative merits of locks and aqueducts, or to explain the finer points of puddling."

It was pointless to dissemble, even if Alistair knew how. Concealing his feelings about a woman, however, was the one form of pretending he'd never mastered.

"You are not mistaken," he said. "I admit this presents a challenge, but it is one I'm resolved to meet."

"How?"

"I don't know yet, but I am determined."

"Car."

"I'll think of something," Alistair said.

Gordy regarded him for a moment, then shrugged. "What am I thinking, to argue with a Carsington? Very well. As you wish. I have nothing to lose by it. *You* might lose your mind, but some men are more comfortable doing without one. On the other hand, in the unlikely event you do succeed, you will spare us a great deal of expense and vexation. The longer this business drags on, the more costly it becomes."

Alistair understood his friend's hurry. He would have been in a hurry as well, if love hadn't slowed his mind.

He knew that every delay would give the landowners time to think of objections and raise the price of overcoming them. Beyond a doubt, Mirabel would help her neighbors in this mode of thinking.

"No matter what happens at Wednesday's meeting,

we must press ahead quickly," Gordy said. "Otherwise, we're in mortal danger of your lady love burying the parliamentary committee in a blizzard of petitions and counterpetitions."

Alistair was well aware of this. He knew Mirabel had already communicated with lawyers. In London they'd descend like locusts upon Parliament, where they would spawn swarms of witnesses to testify. Meanwhile, the landowners would have time to discover scores of new accommodations they needed, and the price of property-taking would soar. And along the way, increasing numbers of palms would want greasing.

It would cost a fortune and take forever. He and Gordy hadn't the fortune or the time.

Alistair had less than ten days to stop the woman he loved from ruining his friend, his brothers, and his last hope for himself.

ON Tuesday afternoon, Lord Gordmor's agent Thomas Jackson arrived in Stoney Middleton, a village in the High Peak, about fifteen miles from Matlock Bath.

Jackson had served under his lordship during wartime and was rewarded in peacetime with his present position as the viscount's representative on a number of fronts. He was as deeply devoted to Lord Gordmor as his lordship's bailiff Caleb Finch was devoted to Caleb Finch. Jackson, however, thought the bailiff's loyalties were of the same species as his own. He believed, for instance, that Finch had recently come to the Peak solely to further his master's interests in any and all ways possible.

This was Jackson's first and fatal mistake.

That evening he met with Finch at the Star Inn and Post House, to enlist the bailiff's help in promoting the canal scheme.

"His lordship wants the miners let off, to come to the meeting," Jackson was explaining after they'd tucked away a hearty supper. "He'd like one or two of the more articulate fellows to say a few words for the canal—how their future livelihoods depend on it, and all the ones depending on them: wives, children, and aging parents."

"Isn't a one of them what you call arti-cu-late," Caleb said. "And I don't think there's a one got a wife *and* wee ones *and* aging ma and pa." He lifted his tankard and swallowed. "The old ones has been planted a good whiles by now, rest their pore souls," he added piously. "Them and a lot of them pore wee babes as don't get enough to eat nor no medicine when a sickness comes on 'em. But as the cause is just, there mightn't be no harm in letting on like it was the way you say. All in the good cause."

And all in a good cause—which was to say, in the cause of Caleb Finch—he went on to blame his lordship's mine foreman for the present plight of the miners and their families. Caleb cited bad discipline, unsafe practices, poor maintenance, and inefficient methods, etc., etc.

This was because the mine foreman, to Finch's disgust, had proved an honest, diligent fellow. He'd refused to understand Finch's hints about one hand washing the other. He had, furthermore, let it be known that he'd heard some dark rumors about Finch's past in Derbyshire.

It was crucial, therefore, that the foreman be swiftly dismissed and utterly discredited. Finch had dismissed him first thing Monday morning and promptly set about the business of character assassination. The foreman was still reeling from the blow. Finch knew that Jackson would carry the slander to Lord Gordmor before the victim recovered sufficiently for a counterattack.

But this was by no means the most important matter to lay before his lordship's trusted agent.

"I'm worried his lordship don't know what he's up against," the bailiff told Jackson.

"All the good families are with us," Jackson said. "I and a half-dozen other men will be going from village to village, doing what we can to win support."

Everyone knew how this was done. Lord Gordmor's agents would be spreading goodwill in the form of good coin and good drink—the same method used so effectively during Parliamentary elections.

"Last I heard, you didn't have *all* the good families," Caleb said. "Last I heard, Miss Oldridge was dead set against any canal anywhere near her property."

"One woman," said Jackson dismissively. He lifted his tankard and drank.

"Like I said," Caleb said. "You don't know what you're up against. Was I in your place—" He put up his hand. "But never mind me. You're in charge of the politics. My business is looking after the property. You don't want my advice, even though my family lived here almost as far back as hers, and I know what she's like."

Jackson signaled for more ale. Then he leant toward Caleb and said, "I want what is best for his lordship. If you have useful information, let's not stand on ceremony or fret about who's in charge of what. We must work together."

"Well, all right then," said Caleb. "All in the good cause."

Sixteen

"... *whereas such a navigation would be of great utility to trade, and in particular benefiting the county of Derbyshire, a meeting will be held at the assembly room of the Old Bath Hotel, in Matlock Bath aforesaid, on Wednesday, the 11th day of March, 1818, at 10 of the clock in the forenoon, to consider of the proper ways and means to effect such navigation, at which meeting the nobility, gentry, and clergy of the said county, and all others who deem it their duty to interest themselves in a matter of so great importance are requested to attend.*"

His announcement appeared not only in the newspapers, as required by law, but, to Lord Gordmor's chagrin, in abbreviated form on placards in shop windows, on posters plastered to walls, carts, and wagons, and on pasteboard signs carried like battle standards about the streets of every village between Cromford and Little Ledgemore, the hamlet nearest his mines.

Consequently, even those who failed to read the newspapers or missed the notice printed therein, could not fail to be informed.

Though far from delighted, he was not surprised, on the specified date, to find the Old Bath's assembly room filled to overflowing. Men of every degree packed the floor, and a similar assortment of women crammed the music gallery.

No one needed to identify Miss Oldridge, sitting in the gallery's front row. The looks Car sent her from time to time—which she affected not to notice, the heartless creature—would have told Lord Gordmor who she was, even if Sir Roger Tolbert, the meeting's chairman, had not graciously performed that office.

Clearly, the lady in the repellent green bonnet had not been idle.

Neither had Lord Gordmor. Scattered through the crowd were men who worked for him. His agents had spent the last week drumming up support and gathering information in every inhabited corner of the Peak.

True, Jackson had returned to Matlock Bath last Wednesday with troubling news about Miss Oldridge's influence in the area. But the worst became known late yesterday afternoon: Mr. Oldridge was so vehemently opposed that he would abandon botany for the morning in order to speak at the meeting.

But Jackson had been prepared for this, and moments ago had whispered that the situation was in hand. Apparently so. As the meeting began, Sir Roger Tolbert leaned toward Gordmor and murmured, "Appears Mr. Oldridge was otherwise engaged. Well, not surprising, not at all. Meant to, of course. But these philosophers, my lord—" He tapped his balding head. "Knowledge box much occupied, you know."

If Mr. Oldridge had not wandered off on his own, then one of Jackson's men had helped him. The agent said it would not be difficult. One need only mention spotting an interesting piece of fungus or moss or lichen. The old gentleman wouldn't be able to resist going to have a look at it.

Whatever the cause, the most significant landowner and sole opposition had failed to appear, and it would be highly improper for a lady to address such a gathering. Women were banished to the gallery for a very good reason. It was men who arbitrated matters of such economic importance. Women looked on and gained what edification their weak little minds could absorb.

Lord Gordmor relaxed. The rest of his team were upon the platform with him. His engineer had arrived on the previous Wednesday and spent the next several days with Carsington, going over the original canal plan. They had made a number of adjustments, which they would reveal to the public for the first time today.

Also in attendance were two members of Parliament for somewhere or other, one of whom informed the citizenry—at length and with a great deal of flowery oratory—that his lordship's proposal would be looked on favorably as a project of lasting benefit to the area and thus to the nation as a whole.

When the windbag part of the business was done, the engineer made his much shorter and less tedious presentation. When he'd done talking, Carsington unveiled the new plan.

It stood on an immense easel upon the platform, and was done on a large scale, simply, in thick black ink.

From her perch above, Miss Oldridge could easily see it, as could most of the other important landowners.

For the benefit of those who could not make out details, Car described the route and the changes made, "to accommodate the special requirements of individual parties."

The new route lay at a greater distance from houses, gardens, and parks. In the case of the Oldridge property, the canal made a convoluted detour. This lengthened the route, making it meander when it might far more easily have gone straight; however, it would cause virtually no disruption to Miss Oldridge's arrangements.

Car and the engineer had made handsome accommodations for the other landowners as well. No rational person could possibly object, and none did. His lordship discerned in the audience not only pleased expressions and nods but clearly audible approval.

Gordmor looked up at the gallery. Even Miss Oldridge was smiling.

Wonder of wonders, Car had done it, as he'd vowed.

ALISTAIR did not find the smile as comforting as his friend did.

He'd learnt to read Mirabel's vast vocabulary of smiles. The curve of her mouth was cold, not sunny at all, and the feeling swiftly came of something about to spring at him from out of the darkness.

There was nothing he could do but brace himself and wait.

He was vaguely aware of voices, of the meeting going on and on, endlessly, it seemed, while he sat in a state of suspense. His leg, which could abide neither tension nor immobility, expressed its displeasure by hammering pain from his thigh to his ankle.

Then Captain Hughes stood up, resplendent in the uniform of His Majesty's Navy. He asked if the ladies and gentlemen would indulge him a few minutes of their valuable time. "I have a letter from my neighbor Mr. Oldridge of Oldridge Hall, Longledge," he said. "The gentleman having been detained elsewhere, I've been delegated the task of reading it."

What had Mirabel said the day they met?

I am thinking of putting that up as his epitaph: "Sylvester Oldridge, Beloved Father, Detained Elsewhere."

Here it was, then, the attack Alistair was waiting for.

The captain read in the clear, ringing tones of Authority.

This same commanding voice had for about two decades read, once a month, the thirty-six Articles of War to a ship's company of several hundred battle-hardened officers and men.

To his listeners he must personify England's invincible navy and the great nation it served.

Small wonder the room instantly fell silent, and the faces became soberly attentive and respectful.

Miss Oldridge could not have chosen a better representative.

When Captain Hughes compared the advantages to be derived from the canal to the disadvantages, citing concerns of respectable tradesmen—and noting their labor and sacrifice during the late wars with the French—heads began to nod. Water issues constituted one of the gravest anxieties, he read. He sincerely hoped the gentlemen had taken into consideration the dryness of Derbyshire's limestone hills. Had they accurately estimated the size of reservoir required, and the costs of building this leviathan? Had the gentlemen calculated this, that, and the other thing? Had the gentlemen included such-and-such in their calculations?

This part of the letter, which threw a glaring light upon the plan's every weakness and inaccuracy, was mercifully brief, though disturbing.

Then the captain began calling out names, and putting specific questions to the men he addressed: "Is it not true, Jacob Ridler, that . . . ?" "Is it not the case, Hiram Ingsole, that . . . ?"

Thus appealed to, the men stood up, one by one, and admitted, most reluctantly at first, to reservations. Once they'd opened their mouths, however, they grew less shy. Their objections became more articulate and more vehement. Their fellows—along with the wives, daughters, sisters, and mothers packed behind the ladies in the first row of the gallery—applauded and cheered.

When the tradesmen and farmers had finished with their grievances, the vicar Mr. Dunnet discovered he had some reservations, after all. After him, a few other gentlemen found something to object to as well.

By the time the gentlemen were done with their complaints, the crowd, which had begun so meek and accommodating, was growing noisy and hostile. They booed Gordy's answers and wouldn't let the engineer speak. Sir Roger banged his gavel in vain. The politicians suddenly discovered previous appointments and fled. A few of the ladies also departed.

Alistair looked up at Miss Oldridge. She wore an expression of blank innocence, as though she not only had nothing whatsoever to do with the pandemonium breaking out below her but did not find any of it—including him— particularly interesting.

The look was a gauntlet flung down, and he was too much a Carsington to retreat before a challenge.

He had agreed, albeit reluctantly, to make his presentation, and no more. "You are too scrupulous and softhearted," Gordy had told him. "Nothing gets done in politics without influence and money. As we are not exactly flush of money, we must make the most of influence."

What this meant, Alistair had learnt last night, was that he was to look handsome and gallant and hold his tongue. He was to leave all negotiating to Gordy.

He would have done this, sat clenching his hands and biting his tongue, if Mirabel Oldridge had not worn the provoking smile—after all he'd done to please her.

She had told him she would fight him with every weapon at her disposal. She had warned him that she was not overscrupulous.

Perhaps she'd assumed he'd chivalrously decline to fight back. Perhaps she thought the only weapon in his arsenal was looking beautiful. Perhaps she believed that overawing the yokels with his fame and family influence—and seducing the one woman who wasn't overawed—was the only strategy he was capable of executing.

He couldn't be sure what she thought. It didn't matter. The look infuriated him. He couldn't remain mute. Honor, pride, loyalty, and duty all demanded he fight—and fight to win.

He stood up, ignoring his leg, which viciously protested with sharp, burning jabs from hip to heel.

"Gentlemen," he said. He did not raise his voice. Carsingtons rarely needed to. They needed only to exert the force of their personalities.

His low rumble carried to the farthest corners of the hall, and the noise subsided slightly.

"Gentlemen," he repeated, "and ladies." He sent a quick glance up at Miss Oldridge.

The uproar dulled to a buzz, then murmuring, then silence.

"I shall consider it a great honor to address your concerns, one by one," he said. "Let me begin with the crucial matter of water and reservoirs."

ABOUT this time, Mr. Oldridge was ambling in the wrong direction—toward Longledge Hill rather than toward Matlock Bath—in the company of his former bailiff.

They had met quite by carefully arranged accident.

Caleb had been strolling casually toward Matlock Bath when he met Mr. Oldridge, also on foot, cheerfully resolved to do his duty, as his daughter had begged him.

He was surprised, but not disagreeably so, to see Caleb Finch. At the time of Finch's dismissal, Mr. Oldridge had been sunk in the lowest depths of the melancholia from which he'd only recently begun to emerge. His daughter had seen no reason to trouble him with unpleasant details. She'd simply told him that Finch had decided to leave.

Consequently, he greeted Finch affably, asked about his health, his family, his work.

Caleb was vague about his work but very precise about a recent discovery. It was this the two men were discussing while going the wrong way: away from rather than to the crucial canal committee meeting.

"Are you quite sure of the shape?" Oldridge was saying. "Like little cigars?"

"Precious little," Caleb said. "Smaller than an ant. And brown. At first I thought it was only dirt, but something made me take a closer look. I was sure I seen it before. And now I'll take my oath I did. My next to last position, in Yorkshire. I had to set the men to scraping it off a wall on account mistress didn't like it. I thought it was a shame, sir, as it was so interesting-like."

"It is, indeed," said Oldridge. "I have never heard of such a moss. And you have encountered it again, you are quite, quite sure?"

"Up on the hill, sir," Caleb said, indicating the lengthy ridge ahead. "Not five miles away."

To Mr. Oldridge, who often covered twenty miles in a single day, a five-mile walk up Longledge Hill was nothing. He would be back hours before dinner.

It was a long while before he remembered that dinner wasn't the only thing he needed to be on time for this day.

And then it was too late.

THE meeting dissolved shortly after noon.

It ended in victory. A majority having voted in favor of the canal, a committee was formed. The members swiftly drafted the petition to Parliament, after which the room emptied.

Only Lord Gordmor and his partner remained.

His lordship was too shaken by recent events to attempt his usual nonchalance.

"That was a near thing, a dreadfully near thing," he said. "For a time I felt as though I stood upon a storm-tossed ship. I contrived to hold on until the vicar—that sweet, amiable man—chided us. *Et tu, Brute?* I thought. Then overboard I went, and swiftly sank. Doubtless we must blame the piratical-looking sea captain, in his gleaming uniform and dashing whiskers, for these nautical metaphors."

Carsington said nothing. He seemed preoccupied with rolling his canal plan into the smallest possible circumference.

"What a fool I was, telling you to hold your tongue and look decorative," Lord Gordmor went on, eyeing his friend uneasily. "I should have remembered how very different a fellow you are when your fighting spirit is roused. I hope you will forgive me. I had been under the mistaken impression that Waterloo beat the fight out of you."

Carsington turned sharply toward him. "You thought I'd turned timid?"

What the devil was wrong with him? They'd won a great victory this day, over seemingly impossible odds.

Oh, Lord, was he brooding about the plaguy female?

"Don't be absurd," Gordmor said. "And pray don't mope about Miss Oldridge. Not today. You will bring her round eventually. Meanwhile, you've won a great triumph. You have plucked us out of the jaws of—of something. Ah, yes, victory. Snatched from the jaws of defeat. By gad, I'm so relieved, I'm tongue-tied. That letter. That brilliant, cruel letter. I collect it was entirely her doing."

"She warned you, Gordy."

"So she did. As did my sister. She told me the lady was dangerous. Who'd have guessed Henrietta could be guilty of understatement?"

"As it is, I'm amazed we got off so easily," Car said.

"Are you serious? She all but *annihilated* us. If you hadn't stepped in . . ." Gordmor trailed off. He could scarcely think of it without trembling: Everything, everything on the brink of being destroyed, utterly. All his careful scrimping and saving and planning. And all of Car's money and hopes: The man had taken the last of his allowance to the gaming tables, then given his winnings to Gordmor to put into their "company."

If Car hadn't stood up and done a stunning imitation of Lord Hargate at his most compelling and eloquent, the redhead in the unspeakable bonnet would have ruined them.

"Dangerous" was a laughable understatement. The woman was diabolical. Since Car, clearly, couldn't manage her, it was up to his friend to solve the problem.

BY the time the two men emerged from the hotel, the meeting attendees had departed. The area, which in the tourist season would have been thick with walkers and gawkers, was deserted.

As they stepped into the promenade, though, a neatly dressed fellow, whom Alistair recognized as one of Gordmor's agents, hurried up toward them.

Several of these men had followed his lordship to Derbyshire and thrown a bit of his money about to win favor with the locals. It was nothing out of the ordinary. This sort of thing went on at elections, and most certainly had occurred wherever canals were under consideration. Alistair had no doubt that Mirabel's agents had done the same.

Gordmor had told his men to keep their eyes and ears open as well. Accordingly, this fellow hastened to alert his lordship: Miss Oldridge and Mrs. Entwhistle had set out for London.

"London?" Gordy exclaimed. "Already?"

"They had a traveling chariot packed and ready, sir," the agent—by name of Jackson—said. "The ladies were the first out of the assembly hall, I was told, and scarcely a quarter hour passed before they were in the carriage and on their way. As soon as I heard of it, I came to tell you."

Alistair did not wait to hear more but strode down the promenade until he had a clear view of the Parade. It was busy today, with vehicles and pedestrians going to and fro. These he barely heeded. He stared in the direction Mirabel had gone, and tried to understand.

She had dealt them a devastating blow. She had very nearly destroyed them. And yet—and yet . . .

"She knew," he murmured. "She knew we'd win." Otherwise, why have the carriage packed and waiting for her?

A minute later, he heard Gordy's voice behind him: "It seems the lady does not mean to give us time to catch our breath."

"She promised to show us no mercy," Alistair said.

"Indeed, I have sadly underestimated her, else I should have been packed and ready to leave as well," Gordy said. "We cannot risk giving her a minute. She has influential friends in London. Do not forget that her father's sister is Lord Sherfield's wife, and believed to wield no small influence over him."

Alistair turned to his friend. "Sherfield? Aunt Clothilde is *Lady Sherfield?*" The Countess Sherfield was one of his mother's nearest friends.

"Surely you knew they were related," Gordy said. "Lady Hargate must have mentioned the connection when you told her where you were going."

"No." Alistair continued briskly down toward Wilkerson's, aware of the puzzled glances Gordy cast his way as they walked.

"That is very strange," Gordy said.

"Hardly," Alistair said. "When I called upon my mother before I left, I was full of our brilliant plan and the wonders of modern invention we'd bring to a remote outpost of civilization. She couldn't get a word in edgeways."

"Waxed oratorical, did you?" Gordmor smiled. "Well, I doubt it makes much difference whether or not you knew beforehand. Miss Oldridge has useful friends, true. So do we. Moreover, we have every practical point in our favor, as you so eloquently explained a while ago to the mob."

Theirs was to be a relatively short canal in a thinly populated part of Derbyshire, Alistair had reminded his listeners. The route lay along fairly level ground, requiring no aqueducts, tunnels, or long flights of locks. The recently enacted Poor Employment Act of 1817 provided government loans for projects that employed the poor. This reduced the sum they must raise from investors.

He knew the plan was sound. The many politicians he and Gordy consulted had promised that so simple and inexpensive a canal scheme could proceed from the first committee meeting to the Prince Regent's signature in two months or less.

If this hadn't been the case, he and Gordy could not have undertaken it. They hadn't the money for elaborate schemes and couldn't hope to raise such funds, given the sour economic conditions following war's end. Last year's poor harvest had not improved matters.

It was by no means a villainous plan in the first place. In the second, Alistair had added nearly five miles to the route to please his lady love.

Yet she turned up her nose.

"At the moment, I'm more concerned about your well-being," Gordy said. "Do have a care for your heart, Car. I don't wish to slander your beloved, but you deserve a warning at least. Henrietta says the lady jilted a fellow some years ago and had to leave London under a cloud."

"I know about that," Alistair said. "More than Lady Wallantree does, I'll wager. There were difficult circumstances. Not that I care if Miss Oldridge jilted a dozen fellows. It was in the past, and my own is nothing to boast of."

He would never believe that the girl he'd made love to could be cruel and coldhearted. If anything, her nature was too open, too compassionate. The cool detachment was only on the surface, shielding her true feelings. He understood the need to protect tender places. Still, he did not understand what she was about at present.

And he was disappointed in himself. In spite of all his efforts, he'd failed her.

"Car."

Alistair came back to the moment, the present crisis. "Her past is irrelevant. The canal is what signifies. I should like to know what troubles her. I was sure my plan addressed her personal objections. If there's another difficulty, I'd rather know about it before we're in front of a parliamentary committee."

He'd become accustomed to things springing out of the darkness and the sudden metaphorical blows to the head. He found the surprises stimulating, actually.

This didn't mean he could let himself be ambushed in Parliament. The thought of being rendered tongue-tied, even for an instant, before his father's colleagues and minions made his blood run cold.

"Very wise," Gordy said. They had reached the entrance of Wilkerson's, and he lowered his voice. "Do you go on ahead and learn what you can from the lady. I'll settle matters here and catch up with you as soon as I can."

AN hour later, Jackson was staring in dismay at the motionless figure stretched out upon a mossy piece of ground in a wooded part of Longledge Hill.

"What have you done?" he demanded of Caleb Finch. "Didn't I tell you what his lordship said?"

"He's all right," Finch said. "I only give him some medicine."

"What kind of medicine?"

"Some of that Godfrey's Cordial. Told him it were my dear old auntie's elderberry cordial."

Opium was one of the main ingredients of Godfrey's Cordial.

Jackson stepped closer. The old gentleman seemed to be slumbering peacefully. His dreams must be pleasant ones, because he smiled. He had a sweet smile, did Mr. Oldridge. Quite a harmless fellow. Jackson did not like seeing him lying on the cold ground. He also didn't like Finch's failure to wait for orders, and said so.

"And if I waited, like you say, until tomorrow or the next day," Finch said, "what do you think was the chance I could talk him into coming away again? As it was, he was on fire to run back to the meeting, even when I told him it was close onto noon, and it'd be long over by the time he got there. Besides, his lordship wants him to disappear, don't he? Well, it'll be easier now. We'll just load him onto a cart and take him away."

"We don't have a cart," Jackson said.

"Yes, we do," said Finch. "I borrowed it from the colliery. And a horse to pull it. They're down that track a ways." He nodded toward an ancient, overgrown packhorse trail. "I told you Miss O had a hundred tricks up her sleeve, didn't I? And wasn't I right? You let her get going in London, what with her lord and lady relations, and she'll grind you down to powder. I knew how it would be, and I come prepared. Well, I don't expect thanks, not a bit, not for doing my duty."

It was as well that he didn't expect thanks, because Jackson was disinclined to offer them. A man was supposed to follow his superior's orders. A man wasn't supposed to rush ahead and do whatever he took it into his head to do.

But Finch had gone ahead and done it, and they couldn't release Mr. Oldridge now.

"It's the same plan as his lordship wants," Finch said. "It'll work perfect. Miss Oldridge'll hurry back from London as soon as she finds out her pa's missing. While she's here looking for him, master gets his canal act through Parliament quick and painless. Meanwhile, we'll have Mr. O in Northumberland, safe and snug. As soon as Lord Gordmor gets his papers signed, we send the old gentleman home. Only think how happy they'll all be at the house, like he come back from the dead. Like Lazarus."

"You'd better make sure he does come back, in the

same condition he left," Jackson warned. "His lordship reminded me several times that the gentleman was not to be harmed in any way. I recommend you be careful with your cordials, Finch. If you give him too much and it kills him, I'll see you swing for it."

Seventeen

THOUGH they were ladies, encumbered with all the baggage, servants, and outriders deemed necessary for a long journey, Mirabel and Mrs. Entwhistle had covered some sixty miles by the time they stopped for the night at an inn in Market Loughborough.

Following a fine dinner Mirabel mainly played with, they adjourned to a sitting room to await their tea.

When the inn servant carried in the tea tray, she informed the ladies that a Mr. Carsington wished to speak to them.

"Heavens, he has lost no time," said Mrs. Entwhistle.

Mirabel said nothing, merely sat straighter, while her heart performed noisy calisthenics within her bosom.

"Pray show him in," Mrs. Entwhistle told the servant.

He entered a moment later, his countenance marked with lines of weariness and his eyes dark. He was otherwise point-perfect, as usual: every hair neatly arranged to appear romantically windblown, every neckcloth fold precisely in place, and not a crease or wrinkle in sight.

Mirabel experienced a mad urge to leap up and rumple him. She reminded herself that it would be fatal to soften. He would wrap her about his finger. She must pretend he was her worst enemy. Otherwise, she would be lost, and all she'd done these last ten years and more would have been done for nothing.

She gave a cold nod in response to his bow and greetings and kept her hands tightly folded in her lap.

She invited him to join them for tea.

"I didn't come for tea," he growled. He threw his hat down and advanced upon her. "I added five miles to my canal, solely to please you, though it inconveniences my partner and increases our costs. I came to find out why you insist upon being so thoroughly unreasonable."

"I should ask the same question," she said. "I fail to understand why you and Lord Gordmor persist, when I have promised to do everything in my power to thwart you."

"If you no longer care for me, you had better say so," he said. "In ordinary circumstances, it would be unsporting to trifle with my affections in this way, but—"

"I, trifle with a man whose affairs have become the stuff of legend?" she said. "Don't be absurd."

"In this case, my affections are of no consequence," he went on as though she hadn't spoken. "You are welcome to break my heart, if this is what you wish. But you must find another way. You cannot know the harm your actions will cause others."

"Break *your* heart?" She went cold inside. Even William had not accused her of toying with him, though everyone else did. After she broke off with him, half her acquaintance became cold and aloof, and those who didn't snub her held back only so that they could tell her what the rest were whispering behind her back.

She was a jilt, people said. She'd used William Poynton shamefully. The letters followed her home. People who saw him in Venice claimed he was going into a decline, dying of disappointed hopes. They said he'd scarcely the heart to lift a paintbrush . . . collapsed after completing the mural . . . traveled to Egypt . . . would never survive the journey . . . vowed he'd never return to England.

All her fault.

For a moment memories from those first two dreary years after she'd given up William engulfed her, and she felt the old despair, that her life would never come right again.

She wanted to sink to the floor and weep.

And the wish to give up and weep made her angry— with this man, for making her so weak, and with herself, for letting him reduce her to this state.

She stood up, trembling with indignation. "I have been playing with you, have I? So this is your opinion of me."

"That is not what I meant. It is your opinion of _me_—"

"I should have realized my forward behavior would lower me in your esteem," she said. "Yet never in my worst imaginings did I see you casting my errors in my teeth."

"_My_ esteem? I am not—"

"You believe I oppose your canal merely to torment you? You think me so petty, so contemptible?"

"Of course not. Why do you twist my meaning out of all recognition?"

Mirabel looked at Mrs. Entwhistle. "Am I off the mark?" she said. "How would you interpret his words?"

"I haven't the least idea," Mrs. Entwhistle said, calmly serving herself a slice of cake. "It has been a long day, and I am far too weary to sort out such complicated matters. If you must dispute, kindly take your quarrel to the dining parlor and let me have my tea in peace."

MRS. Entwhistle might have been a stick of furniture for all the notice Alistair had taken of her. All he'd seen when he entered the sitting room was Mirabel. He hadn't noticed whether the servant had lingered. For all he knew, a crowd of them had gathered upon the stairs to eavesdrop.

Typical, he thought bitterly. Nine and twenty years old, and he still had no notion of discretion.

Furious with himself, he followed Mirabel into the adjoining room and pulled the door closed behind him. She crossed to the farthest corner, by the banquette under the windows overlooking the street, as though she could not get far enough away from him.

He hardly blamed her. He could not believe how clumsily and offensively he'd spoken. He'd been articulate enough at the canal meeting. Why must his brain shrink to pea size when he was with her?

"I didn't mean . . ." he began. Yet even now, he could not string intelligible words together. He didn't want to talk. He wanted to hold her, beg her pardon, bring the warmth and trust back. She was pale and stiff. He'd hurt her.

"Forgive me," he said. "I had wanted so much to please you with the new canal plan, and I failed, and so I was beside myself."

"You did not fail." Her voice was brittle. "You have won the first battle. We must see who will win the last."

"Can you not tell me what I've done wrong?" he said. "I want to make it right, but I am all at sea. Perhaps I was overhasty, assuming we would wed could I but bridge this one gap between us. You have told me no, but I assumed only the canal stood in the way. Was I arrogant to suppose this? Are your feelings . . ." He searched for words. "I have cast lures. I have seduced you. It was not honorable of me to try to win you that way, but I did not care very much how I did it. Perhaps I have merely seduced you, not won your heart, after all. If that is the case, I beg you will do me a kindness and tell me so, and I shall stop plaguing you."

He would do it, too, and it would kill him.

Her hair glowed like burnished copper in the candlelight. He remembered it tumbled upon the pillows and his fingers tangling in it. He remembered tearing the bonnet from her head and dragging his hands through the unruly curls, and her laughter when she knocked the hat from his head. He remembered the way she'd kissed the top of his head, the tenderness, the utter trust.

He remembered what she'd said.

You make me happy. You make me feel like a girl again.

But he'd made her unhappy. She stood stiffly, her gaze so dark and solemn, her hands clasped tightly at her waist.

"That is all I need do?" she said finally. "Tell you I do not care for you? How easy it sounds. How impossible it is. I have told you so, many times, but each time it becomes a bigger lie, and you always know I am lying."

"My love." He started across the room.

She put up her hand. "If you truly care for me, you will keep a distance. If you touch me, I shall become irrational. That is taking unfair advantage."

He wanted to take every unfair advantage.

He made himself retreat.

"You are not to speak sweetly to me, either," she said. "You are too persuasive. This morning, you had me almost convinced that Providence could bestow no greater blessing upon Longledge than your canal."

"Only 'almost,'" he said. "That is the trouble. That's why I came." He gave a short laugh. "No, that isn't why I came. It's the reason I gave Gordmor for hurrying on ahead: to find out where my new plan failed you. I still don't know. What would you have us do?"

"Go away," she said. "Give it up. I cannot believe you are both so foolish or obstinate as to persist. I am not a stranger to business or politics. I know how these matters are conducted. You may win in the end, but it will cost you more than you bargained for, perhaps more than you can afford. Certainly, it will be more than what those mines are worth."

"My dear," he said, "as little as they are worth at present, those mines are all we have."

Her eyes widened, and color rose in her cheeks. She sat down abruptly on the banquette.

Alistair remained where he was, wishing someone would do him a favor and cut out his tongue. "I do wish," he said, "my tongue would consult with my brain now and again. Our financial affairs are not in the least your concern."

"Not my concern?" Her expression became exasperated. "No wonder Lord Gordmor has been so infernally obstinate. What a fool I am! When I wrote to Aunt Clothilde, I should have enquired about him as well as about you. It would have been far more useful to have financial details than the catalogue of your *amours,* entertaining as that was."

"Entertaining?"

"You ought to write your memoirs," she said.

"My *memoirs?*" He had grown so used to being clubbed in the head that he didn't even blink.

"It will bring in more money than those paltry mines."

Alistair walked to the fire and watched the tiny tongues of flame licking the coals while he debated how much to tell her. At length he turned back to her. She watched him intently.

"Mirabel, there isn't time," he said.

"You are not yet thirty," she said. "As exciting as your life has been, the tale is relatively short. If you applied yourself, you could easily write your memoirs in a matter of months, for you do have a way with words."

"There isn't time," he said. "I've only seven weeks."

In a few crisp words, he told her: about his meeting in November with his father and the list of Episodes of Stupidity, and the choice his father had given him.

She listened, her head tipped to one side, as though he were a vastly complicated puzzle. When he was done, she said, "I do not understand what the problem is."

Alistair knew he was not as articulate as he wished to be when speaking to her. Still, he'd told the story in terms so simple, a child could not misconstrue them. He tried again: "If Gordy and I fail to get our canal act passed by the first of May, I must marry an heiress."

"But you've said, several times, that you wish to marry me," she said.

"I have never wanted anything so much in my life," he said.

"Well, then," she said.

"Well, then, what?"

"I'm an heiress," she said.

MIRABEL waited through a short, churning silence.

Then, "No," he said.

He paced from the fire to the door and back. He sat in a chair and got up again. He started toward her, then away again. He returned to scowl at the fire.

It was not the reaction she'd expected. She had never dreamt the problem was so simple. Still, it remained a problem to him, and how could she expect otherwise?

William Poynton had loved her, too, but the sacrifice required of him was too great. He could not give up his dreams and ambitions any more than she could abandon her home and her amiably oblivious father, whom every scoundrel and sharper for miles around was busily duping and defrauding.

"I would not expect you to turn country squire and stay in Derbyshire all the time," she said, her heart beating frantically. "Naturally, you would wish to be in London in the spring, during the Season."

"If you think I would leave you alone in Longledge, in the height of the tourist season, when the place swarms with idle men, I strongly recommend you think again," he growled at the fire.

The flickering light deepened the shadows under his eyes and hardened the lines of his angular features.

"You cannot imagine I can leave the estate unattended, especially in the spring and early summer, when there is so much to do," she said, lifting her chin even as her spirits sank. "We had better settle this now. Certain points are not negotiable."

He turned to her, his eyes cold and hard. "There is nothing to settle," he said. "I shall not come to you penniless. I have been a parasite upon my father. I refuse to be a parasite upon my wife."

"A parasite?" Mirabel stood and faced him, though she wanted desperately to run away, so mortified she was. "I see. I have thrown myself at you in every possible way, yet you doubt me. You have said repeatedly that you wished to marry me—until now, though it will solve all your problems at once. You find this intolerable? Why? Your pride won't bear it? Perhaps you imagine I shall make a lap dog of you, as Judith Gilford tried. If that is what you imagine, then you cannot know me at all, and this professed love of yours is like all your other passions: intense, but lacking the strength to deal with the practicalities of ordinary life."

"I can deal with them very well, thank you," he said curtly. "And I mean to prove it."

He went out, his limp more pronounced than usual. In spite of her shame and anger and despair, Mirabel winced for him, for the unceasing pain he lived with and his constant struggle to keep it from showing.

She told herself it was all pride, and he had more than his share—far too much. Still, she knew a part of what drove him to behave as he did was courage. Angry though she was, she knew as well that the same pride and courage made her love him all the more.

No, not love. Of course not love. She'd known him only a few weeks.

Yet it had been more than time enough, she now saw. Somehow, without her quite realizing, he'd stolen the very last bit of her heart. Then out he went, with her heart in his keeping—her *heart*—as though it were nothing more than a handkerchief embroidered with his initials.

Let him go then, with his precious pride and his beastly canal. If he didn't want her money, that was his problem. She would proceed as originally planned. Nothing had changed, really, she told herself. She knew he'd make her wretched. She'd accepted the fact that she'd pay for a brief happiness with a long misery. It was no more than she'd bargained for. She was quite resigned.

It must have been resignation, then, that caused her, when she'd heard him take his leave of Mrs. Entwhistle and go out, to pick up the nearest breakable object—a pitcher—and throw it against the fireplace.

CREWE carried in a supper tray shortly after Alistair returned from his tumultuous encounter with Mirabel.

He picked at his food, then, weary and sick at heart, undressed and went to bed. It was only to rest his limbs after the afternoon's hard traveling. The hour was far too early for sleep—not that he expected to sleep, given the recent encounter with Mirabel and its stunning revelations.

An heiress! Why hadn't Gordy told him?

He must have assumed Alistair knew this, along with everything else he should have known but didn't. Given the size and prosperity of the estate, he'd assumed, naturally, that she must have a respectable portion. He'd also assumed, however, that the property must be entailed, as his father's was, upon the nearest male in the paternal line.

But the way she'd offered herself as the solution to all his problems told him that her funds must be substantial. She knew he was expensive. She'd probably estimated the cost accurately to the nearest shilling. Unlike most other women, she'd had to learn what everything cost and how to weigh the advantages and disadvantages of buying this or that, how to decide whether repairing or replacing was the sounder economic choice. She would not have suggested he marry her to solve his problems if she hadn't been certain she could afford him.

But he didn't want another—any other, but most especially her—to buy him out of his present difficulty.

If he could not solve this problem himself, he would lose the last scrap of self-respect he had remaining. He would not deserve her love or his father's respect or Gordy's friendship.

All the same, he felt like a beast for rejecting what she offered. He'd hurt her. Again. His brain had shrunk while his masculine pride swelled to monstrous proportions. He should have explained. But it was not until he was alone in his bedchamber that matters sorted themselves out. While with her, all he'd known was frustration and shock and anger. He couldn't think, let alone speak clearly.

Despite all this turmoil, however, he fell into a deep enough slumber to dream the Waterloo dream again, in more detail and length than the previous night. Every night it started a moment earlier in the battle and shed light in places previously dark. Every night he saw the carnage more vividly and relived his feelings more intensely. Every night he woke himself or his valet with his ravings.

This night Crewe stood over him, gently shaking him. "Wake up, sir. You're dreaming again."

Alistair struggled up to a sitting position. "What time is it?"

"Close to midnight, sir."

"Has Lord Gordmor come?"

No, his lordship had not yet come, and Crewe thought it unlikely he'd arrive this night. The weather had turned very bad since the master had gone to bed.

Alistair got up and looked out the window. He could see nothing. He could hear the pounding rain and roaring wind, however, which sufficed to make him agree with Crewe. As great a hurry as Gordmor was in, he would not risk either his people or his horses. He'd have stopped at the nearest inn as soon as the weather took a turn for the worse.

In any case, there wasn't room for everyone here. Miss Oldridge and her entourage had left only a few rooms unoccupied. These were the smallest and darkest, overlooking a narrow alley at the back of the building.

Still, when he heard the knock at the door, Alistair assumed Gordy's panic had overcome his caution. Expecting his friend, he did not hurry to throw his dressing gown on over his nightshirt when Crewe answered the door.

Alistair heard a whisper.

Crewe said softly, "Yes, he's awake, but—"

He was unceremoniously thrust aside, and Mirabel flew in, in a flutter of delicate ruffles and . . . lace?

She came halfway across the narrow room, then stopped short. "Oh. I didn't realize. I thought Crewe meant you hadn't yet gone to bed." She flushed and looked away.

Alistair looked wildly about. Crewe hurried to a chair, snatched up the dressing gown, and swiftly stuffed his master into it. He mumbled something about a hot drink, and vanished.

When he had gone, Mirabel turned back to Alistair. She wore a dressing gown of fine, oyster white lawn, trimmed with exquisite silk lace, over a matching nightgown with a ruffled hem. She looked like a princess in a fairy tale. His gaze moved slowly, disbelievingly, from the dainty silk slippers up over the deliciously feminine confection to her face.

Her cheeks were a very deep pink, and the candlelight made twin stars in the twilight blue of her eyes. Her red-gold hair tumbled over her shoulders, and a fiery froth of curls danced about her face.

She clasped her hands at her waist.

"I withdraw my opposition," she said.

OUT of doors, the storm continued unabated. The wind whistled and wailed, and rain beat against the windows. Within, the fire crackled and hissed in the grate.

Mirabel would have felt safer outside, in the middle of the storm, than here in this small room.

She stood where she was, as she was, barely dressed, her hair undone. She wore the frothy concoction Aunt Clothilde had sent, without explanation, along with the letter describing Mr. Carsington's indiscretions.

The nightclothes were provocative. It was an unscrupulous tactic, but Mirabel didn't care. She would do whatever was necessary to win him over. She was in love, truly, deeply, hopelessly in love this time, and this time she would not give it up.

"I should not have let you go before," she said. "I should have tried harder to understand. But I was too mortified and angry to think clearly."

She'd had hours since then to calm down and sort it out and make up her mind what was most important: a house and a piece of land or the love of a lifetime.

He still gazed at her in that blank way. Had he shut his mind and his heart to her because of his pride? Did he see her differently now? In his eyes had she become another Judith Gilford—the heiress whose petty tyrannies, Aunt Clothilde believed, had driven him away?

It didn't matter what he saw, Mirabel told herself. She would not give him up, no matter what it cost her.

She stood firm, chin up, her hands clasped to white-knuckled tightness and pressed against the knot of fear that was her insides.

"I was unreasonable," she said. "Captain Hughes approved of your revised plan. He read my letter only because he'd promised he would."

She'd known her father would not appear at the canal meeting, no matter how earnestly he promised. He'd insisted on setting out early, and walking, as he always did. She could hardly force him to drive with her and Mrs. Entwhistle in the carriage. She'd prepared the letter for the likely eventuality of Papa's nonappearance, and given it to Captain Hughes the day before the meeting.

"I should have signaled or sent word to him not to read it," she said now. "Your new plan was most accommodating and well thought out. I've been silly not to accept it. I cannot expect everything to remain exactly as it was. The world changes, and we must change with it. I ought to be happy and grateful for all the trouble you took on my account, instead of causing you more difficulty."

"It *was* a good plan," he said.

"Yes, very good."

"But not good enough," he said.

"No plan could be good enough," she said. "I wanted Lord Gordmor to close up his mines and go away and stop troubling us with his transportation problems. I didn't want any more Lord Gordmors or any other enterprising men, including my neighbors, finding new ways to make fortunes on Longledge Hill. I didn't want increased trade. I wanted the peaceful, simple country life I'd grown up with."

"Then I shall find a way for you to keep it," he said.

She looked down at her still-clasped hands, then up into his starkly handsome face. The tenderness she saw there lightened her heart. "You are not to waste your time on any such thing," she said. "You are not to risk everything you have worked so hard for. I came to tell you so. Mine would be a poor sort of affection if I could not sacrifice a very little comfort for your sake."

"I think you'd lose more than a *little* comfort," he said.

Yes, the truth was, it would break her heart to see her home changed. But she knew what he, what any reasonable person would think. One couldn't make time stand still. Times were changing, and she must change with them.

Her mother had been dead for half her life, and re-creating the world Mama had lived in and making her dreams come true would not bring her back. This man was very much alive, and Mirabel loved him. She'd rather make a life with him, under any conditions, than go back alone to her solitary life in her beautiful arcadia.

She said, "I have been in love before, you know, and let it go because I could not abandon my land and roam the world as he wanted—as he needed—to do. I broke off my engagement, and came home, and resigned myself to spinsterhood. Yet it seems I am not fully resigned. I asked myself a short while ago whether I was willing to sacrifice my affection for you. I decided I was not."

"He was a fool to go," he said, his voice low and fierce. "He should have stayed and fought for you. But I'm glad he was a fool, because I'm selfish. I want to be the one who fights for you."

Her hands unclasped, and her heart banged crazily. "You don't have to fight," she said. "I'm won. I'm yours."

"Are you, my love?" He smiled then, and opened his arms, and she ran straight into them.

As soon as those strong arms closed about her, she knew she'd made the right decision. She'd learnt to take care of herself, to do without a man's protection or even affection. She could do without his if she must, but only if she had no other choice, only if he abandoned her.

She would do everything in her power to make sure he didn't.

"I must send you back to your room," he rumbled into her hair. "In a moment."

His hands came up and tangled in her hair. He kissed her forehead and her nose. She tilted her head back, offering her lips.

"We had better not," he murmured, raising his head.

"No, we really mustn't," she said.

Liar, liar. She didn't care what they must or mustn't do. It was late, and they were alone, and the storm seemed to shut out the world.

He slid his hands down to her shoulders. He gazed deep into her eyes, as though she harbored unfathomable secrets—as though she had anything left hidden from him.

She'd opened her heart. She'd let him see and touch— and do things she had no name for—to parts of her body she'd once felt depraved merely looking at.

"I want to be good," he said. "I've taken appalling advantage of your inexperience."

"Yes, it was very bad of you," she said, drawing away. "And it was bad of me not to discourage you. It was bad of me to come tonight in all my dishabille. Despicable, really. I am not wearing a scrap of undergarments. And this gown—what was Aunt Clothilde thinking, to send such a frilly, flimsy little nothing to a respectable spinster?" She looked down and fiddled with the ribbons at the front of the low neckline. "I suspect it is French. No decent English dressmaker would make such a thing."

"Mirabel." His voice had thickened. "Please. I am not made of iron."

"I know that." She smiled. "You are flesh and blood. Very muscled. And the hair on your chest is more generally golden than on that your head." She untied the topmost ribbon. "Whereas I am quite, quite smooth in that area." She glanced down. "But a good deal more rounded."

"Yes." One strangled syllable. "I think your body is perfection, but I must not look at it now. Mirabel, you are not to untie the next ribbon. It is the worst sort of cruelty. You know I must resist you. We shall be wed, and I absolutely will not anticipate the wedding vows."

She untied the second ribbon. "I thought you already had," she said. "Twice."

"That was irresponsible and selfish. And anyway . . . Anyway, you are intact—barely—by the grace of God. Oh, why am I talking about this? You must go. Good night." He limped to the door and opened it.

She stood where she was. She untied the last of the ribbons and shrugged out of the dressing gown.

He shut the door.

"Don't," he said.

"I won't," she said. "I want you to take it off me. You are so good at dressing and undressing."

He stalked to her, eyes flashing gold sparks, and she wondered if he meant to pick her up and eject her bodily from the room.

He grasped her shoulders. "You," he said. "You."

"Yes, this is truly me." She reached up and dragged her fingers through his sleep-tousled hair. "I did not know a wanton lived inside me. You found her and set her free. Now you must live with the consequences." She tugged him down, and her mouth sank onto hers, and in an instant he swept her into another realm, where she was young again, and fresh, and utterly happy.

She curled her hands round his neck and stood on tiptoe, trying to get more of him. He deepened the kiss and dragged her down into a drunken darkness. No fruit of the poppy could be half so intoxicating as the taste of him. With his tongue he played inside her mouth and made her remember the more intimate way he'd played with her not ten days ago. Heat skittered along her skin and under it. Dry reason evaporated, and pleasure seeped in, cool and dark and dangerous, to make her someone else, the wanton he'd brought to life. No longer cautious, no longer responsible, no longer in control.

She moved her hands over his shoulders, his powerful arms, and relished the answering caresses, his long, skillful hands sliding over the frilly nightgown, making it whisper under his touch as though it were alive. He made everything come alive, created a wild, vibrant world, mysterious and exotic and yet so familiar, as though it had always existed inside her.

She slid her hands down to the sash of his dressing gown. His hands got in the way, nudging hers aside, unfastening the ribbon of her nightgown, loosening the bodice. He pushed the thin fabric down, and she caught her breath as his hand closed over her breast.

"Perfect," he murmured against her mouth. "You're perfect."

She leaned into his caressing hand, savoring the touch and seeking more. She wanted him to touch her everywhere. The neckline of the gown slid down her arms, to her waist, and she felt the cool air of the room on her naked torso. She hardly noticed the coolness. All her being was fixed on the warmth of his hands kneading her breasts. They ached and tautened, and her whole body seemed to ache, hungering for more, more, and still more.

She was distantly aware of being led somehow, back, and back again. Something hard against her spine. Something to hold onto. She leaned against the bedpost, dizzy with the feeling swirling in and around her, and watched, as though from a long way away, her nightgown slide down, down, to the floor. She looked up, dazed and stupid. The firelight glinted in his eyes, so dark now.

"Beautiful," he said, his voice pitched so low it might

have come from the floor, where her gown lay. He slid his hand from her throat, between her breasts, and down to the place between her legs where he'd pleasured her. "My beautiful girl."

But he was more beautiful than she. She reached again for the sash, and this time he let her. She untied it and pushed the garment down from his shoulders, down his long arms, and watched it slither into the folds of her discarded nightgown. She reached for his nightshirt, but too slowly. He yanked it off and let it fall among the rest.

The flickering light glimmered gold in his thick brown hair and glowed in his eyes. It traced the sculpted contours of his face and played over the rippling muscles of his torso and limbs. She reached out and slid her hand down as he'd done to her, from his throat to his taut belly, but he pulled away before she could do anything bolder.

Then he bent and made a tingling path of kisses down from her shoulder to her breast. He lingered there, his tongue playing lightly over her skin, then pausing to suckle. She moaned and pushed her fingers through his hair and held him there, though the pleasure—the ache—whatever it was he did to her, was nigh unbearable. And when he lifted his head, she nearly cried out, but he wasn't done yet and tortured her a little longer.

Then down again, his mouth, so wicked, between her legs. *Sin, sin, sin.* Her mind was black and hot. She wanted . . . She didn't know what it was. He must tell her. She reached for him, dragged him up. "Yours," she gasped. "Make me yours."

He made a choked sound, and caught her up in his arms, and lifted her onto the bed. He knelt at her feet and stroked upward from her ankles, and she opened her legs and would have dragged him up over her if she could have reached him. But he was just beyond her reach, and she sank back and let him turn her into hot liquid. She writhed under his touch, wanting more, still more. He kissed her knees and licked the beauty mark, and she wanted to scream.

He shifted upward, sliding his hands up her legs as he went. And then she felt his thumb between her legs, in the place where he'd tortured her before, but this was beyond anything, pleasure beyond bearing. She was reduced to feeling, to hot, pounding need. And then it came, a splintering joy that made her shriek. His mouth covered hers while pleasure erupted from what seemed the very core of her, and spilled outward in cascading sensations.

And in the midst of it, she felt him thrust into her. She stilled, conscious of a strange, uncomfortable pressure.

"Sorry." Two rough syllables against her mouth. "I meant—"

"Oh," she said breathlessly. "That's *you.*" She squirmed, trying to get more comfortable.

"Mirabel."

She squirmed the other way.

"My love."

She felt his hand caressing her in the place where they were joined. By degrees, the pressure eased. Then it was all right, oh, very much so.

She smiled stupidly up at him. "Oh," she said drunkenly. "It feels *good.*"

He made the strangled sound again. "Yes," he said. "Yes, it does."

"Can we do it again?" she said.

"We're not nearly done yet," he said.

Then he began to move inside her; and the world changed again, completely. She held on, letting him take her where he would. They went slowly at first, until the wild pleasure again took hold. Then she was moving with him, seeking something, some place in the hot darkness. The world went away and with it whatever remained of thought. Only feeling remained, for him, given by him, a happiness almost painful and a need she couldn't satisfy. She thrust against him, instinctively seeking more, and her fingers dug into his back.

"I love you." His voice, low, reverberated through her. "I love you."

Her lips formed words, but she was beyond speech. Her body was caught on a powerful current, tearing along faster and faster, then flinging her onto a wild, stormy shore. A heartbeat later, a powerful tremor went through him and traveled through her, like lightning, and blasted the world into shimmering pieces.

Eighteen

FOR a time afterward, Alistair lay stunned. Then he drew her up against him, and they nestled like spoons.

The perfect derrière snuggled against his groin. His hand clasped one perfect breast. Silken curls tickled his face. He pressed his mouth to her neck and inhaled her scent, and that was perfect, too.

His life, at this moment, was absolutely right.

She reached back and stroked the scar. When it wasn't actively harassing him, the pain always hovered in the background. Yet it retreated under her gentle touch.

She didn't mind touching it or looking at it, though it was hideous, the gnarled, shiny lumpish skin.

"Do you hate it?" she said, her voice still husky in the aftermath of passion.

The huskiness confused him. "Hate what?"

"Your injury."

He wanted to say he never gave it any thought, but that was a black lie. "It is an infernal nuisance," he said. He hesitated, then added, "And it is ugly, and I can't . . ." He dragged in air, let it out, and buried his face in her neck. "Must I tell you everything?" he murmured against her skin.

She turned in his arms and brought her hand up to his cheek. He turned his head to kiss the palm of her hand. He loved her hands. He loved her touch. And she seemed very well pleased with his lovemaking. He had nothing more to wish for, except a speedy wedding.

"What can't you do?" she said.

"I wish it did not make me walk so awkwardly," he said, and winced inwardly. It sounded so childish, so ungrateful. He was lucky to be alive, and he whined about being lame.

"I don't doubt it seems more awkward to you than to others," she said. "You will not believe me—you will say I'm blinded by love—but the way you walk has a strange effect. Perhaps it is me. Perhaps it is part of the derangement of my advanced age, but the small hitch in your walk awakens carnal feelings in me. I did not know what they were at first, only that they were both pleasant and disturbing."

The invisible club struck again. "Carnal feelings? You mean lust?"

She nodded.

"You're roasting me," he said.

She laid her head on his chest. The unruly curls tickled his chin. "I would never tease you about such a thing. It is embarrassing enough to admit it—but then, I am past all shame now."

She thought his limp was erotic.

Of all the notions that might have occurred to him, that was not even last. It was nowhere within the realm of possibilities he'd imagined. But then, she had not been within his realm of possibilities. He could not have imagined such a woman, and he'd only begun to discover her.

She sighed. "Even if I am past all shame, I must conceal it and pretend to be good. How I wish I had thought to drug everybody in the inn before I came! But since it did not occur to me, I must return to my room. At least I have devised a plausible excuse for having left it."

He did not want her to leave, ever again. But he didn't want her reputation sullied, either. He shifted up to a sitting position, taking her with him. "I long to hear your excuse," he said.

"I had a bad dream and woke up disoriented, thinking I was in my own house," she said. "After wandering about for a time in confusion, I gradually regained my wits and made my way back to my room." She leaned toward him and kissed him lightly on the mouth.

The perfect pink buds brushed his chest. Her mouth was so soft, the taste of her so sweet. Her scent swam in his head and wafted from the bedclothes.

He told himself to be a man and endure it. He dragged himself from the bed. "I will let you go, and you may tell whatever fib you wish," he said, "as long as you remember that we are to be wed, as soon as possible."

"Does that mean you will marry me, canal or no canal?" she said.

He was aware of her watching him as he limped to the washstand. "It means I will solve the problem," he said. "And don't say, 'What if you cannot solve it?' because I shall. I have made up my mind." He poured water into the washbowl, collected a towel, and carried them to her.

She washed quickly, too quickly.

He gathered up the frothy dressing gown and nightgown, allowed himself one last, lingering study of her sweetly shaped body, then helped her into her garments.

As he tied the ribbons of the dressing gown, he said, "Does your aunt send you such fetching attire often?"

"No," Mirabel said, and blushed.

She did not blush often or easily.

"I thought not, else I'd wonder why you dress as you do. Why did she send it, then?"

"She didn't say. I must leave."

"Mirabel."

"I shall be staying with her in London. I shall ask her. I

am glad you approve of her taste." She spoke hurriedly. "She will take me shopping. I had been dreading that. It takes so much time, and I had so much to do, with my political machinations. But now I shall have plenty of time to shop." She darted him a smile: "For my trousseau."

"No, no, no," he said.

Her startled gaze met his.

"Yes, you will shop for a trousseau, but later, with me," he said.

"You don't approve of my taste," she said.

"With the present exception, you have no taste to speak of," he said. "That is not the problem. The problem is, you must not abandon your campaign."

"Mr. Carsington," she began.

"Alistair," he said.

"Alistair," she said, and his Christian name had never sounded like this before. It was infinitely different when uttered in that whispery night voice. And he, he realized, was a different and better man, here, with her.

She laid her hand on his chest. "Pray recall that the object of my campaign was to destroy your canal scheme," she said. "This, it turns out, would ruin your best friend as well as your younger brothers. I cannot be responsible for so much carnage, certainly not on account of a narrow strip of waterway hardly twenty miles long."

"A better solution exists," he said. "It is there, in the back of my mind somewhere. I will never get to it unless you keep challenging and provoking me."

He gently grasped her shoulders and gazed into the twilight of her eyes. "All my life, it has been too easy," he said. "I always knew someone would be there to solve my problems. As a result, nothing was ever at stake. Nothing was important enough to make me exert myself. Nothing ever tested my intellect or ingenuity. Until now. Until you. You will not let anything be easy. You have made me re-examine everything. You have made me *think,* and plot and contrive. You must not surrender now. I have never been so plagued and beset with problems in all my life—and I know it is good for me. I have not felt so alive since—gad, I can't remember when. Do you understand, my dear, troublesome girl? *I need the aggravation.*"

She studied him in that direct way of hers, not hiding her attempt to puzzle him out. Then, "Oh," she said. And, "Oh, yes, I quite understand." She smiled, a great rising sun of a smile. "I am so relieved."

She kissed him, hard, upon the mouth, the way he'd kissed her good-bye that day at the mausoleum. Then she hurried from the room in a flutter of ruffles and lace.

MIRABEL made it to her room without attracting attention and slipped under the bedclothes, though she knew she would not sleep a wink.

The next she knew there was a stir about her, footsteps hurrying to and fro, muffled voices. She glanced at the window. The sky was still grey, the sun not yet risen. There was a tap at the door connecting her room with Mrs. Entwhistle's. A moment later, the lady herself appeared in an amazing profusion of ribbons and ruffles. Her sleeping attire was, though it hardly seemed possible, even more frivolous than Mirabel's seraglio costume.

"My dear, I am so sorry to burst upon you like this," she said. "But Jock has come with distressing news."

Papa. Something had happened.

Heart hammering, Mirabel leapt up from bed, threw on her dressing gown, and hurried out to the hall, where a sopping-wet Jock stood.

A bad sign, a very bad sign, if the groom had been sent to her in bad weather in the dead of night.

He apologized for disturbing her, but Mr. Benton had said they must not lose a minute.

"Master never come home to dinner, miss," the groom said. He said more, though no more needed to be said.

Not long afterward, she and Mrs. Entwhistle, their entourage and outriders, were all racing back to Oldridge Hall.

• • •

THE clamor outside—of horses being put to harness and servants bustling between inn and carriage—woke Alistair, but only briefly. He glanced toward the window, saw it was still dark, and groggily assuming the noise he'd heard was the storm, returned to sleep. It was the soundest sleep he'd had since arriving in Derbyshire a month ago.

He dreamt he was riding in a carriage towed by Mr. Trevithick's locomotive steam engine, *Catch-Me-Who-Can.*

Alistair was going round and round the circular track at Euston at the mad pace of twelve miles per hour. Gordy was shouting at him to get off—it was dangerous, bound to explode—and Alistair only laughed. He was young, and whole, and fearless—or at least believed he was. Waterloo lay years ahead, in a future his still-immature mind couldn't possibly imagine.

The carriage shook violently, and he could barely hear Gordy over the engine's shrieking.

"Sir, please. It is nearly nine o'clock."

Alistair opened his eyes. The room was only a degree less dark than before. Crewe was regarding him worriedly.

"Nine o'clock?" Alistair repeated. He struggled up to a sitting position. "Why is it so confoundedly dark?"

Though the storm had passed hours earlier, the sky remained thickly overcast, Crewe told him.

Alistair remembered then that Mirabel's party had taken over the better rooms, exiling him and Crewe to this dismal corner of the inn, where what feeble daylight there was could scarcely penetrate.

He prayed the isolation had worked in her behalf. If anyone knew of her prolonged stay in this room . . .

Surreptitiously he began to feel about the bed for stray hairpins. Then he remembered her entering, her glorious sunrise colored hair tumbling about her shoulders. She had worn only the nightgown and the dressing gown, both of which fastened with ribbons. And the silk slippers. She could not have left any stray bits of attire behind for nosy inn servants to find.

His eyes widened. He had deflowered her! The sheets! He leapt from the bed and flung back the bedclothes. Nothing. Not a spot.

Before he could consider the meaning of this lack of evidence, Crewe called his mind elsewhere.

"Sir, I must beg your pardon," the valet said. "I overslept, else I should have wakened you long since."

"You were standing guard again, I collect," Alistair said. "Far into the early morning hours."

"I knew you would not wish a certain lady's visit to be misconstrued by malicious persons," the valet said tactfully. "I am happy to assure you that the lady returned to her rooms without attracting any notice. The inn staff were busy below, in the public dining room, accommodating travelers the storm had waylaid. They hadn't time to be spying upon other patrons."

"Remind me to nominate you for sainthood at the first opportunity," Alistair said as he headed for the washstand. "Meanwhile, as soon as my business affairs permit, I shall double your wages."

"I wish I deserved it, sir," said Crewe. "As it happens, I was asleep at my post and failed you."

Aware that Crewe's standards of service were impossibly high, Alistair poured water into the bowl. "That I rather doubt," he said. He began splashing water on his face.

"Miss Oldridge and her party departed some hours ago," Crewe said. "For home."

Alistair straightened, his face streaming water. "She's turned back?" But she'd agreed to continue to London, and go on plaguing him.

"Her father has gone missing, sir."

JACKSON would not go away.

According to the plan, he was supposed to make sure Caleb had matters in hand and enough money for the trip to Northumberland. Then Jackson was to return to assist his master in London.

But all because Caleb had encouraged Mr. Oldridge to swallow a few drops of Godfrey's Cordial, Jackson decided to play nursemaid. When the storm came on Wednesday night, it was Jackson who made them stop at the mine foreman's deserted cottage.

It was no good Caleb telling him there was no harm in Godfrey's Cordial. Doctors made their patients swill buckets of it, didn't they? Jackson only looked sour and fussed over the old man like it was his own dear pa.

Mr. O was no dear pa to Caleb. He was an aggravating old man, half-senile, and no good to anybody. Amiable, was he? Then how come he never put his little red-haired hussy daughter in her place? How come he let her stick her nose where it didn't belong? How come he never had one good word to say for Caleb, after all those years serving him faithful? Instead, the old fool let her turn off Caleb without a character. It was as good as slandering him, to dismiss him without any explaining to anybody what she was about and refusing to write even ten words commending him to the next employer. Because of her, people wouldn't talk to him. No one would take him on—him, who'd lived among them his whole life, and his parents before, and their parents before that. It was worse than if she'd blackened his character outright or had him put in the stocks.

But she didn't dare have the law on him, because she knew she didn't have a scrap of real evidence against him.

She'd persecuted him, and it was the old man's fault, for letting her do as she pleased. He let her run roughshod over people who knew more than her, never caring if it was almost the same as sending a man to the workhouse.

This was Caleb's thinking, and the more he stewed about it, the less he liked the idea of traveling all the way to Northumberland, nursing the old dodo and looking after him like he was royalty.

If Jackson had only gone away, like he was supposed to,

Caleb could have poured some more cordial down the crackbrain's gullet early last night and dropped him into the nearest abandoned mine. The hill was honeycombed with old mines and shafts. Accidents happened all the time. People would think Mr. O took a tumble, like he was bound to do, sooner or later, with his wandering the hills like he did, in every kind of weather. No one would be surprised when they found his body. If they ever found it.

But Jackson wouldn't go, and now they were stuck, the three of them, in this smoky little hovel—and Mr. O, being a gentleman, got the one bed, and all the best victuals, and even wine, if you please.

Wednesday night passed into Thursday morning, and the cordial's effects having worn off, the old man tried to give them the slip. After that, they had to start dosing him regular with the laudanum Caleb happened to have on hand—in case of mining accidents, he said.

But Jackson was the one who dosed their prisoner, and he was almighty stingy with the drug—only enough to keep Mr. O smiling and dreamy and happy to sit in one place, looking at an old twig or a feather for hours on end.

As the morning wore on, Caleb's patience wore down, too. "The day's wasting, and Northumberland ain't getting any closer," he told Jackson.

"I'll see about hiring a carriage," Jackson said. "I'll be back as soon as I can."

He soon left, taking their one horse and, to Caleb's vexation, the laudanum bottle.

ALISTAIR did not reach Oldridge Hall until well into afternoon. He found the place nearly deserted, most of the staff being out assisting with the search for Mr. Oldridge.

Three separate parties were out combing the botanist's usual haunts. Sir Roger Tolbert had organized a party to search the area about Matlock and Matlock Bath. Captain Hughes and his group were covering the southeasterly portion of Longledge Hill. Mirabel and her servants were working their way over the vast estate itself.

Mrs. Entwhistle remained at Oldridge Hall as search coordinator, receiving and dispatching messages from the various parties. When Alistair was shown into the library, he found her at the writing desk.

She did not waste time with social niceties but promptly apprised him of the situation.

Mr. Oldridge never missed dinner, she reminded him. It was only very rarely that he could be prevailed upon to dine away from home. When he failed to appear Wednesday evening, Benton immediately surmised a mishap. Mr. Oldridge never became so lost as to fail to return home in time for dinner. He was never hindered by inclement weather, and yesterday had not become inclement until well past the appointed dinner hour. The only possible explanation was that he had met with an accident. This was why Benton instantly sent word to his mistress. As he reasoned, if Mr. Oldridge turned up in the interval, it would be easy enough to send another messenger to intercept Miss Oldridge as she was returning.

Mr. Oldridge did not, however, turn up in the interval. He had not dined elsewhere.

"Consequently, one can only hope the mishap was a minor one," Mrs. Entwhistle said.

Alistair remembered his own tumble into the Briar Brook. A sprained ankle. A minor concussion. He might have broken his neck.

"Mr. Oldridge has been wandering the countryside most of his life," he said. "He is nimbler than I—really, he is as nimble as a boy, I think. Who knows these hills and dales better than he? It cannot be anything but a minor accident. And with so many engaged in the search, he is sure to be found before the day is out. Please tell me how I can help."

"You'd better go to Mirabel," the lady said. "She knows what she's about, but she could do with moral support." The ex-governess fixed him with a steely stare, which was a disconcerting contrast to her plumply feminine appearance. "You *are* capable of providing that, I trust?"

While disconcerting, the stare—which had surely reduced erring children to terrified obedience—was nothing to the Gorgon glare his paternal grandmother could administer. "Certainly ma'am," he said, quite uncowed, "that and whatever else the lady requires."

Nearly an hour later he found Mirabel at the outlook where, he now realized, his perceptions of Longledge had first begun to change. She was mounted upon the imperturbable gelding rather than the high-strung Sophy, but she was alone, and in a very short time it would grow dark.

He had come in the nick of time.

She heard his advancing hoofbeats and turned his way.

"You are vexed with me," she said, reading his countenance all too easily.

"Of course I'm vexed," he said. "You're alone, the ground is still slippery from last night's storm, and I know you hadn't much sleep. It is a dangerous combination."

"Have you come to look after me?" she said.

"I am your betrothed, not your nursemaid," he said. "I've come to help you look for your father. You should have sent word to me before you left this morning. But you were too upset to think of it, I daresay. Come, you cannot remain here staring at the moors and making yourself heartsick. We shall find him."

"I didn't want to wake you so early," she said. "You never get enough sleep. And I'd hoped it was a mistake: that Papa had appointed to dine with one of the neighbors, and as usual forgot to tell anybody. All the way home, I was expecting to meet with a messenger telling me he'd dined with the Dunnets, for instance, and ended up spending the night because of the storm. I kept telling myself, 'Any minute now, I shall turn back, and go to London, where I shall cause Mr. Carsington no end of aggravation.'" Her voice wobbled. "Alistair, I mean. It will take me a while to get used to provoking you by your Christian name."

"You may provoke me by any name you like," he said. "Only come away from this place. It is desperately romantic, but at present not conducive to optimistic thinking. One ought to come here to brood, Mirabel, not to plan how best to run a missing parent to ground."

She turned away from the moors and started with him down the path.

"He cannot be in any danger," Alistair told her. "He knows the place too well, every last twig, moss, and lichen of it. You must not make yourself anxious."

"Yes, he is somewhere safe at this moment, no doubt," she said. "Perhaps in one of the hamlets he likes to visit. He is probably quite comfortable in someone's parlor or the local inn, talking about Sumatran camphor trees and reducing everyone in hearing range to a helpless stupor."

MR. Oldridge was far from safe, though he was reducing his lone listener to a helpless stupor.

The sun was setting, the laudanum was wearing off, and the old dodo was lecturing Caleb Finch about Egyptians and poppies.

It had started out in Greek, which Caleb couldn't understand a word of, and didn't see any reason to, he said, as it was a heathen language, made to worship false gods.

"In eastern parts," said his aggravating prisoner, "it is the language of the Christian church, and no more a pagan tongue than Latin."

"Popery is as good as paganism," said Finch.

Mr. O sighed and said, "In his great work, the *Odyssey,* Homer tells of Helen, a daughter of Zeus, who poured nepenthe into the wine the men were drinking at the feast, to make them forget all evil. She learned of this medicine, Homer tells us, from the wife of Thos of Egypt, where the fertile land produces so many balms, some good, and some dangerous. The men at the feast were grieving for their friends and family lost in the Trojan War, you see, and the opium mixture she put into their wine gave them temporary forgetfulness. A respite. That is all I meant," he said, half to himself. "A way to think of terrible things with less distress. I thought he might sleep better, poor boy. Virgil wrote of the poppy, as did Pliny the Elder."

"I wish I had some of that elderberry cordial," Caleb said under his breath. "That and the bottle Jackson took. I'd help you forget, all right."

He walked to the door—the hovel was windowless—and looked out. As soon as it was dark, he promised himself, he'd lead the old man out. A blow to the head, a long drop into a mine shaft, and that'd be the end of his preaching and rubbing it in how he was an educated gentleman who knew Latin and Greek. That'd be the end of his prattling on and on about mosses, poppies, and heathens.

Then the red-haired hussy would be sorry. And in time she'd be sorrier still. Pretty soon Lord Gordmor's canal would cut right through her fine meadows and farms and precious trees. Every day, all the rest of her life, she'd have to look at it.

Caleb stood in the doorway and watched the sky darken.

ALISTAIR, too, was studying the sky, as the horizon began swallowing the sun.

Mirabel watched him. At a respectful distance, her search party waited. She had told them to rejoin her here at sunset. At the time, she'd assumed they would have found Papa long before now. At present, she saw no choice but to give up for the day and let everyone go home. They were all tired and hungry. The others would be able to eat and sleep. She would try to do so, for her father's sake. She would try to wake tomorrow refreshed and hopeful.

Alistair turned to her. "The sky has cleared considerably," he said. "The moon will be up in a few hours. It isn't quite full, but it will give some light. I suggest we use the interval to eat and rest. An hour's nap will do a world of good. I asked Mrs. Entwhistle to prepare provisions.

Someone should be here soon with baskets of food. Those who choose to return to their homes may at least do so on a full stomach."

"You mean to continue?" Mirabel said. "To search through the night?"

"Yes, since we shall have some moonlight," he said.

Then she remembered: his friend had searched for him at night. Had Gordmor not done so, Alistair would not be here at this moment, so sure and confident. While she listened to him, her own flagging spirits lifted.

He was so certain, it was impossible to doubt.

He rode over to the group of men and told them the nighttime strategy. They would divide into two groups. One group would remain. The others would return home, get a good night's rest, and rejoin them as the sun came up. At that time—if Mr. Oldridge had not yet been found—those who'd searched through the night would return home and get their rest.

The provisions arrived as he finished his short speech. He rejoined Mirabel. The men made quick work of their food, then divided themselves into two groups.

Mirabel watched from where she sat with him, upon a large, flattish rock. "They are so orderly," she said, watching the mysteriously chosen half depart. "Like soldiers. I could not believe it when you left it to them."

"Why are you surprised?" he said. "You know I am irresistibly charming."

"I think it is something greater and deeper than charm," she said. "I think you are a born leader."

He withdrew a sandwich from the heavy basket, cut it in half, and gave half to her. "Yes, that, too." His voice dropped to the lowest rumble as he added, "I led you astray with very little difficulty."

"I beg to differ," she said. "It was I who led you astray. Pray do not forget who made the first move. Pray recollect who was first to disrobe. On more than one occasion." She bit into the half sandwich.

"That was all part of my diabolical plan," he said.

"I can almost believe that," she said. "You are a gifted planner. I hadn't considered whether we'd have moonlight or not. I didn't think of ordering provisions. I didn't think of dividing up our search party."

"I had plenty of time to work out a strategy on the way here," he said. "I hadn't an army of attendants to deal with. I did not have to work out how to coddle the vanity of both Captain Hughes and Sir Roger—two men accustomed to ordering others about—and try to guess which assignment would best please them. Furthermore, as much as I like Mr. Oldridge, he is not my father. I have not your attachment and cannot feel as deeply as you do. It is easier for me to view the situation with a degree of objectivity impossible for you. Do stop criticizing yourself and eat your sandwich."

Mirabel ate, though she didn't want to. Later, when he put down blankets for her, she rested, though she couldn't sleep. She closed her eyes and listened to his voice as he talked quietly to some of the men. She could not hear what he said, but the sound of his deep voice comforted her.

She must have fallen asleep, because the next she knew, he was rumbling her name. She opened her eyes and saw first the moon, not quite full, but bright, then him.

His expression was very grave.

She came full awake then, and was up and upon her feet in an instant. "What's wrong?" she said. "What's happened?"

"I'm not sure," he said. "What do you know of a man named Caleb Finch?"

Nineteen

CALEB Finch considered himself a peaceable man, who never raised a hand against his fellows. He'd much rather outwit his fellows or trade favors.

At the moment, though, he had a powerful urge to dash Mr. Oldridge's skull against a rock.

He'd been rattling on for the last hour about some tree that grew in some cannibal country in Africa or China or one of them godless places, and didn't seem like he was anywhere near the end of it.

Caleb couldn't put an end to it, because Jackson was there. He'd come back minutes before the inky blue sky blotted out the last streaks of sunset.

"Kœmpfer said, '*Sed hæc arbor ex Daphneo sanguine non est,*'" Mr. Oldridge said. "It is most definitely not of the *Laurus* genus, but *Dryobalanops,* as Gœrtner declared. However, Mr. Colebrook proposes to name it *Dryobalanops camphora,* rather than *D. aromatica.* The trouble is, he is not a botanist, and his description is not altogether satisfactory. Furthermore, the specimens he received did not survive the cold weather, and he had only the seeds upon which to base his conclusions."

Caleb turned his scowl upon Jackson. "I been listening to that the livelong day. You going to give him some medicine or let him turn us both into drooling bedlamites, like him?"

Jackson poured a glass of wine and added a stingy dose of laudanum to it. He set it down on the table in front of the prisoner. "Best drink it down, sir," Jackson said. "We're going to be traveling, and it'll make you more comfortable."

"Very well," said Mr. Oldridge. "We shall be dining soon, I trust?"

"Yes, sir. I've ordered a hamper for the carriage."

"A hamper." Caleb rolled his eyes. "And gold plates for him to eat off of, I suppose."

Mr. Oldridge raised the glass and mumbled something about old friends and sons-in-law, and drank it down.

When the glass was empty, Jackson turned a narrow look on Caleb. "Don't be making those martyr faces at me," the agent said in a low voice. "You've caused enough trouble, with not waiting for orders, and rushing everything. I said you were too hasty, didn't I? Do you know they're already looking for him?"

"She started out for London straight after the meeting, you told me," Caleb said. "They couldn't've got word to her so quick. Not to mention that no one there'd sneeze without she said so."

It was almost a hundred fifty miles to London, a fifteen-hour journey at least—and that was mail coach style: pushing the horses, and quick changes en route, and hardly a stop to drink or eat or empty your bladder. A private carriage bearing ladies—and them with a train of servants and baggage—would need days. By the time the household took alarm, Miss Hussy would be in Town. Caleb had worked it all out beforehand.

"Mr. Oldridge is like clockwork, I'm told," Jackson

said. "When he missed his dinner, the butler took fright and straightaway sent for the mistress."

The messenger caught up with her before dawn at the inn where she stopped for the night, Jackson went on. Meanwhile, the whole neighborhood started searching for Mr. Oldridge at daybreak.

"If you'd waited, the way master wanted, until she reached London, we'd have time," Jackson said. "But you didn't wait, and now we've barely half a day's start of them. Thanks to you, half of Derbyshire knows he's gone. We'll have to set out right away and travel this fiendish mountain in the dead of night—and pray they're too cautious to try the same. And if we end up in pieces at the bottom of a ravine, we'll have you to thank for it."

Caleb pretended to look chastened. The truth was, Longledge Hill didn't frighten him, even though this was the steepest and rockiest part of it. He'd grown up in the Peak and wasn't afraid of its hills and dales, summer or winter, day or night. There'd be an accident, all right, he thought. But he wasn't the one who'd end up in pieces.

MIRABEL told Alistair about her experience with Caleb Finch as they slowly made their way to the far end of Longledge Hill, toward Lord Gordmor's coal mines.

Their destination was the result of conjecture, which in turn was based largely on rumors—one article the dry limestone hills produced in abundance. One of the women who'd helped carry provisions from Oldridge Hall said she'd seen a tall scarecrowlike fellow, who looked like Caleb Finch, skulking near her neighbor's milk shed early Wednesday morning.

There were other rumors: Finch spotted at church in Ledgemore one Sunday and someone who looked like him at the posting inn in Stoney Middleton a week or more ago.

Because Alistair was Gordy's representative, he was also told an apparently unrelated story about his lordship's mine foreman losing his place suddenly, because Lord

Gordmor's bailiff took a dislike to him. The foreman was muttering about going to the law, the miners weren't happy, and the grumbling had traveled from cottage to public house to posting inn, to reach Longledge this week.

Alistair, who'd visited the mines less than a fortnight earlier and found all in order, was beginning to develop a theory. He said nothing of his suspicions to his informants but promised to look into the matter.

All this had happened while Mirabel rested.

Now she knew that Caleb Finch and Lord Gordmor's bailiff were one and the same man—a man who might have been nursing a grudge against the Oldridges for eleven years.

SINCE no carriage could negotiate the narrow, rutted trails hereabouts, Oldridge had to travel in the coal cart. While Jackson was outside, laying down blankets so the great philosopher's tender bottom wouldn't be bruised, Caleb emptied a sizable dose of laudanum into the wine bottle and pushed it in front of the old man. "Drink all you like," he said. "It'll make the journey more peaceful-like."

Oldridge frowned at the bottle. "I hope Cook does not take offence and give notice," he said. "How many dinners have I missed? I lose count. One must take care with artists. Their feelings are so easily wounded." He looked up at Caleb. "Perhaps someone would send Cook a note? Merely to tell her I've been unavoidably detained."

"Whatever you wish, sir," Caleb said, humoring him. "A very good idea. A business engagement, eh? Called away sudden-like. Business in the north."

"I have not attended much to business," the old man said sadly. "It was remiss of me. The great Dr. Johnson suffered from melancholia, you know. A strange ailment, indeed. How ironic that one should read about it in order to understand a young man, only to discover it in oneself."

"I'm sure it is strange," said Caleb, to whom the words were gibberish. "Do have another glass, sir. Won't get another chance until we get to the carriage. A precious rough ride until then. But this'll settle you nicely."

IT was long after midnight when Alistair and Mirabel reached the colliery. They'd hurried up the packhorse trail as fast as they dared and were now far ahead of the others, who continued systematically scouring the rugged hillside, looking for Papa under bushes, between rocks, in caves and crevices.

The colliery was deserted. Not so much as a watchman.

No witnesses, Mirabel thought. With the foreman dismissed and the men given a holiday, Finch would be free to do whatever he liked.

She would not let herself imagine what might have happened.

"I want to check the foreman's cottage first," Alistair said. "A while ago, I thought I saw smoke coming from this direction."

She followed him to the cottage, half a mile away. It looked deserted. They dismounted, and Alistair cautiously tried the door. It opened easily.

The structure was only a slight improvement over a miner's hut. The candle Alistair lit revealed a single room containing a small, thickly blackened fireplace. The room still smelled of smoke, which meant its occupants must have left fairly recently. The single cot had been stripped bare. A few pieces of crockery stood on the one narrow shelf above the fire, an empty wine bottle on the scarred table.

"Do you see anything?" Alistair asked. "Anything of his, any sign he was here?"

Mirabel moved slowly through the small, dirty room, searching for a sign. If Papa had not been here, he might have been thrown into a mine. He'd be sick, hungry, hurt, and cold. How long could a man approaching sixty, accustomed to ample meals and every material comfort, survive in such circumstances?

If, that is, he'd been left there alive.

She should have had Finch prosecuted when she had the chance. She should not have let her romantic trials cloud her judgment. She should have had more backbone.

She told herself to stop fretting about the past. It accomplished nothing. The present was what mattered. Yet her anxiety must have shown in her face, because Alistair spoke sharply.

"I beg you will not entertain morbid fancies," he said. "You have described Finch as a greedy, dishonest creature. What would he gain by injuring your father?"

"Revenge," she said. "On me."

"Revenge won't line his pockets," Alistair said. "I'm sure whatever he does is done for gain." He lifted an empty wine bottle and sniffed it. "He drinks good wine. Stolen from Gordy, I shouldn't wonder." He started to set it down again, then paused, the bottle in midair, his gaze on a spot on the table.

Mirabel joined him. Something gleamed in one of the table's many cracks. Alistair took out his penknife and worked the object out of the crack.

A gold toothpick.

He handed it to Mirabel. "Your father's, do you think?"

She studied it. "It could be Papa's. I cannot imagine Caleb using a gold toothpick, though it is possible. It cannot belong to the mine foreman. Perhaps—" She broke off as Alistair bent to peer more closely at the table.

"Something is scratched here," he said. "N. T. Is that an H?"

She squinted at the marks, tiny ones, running vertically. One might easily mistake the faint line of letters for scratches. "Or an N," she said.

"N. T. H or N. Then an M, an L, and a rectangle that could signify an O or a D."

He studied it for a long time, while Mirabel tried out various words and word combinations. "Perhaps it's a code?"

Alistair shook his head. "Why leave a message in code?

If your father left this . . ." He trailed off, and his gaze became remote.

"What is it?" she said.

"Northumberland," he said. "Finch is Gordy's bailiff, recollect. The ancestral home is closed up, most of the staff let go. Finch must have handpicked the few remaining. Gordy hasn't been there in years. Depresses his mind, he says."

She could easily imagine how Lord Gordmor felt. Finch must have run his estate into the ground, the way he'd almost done her father's.

"We must have the mines searched," Alistair said, "but I think you and I should continue northward. I feel certain your father left this message. The table is freshly scratched, so it was done quite recently."

"Unless it is a trick."

"Do you think Finch so clever?"

Mirabel considered. "I don't know. I haven't seen Finch since I dismissed him. I was young, and half my attention was elsewhere. Perhaps he is clever. On the other hand, if he is so brilliant a deceiver, how is it he couldn't deceive a twenty-year-old girl preoccupied with losing the love of her life?"

"If you believed Poynton to be the love of your life, any half-wit could pull the wool over your eyes," Alistair said.

She smiled, in spite of her worry. "Yes, of course. How good of you to point that out. Clearly I'm overestimating Finch's intelligence."

SINCE Caleb considered himself a deep and knowing man, he hated admitting he'd made a mistake. But there was no avoiding the fact: He'd misjudged the effects of a large dose of laudanum.

Instead of falling unconscious—or dead—the vexatious old man set to puking.

And Jackson, tenderhearted blockhead, stopped the cart, "because the motion upsets him, don't you see?"

These fine gentlemen had delicate digestions, Jackson said. Mr. Oldridge probably couldn't stomach the plain, peasant fare he'd had for breakfast, or the steak and kidney pudding he'd had at noonday, or the fried slices of leftover suet pudding he ate at tea. It was all coming back to haunt him, like the ghost at the feast in *Hamlet*. Jackson had seen the play on the stage in London not long ago and now fancied himself a scholar.

They wasted an hour waiting for the old man to empty his gut, and after that they crawled along, Jackson walking alongside the cart, promising a good, hot cup of tea the instant they reached Ledgemore, where the carriage waited.

A snail could have beat them, easy.

They crept along for hours in the wooded part of the hill, with the weather getting ready to turn foul again, and Caleb's temper turning uglier by the minute, while the old man lay curled up in the cart, sleeping like a baby, with Jackson hovering nearby, like he was a nursemaid.

But when Jackson stepped away to answer nature's call, Oldridge jumped up out of the cart and bolted for the woods.

It happened so sudden that no one was ready. Jackson needed a moment to finish and button himself up, and Caleb, who was quicker off the mark, tripped over a root and went down, head foremost. He got up in time to see Oldridge disappear behind a rise.

Caleb ran after him, cursing under his breath, because Jackson was shouting, fool that he was. He should save his breath to catch the sneaking rascal. They'd hear Jackson's roaring down in the valley, sure, or at least the dogs would, and set to barking, and wake everyone.

Long minutes later, muscles and lungs burning, Caleb finally closed in on the runaway. He was slowing down and stumbling. Not enough wind in him to outrun a man more than ten years younger, Caleb thought smugly. He stretched his long legs and ran, leaping over rocks and fallen branches. In a last burst of speed, he jumped, and tackled Oldridge, and brought him down hard. Then Caleb dragged him up, and while the wicked old reprobate was gasping for breath, drew his knife and laid it against his neck.

"Your nursemaid ain't here now," Caleb said, gasping, too. "It's time for your accident."

He pulled the man with him, the knife at his neck, while he looked for a likely place.

Ah, yes. There. A good long tumble onto a pile of broken rocks.

ALISTAIR had paused to look up at the sky, which was swiftly clouding again. If he hadn't stopped, he might not have heard the shout and realized it was connected to the subsequent cawing and screeching of irate fowl. The birds were soaring up from the trees, complaining about the intruder who'd disturbed their peace.

If he hadn't heard the shout, he would have guessed a dog or cat had wandered into their midst.

He turned his horse in that direction, though there was no path visible in the rapidly dwindling moonlight. The horses had been picking their way along an old, rutted packhorse road, as they followed the signs of recent passage: the grooves a pair of wheels had made in the dirt, the marks of feet and hooves, and fresh droppings.

Here, in the swiftly dimming moonlight, Alistair distinguished nothing like a trail or path. But the uneasiness he'd carried for all these long hours deepened into anxiety, and he urged his tired animal to more speed.

Yet by the time he and Mirabel reached the patch of woodland, the birds had settled again, and all was silent.

They halted and listened. They were well ahead of the others and heard no voices, only the wind sighing through bare branches and whispering among the pines.

And then a scream broke the quiet, a man's scream, short and terrible, and near at hand.

They dismounted and ran toward the sound.

• • •

THE warning shout stopped Alistair in his tracks.

"Have a care, have a care." Mr. Oldridge's breathless voice came from nearby.

"Papa!"

Mirabel would have rushed toward the sound, but Alistair held her back. "The sound is coming from below," he said. "Wait here."

He walked forward cautiously, straining to see the ground ahead. Thick clouds were swallowing the moon and releasing a cold drizzle.

"Here, here," Mr. Oldridge called. "An air shaft. Have a care, I beg."

Alistair got down on hands and knees and crept toward the voice. He paused when he saw the hole, a ragged shape, only a shade darker than the surrounding darkness. He drew as near as he dared and peered down. He could see nothing.

"Mr. Oldridge," he said. "Are you all right?"

"Yes, yes, certainly."

"We'll fetch a rope and have you out in a trice."

"I fear it is more complicated than that."

Mirabel crept up beside Alistair. "Papa, are you injured? Is anything broken?"

"I think not, but it is difficult to be sure. Caleb Finch fell on top of me. He is . . . dead."

Nausea welled up. Alistair took a deep breath, let it out. He remembered. The mud. The cold, stiffening body keeping him down. The stench. He thrust the memory away.

"In that case, I'll come down to you, sir," he said.

"Alistair."

He could not read Mirabel's face in the darkness, but he heard the fear in her voice. "If you both are trapped there," she said softly, "how shall I get you out?"

"We won't be trapped," Alistair said. "I must go down." More audibly he said, "Mr. Oldridge, can you tell me anything more? It is difficult to see."

"I saw the telltale depression in the ground, and hesitated," Oldridge said. "Then Finch caught me, and when I tried to warn him, he thought it was a trick. It is one of the old air shafts. The hill is honeycombed with them. This one has succumbed to age, weather, and gravity and—in short, it is caving in. We seem to be resting upon a heap of debris that partially blocks the hole."

"You are not at the bottom, then," Alistair said.

"Oh, no. We are wedged over the opening." He wasn't sure how deep the shaft was, he added. Given its position on the hillside, he estimated at least another twenty feet to the bottom.

"I am not sure it would be wise for me to attempt to break through to get to the bottom," Oldridge said.

"No, most unwise," Alistair said. The shaft must lead to an old mine tunnel, but that was more than likely blocked with debris or flooded. Which meant that if the lump of debris supporting them gave way, the two men would fall to the bottom with it. If the fall didn't kill the one still alive, he'd be buried alive or drowned.

"I think it would be best to send for help," Mr. Oldridge said. "I am quite prepared to wait."

And if the rain increased, and became one of the sudden torrents, like the one Alistair had experienced weeks ago? The walls of the shaft could give way, to bury Mr. Oldridge alive or send him to the bottom. They would never be able to extricate him in time.

It had to be now, and Alistair must do it.

"We'll need a good length of rope," he told Mirabel.

ALISTAIR tied the rope around the nearest sturdy tree and dropped the other end into the hole.

The rain was building steadily.

He climbed down, fingers tight on the rope. It was slippery. If his grip failed, he'd crash through the unstable pile of debris and fall to the bottom, taking Oldridge and the corpse with him.

With every move, clumps of dirt and rock gave way.

The rain beat on his head and spattered mud in his face. As he went lower, he became aware of the smell that wasn't wet earth. It was all too familiar. Blood. And excrement. The smell of sudden, violent death. A very different matter from a quiet passing in bed.

He wanted to retch, but he wouldn't let himself. If he gave way to sickness or panic, the woman he loved would lose her father and her future husband at once. Even now she might be carrying his child.

The thought of the child—his child—steadied his nerves and took him down to the uncertain pile of debris where the two men were wedged. He could hear one's breathing. His eyes grew accustomed to the darkness, and he made out the shape of Mr. Oldridge's genial face.

"Can you reach my hand?" he asked, bending down toward Oldridge. He heard a shuffling sound, then dirt and gravel clattering to the bottom. Was that a distant splash he heard? In the rain, it was hard to tell.

"I must get him off first," Oldridge said.

"Let me see if I can help," Alistair said.

He inched down nearer. Still holding onto the rope, he felt with his free hand until he found an ungiving limb. "I've got him," Alistair said. "Which way do we move him?"

"To my left."

"Together now, then, on three, but gently, gently. One. Two. Three."

He tugged and Oldridge pushed, and they shifted the corpse to one side. Another clump of earth gave way.

"We'd better make haste," Alistair said, glad the beating rain drowned out the pounding of his heart. "Take my hand."

Oldridge grasped his hand.

"Can you climb onto my shoulders?" Alistair said. The ground was sliding away from under his feet. He edged back from the crumbling dirt. "You'd better do it *now*," he told Oldridge.

For any other man, even a much younger one, this

would have been next to impossible: The hole was
cramped, its sides unstable, the ground beneath their feet
threatening to give way any minute. Oldridge was far from
young, probably bruised and stiff, and that might be the
least of his troubles. But years of clambering over the
Peak's hills and dales and negotiating slippery paths had
kept him strong and nimble. Though he moved more stiffly
than usual, the botanist managed to climb onto Alistair's
shoulders.

Alistair carefully straightened. "Can you reach?" he
gasped.

"Ah, yes."

At the top of the hole, the blackness lightened to dark
grey. He saw Oldridge's head mere inches now from the
top. Then Mirabel's face. She lay on her stomach, her hand
outstretched.

"Come, Papa," she said.

With her help, Oldridge shimmied and heaved himself
up and over the edge.

Alistair then turned to deal with the corpse. But as he
bent toward it, the body slumped and the dirt—turning to
mud—beneath Alistair's feet shifted and slid away. He
edged back, tightly clutching the rope, and listened to the
rattling dirt and rocks falling into the darkness below.

"Alistair," Mirabel called. "Please."

"I can't leave him—it—here."

He reached again for Finch, but as he moved, the mud
beneath the corpse sagged, and the body slid out of reach.
Another piece of the shaky ledge gave way.

The rain fell faster and heavier, beating on Alistair's
head. Mud and pebbles rained down, too, from the disinte-
grating rim of the hole.

The rope was wet, his hands numb. Merely standing
still, putting little weight upon it, he could barely hold on,
and the ground beneath his feet was crumbling away. If he
tried to climb, and put his full weight on the rope, he'd lose
his hold and fall. If he tried to climb the crumbling shaft
wall, it would collapse on him.

He looked up at the face he could barely see. He didn't need to see it. He had her memorized, carved into his heart. "I love you," he said.

MIRABEL understood what was happening, why he said the three words.

The hole was caving in, and he was going to be buried alive.

She was vaguely aware of a voice, some distance behind her. An unfamiliar voice, talking to her father. She couldn't make out the words, didn't care. All her consciousness was riveted upon the man below. Her heart was pounding in her ears. She had to get down there somehow. She had to help him. She couldn't lose him. She wouldn't.

Then Papa called out, "It's all right, my dear. We've run the rope through the stirrup leather. The horse will pull him out. I'll guide the animal. You assist Mr. Carsington."

"The rope's wet," Alistair told her. "I can't pull myself up, and the shaft wall is likely to give way if I try to get a toehold."

"No, don't try it, sir," came the stranger's voice. Its owner lay down on his stomach next to Mirabel. "Just leave it to us to pull you up."

They let down more rope, and the man told Alistair to loop it about his waist, then round his hand.

"We're going to tow you," the man said.

Mirabel couldn't speak. She could scarcely breathe. She didn't think, but blindly did as she was told.

It was slow, and twice he slid back, but with the stranger's help, they got Alistair up. A mere six lifetimes later, his ice-cold hand was grasping hers.

Another minute and they'd pulled him out and over the edge. He was wet and filthy, and probably in unimaginable pain, but he was safe, and she dared to breathe again.

She threw her arms about him, and felt the ground shift. He pulled her clear, and a heartbeat later, the hole caved in.

They watched silently as the earth swallowed Caleb Finch.

For a long while afterward, no one spoke. They stared at the place for a time, then turned away.

After they'd helped her father onto a horse, the stranger finally broke the silence.

"I'm sorry, sir," he said to Alistair.

"Jackson?" Alistair said. "I thought I recognized your voice."

"Yes, sir," the man said. "I truly am sorry, sir. This is all my doing—all mine—but I never meant for it to turn out like this, I swear."

Twenty

ALISTAIR did not intend to stay at Oldridge Hall. He wasn't satisfied with Jackson's confession and wanted to think it over. If matters were as he suspected, honor forbade his accepting Mr. Oldridge's hospitality. In any case, the farther Alistair was from Mirabel, the clearer his thinking would be.

But Mr. Oldridge proved amazingly obstinate.

They had ridden to the house, and Alistair—intending to go on to Bramblehurst and impose upon Captain Hughes—was trying to brush off the older man's thanks and graciously decline the invitation.

"No, no," Mr. Oldridge said. "It is not convenient for you to depart. I cannot be chasing you all over the neighborhood. You are here now, and I don't doubt Benton has already ordered hot baths. He thinks of everything, you know. You will bathe, and sleep, and we will wake you in time for dinner. Someone will find your servant between now and then, I daresay. But if we cannot find him, you must dine in a dressing gown and refrain from going into a decline because of it. You will not die because you lack a starched neckcloth or whatever it is you make such a fuss about. I shall see you at dinner, then, and we shall talk."

Throughout this speech, Mirabel stared at her father, her eyes opening wider and wider.

Mr. Oldridge met her gaze. "Caleb Finch was holding a knife when we fell," he said. "On impact, it might easily have entered my body instead of his. A great deal passed through my mind between that time and your arrival. Nothing on earth is so dear to me as you. I am heartily sorry that I've been like a stranger to you, and that it wanted the recent series of shocks to bring me to my senses."

He gave neither of them a chance to respond but hastily dismounted, and hurried into the house.

CREWE was there to wake his master at the appointed time, and to apprise him, during the dressing process, of all that had occurred while Alistair slept.

Mr. Oldridge had refused to bring charges against Jackson, who'd been allowed to set out immediately for London.

He'd set out to alert Gordy, of course.

Gordy, the traitor.

"All Jackson's idea, indeed," Alistair muttered, as he buttoned his trousers. "As though he'd dare do such a thing—abduct a gentleman—without his master's express order. 'I'll settle matters here,' Gordy said. I can guess what he was whispering to Jackson behind my back."

"Sir?"

"It cannot wait," Alistair said. "First thing tomorrow, we must set out for London. See to it, please."

"Yes, sir."

The dressing continued through a long silence, finally broken by a small, meditative cough.

Alistair sighed. "What is it?"

Crewe handed him a neckcloth. "I merely wished to observe, sir, that you slept undisturbed."

"No, I did not." Alistair wrapped the linen about his neck. "I dreamt of the circular railway at Euston."

He remembered the dream clearly: the locomotive steam engine racing round and round the track, Gordy shouting at him to get off.

In reality, Alistair had ridden the machine safely, all those years ago. But a short time afterward, the locomotive had fallen off the track. Trevithick hadn't funds for repairs. Others had made the device work elsewhere, though. Weren't they using locomotive engines running on rails, to carry coal in Wales?

The rail track was the great advantage. Locomotive engines were not much faster than horses, except on level ground. But horses could not gallop endlessly for hours, where the steam engine would go on as long as it was fueled. But the great advantage was the rails. They made the way as smooth as water. A horse could tow a much heavier load traveling on water—or along the rails of a tramroad—than it could carry on its back.

Rails, however, could be laid almost anywhere. You didn't need locks or aqueducts to get over inclines. You didn't need great reservoirs.

His mind busy with engineering matters, Alistair quickly tied his neckcloth. He was only distantly aware of Crewe's shocked look as he helped his master into his waistcoat and coat.

"I want you to pack," Alistair said. "We must set out for London, first thing." Without so much as a glance in the mirror, he hurried out.

MR. Oldridge continued in tearing good spirits at dinner. He made light of his recent travails, calling them adventures, and was delighted when Mirabel explained how Alistair had discovered and interpreted the message hastily scratched on the table.

After dinner, when they retired to the library, he became more solemn. As soon as the tea was brought in and the servants had gone out, he said to Alistair, "You must not be too hard upon your friend. He was under a very great strain—and Mirabel's writing to him that you were not right in the upper story did not help matters."

Alistair was too astonished by the man's prescience to answer.

Mirabel tried to say something, but her father held up his hand. "A moment, pray. I signed those letters to Lord Gordmor and the Hargates because I was deeply worried about Mr. Carsington, too, as was Captain Hughes. He'd sought me out that day in an attempt to comprehend my theories about Mr. Carsington's ailment."

"But it is no great mystery," Alistair said. "I suffer from insomnia."

"He was dreaming about Waterloo, Papa," Mirabel said. "It turns out that Mr. Carsington had amnesia, and the bad dreams began when his memory returned."

"A conscientious captain prefers a happy ship," Mr. Oldridge said as though he hadn't heard her. "The men are united, and work and fight better. A good captain is closely attuned to the mood of the vessel in general as well as in the particulars."

Mirabel looked at Alistair, whose mystified expression mirrored her own.

"They live in such close quarters, you know, so many men crammed together, isolated from the outside world for days, weeks, months," Mr. Oldridge continued. "It would be difficult *not* to notice when one of the officers, for instance, becomes dispirited or withdrawn into himself, or grows dangerously reckless in battle, or otherwise undergoes a radical change of behavior. Captain Hughes, I reasoned, was therefore more likely than the average civilian to have encountered and attempted to deal with ailments of the mind and spirit. He must have seen more of such things than the average country physician. But I was unable to make my meaning clear to the captain."

Dispirited. Withdrawn.

Shaken, Alistair set down his tea, got up from his chair, and walked the length of the library, to the windows. He looked out, and recalled the first day he'd come here. He'd looked out of the drawing room windows, unmoved by the scenery, his attention riveted upon Mirabel, the single bright spot in the dreary landscape.

But the view had changed since then. The world beyond the windows was beautiful, changeable, ripe with possibilities. And it was welcoming. It was . . . home.

He turned and found two pairs of blue eyes watching him.

"I had always thought of dandies as frivolous, shallow creatures, not overly intelligent," Mr. Oldridge said. "When Mirabel proclaimed you one of the species, I was deeply puzzled. My botanist's instinct told me your attire was armor of some kind." He glanced at Mirabel. "Cactus spines."

Armor, to protect what was inside, Alistair thought. What had he been trying to protect? What was he hiding from? Uncertainty, perhaps. The chance that the battle had damaged his mind permanently. And always, in the background, even when he couldn't remember the details of the battle and its aftermath, there hovered a vague sense of shame.

He now knew that the carnage had shocked and sickened him. Every time he'd fallen, a part of him had wanted to stay there and weep for the dead, strangers and comrades alike. Young men, boys had died about him, some in horrible agonies. He'd gone on fighting, though, mindlessly, because thinking would only yield grief and despair.

He now knew as well that he'd been terrified of the surgeons' instruments—he, who'd always believed fear was for women and the weakest of men.

Mr. Oldridge's voice called him out of the reverie.

"Perhaps I recognized your difficulty because it was something like my own," the older man said. "I did not retreat from the world on purpose after my wife's death. The thing came upon me, like a sickness or a pernicious habit, and I could not break its hold upon me. I found myself wondering if your grievous experience at Waterloo had a similar effect upon you. I retreated into botany, and you . . ." He smiled. "And you into the arcane science of dress."

"Good heavens," Mirabel said, eyes wide as she regarded Alistair. She rose from the sofa and crossed the room and looked him up and down, as though she'd never seen him before. "I had too much on my mind to take proper notice. But now that I do notice, I am astonished. My dear, you are all—" She flung her hands up, clearly at a loss. "Your neckcloth. Words fail me."

Alistair looked down and blinked. He had tied the thing any which way. How had Crewe let him out of the room looking like this?

He looked at Mr. Oldridge, who was smiling. Alistair grinned. "If your theory is correct, it would appear that I'm recovering, sir," he said.

"I'm relieved to hear it," said the older man. "And to see it." He walked to a set of bookshelves and plucked out a volume. "Since you've shown signs of returning to sanity, I shall await a private interview in my study. I believe you have something particular to say to me regarding my daughter." He walked out.

London

HAVING received yet another express letter from Oldridge Hall on Saturday night, and not long thereafter a report in person from a greatly distressed Jackson, Lord Gordmor was unhappily aware of all that had transpired in the previous two days.

He sent Jackson to Northumberland to survey the devastation there and untangle matters as best he could. Meanwhile, his lordship stoically awaited public disgrace and possible private dismemberment.

He had a long wait.

The message from Carsington arrived ten days later. It requested his lordship appoint a time and place for a meeting.

Lady Wallantree was visiting her brother when the curt note arrived, and as usual had no scruples about snatching it from his hands.

"He is challenging you to a duel?" she cried. "But you must not fight him, Douglas. He is not in his senses. And he always was the better shot, as well as the better swordsman. I am not at all confident that his crippled leg will give you much advantage."

Lord Gordmor gave her a mildly puzzled look. "Since when have you become an expert in affairs of honor, Henrietta? But why do I ask? What is between Carsington and me is none of your affair, and never has been. You always prophesy catastrophe, always discern the thundercloud within the shiniest silver lining. You make Cassandra seem jolly by comparison."

"No one heeded her, did they?" she shrieked. "That was the curse of her gift. It is my curse as well. You mock me. You refuse to hear the truth."

"It is truth distorted out of all recognition," he said. "I have allowed your hysterias to disrupt the peaceful tenor of my life once too often. The last time constitutes a mistake I shall regret to the end of my days. However, if your clairvoyant powers prove accurate for once, those days may be mercifully few."

Lady Wallantree promptly fell into a fainting fit.

Lord Gordmor summoned a servant to attend to her, called for his hat and cane, left the house, and went in search of the man who'd been his closest friend for twenty years.

ON the same day, the Monday following Easter, Alistair was pacing the richly carpeted floor of London's most sought-after and expensive modiste.

At length his bride-to-be emerged from the dressing room. She paused before him. He shut his eyes.

"Lavender," he said in martyred tones. "It is a gift, a veritable gift, I vow. A rare knack for finding—among a collection of gowns so elegant that even Parisians must weep with envy—the one that turns your complexion grey."

"Alistair," Lady Hargate said reproachfully.

He opened his eyes and stoically regarded his mother. She sat with Lady Sherfield, a handsome woman bearing a strong resemblance to her niece. They were looking over fashion books.

How he missed Mrs. Entwhistle's lackadaisical chaperonage! His mother and Lady Sherfield were always about. He had not had one moment alone with Mirabel since they'd arrived in London the previous Thursday.

"If you are bored with this business," his mother went on, "kindly take your ill humor elsewhere. Otherwise, Miss Oldridge might have second thoughts about marrying such a tactless, sarcastic brute."

"I am never to wear lavender?" Mirabel said.

"No," he said. "You must keep to warm, rich colors. That is a cool, pale color. It is not for you. And anyway, it looks as though you are in half mourning, when you are supposed to be a deliriously happy bride-to-be."

"I like cool, pale colors," she said. "They are so soothing."

"Leave it to me to soothe you," he said. "Leave it to your clothes, I beg, to become you."

"You have not been soothing company this morning," she said.

He cast his gaze meaningfully toward his mother and her aunt, both again engrossed in the fashion plates, and made a pantomime of tearing out his hair.

"Yes, shopping is very tedious," she said. "But you were the one who insisted on my replacing every stitch of my wardrobe."

"You were also the one, Alistair, who insisted upon participating in these tiresome proceedings," said his mother, without looking up.

"I did not insist she do it all at once," Alistair said. "I had hoped to show my betrothed something of London. I had thought we might at least take a turn in the park. If we do not appear, people will wonder what we are hiding."

Both older ladies looked up then.

"I believe they will also wonder why we need such close chaperonage," he went on. "We are betrothed, after all. The notice appeared in the paper. We are to be wed in two days. We really ought to be allowed to go out alone in public. Do you not agree, Miss Oldridge?"

"Oh, yes," she said. "An excellent point. We do not wish to cause talk. Only let me get this horrid thing off, and I shall be out in a trice."

THE whole business took rather longer than "a trice."

They were obliged to take the chaperons home, and Miss Oldridge must change while Alistair borrowed his younger brother Rupert's curricle. As a result it was close to four o'clock before they reached Hyde Park. In another hour, the place would be crawling with people. He and she not only would have no privacy but would be interrupted every few minutes as people came seeking introductions to his affianced bride, and to offer good wishes while appeasing their curiosity.

A number of men would be sick with envy as well, Alistair had no doubt. Mirabel's moss green carriage dress was not only becoming, but au courant. They'd had it and several other items made up in a hurry. Though the fittings bored Mirabel witless, she was happy with her pretty new clothes, and this day she had let the maid take time with her hair.

"You are ravishing," he told her after they'd entered the park, and he no longer needed to give his full attention to negotiating the congested London streets.

"I think you are blinded by affection," she said. "But I

don't mind. It is such a relief to have you choose my clothes. I am rarely indecisive, except when it comes to dress. The choices and all the vexing details overwhelm me. And recollect that until now, my situation required me to dress plainly and simply. I had so often to deal with men in the way of business, and they are so easily distracted. But it is most agreeable to have pretty things again."

She had not refused a single pretty item presented to her. When given three gowns to choose from, she chose all three. The same held for bonnets and shoes. As to her underthings, Alistair had been kept out of those transactions, but he'd seen the heaps of boxes when she returned with her aunt from a shopping trip.

"I'm glad you're pleased," he said. "I had not guessed that you could be as extravagant in that way as I. But I am changing my ways. If I forgo my old spending habits, we should have no difficulty living within our income."

She tipped her head to one side, studying his profile.

"What is it?" he said. "What have I said that is so puzzling?"

"My dear," she said, "did you not read the marriage settlements before you signed them?"

"Certainly I read them," he said. They would be wed on Wednesday, by special license, which would allow them to dispense with banns and marry when and where they chose. Lord Hargate had wasted not a moment in procuring the document or in getting the settlements drawn up and signed.

"Whether I understood them is another matter," Alistair added. "In the first place, there is the villainous law hand, which is indecipherable. In the second, there is the villainous law language, which is incomprehensible. I do recall a great many noughts in some of the figures, and an error in computation, to which I called my father's attention. He laughed heartily about it, and I donned an expression of heroic resignation and wrote my name where I was told."

"My dowry is two hundred thousand pounds," Mirabel said. "In addition, there is—"

"I beg your pardon," he said. "Something is awry with my hearing. I thought you said *two hundred thousand.*"

"That is what I said."

The club had struck again.

"My dear, are you unwell?" she asked anxiously. She reached up and laid her gloved hand against his cheek.

Alistair stopped the horses and turned his head to press his mouth against the palm of her . . . glove. It was not very satisfying. He pressed his lips to the narrow bit of skin showing at her wrist, then drew away.

"It doesn't signify," he murmured. "A momentary faintness, that was all. Two. Hundred. Thousand. No wonder my father laughed."

"You did not know?"

"I thought someone had misread, and counted too many noughts," he said. "I assumed twenty thousand or thereabouts." The daughter of the Duke of Sutherland, one of England's richest men, had brought twenty thousand to her marriage. "I did not dwell on the matter, because it is vulgar to speak of money."

"Mama inherited her family's banking fortune," Mirabel said. "Papa's inheritance was substantial as well."

"I see," Alistair said faintly. He looked about him, dimly aware of trees putting out their new green leaves, and birds twittering, and a few figures on horseback. In a short time the park would be packed with Good Society, riding expensive horses or driving elegant vehicles, dressed in the latest modes and exchanging the latest gossip.

"You are upset," she said.

"No wonder my father was so excessively affectionate," Alistair said. "After I had signed the papers, he actually patted me on the shoulder."

"Well, you are very expensive," she said. "He would have worried about your finding a girl who could afford you."

"I am not *that* expensive," he said. "Only the Prince Regent is that expensive. And may I remind you, dressing him requires a much greater quantity of material than does dressing me."

The Prince Regent's figure had grown elephantine with the passing years.

"I recall what you said about refusing to be a parasite upon your wife," she said. "I hope you will not brood about it and make yourself unhappy. There is nothing out of the way about a younger son's marrying money."

Alistair studied the woman who'd soon be his wife. Hair: sunrise. Eyes: dusk. Voice: night. He'd seen all this at the first glance. That was before he'd learnt the dizzying changes of her countenance, the quickness of her mind, the openness of her nature, and the kindness of her heart. It was before he'd held her in his arms and discovered how completely, trustingly, and uninhibitedly she could give herself to him.

He smiled.

"I have said something amusing?" she said.

He leaned toward her. "I was thinking of you naked," he whispered.

"A thousand pardons for interrupting, Car," came a familiar voice nearby. "I do regret it, but there is only so much suspense a fellow's nerves can stand."

MIRABEL, who'd become oblivious to her surroundings, started. Alistair did not. Instead, he went rigid and slowly, stiffly, drew away from her.

"Gordmor," he said coldly.

A dull reddish color suffused the viscount's previously pale countenance. "Miss Oldridge," he said, doffing his hat.

She nodded politely.

"I beg you will forgive the intrusion," Lord Gordmor said.

The atmosphere, already thickening, grew thunderous.

Mirabel looked about her. The park was all but deserted. Moments ago, she'd been thrilled to have a moment alone with Alistair at last. Now she regretted the isolation.

There was no one about to intervene or to interrupt the confrontation now threatening.

"Your effrontery passes all bounds," Alistair said to his friend, his voice dangerously low. "Even if you are without any sense of shame, you might consider the distress your presence must cause Miss Oldridge."

"I do consider it, Car," said his lordship, "and that is why I have come. I could have blown out my brains, or cut my throat, but I've never been dramatic. Also, I doubt I could do it with the proper elegance, and would only make a hash of it—"

"Blow out your brains?" Alistair cut in. "What are you talking about?"

"I am not at all sure," Gordmor said. "But I could not bear to do this through outside parties. If we are to fight, Car, let us do it without—"

"Fight?" Mirabel turned to Alistair. "Tell me you have not challenged him to a duel."

"Certainly not," Alistair said. "He's a terrible shot, and liable to kill an innocent bystander."

"Terrible shot?" Gordmor said. "I am an excellent—"

"His swordsmanship is even worse," Alistair said.

"You think so because I *let* you get the better of me now and again," Gordmor said. "Out of pity."

Alistair's eyes narrowed to golden slits. "Pity," he growled. "For my infirmity, you mean."

"You were infirm long before you let those foreigners scratch you up at Waterloo. I have spent most of my life looking out for you."

"You were looking out for me to rescue you," said Alistair, "from the first day of school."

Gordmor turned to Mirabel. "I cannot count the number of times I have had to rescue this dolt from one scrape or another. That little blonde girl—what was her name? When we were at Eton. The caretaker's girl."

"Clara," said Mirabel, recalling her aunt's letter.

"Clara." Gordmor pointed to his nose. "This used to be straight—until one of Clara's brutish lovers broke it. Then there was Verena."

"You did not rescue me from Verena," Alistair said.

"I warned you. How many times have I warned you?" Gordmor turned back to Mirabel. "He has never had a particle of sense about women. He never sees what is obvious to everyone else who is not deaf, dumb, and blind."

"Gordy, may I remind you that you are addressing my future wife," Alistair said.

"I was not referring to Miss Oldridge," Lord Gordmor said. "But you have discomposed me so, I cannot think straight. I came, intending, as I recollect, to apologize."

"Then get on with it," said his friend.

"Miss Oldridge, I behaved very stupidly, and I sincerely regret it," his lordship said. "I made so many errors of judgment, it would take a week to enumerate them. I shall never forgive myself for placing your father in danger, though I assure you it was not intentional. I meant only to create a diversion that would keep you out of London while our canal act was considered. I was about to offer—before Car cast aspersions on my marksmanship—the most abject of apologies. I was also about to admit—before he started quibbling about Verena—that my recent Episode of Stupidity far surpasses all of his combined."

"Thank you," Mirabel said.

Gordmor looked at Alistair.

"If Miss Oldridge is satisfied, I suppose I must be," Alistair said stonily. "I collect I must invite you to the wedding now."

"It would be the nobly forgiving thing to do," Gordmor said.

"I am not that noble," Alistair said. "The trouble is, if you don't come, one of my brothers will stand up for me. You are a fraction less tedious than the older ones and a degree less annoying than the younger ones."

• • • •

THE following morning found Alistair in Lord Gordmor's dressing room as the latter was preparing to go out.

His lordship, who was working on his neckcloth, did not look away from the mirror when his friend entered. "I am trying to invent a new style," he said. "Primarily because I have such an infernally difficult time arranging the ones that have already been invented. I am not sure I shall be able to concentrate properly, however. I am all agog to learn what tore you from your bed at this early hour. The noon bells have hardly ceased tolling."

"I want to talk to you about a railway," Alistair said.

Gordy gave up on his neckcloth, turned away from the mirror, and looked at him. "A railway," he said.

Alistair explained the plan he'd discussed with Mr. Oldridge when he'd sought his blessing for the marriage. Mr. Oldridge had approved of both tramroad and wedding plans.

Instead of building a canal, they'd lay down rails directly from the mines to the lime burners and others to the north. They could install stationary steam engines to draw the carts up steep inclines. They wouldn't need to follow level ground. They wouldn't need locks or aqueducts. They would need only enough water to run the steam engines. It would cost less than building a canal, and take less time. It would carry the coal, cheaply and speedily, from their stony piece of Longledge Hill to the nearest customers. They wouldn't need to go through the Oldridge property, or any of their neighbors' lands.

"A tramroad," Gordy said when Alistair had finished. "Why didn't we think of that in the first place?"

"Because Finch, your trusty overseer, suggested a canal, and we got the idea fixed in our heads," Alistair said. "And because I failed to exercise my imagination sufficiently."

Gordy considered. "I take it Miss Oldridge approves of this plan?"

"It's to be a surprise. A wedding gift. I did not want to

tell her about it until I was certain you would cooperate."
He'd promised Mirabel he'd solve the problem, and he
had.

"Of course I'll cooperate. I'm grateful that she didn't
hold my idiotish behavior against you." Gordmor tore off
his neckcloth, tossed it aside, and picked up another from
the stack of neatly folded linen placed on a table near the
mirror. Then he put it down again and turned to Alistair.
"Car, I must beg your pardon," he said.

"You already did. Yesterday, in Hyde Park."

"No, I begged Miss Oldridge's pardon. But all the trouble began because I did not believe in *you*. My sister
harped ceaselessly on how much you'd changed since Waterloo, and had me half-convinced you were non compos
mentis. She was prating about pernicious melancholia, and
I didn't know how to argue with her. You seemed to have
lost all your passion and energy since Waterloo. You hardly
noticed women, though they were throwing themselves at
you, left and right."

"Perhaps she was not far wrong," Alistair said. "It was
a melancholia of some kind, apparently, though I have
never heard it called 'pernicious.' And it did come upon
me after Waterloo. I am told that such things are not un-
heard of among former soldiers and sailors. Some don't recover. But my case could not have been so very
pernicious."

Gordy studied him for a moment. "No, today you are
like the Car I always knew, not the stranger who came
home from the Continent."

"I don't understand how I came to be that way, or why,
exactly," Alistair said.

"I should think that time in the surgeons' tent would be
enough to disorder any man's mind," Gordy said.

"I was terrified," Alistair said. It was the first time he'd
admitted it, aloud, to anybody. He had not even told
Mirabel yet. He would, though.

Gordy did not even blink. "You covered it well," he
said. "I had no idea. But then, I was too terrified myself to

pay close attention to you. I knew I must stand by you, Car, and I should have done it, too, but I should have disgraced us both, and been sick—and probably swooned dead away. I know it will sound mad and inexcusably selfish, but I was vastly relieved when you declined the surgeon's kind offer to amputate."

"You were sick? Really?"

"It was worse, infinitely worse, than the actual fighting. Then, at least, one is caught up in the heat of battle. Gad, I couldn't wait to get us both away from that ghastly place."

"That saw," Alistair said, "caked with blood."

"The surgeons," Gordy said, "covered with blood and God knows what else. And the stink of the place."

"If I could have run, I'd have run away screaming, like a girl," Alistair said, his heart lightening.

"I would have been right behind you," Gordy said, "screaming louder and at much higher pitch. I have not your manly basso, you know."

And in another moment they were laughing at their so very non-nonchalant reaction to that glorious, horrendous day, and Alistair had no trouble remembering why Gordy had always been his dearest friend.

Twenty-one

THE day of the wedding dawned bright, and the groom was wide awake, dressed, and pacing his bedchamber at Hargate House well before the appointed hour.

Crewe had had a Premonition.

"Why did you not have one the day Mr. Oldridge went missing?" Alistair said. "Why must you have one now?"

"I apologize, sir," his valet said. "Perhaps it does not signify. Perhaps it is merely prenuptial nerves."

"You are not getting married, Crewe. I am."

"Indeed, sir, but we are changing our circumstances. Ours is no longer a bachelor household." The manservant gave a small, anxious cough. "My mind is most uneasy about the linen. Mr. Oldridge and you have different views regarding the starch. He prefers his linen a degree less stiff. And the chief laundress at Oldridge Hall is a singularly forbidding female."

Alistair ceased pacing to stare at his valet. "You are afraid of the laundress?"

Crewe coughed an affirmative.

"We shan't be at Oldridge Hall all the time," Alistair said. "We shall have our own townhouse here, as soon as we find a suitable place. Then I give you leave to choose our London laundress and demand all the starch you wish. I am sure it will not matter to Miss Oldridge one way or another. Perhaps, in Derbyshire, on the other hand, we might be a degree less—er—starched, than in London."

"Are you sure, sir? It will be—" A very small, deprecating cough intervened. "—an adjustment."

"I am told that married life requires a great number of adjustments, Crewe. And bear in mind that Miss Oldridge must also make certain changes to accommodate a husband. She has been accustomed, these ten years and more, to arrange all matters as she sees fit. Now she will have both a parent and a spouse putting their oars in."

Not, Alistair thought, that her father had not already put an oar in. He had a growing suspicion that some sort of communication had passed between Oldridge Hall and Hargate House prior to his arrival in Derbyshire last month. Lord Hargate had not seemed the least surprised at the news of the impending marriage. He had looked, in fact, smug—and most especially so when the marriage settlements were being signed.

Alistair was marrying an heiress, just as his father had recommended in November.

"But it was impossible for them to conspire," he said, half to himself as he studied his reflection in the mirror for the seventeenth time. "Mirabel opened all her father's letters. It was the merest accident that she did not see mine."

Crewe coughed.

"Yes, what is it?" Alistair said.

"I only wished to observe, sir, that certain letters have been known to make their way directly into Mr. Oldridge's hands. They would be enclosed in one addressed to the head gardener. Lady Sherfield used this method from time to time."

Lady Sherfield, his mother's bosom bow.

Alistair had left his letter to Oldridge in the tray with the others, for his father to frank.

His father must have enclosed it in one addressed to the gardener.

That was how Mr. Oldridge had received it.

He'd sent a positive, encouraging answer to Alistair, though the botanist had not wanted a canal through his property any more than his daughter did.

Why?

"Matchmaking," Alistair told his reflection.

"Sir?"

"I was lured there," Alistair said. "On purpose. They set a trap, the two of them. My father saw the opportunity, and he took advantage. It was Machiavellian." He turned away from the mirror and smiled. "And exceedingly good of him. I might not have discovered her otherwise."

Someone tapped on the door.

Crewe went across and opened it.

He came back to Alistair bearing a small tray on which rested a note bearing Lord Sherfield's seal.

Heart pounding, Alistair opened and read it.

Then he ran from the room.

THE wedding was to take place at Hargate House at eleven o'clock.

It was a quarter past ten, and the bride, at Sherfield House, had chased out her maid and locked herself in her room at a quarter to, saying the wedding must be called off.

"I have tried to speak to her," Mr. Oldridge told Alistair when he arrived. "My sister assured her—through the door—that it is only a last-minute attack of nerves, which happens to everybody. But neither Clothilde nor I, nor even Mrs. Entwhistle could obtain any sort of response. Lord Sherfield fears she is ill and wishes to break the door down. I confess I am anxious on that head, though Mirabel never takes ill. But she is never so unreasonable, either."

Oldridge frowned. "At least, I'd always supposed she was not given to irrational or temperamental behavior. But I had not paid close attention, as you know."

"She is not unreasonable or temperamental," Alistair said. "Very likely she has qualms. Perfectly reasonable, in the circumstances."

He recalled what he'd told Crewe, about two men putting their oar in, when she was accustomed to being in command. Her life was about to change dramatically. She needed more time to get used to the idea. Alistair should not have rushed her. But he was worried that she was pregnant. And yes, he was in a fever to be wed and be rid of all the dratted chaperons. Selfish brute. He should have been reassuring her yesterday, instead of reassuring himself with Gordy.

All this was passing through his mind as Mr. Oldridge led him to the staircase. Lord Sherfield was pacing at the foot of it. Lady Sherfield was talking to Mrs. Entwhistle. She broke off as Alistair approached.

"I do not understand," Lady Sherfield said. "She was so cheerful when I went up earlier. And Mirabel is not given to moodiness."

"I think she has retreated to the dressing room," said Mrs. Entwhistle. "You will have to shout at the top of your voice to make her hear."

Alistair paused on the first step. "I am not going to shout at my bride on our wedding day," he said.

He considered. Then the idea came.

THE dressing room door shut out the voices. It could not shut out everything, however.

Mirabel sat well away from the dressing table on a footstool at the far end of the room, out of the window's light. She did not need the voices to make her aware she was behaving badly. Abominably. But she could not go through with it. And she could not explain. They would not understand. They would tell her she was being silly, that it was merely a case of last-minute anxiety, which everyone experienced. They would assure her that nothing was wrong and gently remind her that she would embarrass Alistair's family and inconvenience the guests. Alistair would be humiliated. She shut her eyes. She could not do that to him. She must go through with it.

She rose, but her courage instantly failed, and she sank onto the footstool again, her head in her hands.

A loud clattering, as of hailstones against the window, shot her upright again.

Heart pumping, she went to the window and looked out. The sky was still blue, dotted with fluffy white clouds.

Then she looked down.

And blinked.

And opened the window.

From the bottom rung of a ladder, Alistair gazed up at her.

"What are you doing?" she said.

He put his index finger to his lip and swiftly ascended. "I've come to rescue you," he said. "I shall carry you away on my snowy white charger, to wherever you wish. Or rather, behind a pair of greys, as I was obliged to borrow Rupert's curricle again. I thought the carriage would be more comfortable for a longish flight." While he spoke, he was climbing onto the ledge, then over it, into the room. "You've had second thoughts about marrying me," he said. "I don't blame you. I was insufferably arrogant. I told you to marry me. I never asked you properly."

"That is not the problem," she said, backing away.

"I am not the hero you imagine me to be," he said. "I should have told you the real reason I refused to be amputated. The truth is, I was far more frightened of the surgeons than of the enemy."

"It was sensible to be alarmed," she said. "You would not have survived an amputation. That is not the problem."

"I haven't told you the worst," he said. "I was frightened witless when I went down into that hole after your father."

"But you did it anyway," she said. "That is true courage: to act in spite of fear. And it was a rational fear. I had never been so frightened in all my life as I was then. That is not the problem."

"I've kept things from you." He walked to the looking glass, made a small adjustment to his neckcloth, then came back to her. "Your father and I have been plotting behind your back. I have a new scheme. Instead of a canal, Gordy and I will build a railway from the mines to our customers. Your father approves the idea, and Gordy is delighted. I should have told you first, but I wanted it to be a wedding gift. I imagined you would swoon with admiration of my brilliance."

A railway. She had searched and searched for a solution, but always she'd assumed they must have a canal. A railway had not even occurred to her.

She pressed her fist to her bosom. "It is brilliant, and I should swoon if I knew how. Perhaps I learnt the art but it was long ago, and I've forgotten. It is merely one of a number of feminine skills I lack." Her eyes itched. "You told me you would find a solution, and you did. It is a wonderful surprise. It is a perfect gift. It is certainly not a problem."

He came to her then and gently grasped her shoulders. He gazed at her in that way of his, making her look up, straight into his golden eyes, making it impossible to pretend anything.

"It does not matter that I was not the first," he said gently. "I have had a twinge of jealousy now and again, I admit. It is absurd, of course. It is not as though I have lived like a monk. But my nature is somewhat possessive, and I did not wish to share you with anyone, even if the sharing happened in the distant past, practically before I was born. But that is all—pride and possessiveness. It does not alter my feelings for you a whit."

"Not the first?" she said, bewildered. "Not the first what? To be jilted by me? But I am not jilting you. That is, not—"

"I know I am not your first lover," he said. "It does not matter. You were not obliged to tell me. It is ancient history, no more relevant than my own episodes. Merely because men are customarily allowed more latitude in these matters does not make it right or just."

Mirabel drew back, stunned. Had someone in London who knew her in the past whispered slander in his ear? William Poynton had been very popular. A great many ladies had been jealous of Mirabel. Some may have blamed her for his leaving England and never returning. Could they still be holding a grudge, after all this time?

"I don't know who told you this," she began.

"No one told me," he said. "I saw the evidence. Or rather, the lack of evidence. After we made love, at the inn. The sheets. Not a spot."

"Not a spot," she repeated. Then, finally, she realized what he was saying, and in spite of her misery, she smiled. "My love, I am one and thirty," she said. "Did it not occur to you that my hymen might have shriveled up and died—of despair, most likely."

"Of course it didn't occur to me," he said. "To me you are a girl." He let her go and stepped back, his expression perplexed. "My dear, I am at a complete loss now as to what troubles you. But I don't need to know. All that matters is that you are in difficulties of some kind and want to call off the wedding. I shall not attempt to force—"

"I can't do it!" she cried. "I cannot." Her shoulders sagged. "Look at me."

"You look beautiful," he said. The gown was a warm, oyster-shell white, trimmed with fine lace, rather like the fetching nightgown she'd worn that night at the inn.

She stared at him. "What is wrong with you? Not my gown. That looks well enough. It is my hair. I cannot believe you didn't notice. It is *all wrong!*"

He blinked. "Your hair," he said. "You want to call off the wedding because your hair is not right?"

"Can't you see? Aunt Clothilde's maid did it, and it is too high on the forehead, and here are these untidy clusters dangling at my ears, and it took her forever, and I am stuck with a thousand pins, and there isn't time to pull them all out and start over again, and I know you will not be able to concentrate on the service because you will be in agonies about it, and I will embarrass you in front of your family and friends."

There was a short silence.

Then, "It is the latest fashion," he said. His mouth twitched.

"Oh," she said.

"It would not matter to me if it were the fashion of last century," he said. "The only agony I shall suffer is impatience for the wedding night. It has been a very long time since I held you in my arms."

"Yes, it has been tedious and annoying," she said. "A turn about the park in an open carriage—with half the world looking on and the other half interrupting to chat—is not very satisfying."

She drew near to him again and tipped her head back. "We are entitled to a kiss, I should think."

"To sustain us through the trial ahead," he said. He bent his head.

The instant his mouth touched hers, the world came right again. She reached up and curled her hands about his neck, and his hands came round her waist. She loved his hands, and the clean, masculine smell of his skin, mixed with starch and soap. She loved the way his mouth moved over hers, the light pressure coaxing her to part her lips, and the taste of him. She shivered and pressed closer, and his hold tightened.

She'd felt so unsure, so cold and alone. Now she was warm again, and wanted. His hands moved over her back, and she sighed with pleasure. "I've dreamt of this," she murmured against his mouth. "Your hands, your wonderful hands."

"I've dreamt of it, too." He nuzzled her neck. "We have to stop."

"Oh, yes."

He made a cascade of kisses from the tender place behind her ear to the neckline of her gown. With his finger, he drew the neckline down and trailed his finger inside, against her skin. He made another path of kisses from her shoulder to the very edge of the fabric, over the upper swell of her breasts. The tender caress of his mouth made her ache.

She strained toward him, her hands sliding to the back of his waist. There was so much in the way. She dragged up the coat, and her hands slid over the silk waistcoat and down, over smooth wool and the taut curve of his buttocks.

He tensed and growled something against her neck, and she pressed against him. Even through the layers of her gown and petticoats and his trousers, she felt his arousal. It would be hot there, and hard.

She remembered that heat thrusting into her, and heat eddied through her to sink to the pit of her belly. Her mind sank, too, into a deep, dark place, while the world slid away.

"Don't make me stop," she begged, her voice low and thick, the words dragged out between ragged breaths. "I want you inside me." She drew her hand over the front of his trousers. "Now."

THE bold caress took his breath away and sapped his will. He lifted his head and looked at her. Her eyes were smoky blue, half-closed. With every inhalation he drew in the scent of her, and it clouded and thickened his mind.

Yet some awareness remained. They couldn't continue. The wedding. The waiting guests. He drew back and tried to catch his breath and regain his balance.

She advanced, tugging at the bodice he'd disarranged. Her breasts swelled, pearl smooth, above the lace. She slid her hands over them, down over the dainty waist, and down further, over her hips. Her fingers tightened on the skirt, and she dragged it up. His gaze slid down to the soft kid slippers, and up: the white stockings . . . the pretty turn of her ankle . . . the perfect curve of her calves.

He backed away another step, and she advanced, drawing the gown up higher still, nearly to her knees. A little more, and he'd see the misshapen, upside down heart, so like her, turning his mind and heart, his world, topsy-turvy.

He shut his eyes. No. The wedding. The guests. Waiting.

He backed away another step, and struck something, and stumbled backward. He came up against the wall, but his bad leg gave way, and down he slid, onto the carpet.

And before he could think of rising, she was there, standing astride him, her skirts still gathered in her hands. She was looking down at the front of his trousers, and her mouth curved into a wicked smile.

She reached up under her gown and untied her drawers, and down they fell onto his belly. His cock, hardly affected by the fall, stood at attention.

Down she came, onto her knees, her femininity mere inches from his eager member.

He slid his hands up her sweetly rounded thighs, over garters and the tops of her stockings, to the soft skin. He trailed his fingers over the curve of her belly, the smooth place just above the feathery curls. She uttered a low moan and moved against his hand. He let his thumb slip lower, where she wanted, and stroked her, though his hand trembled and his mind was a wild place, all need and animal instinct. She was so near, warm and ready, the tender place under his thumb so soft and dewy.

He felt her tremble against him. She pushed his hand away, and rose a little, and grasped his rod, and eased herself onto him, slowly. "Oh," she said, and it was half-moan, half-sigh. She bent to him then, and he reached up and caught her, his fingers dragging through the thick, wild curls, and brought her down, brought her mouth to his.

"You are in command," he murmured.

"Yes."

He felt her smile against his mouth. She lifted herself,

and came down, and his mind went black. Nothing left but feeling, heat coursing through him as she rose and fell, as he rose and fell with her, slowly at first, then faster and faster . . . until she reared up, and let out a cry, and shuddered, again and again, as she took him to the pinnacle with her, to a burst of fiery brilliance. Then they fell together into a sweet, cool darkness, and her mouth found his again, and she breathed, "I love you."

"I love you," he answered hoarsely. "My wonderful, wicked girl."

IN the drawing room of Hargate House, Captain Hughes took out his pocket watch and frowned.

Mrs. Entwhistle, standing beside him, dug her elbow into his ribs. "This is not the Royal Navy," she said in a low, disapproving voice. "Our lives are not run by the clock. Six bells for this. Three bells for that. Haste, haste, haste. Must not lose a minute."

He put away his watch and turned his frown upon her. "I had supposed that even a pair of civilians might contrive to be on time for their own wedding."

He most certainly would be on time for his, if he could ever persuade this lady to look kindly upon him. That, he calculated, given the present rate of progress, would take a few years. He hoped his teeth and hair would not fall out before then.

"They are but a few minutes late," she said. "There was a difficulty. But Mr. Carsington promised to sort it out and told us to go on ahead."

A moment later, the buzz of conversation dulled to a murmur. The groom strode to his place before the minister, his groomsman joined him, and the drawing room doors opened to reveal the glowing bride, leaning on her father's arm.

She was more than glowing, Captain Hughes observed. She was flushed, and her hair . . .

His gaze went to the groom—the famous dandy who

came down to breakfast dressed to the inch, whose idea of dishabille was a silk dressing gown instead of a coat worn over his usual silk waistcoat, a freshly pressed shirt, and a starched neckcloth tied in knots so complicated that even the most experienced seaman must regard it with mystification and despair.

This was the man who'd declined Oldridge's hospitality on one of the worst nights of the winter and ridden two hours to Matlock Bath in an ice storm. All because he hadn't brought a change of clothes with him.

At present, Mr. Carsington's hair appeared to have recently survived an Atlantic gale. His neckcloth was crooked, the knot so simple that a seven-year-old midshipman, half-blind, with one hand tied behind his back, could manage it.

Captain Hughes smiled. He had no idea what the difficulty had been, but he could guess how the bridegroom had sorted it out.

"What are you smirking at?" Mrs. Entwhistle whispered.

"I am not smirking," he whispered back. "I am smiling benignly upon the happy couple."

"You are smirking. I can guess why. It is bad of you to notice."

"You were her governess," he said. "I must wonder what you taught her."

To his delight, the widow's cheeks turned pink. "Lionel, you are incorrigible," she said.

Lionel. Oho. Perhaps not so many years after all.

"Dearly beloved," the minister began, and they fell silent, turning their attention thither.

LORD Hargate had waited what seemed an intolerable length of time for the ceremony to begin. He had heard of the bride's balking even before the bridegroom did. Yet his lordship had chatted amiably with his guests, then taken his proper place in the drawing room at the scheduled time. He had stoically remained in that place while the minutes ticked by, while paternal instincts urged him with increasing shrillness to hasten to his third's son rescue.

Consequently, he drew a deep sigh of relief when it appeared that Alistair had handled the crisis on his own. Lord Hargate did not question the means of persuasion employed. He was a politician, after all.

All the same, he did not breathe easy again until the ceremony ended.

Then he glanced at Mr. Oldridge, who gave him a conspiratorial smile. For all his absentmindedness and preoccupation with matters botanical, he had managed to discern the rightness of this particular match.

The earl turned to his wife. "Well, Louisa?" he murmured.

"Well done, Ned," she said under her breath. "Very well done, indeed, my dear."

Yes, it was well done, Lord Hargate thought. One bachelor son safely shackled. Only two more to go.

Afterword

ON 2 May 1825, royal assent was received for *"An Act for making and maintaining a Railway or Tramroad, from the Cromford Canal, at or near to Cromford, in the parish of Wirksworth, in the county of Derby, to the Peak Forest Canal, at or near to Whaley, (otherwise Yardsley-cum-Whaley) in the county palatine of Chester."*

Among the hundred and sixteen members of the Cromford and High Peak Railway Company was a woman, the Dowager Viscountess Anson.

The railway, which opened in 1830, was considered one of the most remarkable and daring building feats of the age.

Joseph Priestley, author of *Historical Account of the Navigable Rivers, Canals, and Railways of Great Britain* (first published in 1831), called it a "grand scheme, for passing such a mountainous tract of country."

BERKLEY SENSATION
COMING IN APRIL 2004

He would offer her everything a woman could want—except his heart...

The Souvenir Countess

by
Joanna Novins

Alix de la Brou is on the run from French Revolutionaries, and only one man can help her—Rafe Harcrest. When Rafe's solution is to get married, Alix realizes that she can't bear the thought of Rafe not loving her as a true bride.

"NOVINS BRINGS A RICH, NEW VOICE TO ROMANTIC FICTION."
—JULIA LONDON

0-425-19387-X

Available wherever books are sold, or to order call 1-800-788-6262